in the midst of lions

Arc of the Oracles
Book One

gordon bonnet

To the Bumbershoots.

Thanks for being my cheerleaders, support team, and friends. Y'all are amazing.

Have pity on me, O God, have pity on me… for I lie prostrate
in the midst of lions that devour men.

Psalm 56

part one
the oracles

one

. . .

M onday, April 2, 2035

Signs and portents are the stuff of fiction. Great changes in the fortunes of humanity are rarely ever presaged by thunder, and black skies and the lash of lightning bolts seldom mean anything except that it's going to rain.

So it might well mean nothing that it started and ended with earthquakes. But even so, long after the details had faded from the collective memory, long after the names of the people who lived through it were forgotten, people remembered that.

The first one wasn't a big earthquake, especially given that Seattle sits near an active and dangerous fault line. Still, it jolted Mary Hansard hard enough as she walked across the parking lot that she stumbled and dropped the armful of student work she was bringing home to grade, and was able to keep her feet only with an ungraceful effort.

"Are you okay, Ms. Hansard?" A concerned voice came from behind her, and still a little wobbly, she turned to see

Brian Nehring, one of her students, rushing up toward her. "Here, let me help."

"Thank you, Brian." She knelt next to him in the parking lot, picking up papers now hopelessly disordered.

Brian jogged after one that had been caught by the spring breeze and was flipping its way across the asphalt. He came back as she stood up, adding the errant worksheet to the top of her stack.

The young man gave her a grin. "No problem. That was a surprise. Biggest quake we've had in a while."

"I wonder where the epicenter was. I hope no one got hit too hard." She dusted off the knees of her slacks. "Anyhow, I'm none the worse for getting jolted around. Thanks for the help."

Brian gave her another quick smile and turned away to rejoin some friends.

Handsome boy. Nice, too. A pity he's going to die so soon.

The thought came without warning, and with none of the tentativeness of the typical anxiety-laden worries everyone has. In fact, it was completely devoid of emotion. Or, more accurately, the emotion came afterward. She knew, knew without doubt, that Brian Nehring was going to be dead in a few short weeks. It felt as dispassionate as a newspaper headline about a total stranger, and as certain. The flood of sadness that came afterward was like times she'd received unexpected bad news.

Only here, it wasn't news about something that had already happened. It was news about the future.

"I'm losing my mind," Mary said under her breath. She looked back toward Brian, who was chatting and laughing with a girl—Leah something? Mary recognized her, but hadn't taught her before—and then it happened again.

Leah Chambers. Her name is Leah Chambers. And she's going to die, too.

Mary clutched her papers to her chest, turning away from

the pair and heading at a jog toward her car. She had to sit down or she was going to faint.

She unlocked and opened the door and collapsed behind the steering wheel, tossing the stack of papers into the passenger seat and increasing their disarray. She looked at the loose pile, worksheets on kinetic and potential energy from her physics classes.

How appropriate. Entropy. She could expend energy to stack the papers back up, reorganize them by class as they had been when she left the building, but it was no good. Things were falling apart, everything spiraling into chaos. You could try to slow it down, decrease the disorder locally and temporarily, but eventually you were bound to lose.

Entropy always wins.

Mary closed her eyes and leaned her head back against the headrest, trying to halt the whirling vortex of dizziness she'd fallen into. She had to get a hold of herself, at least enough to get home. If she sat in the parking lot much longer, some of the teenagers still hanging around campus would see her and come up to check if she was okay. It was endearing—she was on friendly terms with nearly everyone, students and staff, and was one of the most liked teachers at Shoreline High School—but at the moment their concern was the last thing she wanted.

How would she explain herself?

She took several deep breaths and opened her eyes. Looking in the rearview mirror, she saw Brian and Leah looking in her direction with a frown.

Don't stare at me, you're both going to die and I can't deal with knowing that I can't stop it, please look somewhere else…

With some effort she fished her keys from her purse, put them in the ignition, and started the car. When she put her foot on the brakes and shifted into reverse, the two young people evidently saw the brake lights. They turned back to their conversation. Whatever was wrong with Ms. Hansard, it wasn't bad enough to keep her from driving, so everything must be okay.

It wasn't okay. It was far from okay.

She backed out of her parking space and headed out toward the road. But it kept happening. Every time she passed someone, glanced to her side and saw another driver or pedestrian. All of them were strangers, but when the voice spoke in her mind, it knew their names.

Albert Dunn. He's going to die by drowning.

Lila van Cleve. She's going to be killed by her next-door neighbor.

John McNamara. Killed during a riot, hit by a stray bullet.

Edith Quinn. Starved to death.

Stopped at a stoplight, she turned to look at the little old lady her mind had named as Edith Quinn. The woman saw Mary staring, and returned a friendly smile and little wave. She was walking down the sidewalk slowly, leaning heavily on an aluminum cane, but had a rosy-cheeked appearance, like the storybook grandma.

The words hit her again.

Starved to death.

Then water, a rising tide of water, obliterating everything in its path. She fought back the sensation of drowning. Once again a voice, seeming to come from somewhere outside her own mind, said, "All springs reduce their currents to mine eyes, that I, being governed by the watery moon, may send forth plenteous tears to drown the world…"

What was that? It had the cadence of Shakespeare. It sounded familiar—she'd seen a performance of *Richard III* up at the University two months earlier—but as a rule, she didn't remember lines of dialogue, and this one sounded verbatim. In a woman's voice, but not her own…

"What is happening to me?" Her voice sounded thin in her own ears. The blare of a horn behind her jolted her awareness back to the present. The light had turned green without her noticing. She gave a feeble wave to the angry face of the man in the car behind her.

Michael Tamura. His name was Michael Tamura.

And he was going to die, too. Stabbed in a street fight.

Mary pulled into her parking space at her apartment complex and somehow made it to her home on the third floor, hardly aware of how she'd gotten there. She let herself in, shut and locked the door behind her, and only then realized she'd left the stack of student papers sitting on the passenger seat in the car.

Shouldn't worry about it, the mental voice that was not her own said. In a couple of months they're all going to be…

"Stop it!" she shouted. The voice halted as if she'd flipped a switch.

Was this the beginning of schizophrenia? Was it incipient psychosis? She had a distant cousin, some relative on her mom's side of the family, who was schizophrenic, and was in an institution. Heard voices, Mary's mom had said. Sad case, he became paranoid and eventually a danger to himself and others, so they locked him away.

Maybe that's where she was headed. Locked away, just her and the voices.

No. The voice sounded almost cheerful. *That's not what will happen to you. Bide your time for now, you'll have plenty to do very soon.*

Vertigo. Sudden, powerful, overwhelming. She had the sense of standing upright on a tilted floor. Her eyes told her different—the floor was level, the windowsill parallel with the skyline, everything as it should be—but her body was caught in two places at once, the ordinary plumb, right-angular world and one that had been shattered, the pieces jutting up at crazy angles. Clenching nausea rose in her belly, and she knew if she waited moments, she would be unable to walk.

She made it to the bathroom before the vomiting started. Barely.

Mary had never missed three days of school in a row, not in nineteen years as a teacher. She couldn't get out of bed without the vertigo knocking her back down. She considered calling 911 and getting an ambulance to the emergency room, but was dissuaded by the fact that to do so, she would have had to get to the living room somehow, where she'd left her phone when she'd stumbled in.

So she decided to ride it out.

The nausea, fortunately, didn't last long. The dizziness was slower to abate, but by the middle of the third day she was able to walk without falling. But over the three days in bed, she became aware of another, more troubling fault in her mental processes.

She couldn't keep the past and the future straight.

She remembered some things that were clearly in the past. Her childhood, for example. But when she thought of an event since she became an adult—something that had occurred in her classroom, for example—she honestly didn't know if it had happened already, or was going to happen in the future. She knew, rationally, that there was no way she could know the future, but she saw the building across the road on fire, burning wildly with no firefighters there to stop it, and was convinced it was a memory until she staggered her way to the window and confirmed the building was still there, intact, where it always had been. Even after seeing it, when she turned away, in her mind were two images. The burning building and the intact building. Both of them felt like memories.

But one of them hadn't happened, at least not yet.

The more she probed, the more she realized that everything was like that. She remembered conversations with people and at the same time knew she'd never met them. She lay in bed, sleepless, trying to cope with the sensation that the floor was simultaneously flat and tipped at an impossible angle, trying to sort out her thoughts.

There was no such thing as a "future memory." Those had to be delusions, or at best, idle daydreams. They felt completely real, though, and very quickly she figured out that other than instances where she could verify the truth—the burning building, for example—she had no reliable algorithm for telling them apart from actual memories of the past.

The world, it seemed, was no longer sorted into past, present, and future. There were only two categories—present and not-present.

Something in her brain that was not-present could equally well be in the past or the future. Apart from the few she could corroborate, there was no way to determine which was which.

When she got out of bed on the fourth day since her vertigo began, she put on coffee, padding carefully across her kitchen, barefoot and clad in her old terry-cloth bathrobe, and made two phone calls. The first was to her school, telling them she was still sick and wouldn't be in that day.

The second was to her doctor.

Part of the reason was her school's policy that an absence of longer than three days required a doctor's note to qualify as sick leave. She doubted the administration would hold her to that, as she hardly ever called in even when she *was* ill, but might as well do what the contract demanded. The other part was to find out, if possible, what the hell had happened, was happening, to her brain.

She was able to keep back the disordered thoughts as she slowly made her way down the elevator and then to her car, trailing her fingertips along the wall to keep her balance. It was a sunny, pleasant day, and she passed other residents of her apartment complex as she walked, trying to seem steadier than she felt, trying not to attract attention and words of concern. The effort to walk without stumbling, and simultaneously stifle her brain's declarations about the fates of the people she passed, required one hundred percent of her attention. But she was determined to drive herself the three miles to her doctor's office. No way was she calling a cab.

Calling a cab seemed too much like giving in.

She made it to her destination by focusing on one thing—driving safely—which she only accomplished by ignoring everything but the road in front of her. Even that was difficult, because once again she got a dual sensation, that her tires were rolling smoothly along, and that they were bucking and jolting over obstacles, jarring her whole body even though there was nothing there. She gave a deep sigh of relief as she pulled into a parking space (*halfway, I still have to get back*) and once again moving with deliberation and caution, got out of her car and walked into the office.

The nurse who called her out of the waiting room did a cursory check of blood pressure and pulse, asked her for a recap of her symptoms, then told her the doctor would be in to see her soon. "Soon" turned out to be twenty minutes, but honestly, Mary was glad to have a place to sit, alone, without wondering if she was listing in her seat, without hearing pronouncements about all the people around her.

Dr. Kalemba came in smiling, but with concern in her eyes. Mary could hear the thought as clearly as if she'd spoken it aloud—*She thinks I've had a stroke.* The possibility certainly had occurred to her more than once in the last three days, during which her training in the sciences had come up with a number of dire possibilities that might account for her condition. Stroke. Blood clot. Menière's disease, multiple sclerosis, Parkinson's.

Brain cancer.

Mary answered the doctor's questions as she shone a light

in each eye, looked into her mouth and ears, listened to her heart and lungs, checked lymph nodes. After the exam, Dr. Kalemba sat back, her dark eyes filled with concern.

"You said this has been going on for three days."

Mary nodded. "I know, I should have gone to the emergency room right away."

A flash of a smile. "Definitely. But the fact that you didn't, and your condition has improved some, is a good sign. The nausea and vomiting didn't last long?"

"A couple of hours. After that, I didn't exactly feel like eating, but I wasn't throwing up any more. Since then, I've been able to eat at least small meals, and no trouble keeping them down."

"That's also a good sign." She made some notes on the laptop in front of her. "Uncontrolled tremors?"

Mary shook her head.

"Muscle weakness?"

Another negative.

"So at present, the only issue is the dizziness."

Mary nodded, wondering if she should bring up the bizarre psychological symptoms. What would Dr. Kalemba say if she told her, "The only other symptom is that I can no longer tell apart the past and the future"?

"What I've seen so far suggests that you may have something going on in your inner ear. Sometimes an ear infection can cause dizziness, but the sudden onset argues against that. Have you heard of benign positional vertigo?"

"Yes, I think I read about it in *Scientific American* a while back."

The doctor smiled. "Oh, right, I'd forgotten you're a science teacher. Well, just to make sure you have all the facts, I'll summarize. It's caused by crystals forming in the fluid of the semicircular canals, the organs of balance in your inner ear. The crystals brushing against the sensors in the semicircular canals cause disorientation and vertigo. But the 'benign' part is what you should focus on. The condition is usually self-limiting, and there are head-motion exercises you can do that often hasten its resolution." More notes on the laptop. "But just to be safe, I'd like to schedule you for an MRI at the hospital, to rule out anything else going on." She paused. "Do you drink alcohol, or use any psychotropic drugs?"

"No. I mean, I occasionally have a glass of wine with dinner, but I haven't even done that in the last couple of weeks. And drugs? Never. I didn't try drugs when I was a teenager. Too much of a socially awkward science nerd to have the opportunity."

Dr. Kalemba chuckled. "That's not a bad thing. And I probably don't need to tell you this, but avoid alcohol until we resolve whatever is going on here."

"Of course." Mary swallowed hard, trying to figure out how to make the next thing she said not sound either ridiculous or downright alarming. "Doctor, does the condition you mentioned ever cause any… psychological symptoms?"

A quick frown. "Psychological symptoms of what sort?"

"I don't know how to describe it. Errant thoughts. When I see people, or things, my imagination starts speculating about them. Wondering what will happen to them in the future."

"And you haven't experienced this before?"

Mary shook her head. "It started the same time as the dizziness."

Dr. Kalemba tapped a few more notes into the laptop. "I've never heard of benign positional vertigo causing any psychological symptoms. Anxiety, of course, given that the episodes of dizziness can be a little frightening, especially given how quickly they can come on. Can you tell me more about these thoughts?"

She looked away, focusing on the pristine tiles of the examining room floor. When she relaxed her grip on her mind, she could see them broken, muddy, the equipment and supplies in the room scattered and trampled. People fighting, trying to stop thieves from getting in and raiding the medications storeroom…

Mary clamped down again. *Stop it. Just stop it.*

Speaking slowly, keeping her voice steady with difficulty, she said, "Everything I see makes my brain come up with a story about the future. It's never a good future. All I can think of is death and destruction and horror."

A long pause, during which there was silence in the little room. "Do you…" Dr. Kalemba looked upward, thinking. "Would you characterize the thoughts as self-centered? That you're anxious bad things will happen to you personally, or that others might be wishing you harm?"

It figured that'd be the next question. The doctor suspected paranoid schizophrenia. "No. Not at all. In fact, it's never about me."

"Do you feel like the thoughts are impelling you to harm anyone, or yourself?"

Mary shook her head vehemently. "No. The bad things I see aren't caused by me. In fact, they don't involve me at all. They're horrible, and fill me with dread, but it's not for my own safety. You don't need to worry that I'm going to kill anyone." She tried to make it sound light, and failed completely, even in her own ears.

"Do you have those sorts of thoughts when you look at me?"

Okay, she hadn't anticipated *that*. Her eyes flitted away, passing over the spotlessly clean, mud-streaked, intact, shattered walls of the examining room. "It's everyone," she said in a whisper.

Then closed her eyes, hoping Dr. Kalemba wouldn't ask her to elaborate.

She didn't. "That's worrisome, especially given that what you call the 'errant thoughts' started at the same time as the dizziness. We should get you into an MRI as quickly as possible—I'll see if the hospital can put a rush on your referral. The simultaneity of the physical and psychological symptoms is odd, to say the least."

"Could I be having a psychotic break?"

If the bluntness of the question caught the doctor off guard, she showed no sign of it. Probably she'd been thinking the same thing.

"I honestly have to tell you that I don't know the answer to that. It's not classical psychosis, I'll say that much. But I am a G.P., not a psychiatrist, and I'm not qualified to make a definitive assessment. Hopefully the MRI will allow us to rule some things out, but unless it pinpoints a cause, the next step would be a psychiatric referral." She paused. "I'll order a blood and urine screen, just to make sure there's nothing going on with your metabolism or blood chemistry. Sometimes conditions like hypoglycemia can cause psychological symptoms, although from what you describe, I think that's unlikely. If it were hypoglycemia, it would come and go—worse when you're hungry, better when you've just eaten. Same with dehydration. You haven't noticed any fluctuation? Time of day, proximity to meals? Anything like that?"

Mary shook her head.

"Okay, so let's wait till we see the results of the MRI and metabolic screen." She typed a quick note on the laptop, then glanced up and smiled. It looked a little forced. "Do you think you're safe to drive home? We could call you a cab."

"No. I'm okay. I drove here without any trouble. It just takes concentration. And I don't have to drive far. I'll be fine."

Dr. Kalemba nodded. "All right, then. I'll have the nurse come back in for the blood draw and urine sample, and by then the secretary will hopefully have an appointment for you to get the MRI. Once the results for all those are in, we'll talk again."

"Thank you."

"It's no problem. But if your symptoms suddenly become

more severe, or you do start having suicidal ideation—call 911 immediately and get yourself to the emergency room."

"I will."

Dr. Kalemba shut the laptop and left the examining room, and Mary stared at the closed door for several minutes afterward.

How tragic that she was going to die defending the clinic. She was a nice woman and a good doctor.

She deserved a better fate than that.

No. Mary squeezed her eyes shut. It was an irrational anxiety thought. Maybe they'd find she had a brain tumor or something. But these things *couldn't* be true.

That would be scarier than a brain tumor—or the possibility that she might be going insane.

two

. . .

The earthquake jolted loose a pile of books that had been perched precariously on a bookshelf in Brandon Nguyen's art studio and sent them tumbling to the floor.

A couple of them hit Brandon on the way down, because despite it being three in the afternoon, he wasn't painting, he was taking a nap on his sofa. Sitting up with a startled grunt, he flailed his arms to protect his head, but the temblor was over as quickly as it started, and no further projectiles came his way.

He got up and stretched, cupping his hands behind his head and arching his back, yawned prodigiously, and made a quick tour of his house to see if there'd been any damage. He found one drinking glass lying tipped over in the kitchen sink, a long crack snaking its way up the side, but that and his nap seemed to be the only casualties.

He considered going back to the sofa, but a pang of guilt struck him at how easily he accepted choosing sleep over work. His productivity had been languishing for some time now. He made a decent living as a portrait and landscape artist, working on commission, and was good enough that the business was steady. But true creativity? His MFA from the

Rhode Island School of Design had excited him with its promise of a life of making new, startling, visionary art, but the reality had been a disappointing descent into doing the same pedestrian things over and over.

With his grudging acceptance of his prime motivator being making enough money to survive, he found inspiration receding further and further into the distance. He occasionally pulled out some of the pieces he'd done while in graduate school and immediately after graduation, and they had a vibrancy he hadn't been able to access since. Wild scenes of fantastical worlds, visions of scenarios somewhere between brilliance and fever dream. When he looked at them, it was with a real sense of grief over loss. Creating something like those pieces again seemed an impossibility, almost as if they'd been painted by someone else, someone whose genius he could only dimly grasp.

He glanced at the clock. Three-thirty. Was it too early for a drink? He felt like he needed one. If he couldn't bring back the inspiration, he could at least numb the regret.

He trudged into the kitchen, but as he opened the door of his fridge to get a bottle of beer, he froze in place, his mouth hanging open.

Images poured into his mind. It felt like he was not producing them but receiving them, that he'd been turned into an antenna. The colors were vivid, intense, almost electric. He shuddered, let the fridge door go, and it silently swung shut.

Whirling pictures cascaded into him, more real than his run-down kitchen with its stack of dirty dishes on the counter, more real than the fir trees in the back yard, more real than the traffic noise and the block of sunlight and the brush of the spring breeze coming in through his open window. He stood, completely swept away, for nearly ten minutes.

Then he returned to his studio, and picked up a sketch book.

Two hours later he had made some preliminary sketches, and he stood, wincing at the ache in his back and neck from hunching over in the same position the entire time he was drawing. But he wasn't done, not close. He went to his cabinet and pulled out the largest blank canvas he had. He'd been saving it for years—it was too large for the portraits and bland doctors'-office landscapes he created every day—and now it seemed to him he'd saved it for that moment, for that purpose.

He transferred the sketches to the canvas, then got out his oil paints and brushes.

The next time Brandon checked the clock, it was two in the morning.

He stepped back and looked at the painting. It still needed work, it was rough in places, but it conformed perfectly to the vision he'd had in his kitchen, as if his mind or whatever had powered it had connected directly to his paintbrushes. He knew at that moment it was the best thing, by far, that he'd ever done, maybe the best thing he ever would do.

It showed an apocalyptic landscape in crimson and orange and gray. The world was burning. In the near ground, huge blocks of what looked like cement were broken and tilted upward, the dark cracks between them like tears in the fabric of reality. One figure dominated the center of the painting—a tall, well-built blond man, clad in torn and dirty clothing. He was standing front-forward, his arms out to his side, palms opening toward the viewer to indicate the destruction around him, as if saying, *Look at this. Look at what you've done.* His face was turned away to the right, eyes partially closed, his expression radiating shame and accusation.

There was nothing particularly unusual about the man's appearance. Despite this, he was rendered with such photographic realism against the surreality of the background that his body looked solid, like it had actual weight. He was the fulcrum of the entire image, and the position of everything in the world should be calculated relative to where he was. No matter where he stood, he would be perfectly upright—it was the surrounding world that was skewed.

Behind him, shadowed and indistinct, were what looked like dozens of other people. Children, mostly, with a few adults. The blond man's outstretched arms were not only a palm-upward gesture of despair, they said clearly, *These are under my protection. You will not get past me to harm them, not one of them.*

Blinking in the fluorescent light of the studio, Brandon peered closely at the face of the blond man, and—as far as he could see them—the faces of the people behind him, the people he was guarding.

To his knowledge, he had never seen any of them in his entire life.

He scanned the painting again, his exhausted mind trying to determine where the images had come from. Even though his early work had focused on imaginary landscapes, bizarre and sometimes disturbing visions of other worlds, other dimensions, heaven and hell, he was usually able to identify his inspiration for them.

Here, he didn't have the slightest idea. Once it was transferred to canvas, the blond man standing in the destroyed landscape seemed as unfamiliar as if it had been painted by someone else. He studied it in complete bafflement, trying to figure out how he could have created something so deeply profound and still know nothing about what it meant.

But at the moment he was too tired to ponder it. He did a cursory cleanup of his brushes and palette, then stumbled into his bedroom. He was barely aware of climbing into bed, and was sound asleep in under a minute.

When Brandon awakened, it was obviously mid-morning from the angle of the light coming through his open window. He hadn't even pulled the curtains before undressing, and the light from his nightstand lamp was still on. Oh, well, if the neighbors had seen him naked, there was nothing he could do about it now. Hopefully they had enjoyed the view.

He dragged himself out from under the blanket and padded into the bathroom. His brain still felt like it was sunk in a cloying fog. He turned the shower on, adjusted it so it was as hot as he could stand, and climbed in.

As he stood under the scalding spray, he thought about the painting.

Or had he dreamed doing it? His memories of the previous evening were themselves as surreal as the landscape he'd created. Everything after the earthquake was suspect, and for a brief moment, he wondered if the books that had fallen on him had caused a concussion that might account for the experiences of the last eighteen hours. But he ran his fingers through his long black hair, tentatively brushing his scalp, and didn't detect any sore spots or bruises.

Shower completed, he dried himself off and dressed, but was still groggy and disoriented. Coffee and food, that's what he needed. But first, he had to verify that his memories were accurate. If the painting wasn't there, he'd been hallucinating and needed to see a doctor. If it was... well, that wasn't a whole lot more reassuring, but at least it meant some part of his mental faculties was still intact.

He went into his studio, and there it was on its easel, exactly as he recalled. A vision of burning chaos transferred to canvas, and the commanding, solid presence of the central figure, with his gesture of anger, protection, accusation, despair.

Where the hell had that image come from? He was no closer to understanding it than he had been the previous evening. He shook his head to clear away the confusion, then retreated to the kitchen.

Coffee and a light breakfast helped with some of the loopy lightheadedness, but as his mind cleared, he realized that the strange power that had taken over his brain wasn't done yet. He needed to give the finishing touches to the painting he started, but there were other images coming in, all jostling and competing for his attention.

A tall African American woman, elderly but ramrod straight, hands cupped in front of her, light spilling from them like some sort of liquid sunshine. Above her, the sky sagged, and making her appear a latter-day Atlas, bearing the weight of heaven's vault on her narrow shoulders.

A flood swirling around the foundation of buildings, the muddy water dragging along cars, trees, debris... and corpses.

People in a rugged, mountainous landscape watching a rocket taking off. One of the nearest figures was obviously weeping, leaning into the person next to him as though he couldn't bear to watch the craft's ascent.

A woman standing on the end of a collapsed bridge, its broken edge jutting out before her. She was middle-aged, with straight, light brown hair being blown on a stiff wind, and looked off into the distance with a transfigured expression, as if she'd just witnessed a miracle of divine grace. The cracks in the pavement twisted all around her—the piece she stood on looked ready to crumble beneath her feet—but she appeared unaware of her danger, or else didn't much care.

Nighttime, a group of five people surrounding a campfire. It looked like the familiar scene of a friendly campout—but indistinct in the shadows behind them was a tangle of razor wire, and behind that, faces that were desperate, feral, barely human.

What appeared to be a scientific facility. Scattered on the spotless tile floor were dozens of fallen people wearing space suits. The nearest was angled so Brandon could see through the visor, and behind it was the grinning, fleshless visage of a skeleton.

These were only the first of many, and he knew if he let his brain wander, they would overwhelm it. He still retained enough rationality to realize he had to be methodical, that he could only paint one thing at a time. But simultaneously he also knew that even if he set some of them aside, the images wouldn't be lost. They were real, more real to him than his own house and his own world.

Take it slowly and do it right. However long he took, the visions would be there waiting for him when he was ready.

Fortunately. Because what he had already seen could take years to create. Even so, there could be no delay. There was work to do, important work, although what its importance was, he had no idea.

He set down his coffee cup, stood, and returned to his studio.

Five days later, Brandon was having a drink at a nearby pub with his on-again, off-again girlfriend Caria Sahin. Lately it had been more off-again. Caria had seemed to pick up on his loss of enthusiasm and drive, and their dates had become more and more infrequent. It had occurred to him to try harder, or at least talk to her about his slide into depression, but the time was never right, and honestly he didn't have the energy to broach the topic. There was nothing she could do about it, and in any case, he could deal with it, could handle being alone. Caria was probably better off not hanging around him when he was in this frame of mind anyhow. Some dimly-recognized part of him knew this was itself a manifestation of the depression, and that even six months ago just the promise of regular sex would have been enough to impel him to try to salvage the relationship. Their connection had never been deep, but until recently he considered it at least worth pursuing.

Lately, *nothing* had seemed worth pursuing.

But tonight, things had done a complete about-face. He was desperate to talk to her, to be near her, and sweet Jesus he was horny. The visions had plugged him in to some unguessed energy source that was filling his entire body with fire.

He had only a momentary hesitation after her question, "What's new in your life?" It was a risk telling Caria—telling anyone—about something that was so powerful, so deeply intimate, as his experiences over the last week. But at the same time, he was compelled to tell her. He couldn't keep to himself the biggest thing that had ever happened to him. To keep silent was to invite some kind of mental self-destruct, an emotional implosion. Not only was she the only person in his life who might understand, she was the only one with whom he wanted this kind of connection.

So he launched into a description of his work over the last five days. Once started, the words poured from him in a flood.

Afterward, his mind emptied and sated for the time being, he brushed the back of her hand with his fingertips, and an electric charge zinged its way up his arm that was so powerful he was surprised he didn't see actual sparks. The fire was still there, ready to be rekindled at any moment.

"Sorry. I got carried away."

"Don't apologize." Caria looked at him over the top of her wine glass, an amused smile playing about her lips. "But what's gotten into you? I haven't seen you this way in months. I like it."

"I haven't felt this way in months. And I like it, too."

"What caused the change?"

"I have no idea."

"But you said you're painting again. I mean, really painting, not just doing portraits for rich old ladies. Doing pieces you actually care about."

Brandon nodded and took a sip of his beer. "Yes. It's incredible. I don't know why, but all of a sudden, I've reconnected to my creativity." He paused. "That's not exactly right, though. It kind of doesn't feel like me. Like I've been linked to someone else, or something else, that is electrifying my brain, dumping these images into it. It's overwhelming. Overwhelming in a good way."

"Wherever it's coming from, I'm so glad this happened. I've been worried about you. You just seemed so low, and I didn't know what to do."

"Neither did I. But I guess it fixed itself. I don't know how, but it feels good."

"How much are you painting?"

"Twelve hours a day. More. Breaks for food and bathroom, that's about it."

Caria's eyes widened. "Twelve hours?"

"More, some days."

"I work eight hours sitting on my ass doing a stupid desk job and I'm exhausted. How are you not asleep on your feet?"

"I don't know. But the last thing I feel is tired. Some nights I can't sleep, and I get up and work in the middle of the night. All I want to do is paint."

"Wow. When do I get to see these amazing new pieces?"

"Tonight, if you want. When you're done with your drink we can go back to my house. I'll show you what I've done." Brandon grinned at her and lowered his voice. "Plus, after that I want to make love to you. Maybe several times."

"I'd never turn that down." She returned his smile, and stroked the back of his arm with her fingertip. "I could tell the moment I saw you tonight. You haven't looked at me like that in a long while. It turns me on to know you do want me."

"Want you?" He laughed. "If I wanted you any more, I

wouldn't be able to stop myself from taking you right here on the floor."

"Well, I think we need to go to your house, then. I like daring sex, but that's a little over the line even for me."

Three hours later, they were cuddling in Brandon's bed, Caria's head resting on his shoulder.

"Who is that guy in the painting? The big painting, with all the fire?"

"I have no idea."

"So you made him up? He looks so real."

"He *is* real."

There was a long pause. "What do you mean?"

Brandon didn't answer for a moment. Finally he said, "I know he's real even if I've never seen him before and don't know who he is."

"That doesn't make sense."

"I know. Believe me, I know. But all the people I've painted—the blond man, the woman on the bridge, the sniper—they're all real people. I'm seeing real people, real events. They're all out there somewhere."

Now her voice sounded even more tentative, like she was trying to put a rational spin on something fundamentally irrational. Understandable, since that was how Brandon himself felt. "So these are depictions of, like, historical events? Things you've read about, places where there's been war or whatever?"

Another pause, and when Brandon spoke, his voice was quiet. He felt a sudden reluctance to say what he was thinking. What he'd already told her was pretty out there, but this honestly sounded insane. "No, I mean real events. Just ones… ones that haven't happened yet."

three

. . .

Julia Lowell's lips moved as she read, but honestly, she could have recited this bit by heart. Her eyes hardly registered the words before her mouth formed them.

"From Jesus Christ, who is the faithful witness, and the first begotten of the dead, and the prince of the kings of the earth. Unto him that loved us, and washed us from our sins in his own blood, and hath made us kings and priests unto God and his Father; to him be glory and dominion for ever and ever. Amen. Behold, he cometh with clouds; and every eye shall see him, and they also which pierced him: and all kindreds of the earth shall wail because of him. Even so, amen."

Julia looked up from her well-worn Bible with a grim expression. She had been expecting the End Times for years. Even back into her dimly-remembered childhood during the turbulent 1960s, she had a fascination for the Book of Revelation, and had been waiting for it all to start, for the King of Kings to arrive with a flaming sword to defend the righteous and slay the unrighteous, to bring justice to this sad, ailing world.

Every time there was a major upheaval somewhere—

which was frequently—she thought, *This is it*. But it never was. Things resolved, tensions lowered, violence returned to a low simmer, and none of the signs that were promised came. The Antichrist, the Beast With Seven Heads and Ten Crowns, the Four Horsemen of the Apocalypse, the Scarlet Whore of Babylon. Each time her hopes had been raised that perhaps the evils and iniquities of the world were about to end. Each time they were denied, she recited the verse from the Book of Matthew.

"But of that day and hour knoweth no man, no, not the angels of heaven, but my Father only."

Despite her years of study, Julia told herself, she was just one weak and foolish and ignorant woman. She should never presume to know the Will of God, or even show a hint of disappointment in the way things were. That would be to doubt God knew best and was seeing to it that everything spun out in accordance to His infinite knowledge.

So she returned to her Bible and prayed for patience.

But now? Now it seemed all but certain.

The signs were there in the news. The group calling itself the Lackland Liberation Authority was issuing threats on a daily basis to strike hard at the foundation of the nations of the world, to bring them all down in fire and flame. Put the leaders to the sword, leaving nothing but rivers of blood in their wake. The media tried to be upbeat, that the LLA was negotiating with heads of state to achieve redress for their claims of injury, but Julia could read between the lines enough to recognize that this was just a delaying tactic. The LLA leaders were trying to put the secular powers at ease while they laid their plans, make them drowse under layers of falsehood while the fuses were lit that would destroy everything.

They didn't want redress. They wanted revenge. That was clear to anyone who, like Julia, had been raised in poverty, who had been the targets of racism, who understood on a visceral level the deep, deep anger generated by years of facing deprivation and prejudice while watching wealthy white men thrive in their privilege. The LLA had started ten years earlier as a loose, disorganized conglomerate of people who had been dispossessed by the land buy-ups of multinational corporations—thus the "Lackland" part of their name—but in that decade the coalition had gradually tightened, coming under control of very smart people who were also entirely ruthless.

In the last year, the movement had picked up momentum, uniting the angry and resentful regardless where their anger and resentment originated. Some of the LLA members were the poor and desperate, some were excluded and downtrodden minorities trying to escape bigotry, some were political extremists, some were idealists who hated the way capitalism had led to global injustice, some were people who approved of agitating for its own sake. Some were simply criminals who enjoyed rioting and—usually—getting away with it.

The tipping point came when ordinary people began to be caught up in the violence, losing property or jobs or loved ones to the mob. As long as it was just a news story about something happening elsewhere, the average working man and woman could afford to ignore it. When it hit the neighborhoods of the comfortable middle class, anger boiled over, which was undoubtedly what the LLA intended. The government leaders were blamed for the unrest, and became targets for assassination. Sometimes the assassins succeeded. A few of the politicians, like Erik Kimmell, the EU's wily and cautious economic advisor, escaped. In Kimmell's case no one knew where he'd gone for certain, but there were rumors that he'd been on the last space shuttle launch, headed for Tycho Base on the Moon, taking with him only a few personal belongings and his robotic Self-Contained Occupational and Medical Assistant, or SCOMA.

The assumption was that he wasn't going to be back for a while.

Might be safe there, at least for a while. But the anger that drove the revolts still bubbled underneath the surface, even in areas that had been "pacified," which was the corporate code-word for crushing dissent via indiscriminate violence up to and including public execution of the leaders.

Julia Lowell watched all this with a grim acknowledgement of its inevitability. She felt aching pity for the innocent victims of the violence, and even for the not-so-innocent. She said prayers every evening for them. Her fervor and devotion had always been tempered by a deep core of compassion, and more than once in the last six months she'd been brought to tears watching the news. But truthfully, it was all happening exactly as the prophets had foretold. Humanity had been warned, and it shouldn't have come as a surprise that it was all falling apart. Everything she had witnessed during her seventy years on the Earth was only a prelude. This was it, she was sure of it. No longer was the violence confined to specific locales. The LLA was global, and they were set up to bring down not just one government, but all of them.

"Lo, there was a great earthquake; and the sun became black as sackcloth of hair, and the moon became as blood; and the stars of heaven fell unto the earth…and every mountain and island were moved out of their places. And the kings of the earth, and the great men, and the rich men, and the chief captains, and the mighty men, and every bondman, and every free man, hid themselves in the dens and in the rocks of the mountains; and said to the mountains and rocks, 'Fall on us, and hide us from the face of him that sitteth on the throne, and from the wrath of the Lamb: For the great day of his wrath is come; and who shall be able to stand?'"

How could anyone read this and have any doubt? It had already been as clear as glass, even before the day of the earthquake.

The day Julia began hearing the Voice of God. The day she realized that she was not an ordinary seventy-year-old woman, a retired nurse, widowed and childless and living alone in an old duplex in the Capitol Hill neighborhood of Seattle.

She was a prophet, the last in the line of Isaiah and Jeremiah and Ezekiel, tasked with bringing the command for repentance and preparation to the people, before it was too late.

She called Reverend Talcott that evening, and he was less than enthusiastic about her claim, even though she explained it at some length and in unequivocal terms.

After she told him about the messages she'd received, he didn't answer for some time, and when he did, it was slowly, with a tense deliberateness filled with a mix of caution and confusion. "Now, what happened again, Mrs. Lowell? You said after the earthquake this afternoon, you began hearing voices?"

"Not *voices*, Reverend. A Voice. *The* Voice. The Voice of God."

"What..." He seemed to be searching for the right words. "Are you certain what you're hearing is God's voice?"

"What else could it be?" Julia scowled. "You're not trying to tell me what I'm hearing is Satan?"

"N-no, no, of course not. But you see those aren't the only two options. You didn't... you didn't fall during the quake, or something?"

"Reverend, with all due respect, I spent almost forty years as a nurse. I'm not stupid enough that I wouldn't realize it if I'd hit my head or something and was hearing things because my brain was addled."

"I didn't mean that, of course."

"I've been a staunch and upright Christian woman my whole life, and I know the difference between God's Voice, the voice of the Evil One, and the voice of my own self. I have no doubt."

"What did the voice tell you?" Reverend Talcott sounded reluctant to ask the question, but it was really the only pertinent thing *to* ask.

"It said that the prophecies were being fulfilled, that the dark times were upon us. That fire and flood and the sword were coming, coming soon, and the righteous needed to prepare to fight the forces of evil."

"Soon? How soon?"

She responded by quoting her favorite line from the Book of Matthew about how no man knoweth the day and hour.

"Well, of course, I understand that. But I thought if you *were* receiving a divine message, perhaps you might have more information."

"Why don't you?"

Long pause. "Beg pardon?"

"I am nothing special. I dedicated my life to God, as everyone should, but other than that I'm just an ordinary woman. You were called to the ministry. It seems like if anyone should have knowledge of the imminence of the End Times, it would be you."

"God chooses whom he will to speak to." Reverend Talcott's voice was a little defensive. "All I can say is that if He speaks to me, I'm ready to listen."

"'He that hath an ear, let him listen to what the spirit saith.' It says that right in the Book of Revelation."

"Exactly."

There was silence on the phone for almost a minute. Finally it was the Reverend who broke it.

"I don't understand, Mrs. Lowell, what you are asking me to do."

"I wanted you to know. You're the leader of the church I belong to. Since I was the recipient of words of prophecy, you needed to hear it so you could warn the rest of the congregation and stop them from being taken unawares. So they could prepare for what is to come."

"And all of this, you think, has to do with the LLA."

"What else could it be? It's the main threat facing the world today."

"I think perhaps you're overestimating their reach. Maybe if we lived in Germany, where there have been so many riots, I would agree with you. But here?"

Julia snorted in frustration. It was becoming increasingly clear. It wasn't that Reverend Talcott didn't understand what she was saying. He didn't *want* to understand. "When God speaks, our place is not to doubt. Our place is to listen and obey."

"If you're certain it is God speaking."

"I am certain."

Another long pause. "Well, Mrs. Lowell, let me think and pray about this. I don't want you to think I'm discounting what you're saying."

That was exactly what he *was* doing, but Julia decided not to say that. "That's fine, Reverend. But don't think and pray too long. There comes a point where thinking and praying must end. A point where you must act."

"I know that." He drew a long breath that probably was a sigh of annoyance. "But it's the best I can do for now. I will be back in touch with you when I've had a chance to consider what you've told me."

"All right. Good night, Reverend Talcott."

"Good night, Mrs. Lowell."

When the call ended, Julia did some annoyed sighing of her own. She wasn't sure what she'd expected him to do, but it certainly wasn't to dance around and pretend nothing had happened. She recalled the verse from the Acts of the Apostles, "Behold, ye scoffers, and wonder, and perish: for I work a work in your days, a work in which ye shall no wise believe, though a man declare it unto you."

She never would have thought the leader of her own chosen church would have been one of the scoffers, who would reject a message from God even if it was right before his eyes. What a shame. But she couldn't help that. She'd tried to reach him, tried to convince him, and would certainly try again. Despite her compassion for others, Julia Lowell could only be responsible for Julia Lowell's own salvation, and each man and woman was free to follow God's word or reject it.

After all, Reverend Talcott and everyone else—believer and nonbeliever, the ones who accepted the prophecies and the ones who scoffed at them—would find out the truth all too soon.

The next morning, Julia was fixing some coffee, keeping one eye on the news on her television while she did so. There were no further signs of the chaos that was to come. When the collapse came, it would be sudden—she knew that much—but it was good to find out what she could from secular sources during times when God wasn't speaking to her directly.

Once the coffee maker chimed to signal it had done its job, she poured a cup and sat at the dinner table sipping it and considering the dream she'd had the previous night.

In it, she stood in the street, calling to people in a voice louder than she'd known she could produce. They came, pouring out of apartment buildings and houses and condos, jostling toward her in a surging mass of humanity. The faces were taut with emotion, and two predominated—fear and exaltation. They looked like they had been in desperate terror for their safety, but had suddenly found the person who would save not only their lives, but their eternal souls.

"You must follow me!" Julia thundered. "This place has

become the very mouth of hell. If you stay here, if you cling to your homes and your belongings, you will lose everything. If you abandon what you have and follow me, you will find new life in a new place."

There were cheers and whistles and upraised fists.

"The powers of darkness are at our heels. There is no time for wavering, no time for hesitation. Take only what is on your back, and carry only enough food and water for the first day. Trust in the Lord. The Lord shall provide for his faithful."

More shouts of approval.

At this point, the scenario dissolved, but she got vignettes of others, disconnected bits that flashed before her like glimpses through the windows of a moving train, there and gone almost too quickly to interpret. Huddled crowds of people cringing under a howling wind and slashing rain. A woman standing on the end of a collapsed bridge, the roadway beneath her feet crumbling out from under her, but smiling in triumph despite the imminence of her own death. Then Julia herself was standing on the top of a grassy hill, but she turned and looked behind her to see the entire city sinking beneath a raging flood. Next she stood atop another hillside, this one looking down into a tree-lined and sheltered valley, her arm pointing out the way to a ragged, dirty group of people whose gaunt faces were lit up with hope at a promise fulfilled.

She woke from the dream disturbed, and not just by its story of devastation and displacement.

Her role in all this, from start to finish, was the very embodiment of the sin of pride.

She thought, with some shame, of the verse from the Book of Proverbs: "Pride goeth before destruction, and a haughty spirit before a fall; better it is to be of a humble spirit with the lowly, than to divide the spoil with the proud." And there she was, acting like some amalgam of Moses leading his people out of Egypt and Lord Jesus himself telling the apostles to leave behind everything they had and follow him.

Even her deportment with Reverend Talcott the previous evening now seemed to her haughty and self-aggrandizing. He'd doubted her, and why not? Who was she to claim she knew better than him?

Better than *anyone*?

But the thought came to her—what if she *had* been chosen to lead people to safety? If she was doing what the Lord demanded, it wasn't pride, it was obedience. Moses had been a humble orphan before being called by God to save the Israelites from Pharaoh. The apostle Matthew had been a tax collector, Peter and Andrew fishermen, Paul an actual dedicated enemy of the church. All of them, the disciples and prophets and holy ones, had started *somewhere* before they found their life's work.

She looked down at her brown, work-hardened hands, laced together in her lap.

"Lord," she said in a small voice, "how can I know if this is my true calling, a command coming from You, or if it is my own prideful spirit? I don't trust myself, not at all. All I want to do is rely on You. Give me a word, a single word, so that I can know Your will, so that I can cast aside my own, and I will never doubt again."

There was nothing but silence in the tidy, spotless kitchen.

"I know the visions You have sent me are real, Lord. I don't doubt those. What I doubt is myself. I am weak and foolish and vain, and I fear to have my own desires cloud my mind. All my life I have waited for the opportunity to serve You fully, to put my own body and mind at Your will regardless of the risk, to do whatever it took to reestablish Your kingdom on Earth. But now that the trial is laid out before me, I fear to fall short, to take too much credit myself, to set myself up as a prophet not to speak Your word but to garner the praise and adulation of others. Make me a channel, Lord, an instrument, not a leader, so that the people who follow me will know the command comes from You and not from my own pride. Let me debase myself, else I will be tripped up by my own arrogance and fall lower still, to a depth from which I will not be able to rise."

She stopped, looking around her, looking for some sort of sign. Not even an answer, necessarily, but at least a sign her prayer had been heard.

Nothing.

She sat listening for almost an hour, as the remains of her coffee got cold, terrified to move lest she miss what she was listening for.

After a while, she began to cry, in despair for her weakness, doubt, and foolish vanity—and also because she felt completely inadequate to walk the road that was laid before her.

four

. . .

Corine Abraham gave her son a despairing look. "Dr. Lansing, do you think this is just another manifestation of his... his condition?"

Perry Abraham had seen that look a lot of times in his five years, but this time it felt different. This time it seemed like she was giving up.

Dr. Lansing did what he always did. When he wasn't actually talking to Perry, he talked about him as if he weren't there.

"It's hard to say." He smoothed back his thinning gray hair with one hand. "Being on the neurodivergent spectrum is so variable. Thus the word *spectrum*. There's so much we don't know about it."

"I thought... I thought we were managing things fairly well. We enrolled him in kindergarten at Cabell Street School this year, and he really seemed to be thriving academically..."

"His brainpower was never in question," Dr. Lansing interjected.

"Well, I know that. But if you're achieving in school, it means you've adjusted to it, doesn't it?"

"There's more to emotional adjustment than intellectual success."

Corine didn't respond, but her mouth tightened. That was another expression Perry had learned. When his mother's lips disappeared, it meant she was angry. He had no idea why what the doctor said made her angry, but there was no doubt about it.

Dr. Lansing turned toward Perry as if he had suddenly popped into existence. Sort of like the Genie in *Aladdin*. "Perry, how do you feel about school?"

He shrugged. "I like it."

"Do you think the other children like you?"

"I don't know."

"Do you have any friends?"

"I don't know."

"Have you talked to any of your classmates or your teacher about the messages?"

Perry immediately broke eye contact and looked away. "No."

"So right now, your parents and I are the only ones you've told."

"I also told my sister. She didn't believe me." Perry glanced toward the doctor, met his eyes for a fraction of a second, then looked away again. "You don't, either."

"I believe you, Perry. I believe that you think you're getting messages."

"That's the same thing as not believing me."

Dr. Lansing didn't answer for a moment. "Do you think the messages are coming from another person?"

"I don't know."

"Does it sound like someone's voice? Someone you know?"

Perry shook his head and kicked his legs against the chair once, twice, and then sat still again. "It's not like that."

"What is it like?"

"I already told you."

A small sigh escaped the doctor's lips. Perry had learned this also was a sign of irritation, even if it didn't show in his tone of voice.

"Why don't you tell me again?"

Another shrug. "It's like a robot's voice. There's no air in it. It's just dry words. Empty words."

"Empty, like they don't mean anything?"

"No. They mean a lot. They mean too much. Empty like…" Perry frowned, still not meeting the doctor's eyes. Meeting the doctor's eyes made it harder to think. "Empty like a paper bag. Like it's a paper bag talking."

The frustration rose in him. He didn't have the words to say what he meant, and whenever that happened, people either decided they knew what he meant anyhow and invented things of their own to fill in the gaps, or else figured he was just making up childish stuff and stopped listening.

It was why he was so desperate to learn to read. The more words he knew, the more he could get people to understand.

"No emotion." The doctor seemed at least to be trying to help him turn his thoughts into spoken words.

"Yes. Even when it says bad things, it's just… just empty."

Dr. Lansing nodded. "Can you tell me some of the things it's said?"

Perry's mother had told him when things were getting dangerous, you were *walking on thin ice*. He knew immediately this question was *thin ice*.

"It says that this is the way to know stuff now. When the internet's gone, this will be the only way, so we have to learn how to use it."

"Why do you think the internet will be gone?"

He looked up, flashing an angry glare at the doctor. Then his face relaxed again, and he said in an even tone, "I don't *think* so. I don't think anything about it. That's just what it says."

"So you don't know whether anything it says is true or not?"

"Sometimes I do. Not usually."

"Do you want to tell me about other things it has said to you?"

Another shake of the head. No, if the earlier question had been *thin ice*, this was breaking through the ice completely. This was drowning in cold water.

Dr. Lansing waited for a moment, then turned back to Mrs. Abraham. Once again, Perry ceased being a person in the room and went back to being invisible.

"It's troubling, I must admit. He doesn't seem delusional in any other respect. The psychological screen showed no changes from his previous one, with this one exception. I've never seen a case quite like it. But I think as the messages he says he's getting don't seem to be inciting him to *do* anything, we can afford to watch and wait."

"But is it psychosis?" Mrs. Abraham clenched the hem of her dress. Her knuckles were white.

Perry stared, fascinated. What could that mean?

He also didn't know the word *psychosis*. Maybe someone would explain, and that'd be one more word he had available to him.

"It would be extremely rare for true psychosis to occur in a six-year-old. It's much more likely that what you're seeing is his version of the Invisible Friend—a voice telling him things, but not really impelling him to act. In many children, the Invisible Friend is a coping mechanism that intensifies under stress and weakens when the stressor is gone, and almost always goes away completely by age seven or eight. I understand your concern given his diagnosis, but my recommendation is simple observation." He raised one white eyebrow. "And, Mrs. Abraham, I also recommend that you find a way to deal with your own anxiety. Perry is neurodivergent, but that doesn't mean he can't grow up to be a healthy, happy, well-adjusted adult. I can't help but think that your own anxiety over him might be... contributing to the intensification of his condition."

Perry glanced at his mother. Her lips had disappeared again.

"I don't see how motherly concern would contribute to Perry's condition." Her voice was tight, the annoyance rolling off her in waves so strong Perry could feel it even though it wasn't directed at him. "I'm merely trying to do the best I can for my son."

Clearly Dr. Lansing wasn't interested in fighting this battle. He gave her a conciliatory smile. "I understand, and I wasn't trying to assign blame. I'm simply worried about *you,* Mrs. Abraham. It would help you both if you were to relax, and believe me when I say that there's nothing dire wrong with your son. Simply *talk* to him, and if he tells you about other messages, jot them down so we can discuss them. Apart from that, there's no real cause for concern unless things change drastically. At which point you can make another appointment, and we'll deal with that when and if it happens."

Corine Abraham nodded, a sharp, jerky movement. After a few more formalities, during which neither of them looked at Perry, she took his hand and led him out of the doctor's office.

"Dr. Lansing is a nice man," Corine said as she opened the passenger side door to let Perry in.

Why did she do this? She always acted like she had to break the silence. He'd noticed most people were like that. Silence was a space they had to fill with idle chatter, with music, with *anything.* Any time there was a lull in the continuous background noise, something had to be put in its place. To Perry, silence was nice—it meant at least a short respite from trying to figure out the people around him, people whose actions were complex and erratic and unpredictable.

He would have been perfectly happy to sit in complete quiet on the ride home, but he knew from experience his mother would never let that happen.

After getting into the driver's side and settling herself behind the steering wheel, she said, "I hope that what he said didn't upset you."

Perry shook his head. "No, it didn't."

"I don't want you to worry. This appointment was just about making sure there wasn't anything wrong, anything we could work on. Dr. Lansing and your dad and I will make sure that everything goes smoothly. Nothing bad will happen, so you don't need to worry."

Perry turned to look at her. She was facing forward, driving the car slowly out of the parking lot, and if she knew he was staring at her, she gave no sign.

Nothing bad will happen, so you don't need to worry.

Was this a lie, or just a mistake? It certainly wasn't true. But it was impossible to tell if his mother had said it knowing it was untrue, or if she honestly believed it. He'd learned the difference between a lie and a mistake in school earlier that year, and it was always his first thought when he heard someone say something untrue.

But it wasn't always easy to discern the difference.

Nothing bad will happen. That was about as far from the truth as you could get. That was one of the first messages he'd gotten—that everything around him was going to be gone soon. His parents, his sister, his house, the familiar neighborhood. Even people he knew like Dr. Lansing.

All gone.

He slowly swiveled his head to face forward again. Should he tell his mother that? So far, he'd only told her about messages that weren't horrible. That when their family cat escaped through an unsecured back door and was gone for hours, she'd be back by bedtime. That his father was coming home from work early. That his sister was coming down with a cold.

When each time the message was accurate, he expected them to question how he'd known. The cat and his father's early arrival they attributed to wishful thinking. They assumed he'd figured out his sister's cold because he'd heard her cough or sneeze or something.

He didn't correct this impression. It would have raised too many questions he couldn't answer. Each time he'd known, known for sure, because of the messages. Wishing was just another way of lying—trying to make something true because you want it. Even his sister had supported him when he said she hadn't shown any cold symptoms beforehand, but they hadn't believed her, either.

Given their reactions to simple, innocuous messages like those, he certainly wasn't going to tell them about the others.

Especially not the ones about the entire city being destroyed.

When they got home, Corine fixed Perry some lunch, then left him to talk to their new robot, Joe.

Joe was the very latest in educational technology. The first models had been released in early 2034, and they were still prohibitively expensive for almost everyone. Corine and her husband Dan were both top-flight lawyers, and they could afford it, even if Joe had cost as much as a new car would have. Joe was a SCEPA—the Education and Personal Assistant version of the SCOMA—and Perry took to him right away. His interactions with Joe were a lot easier than those with his classmates or teachers.

Joe never had an unexpected reaction. Ever. Perry could tell him he didn't want to play word games any more, and Joe would just say, "Okay, if there is anything else you would like to do, please tell me."

Then he'd sit there waiting, as if completely content.

People, on the other hand? They were full of sudden moods and weird reactions and unexpected responses. When Perry said something, he honestly had no idea how someone would reply. Even when it was a purely factual question—"what kind of bird is that?" or "who were you talking to on the phone?"—it seemed like half the time he'd get a simple, direct answer, and the other half something dismissive or angry, or worst of all, a question like, "Why do you want to know?"

He never knew how to predict which kind of response he would get. It was always sheer guesswork, and it was exhausting.

Joe, though? Factual questions got factual answers. Requests to play a game or hear a story or help with schoolwork were never denied.

Perry often wished his world was populated with Joes.

Now, sitting at the table across from Joe, munching on a sandwich and swinging his legs, Perry said, "Joe, can I ask you a question?"

The robot looked up, and the faint light behind his eyes switched on. "Of course you can, Perry."

"Is there a word that means, when you know something is going to happen before it happens?"

"There are several, but they do not all mean exactly the same thing. There is *foresight*, which is using one's knowledge to predict what will happen in the future. There is *anticipation*, which is looking forward to a future event one believes will happen. There is *precognition*, which is foreknowledge of an event without any direct information as evidence of it..."

"That's it. Precognition." Perry took another bite of his sandwich. "Is precognition real?"

"As of my last update, there has been no definitive

evidence that precognition exists. Most scientists are of the opinion that it is impossible."

"What is psychosis?" That was another thing Perry liked about Joe. He wasn't bothered by abrupt changes of topic.

"Psychosis is a severe mental disorder in which the thoughts and emotions are so disrupted that the person loses touch with external reality."

"They can't tell what's real and what's not anymore?"

"That is correct."

"So how would a person with psychosis know they had it?"

"Many times, they do not. The psychotic thoughts seem as valid as the normal thoughts do, therefore it becomes impossible to tell them apart. However, psychosis often comes with extreme anxiety and emotional disruption. So even though a psychotic person might not recognize that they were suffering from psychosis, they would still know that something was terribly wrong."

"Do you think I have psychosis?"

No hesitation. "You show no signs of it I have observed."

Perry frowned. He'd often had the sense that what he saw and what everyone else saw weren't the same. Stuff that seemed obvious to him made no sense to anyone else, and often what other people did and said seemed weird and random. It was like he saw the world as green and everyone else saw it as red. No matter how much you talked about it, you'd never agree.

But was this psychosis? How could he tell, from inside it?

He decided not to press the topic any more with Joe. "Okay. Thanks."

"It is my pleasure."

Joe fell silent, and after five minutes, the light behind his eyes turned off.

Putting together what he'd learned was a little troubling. What he had suddenly become able to do last week was something scientists thought was impossible, so that meant it was probably in the category of *not real*. When a person lost the ability to tell what was real and what wasn't, they were psychotic.

But internally, he didn't *feel* like anything was awry. He just... knew things. Joe had said psychotic people know there's something wrong with them even if they don't know what it is, and nothing in Perry had changed except for that one thing. Plus, Joe told him he showed no signs of psychosis.

Precognition. Foreknowledge of an event without any direct information as evidence.

Like the absolute knowledge that there would come a day soon that he would say goodbye to his parents, to his sister, to Joe, and he would never see any of them again.

A few days later, Perry was sitting on a bench in the school lobby waiting for his parents to pick him up after school, when his teacher, Mrs. Gray, came over to him wearing a smile.

"Hello, Perry, how are you today?"

"Good."

"You looked like you could use some company while waiting."

Perry shrugged.

"You've seemed lately like you have a lot on your mind."

He flashed her a quick glance. "Did my mother talk to you?"

Mrs. Gray laughed. "Do you know what the word *perceptive* means?"

He shook his head.

"It means you notice things and figure things out quickly. You are very perceptive."

"So *perceptive* means my mother talked to you."

Another laugh. Why was that funny? What made something funny was another of those things that Perry never could seem to figure out.

"Yes, she did. But only that you'd been a little anxious over the last couple of weeks, and that I should know so I could help you if you needed it."

"I'm not anxious."

"That's good. There's nothing that's on your mind?"

"I didn't say that. I just said I'm not anxious."

"Oh, I see. So what have you been thinking about lately?"

He didn't answer for a while, just kicked his legs against the floor once, twice, then stopped. "If you had bad news about someone, should you tell them?"

"What kind of bad news?"

"Like if you knew something bad was going to happen."

"Well, yes, if I knew something bad was coming, I would warn them."

"Even if you knew that warning them wouldn't stop it?"

Mrs. Gray gave him a frown. "How would you know that?"

Perry shrugged again. "I'm just asking what if. If you knew bad things would happen, but you also knew that no matter who you told, it wouldn't make any difference. The bad things would happen anyway."

Mrs. Gray gazed at him in thoughtful silence for a few moments. "Do you know the word *fate*, Perry?"

He shook his head.

"It means that things are meant to happen in a certain way. That even if we can't see the future, it is already out there waiting."

He thought for a moment. "Like in a book. Even if you've just started it, the story is there in the pages you haven't read yet, you just don't know what it is."

"Exactly." She looked at him intently. "So, what you're asking, is life like that?"

He nodded.

"Well, that's a pretty big question. The easiest answer is that no one knows for sure. I always like to believe that things will work out for the best if we let them. I'm an optimist."

"What's *optimist*?"

"An optimist is a person who is hopeful and confident, who thinks the future will be positive. I've always found that a good way to be. Much better than expecting the worst. That's called being a *pessimist*." She looked up and smiled. "But here's your mom to pick you up. It was nice talking to you today. Thank you for keeping me company."

Perry didn't respond, but got up and trotted off to join his mother as she approached. Corine Abraham and Mrs. Gray locked eyes for a moment, and Mrs. Gray gave a tiny, almost imperceptible shrug.

What that meant, Perry had no idea.

But now he had another word to think about, besides *precognition* and *psychosis*.

Pessimist. Perry was a *pessimist*.

Gradually, he felt like he was figuring things out. Maybe Joe could tell him more about *pessimist* when he got home.

He certainly wasn't going to ask his mother about it.

five

. . .

D oyle Mallett gave a frustrated look at the pile of paperwork on his desk. Part of his frustration was the sheer amount of it. He had three offers on homes he was handling for sellers and four others for clients who were purchasing. This meant a lot of work pushing around paper, the part of the job he disliked the most, but it also meant there'd be a nice paycheck coming for this month.

The other piece of the frustration, though, was his sudden conviction that he'd never see the money he'd just earned.

Why he thought that, he had no idea. It just came to him as he gazed at the stack of manila folders with various clients' names. Not only would he never see his paycheck, his clients would never move into any of the houses they'd just purchased. All the excitement and smiles at putting an offer down on a home would not be fulfilled.

Doyle had been having a great many of these worry-laden doom thoughts for about a week now. He figured it was just another manifestation of the anxiety disorder he'd dealt with since his teenage years. He'd been prone since high school to worst-case-scenario-ing everything, imagining what could go wrong and then working himself into a panic over eventualities that were highly unlikely.

In the last week, though, the anxieties had been coming hard and fast even by his usual standards. He had to keep constant vigilance or he could easily ramp up into a full-blown panic attack.

He pushed the thoughts aside. No time for a panic attack today. He had an appointment to see his therapist at the end of the week, so he'd add this to the list of things he wanted to discuss with her.

He checked his watch. Nine-thirty. He needed to pick up his new clients, a Mr. and Mrs. Garrity, at ten, so he'd better get going. He threw some blank purchase offer forms into his briefcase—may as well be hopeful about that at least—closed it, stood, took a deep breath, and headed for the door.

On the way he passed the receptionist's desk, currently staffed by a temp because the regular receptionist, Brittany Tanner, was out on maternity leave. He gave her a smile, and got one in return. She was pretty and friendly—thick brown hair in a complicated braid, dark eyes, a nice figure—what was her name? Lydia something. Lydia Marston? That wasn't quite right, but he couldn't remember and didn't want to ask.

"I'm off to pick up the Garritys," he told her. "They said they had until one o'clock to look at houses, so I'm guessing I'll be back by midafternoon unless they find their dream home."

"Hope they do. You've had a good run of luck lately."

"Right? I seem to have all my stars aligned."

"Maybe they'll stay that way."

"I hope so. I'd better go while they're in my favor."

He smiled again, and turned away.

She can't stand you, you know.

Dammit, there it was again. Stupid anxiety. Why the hell would Lydia dislike him? She'd only worked there three weeks, and all their exchanges had been completely friendly.

She despises you because you're young, nice-looking, and successful.

He resisted the urge to turn back and start talking to her again, if for no other reason to check if she was flipping him off and mouthing *fuck you* as he left.

That wasn't a reality check, though. That was an unreality check. His therapist had told him it was a good thing to challenge his anxiety thoughts with a sober assessment of the real situation, but it was important not to get caught up in the merry-go-round of looking for constant reassurance. Act on rationality, not on your disordered emotional state.

She had also told him *Fake it till you make it*, but he hated that phrase, almost as much as he hated her other favorite, which was *Push the envelope.*

There was no reason in the world why Lydia would despise him. He barely knew her. She seemed genuinely glad he'd made some sales recently, and there was no justification for doubting that her congratulations were completely sincere.

But as he got in his car, the thoughts still plagued him.

You'd like to ask her out on a date, but she'd never go because she thinks you're scum. All of her smiles and friendly words are a coverup for contempt.

"God *damn*," he said as he started his car. "Will you just *stop*?"

Okay, add something else to the list of things to discuss at his next therapy session.

Mr. and Mrs. Garrity turned out to be an elderly couple from Bellingham, Washington who were moving to Seattle to be closer to their children.

"We've lived up there for forty years," Mrs. Garrity told him. "And we love it, but it's kind of far from everywhere. All three of our kids are in the Seattle area, so it makes sense rather than having a two-hour drive to visit."

But his winning streak didn't hold. No miraculous sale on

the first day of showing the clients around. They were polite about what they saw—polite about everything, really—but nothing really spoke to them.

That was the problem with wealthy people looking for an upgrade. They could afford to pay top dollar, but they were also usually in no hurry.

Heading back to the office after dropping them off, he saw along the wall of an underpass something that was becoming increasingly familiar—graffiti with the logo of the LLA, a stylized face made of the letters of the acronym. The horizontal strokes of the two Ls were modified into eyes, the uprights into arched eyebrows. Underneath, the A became a downturned triangular mouth with two long fangs.

Nasty. He'd been hearing about the Lackland Liberation Authority since they first made the news in a big way with a series of deadly attacks in Germany five years earlier, but it had all seemed remote. That they had such a visible presence here was alarming. It was hard to believe that enough people in prosperous, bustling, artsy Seattle bought their message of tearing down civilization that LLA graffiti was scrawled on walls all over the city along with edifying messages like "Save the world, slaughter the wealthy parasites."

He wondered if Mr. and Mrs. Garrity had noticed it. Hopefully not. That could definitely put the dampers on their enthusiasm over moving to Seattle and rob him of a sale.

Not that it was a problem if they chose not to buy, really. He'd already made plenty enough with his recent sales that this month looked like it'd be one of his best ever. He returned his mind to cheerful musings on his good fortune. He was even able to push aside the anxious thoughts about never getting an opportunity to spend his commission enough that he walked into the office with a smile on his face, greeted Lydia cheerfully (*Moreton. Her name is Lydia Moreton*), and generally held it together for the rest of the day.

"So the anxiety has been worse in the last week?" Andrea Lewis, Doyle's therapist for the past two years, gave him a sympathetic look. "Do you have any idea what might have triggered the upsurge?"

Doyle, sitting on the sofa in her tastefully-decorated office, shook his head. "None. It's not like anything bad has happened. I'm not worried *about* anything. Or actually, it's more like I'm worried about *everything*. I can't look at anyone or think about anything I've done without catastrophizing."

Catastrophizing was one of Andrea's favorite words for describing Doyle's thought patterns. Unlike *fake it till you make it*, this one seemed apt enough.

"No other changes you can think of that might have precipitated this? New stressors at work, a change in diet or sleep habits, interactions with family or friends?"

Another head shake. "It just sort of started. The only thing I can think of that happened around the same time is the earthquake last week."

Andrea raised one neatly-plucked eyebrow. "Did your house get damaged by it?"

"No. Nothing. In fact, I wasn't even really aware of it. I was driving to pick up a client, and my car got jolted, but I thought I'd just hit a pothole or something. It was only when I talked to my client that I realized it was an earthquake. When I got home that evening, there was nothing amiss except a couple of things that fell off shelves. No damage."

"You're not phobic about quakes?"

"Not at all. I mean, I don't like them. They're unexpected and startling. But other than that, no."

"Then it's probably unlikely the earthquake is what started the spike in your anxiety."

"Is it really that important to figure out why it happened?"

"Sometimes if we can identify a root cause, we can address it from the standpoint of rationality. Is the source of the anxiety something that is potentially dangerous in reality, or is it just an irrational trigger? But you're right, it's more important to deal with the present anxious thoughts and keep them from interfering with your life."

"Some of them are just plain ridiculous. Like every time I see the temp who is filling in for our receptionist, I keep thinking she dislikes me."

"You haven't seen any evidence of it?"

"None. She's always perfectly friendly."

Andrea nodded. "Have you been doing a reality check when the thoughts occur to you?"

"Yes. Every time. I stop myself, and go back through all the interactions I've had with her that I can remember, and picture her smiling face. There's no basis for it." He paused. "In fact, I haven't even had all that many interactions with her. She's only worked for us for three weeks, since our receptionist went on maternity leave. I say hi to her when I pass her desk, but other than that, the only things I tell her are business-related—when I leave to pick up a client, when I'll be back in the office, when I'm expecting a call. Totally prosaic, and usually just a brief exchange. But nothing unfriendly, or even neutral. She's always pleasant and positive."

Andrea leaned back in her chair. "You're doing the right thing. As you said, anxiety isn't rational, so casting the light of rationality on it often has the result of diminishing its grip. But you said it's not just… what was your receptionist's name?"

"Lydia Moreton."

"Lydia. It's not just Lydia you're feeling anxiety about."

"No." Doyle gave a deep sigh. "It's been kind of constant. Unrelenting. When I look at anything or anyone, if I don't keep a good handle on my mind, I start daydreaming all sorts of awful things."

"What sorts of awful things? Is it like with Lydia, that people dislike you?"

He shook his head. "No, not for most of them. With most of them, it's more that I think about how they're headed for calamity."

"What sort of calamity?"

He shrugged. "It's never very specific. More like… you know that feeling when you're looking down from the top of a building, or over the edge of a big bridge? Anything where there's a long way to fall? It's kind of a clench in your stomach. You picture what it'd be like to lose your balance and go over the edge, and know once that happened there'd be absolutely nothing you could do."

"I know what you mean."

"That's what it's like. It's like everyone and everything has already gone off the bridge. We're all hurtling toward ruin, but most of us don't realize it."

"Do you see any actual signs that we're approaching a catastrophe?"

"Not really. I mean, a couple of days ago I noticed how much LLA graffiti I've been seeing, and wondered if there might be some unrest here, like there's been in other places. But other than that, no."

"The LLA have been here for a while. They're just the latest in a very long line of groups who have a grudge for some reason. In my opinion, anything they'll do will be on a small scale, so it's really nothing the average person should worry about. My suspicion is that you're noticing the graffiti more because you're already anxious, not that there's been any kind of real increase."

"You're probably right."

"So your homework for this week is to practice that kind of

logic. When you look at something and find those anxiety thoughts rising, take a step back and ask yourself how the thoughts line up with what you know the reality to be. If you think, 'I'm at risk,' ask, 'What is the risk *actually*, based on what I've observed and what has already happened?' Don't waste your time arguing with them, or looking for evidence that validates them. Let the cool, calm, rational part of your brain do a real assessment of what you're anxious about. Eventually, this will become such a habit that you won't need to think about it, or to have me remind you to do it." She smiled at him. "At that point, I give you permission to fire me."

With an effort he pushed away the thought that he'd never get the chance to fire her because all of what now seemed like anxiety would be proven true very, very soon.

Assess risk. He glanced out of the window of Andrea's office. A quiet street with a painter's palette of colorful gardens, flowering trees, rhododendrons. Not a hint of catastrophe anywhere.

He took a deep breath. Maybe reality checking *would* eventually become second nature. It seemed to calm him, at least temporarily.

"Don't worry," he told her with a smile. "If I do fire you, it'll be because you've done your job too well."

As Doyle fixed dinner for himself that evening, he had the television on KING, the main Seattle station. The nightly news, today centering on negotiations between the LLA and Governor Andrew Wiedemann over their grievances about land buy-ups in eastern Washington by mining and logging corporations and industrial farms.

"LLA representatives made a persuasive case today that the use of eminent domain law to displace small landholders was harming local economies." The reporter was standing in front of the capitol building in Olympia, her voice modulated to convey the gravity of the situation. "Lawyers for the corporate interests, however, established late last year in the Circuit Court of Appeals that the purchases and consolidation of landholding by their clients was entirely within the scope of the law, so it is uncertain what, if anything, Governor Wiedemann could do to redress the plaintiffs' grievances. He has promised to continue discussing the issue with LLA spokespeople, assuring them that if there are steps to be taken that fall within the parameters established by the Circuit Court's rulings, he would do whatever he could. It remains to be seen if that will be enough to satisfy the LLA." She paused. "This is Linh Tran-Arnette, reporting live from Olympia."

Okay, well, that sounded hopeful. Maybe time to quit while he was ahead. He pulled his dinner out of the oven, and switched the channel to a game show. The chance of his hearing two news stories in a row that didn't jab his anxiety was slim. Probably shouldn't tempt fate.

His therapist's reassurance that with practice, it would become easier to challenge the part of his personality that seemed to enjoy prognosticating doom, didn't really seem to be bearing fruit. Over the next three weeks, Doyle stopped his anxiety-laden thoughts with a firm, "Just hang on a moment," followed by going through the list of reality checks Andrea had recommended. What was the risk, really? Did any of the horrible things he was thinking have a basis in reality? When his mind became convinced that someone disliked him, did the person actually show any sign of it?

Each time, it worked, in the sense that it muted the voices for a while. But they always came back. He mulled over what else he could do to counteract the part of him that was bound and determined to find the worst-case scenario in every situation.

Finally, he decided to ask Lydia Moreton out on a date.

She had still never shown him anything but friendliness—no sign of the loathing he worried about every time he saw her—and he figured that asking her out would be a final test of how inaccurate his anxieties were. He had always had trouble finding the gumption to ask a woman out, explaining why he was thirty years old and had slim experience with romance. Here, though, he had two reasons to steel his courage.

First, she was attractive. Second, it would give him abundant evidence of whether she actually hated him or not.

He also had only a short time to act. The regular receptionist had almost worked through her eight weeks of paid maternity leave, and Lydia would be on to her next temp job. If he wanted to ask her out, he needed to do it soon.

He sat at his desk, trying to slow his pulse down, shove aside the anxious thoughts, and not freak out to the point he'd decide to chuck it and not ask her. He was staring at an open file on his desk, but if anyone in the office had noticed he hadn't written anything on it, or even turned the page, for twenty minutes, no one said anything. Finally, he forced himself to get up, feeling a little like he was standing on the end of the high diving board looking at the swimming pool, tiny and remote and seeming a mile beneath his feet.

He straightened his shirt, smoothed back his hair, and walked to the front of the office.

"Lydia?"

She turned toward him, her face wearing its usual friendly smile. "Yes?"

"I was… I was wondering. Maybe. If you thought you, you know…"

Her smile widened to a grin. She obviously knew where

this was going, but didn't do anything to put him out of his misery, just let him keep stammering on.

"I... I... thought, maybe we could go out for dinner and a movie some time? Only if you want to."

She looked at him in silence for a moment, her amused expression tempered with an evaluative look. "You don't have to be afraid of me. I don't bite."

Okay, that made it worse. His cheeks warmed.

"I know." He swallowed hard. "I mean, if you don't want to, or if you're already in a relationship, or something…"

She laughed. "You also don't need to give me an easy excuse. But I'm not in a relationship, and I'm fine with dinner and a movie. When?"

Doyle had been so certain the answer would be no that he hadn't even thought through where they might go if the answer was yes. He did some rapid thinking.

"There's a nice Japanese restaurant just north of downtown. Near the Space Needle. If you like Japanese food?"

"Love it."

"And I don't know what movies are showing, but if there's something you'd like to see… I could look up what's playing…"

"We'll figure it out." Her grin flashed out again. "Breathe, Doyle."

He forced his body to relax. "Okay."

"One thing, though… I really can't afford anything expensive. I don't make much as a temp. I hate to be this blunt about it…"

"No, no problem. My treat."

She nodded. "Cool. Shall we say Thursday?"

"Definitely."

"Then it's a date." She raised an eyebrow. "That wasn't so hard, was it? What were you expecting, that I'd say, 'No, I can't stand you,' or something?"

He shook his head, because that had been pretty much

exactly what he was expecting. A few moments later, he was able to make a hasty—but hopefully not too awkward—retreat to his desk.

Once seated, he couldn't help himself. He broke out in an astonished smile.

The score for today was Doyle Mallett 1, anxiety 0.

six

. . .

Mary Hansard's MRI and blood work came back completely normal.

She wasn't sure if this was good news or not. She'd always been a solidly rational person—thus her love for science—and it was unsettling not to find an organic cause for what was happening to her. She'd been absolutely certain that *something* would come back with a red flag. Given her symptoms, she didn't like the possibilities of what could be going on, but she knew she was able to deal with bad news.

What she couldn't deal with was uncertainty.

She'd gone back to work a week after the first incident, receiving concerned well-wishes from students and staff alike, and had lied that it had just been a late case of flu, but she was feeling fine now. The truth was, the disorientation was still there, she was just learning how to manage it. It was, she reflected, a little like when she'd gone on a day-long bird-watching trip off the coast of California. The waters had been rough, and even though she wasn't prone to seasickness, the pitching of the boat made it impossible at first to walk without holding onto something. But after only twelve hours her body had acclimated, and by the end of the day she had no problem walking across the deck without stumbling.

Of course, after she got off the boat that evening, she spent the next twelve hours feeling like the rock-solid ground under her feet was swaying.

Here, there was no such external cause, but the symptoms were the same—the vertigo and unsteadiness that came from walking on a tilted surface when her eyes were telling her everything was plumb and level. But in a week, her body had adjusted, and she no longer felt shaky on her feet.

The errant thoughts, however, were harder to manage.

She found that the only thing she could do to remain sane was compartmentalize. To some extent, she was already good at this, from nineteen years in the classroom. You couldn't let on to your classes about every ache, pain, and bad day—a lot of teaching consists of soldiering on with a smile on your face regardless what's going on in your life. So in the week since the earthquake, she had become at least somewhat adept at corralling the death-predictions and other ugliness her brain was coming up with.

A little like the way that back in the day, families would lock an insane great aunt in the attic bedroom. If you can't get rid of the craziness, at least you can contain it. Not the most pleasant of analogies, perhaps, but it seemed apt.

It wasn't that the thoughts weren't *true*. She knew, knew without a shred of doubt, that her own mental crazy aunt was telling the unadulterated truth. The issue was that she still had to do her job and remain reasonably able to look after herself, and attending to the thoughts made that difficult. She quickly gained skill at hemming them in, so that their incessant battering on her mind became an annoyance rather than completely disabling.

The hardest thing was dealing with the confusion between past and present. She'd gone to starting nearly every conversation and class lecture with some kind of verification that her memory of it was, in fact, from the past and not from the future, that she wouldn't end up skipping something important because she thought it had already happened. A quick, "I think I told you before that..." or "Where did we leave off yesterday?" headed off the most glaring stumbles, but still, she was never sure if most of what was in her mind were memories or predictions.

Despite all this, she was confident no one realized anything had gone wrong with her, much less something this frightening.

Dr. Kalemba had given her a referral to a psychiatrist, a Dr. Colin Renfrew, and she had an appointment for a consultation two days hence. When she talked to the receptionist, she had to fight down an impulse to play down her condition, to say, "I'm sure it's nothing, but my doctor just wants me to double-check," or some other vaguely reassuring lie. She resisted it only by reminding herself of the fact that the receptionist undoubtedly talked to dozens of people during the day, many of whom had psychological conditions, and she would have no particular interest in Mary's own. It would be purely to reassure herself that nothing serious was wrong, and she *knew* that wasn't true.

Besides, the receptionist would be dead in a few weeks, too. Shot down while trying to get across the Evergreen Point Floating Bridge on foot.

Mary pushed that thought aside. Nope, can't relax. Get the crazy aunt under control, push her back into her bedroom, try not to pay any attention to the terrifying things she screams through the locked door.

Colin Renfrew turned out to be a tall, slender man with bright red hair, freckles, and traces of a rolling Scottish accent. He looked too young to be a psychiatrist, but Mary thought ruefully that this sort of observation had been happening more and more lately, and as she progressed through her forties, would only get worse.

Dr. Renfrew did a cursory medical exam—pulse, blood pressure, looked into her eyes and ears and throat—then asked her what was going on. His manner was easy, genial, and calm. Pretty critical when dealing with mentally ill patients.

"I'm not really sure," Mary said, attempting a smile of her own. "It's been going on for… what is it, three weeks now? It started the day of the earthquake, but I think that's just a coincidence. I don't have any phobia about earthquakes, or anything."

She'd anticipated that question as she sat in the waiting room, and decided to forestall it.

Dr. Renfrew nodded. "All right, then, tell me what started that day, what you've been experiencing."

"I have these strange thoughts. Things about the people and places I see. When I think them, I'm convinced they're predictions, that they're things that will happen in the future. So— I don't quite know how to word this—the whole time sequencing in my brain is messed up. When I picture something, I honestly can't tell if it's in the future or the past. It all feels the same."

If Dr. Renfrew was shocked by this, he showed no sign of it. It probably wasn't the weirdest thing he'd ever heard from a patient. "You call them *predictions*. Do you mean that some of them have subsequently come true? That what you thought about happened?"

"Yes. Lots of them. Not all of them, though. Some of them are still in the future."

That got an eyebrow raise. "Perhaps you could give me an example or two."

"It happened just today. I'm a high school teacher, and I had in my head a picture of the fire alarms going off, and all of us ending up standing in the parking lot in the rain. I've known about this for a while, but I had no way to tell if it had already happened or was going to happen, and of course I didn't want to ask someone, because that'd sound ridiculous. Then today, just as I'd pictured it, the alarm went off—turned out there was something spilled on a stove top in the cafeteria, and the smoke sensors set the alarms off—and there we were for fifteen minutes, standing out in the rain while they checked over everything and made sure it was safe."

"And you knew this was going to happen today."

"Not today, necessarily, but I knew it either had already happened, and was a memory, or it was going to happen. For that one, I didn't know when."

"For some things, you do, though."

She nodded. Either Dr. Renfrew was humoring her along, or else he believed her. She suspected that in his line of work, it was more likely to be the former, but at least he wasn't dismissing her out of hand.

"For some things, I know exactly when. That's how they're like memories. You know how you have some memories that are clear, but you don't know exactly when they happened? You remember having a nice dinner at a restaurant with a friend, but you couldn't be sure of the date it happened. Other things, you're crystal clear, like if you had a surprise party on your last birthday. It's the same here. Most people can only do this with past events, but I can do it with future ones, too."

His forehead creased with a frown. "Can you tell me one thing you know is still in the future? Something that will happen to us, here?"

"Aha." Mary smiled. "That's what I like, a rational approach. Provide evidence." The smile faded. "But sure. I can see lots of things. I think they're in the future, but I'm not a hundred percent certain. Has an ambulance gone by, down the street, with the sirens on, since I got here?"

Dr. Renfrew shook his head.

"Oh, okay. That must be in the future, then."

A momentary twitch of the mouth was all the reaction he had. Man, this guy was good at keeping "what the hell are you *talking* about?" out of his face.

"There's one other thing," Mary said. "It's the physical disorientation. It's a little like the past and present and future being jumbled together, and it's all around me simultaneously. I feel like the floor is tilted and flat at the same time. It even happens when I'm driving—I sense going over obstacles and potholes that I can see aren't there. Or aren't there *yet*."

"I wonder if you should be driving."

"I try to do as little of it as I can manage. But I've kind of gotten used to it, you know? All it takes is some extra concentration. I can deal with that jumble of sensations without it making me fall down or giving me motion sickness anymore."

"You used to experience that?"

She nodded. "That's how it started. I could barely walk."

"I'm surprised you weren't sent to the emergency room. That could have been the sign of something really serious."

Mary looked sheepish. "I know. My fault entirely. I didn't want to make a fuss, so I just stayed in bed until it got better. My doctor said the same thing, that I should have gone to the ER right away." She brightened. "But it turned out all right. I mean, the MRI didn't show anything wrong, did it?"

"No," Dr. Renfrew admitted. "But there are conditions that cause severe vertigo that wouldn't show up in an MRI. Menière's disease, for example."

"Dr. Kalemba went through some of the possibilities, but she said that none of them accounted for all the symptoms I'm having."

No response other than looking down at his laptop. For a while, there was nothing but silence in the room, except for the distant and omnipresent background of traffic noise.

When he looked up again, his face was impassive. "Do you have any family history of schizophrenia or dissociative personality disorder?"

Okay, she'd been waiting for that question, too. "No. Other than some distant second cousin whom I don't even know. Every else is the pinnacle of normalcy."

"Have you ever taken psychoactive drugs?"

"Never. My blood work was negative for anything of that sort, wasn't it?"

He nodded. "Do you know of..." His voice trailed off, and he met Mary's eyes, his mouth hanging open slightly.

The whine of a distant ambulance siren, increasing in volume as it rapidly approached. The doctor remained silent as it zoomed past, only for a moment its flashing lights piercing the window and reflecting from the white walls.

The doctor's eyes stayed locked on Mary's, but he seemed to be at a loss.

She gave a shrug and a smile. "What were you saying, Doctor?"

"I, um." He looked down at his laptop again, as if giving himself space to collect his thoughts.

"It wasn't just a shrewd guess, Dr. Renfrew. I *knew* that was going to happen. I knew because I saw that ambulance in my memory. I saw it as clearly as you remember the conversation we've been having."

After a moment, his gaze returned to her face. "There is no scientifically admissible evidence for precognition..."

"There is now." She could hear the belligerent note in her voice, something not at all common for her. She considered apologizing, then decided that she didn't care.

"My office is on a busy street," Dr. Renfrew said in a slow, patient voice. "Any time of the day or night..."

"Oh, come on." Mary gave him another shrug, turning her hands palm upward. "Seriously? How often in the past month has an ambulance gone right by your window? This isn't a main thoroughfare. Yes, you can hear them any time, but one down this street? Stretches credulity, doesn't it?"

"No more so than the idea that you foresaw it."

"Look, doctor, I don't have an explanation for it either, much as I'd like to. I'm a rational person. A science teacher for nearly two decades. I don't subscribe to any belief in the supernatural or paranormal or whatnot. Heck, I'm not even religious. If I knew what was going on, I'd tell you." She shook her head. "Actually, if I knew what was going on, I wouldn't be here."

"No, I suppose not." He tented his fingers and looked upward for a moment. "Now, assuming that I accept your basic claim that some of what is in your mind is precognition about the future—and, allow me to state for the record, I am not ready to do that, not without more evidence—is all of what you see coming minutiae, like ambulances and fire alarms and so forth?"

Mary felt her smile fade. Yes, she knew it would come to this eventually. "No. No, Dr. Renfrew, in fact, most of it isn't about minutiae at all. Most of it is… dreadful. Devastating. Foreknowledge of disaster."

"What sort of disaster?"

The terror that she had shut away was banging on the door now. The doctor's questions were natural enough, but their answers sounded insane. "Everything." Her voice was a near whisper. "Everything destroyed. Everything and everyone."

Dr. Renfrew was silent for a moment, his face set in a frown. Finally he said, tentatively, "You must be frightened."

She laughed, a nervous bray completely unlike her usual cheerful laughter. "That doesn't begin to describe it."

"I must admit your symptoms aren't something I've run into before. I'm hesitant to put you on antipsychotics—"

"—good, because I'm hesitant to take them."

He paused and nodded. "Perhaps giving you as-needed

anxiolytics could at least help with the worst of the emotional symptoms. Sometimes clearing out the emotional reaction helps a person to see the other issues in a more rational light. To deal with them through therapy rather than simply medicating them away."

"Doctor…" She met his eyes, gave a short, sharp shake of the head, and looked away.

"Yes?"

She took a deep breath, let it out slowly. "I know you're trying to alleviate how unpleasant this has been, but you know… sometimes symptoms are there for a reason. If you're in pain, it's to alert you that something is wrong so you can take care of it. What if… what if this isn't just some sort of malfunction? I mean, you're approaching this as if these sensations are coming from my own mind. I understand why you look at it that way—mental illness comes from a person's neurophysiology. I get that. But what if this isn't the same thing?"

"How do you mean?"

"What if it's not really mental illness?"

"What do you think it is, then?"

"Maybe it really is precognition."

"As I said before…"

"Me too!" She cut into his quiet, patient voice with an intensity that was nearly anger. "Me too. I don't believe in precognition either. Or didn't. But how much evidence do you need before you just say, 'Okay, I guess I was wrong'? I've had to re-evaluate a lot of things since this started. One of those things is whether my previous rationalistic, scientific notion of how the world works is actually correct."

He tapped his long fingers on the side of his laptop. It was the first gesture of pure nervousness and discomfort he'd shown. "The alternative is devastating."

"I won't argue that. But a person's emotional reaction to something has nothing to do with whether or not it's true. If there's one thing I've learned, it's that the universe doesn't care if I find the truth comforting."

A flicker of a smile crossed Dr. Renfrew's face. "Whatever else may be going on, your logical faculties are intact."

"Good to know. But Doctor... seriously. What do I do with the idea that however it works, I have certain knowledge that everything and everyone here is headed for catastrophe?"

"Ideally, what would you want to do? I mean, suppose you had the power to compel people to do what you wanted. Best case scenario. What would you do?"

"Honestly? Make everyone leave. Get out of Seattle. Now."

"So the calamity you see is confined to the Seattle area?"

"No. It's everywhere. But here was one of the worst places. Or will be." She winced, closed her eyes, and shook her head. "God, it feels so much like a memory. I can't help putting it in past tense, as if it's already happened."

"If you see it all that clearly... what *will* you do? Not what you'd want to do in ideal circumstances, but what will you actually do about all this? If terrible things are going to happen here, why don't you leave and save yourself?"

"Well, first, it's not all that clear. You know how weird memory is? You remember some things with incredible accuracy, others are kind of foggy, some things you forget entirely. My future sense is like that. So it's not like I see every single thing in my future with complete clarity." She paused. "But what I do see... all I can say is that I don't leave. Not yet, anyway. There are things that have to happen first. There are people I need to find, people to help. Once they're safe... well, I don't know."

"Why don't you know after that?"

Another shock of terror zinged its way through her. Here it was, the other thing she hadn't wanted to reveal, and despite that, it had come out anyway.

"Past the point where I've done what I could to help

people… to get some of them to safety… I never can see anything further. I don't know why. But I suspect…" She trailed off. To say the words seemed like bringing them into being, even more than her certainty about the accuracy of her forward-facing memories had already done.

"You suspect…?" Dr. Renfrew urged her, his voice gentle.

Mary took a deep breath, and locked her gaze onto his. "After that, I don't see anything, because I think that's when I die."

seven

. . .

"This piece is called *The Tilted World*."

Brandon Nguyen kept his eyes fixed on Mr. Sawester's face as the older man examined the digital image in front of him, looking for any sign of a reaction, positive or negative. About all he saw was a slight lift of shaggy eyebrows.

Finally, Mr. Sawester looked up. "It's really… quite extraordinary, Mr. Nguyen."

The wash of relief was instantaneous. "You think so?"

A smile played about Mr. Sawester's thin lips. "I don't say that often, or about many works of art, but when I do, it's genuine."

Brandon let out a long breath. "Thank you."

Mr. Sawester used the tip of his thin index finger to swipe through the other images in the file. There were now twelve paintings, all completed in the last three weeks. Brandon had never achieved that level of productivity in his life, and even considering the inevitable difficulty of assessing one's own work, he knew they were good. They were, in fact, the best pieces he'd ever painted.

He couldn't escape the rueful sense that it was almost like they'd been painted by someone else.

"I am quite prepared to recommend to the committee that you have a solo show here at the gallery. I am not the final word on the decision, of course, but I cannot imagine there will be disagreement. Your work is breathtaking."

"Wow. Thanks."

"This one, for example." He gestured at the computer screen, which held a jpeg of *The Hands of the Magician*, showing a thin little blond boy, perhaps five or six, standing in a typical kid's room, with toys and books on the floor. But the boy was looking upward—hovering over his outstretched hands a glowing sphere floated, which if you looked closer seemed to be the Earth.

The ceiling over the boy's head was the black of interstellar space, spangled with stars.

"This kind of imagery draws in the eyes and the mind. One keeps looking closer, and the more one looks, the more one sees. I can only imagine that the effect will be even more dramatic when the actual canvas is before the eyes, not a digital image." He shook his head. "Extraordinary. Truly extraordinary."

"I hardly know what to say."

"Might I ask what inspired these? The images are complex, and are fantastically realistic and completely surreal at the same time, something that can be quite difficult to achieve."

"I'm not exactly sure. It's nothing more than seeing them clearly in my mind, and then painting what I see."

Another faint trace of a smile. "You shouldn't downplay what you have accomplished. Many of us have clarity of mental images, but transferring those images onto canvas is another matter." He swiped to the next image, and peered in closer toward a dark, ominous scene of people around a campfire, with curls of razor wire and feral, desperate faces barely visible in the shadowed background. "Who have you used as models, may I ask? They don't have the generic look many artists fall back on. Not only the central figures, but the people in the periphery of the image—they have a stunning realism. Each one is, quite obviously, a real person."

Brandon was brought back to his conversation with Caria the night he'd shown her *The Tilted World* and she'd asked much the same thing. His answer to her—that the people in his paintings were real even though he had no idea who they were—seemed too out there for this staid, academic gallery director. He'd gotten this far in the process of achieving a solo show. He didn't want to blow it by saying something weird.

He fell back on vague generalities. "I'm not sure. I just visualize people clearly. They're probably composites of people I know and people I've seen."

Mr. Sawester gazed at the image for a few more moments. "Really extraordinary. I can confidently state that I've never seen anything quite like them." He touched a key on his computer, and the image of the people seated around the outdoor fire was replaced by a much more prosaic one of a document that Brandon recognized as his show application.

"We have your paperwork, and everything seems to be in order. When would you be ready to show? I presume you have other pieces in progress."

"Several. But I could show any time, honestly. With a few weeks' notice to give the paint time to dry."

"Excellent. You already know that we have the next three months of shows scheduled, so it's unlikely to be before August. Some time this fall, I expect, once again with the caveat that your application and portfolio have to pass jury."

"Of course."

"I believe we can have an answer to you by early next week. At that point, presuming a positive response, we can discuss scheduling. Thank you again for submitting. Your work is fascinating."

It was obviously a dismissal, albeit an upbeat one. "Thank you, Mr. Sawester." He stood, shook the older man's hand, and left the office.

It was only once the door was closed that he allowed himself to mouth "Yes!" and give an enthusiastic fist-pump in the air.

He'd told Caria he would meet her for lunch after his interview, and he was barely seated in the café before the words started tumbling out of his mouth.

"He loved them. I mean, seriously. I've applied for shows before, and they're usually all neutral, like, 'Yes, interesting, your pieces may work for us, we'll have to discuss it.' This guy was salivating from the first image."

"That is awesome."

He nodded. "I can't believe it. I've always had to struggle to get into shows, feeling like I'm sunk in a huge crowd of artists all vying for attention from a tiny number of galleries. I've never just walked in and gotten a reaction like that."

"Are you still painting every day?"

"Yes. That's another thing. I wouldn't have thought I could keep this kind of schedule, or at least not for long. I'm still working twelve to fourteen hours a day, every day. I think I maybe sleep three or four hours a night, but I'm not tired. I'm never tired."

Caria took a sip of her cup of coffee, and seemed to be trying to figure out what to say. When she finally looked up, she was frowning. "I'm glad your creativity has returned, but doesn't the suddenness of it concern you a little?"

"How do you mean?"

"Before three weeks ago, you seemed completely listless. About everything. Then bam, you're like a creative dynamo." She took another sip. "Aren't you a little worried about where all this is coming from?"

"I wonder, yeah. But worried? Not really. I'm enjoying it too much."

"Have you…" She stopped, her frown deepening. "I don't want to piss you off, or make you think I'm not glad for your success. But…"

"Go ahead."

"This sounds a little like… bipolar disorder. My college roommate was bipolar, and she would soar up to these amazing highs. Like you describe, she didn't want to sleep, she wanted to do stuff round the clock. But it never lasted. She'd plummet, and for days could hardly get out of bed. There was… fortunately there was medication that helped, or she'd probably have dropped out of school. It evened out the highs and lows and made her at least functional."

"You think I'm bipolar? That sort of thing doesn't just come on all at once." The insinuation annoyed him, but he couldn't put his finger on exactly why. She was obviously speaking out of concern.

"No. I'm not qualified to make that kind of judgment. It just worries me that you changed so completely and so suddenly. I'm glad you're happy, but I don't want you to crash and burn at some point."

"I don't feel like I'm going to."

Caria nodded. "I know. Just be aware of it, okay? And if you feel like the flood is drying up, and you're sinking, talk to someone. Or talk to me, and I'll find someone for you."

Brandon gave a quick shrug. "Is it really that extreme? It's not like I just took up painting, or something. I'm still doing what I've always done." As he said it, he knew this was a lie. In three weeks he'd made the biggest shift he'd ever experienced in his life. It was ridiculous to claim that it was anything but a fundamental alteration to his personality.

"Not like this. There's something new, something I've never seen in you, or only seen traces of. Honestly, I have to confess that I thought at first you might be taking drugs. Speed, or acid, or something. The change was that drastic." Her face relaxed into a smile. "But I don't want to take away from your accomplishment. You're doing brilliant work, and I'm so glad you're finally getting the recognition you deserve. It's wonderful to see you enjoying life, and especially enjoying art, again."

Brandon smiled back, but there was still a nagging feeling that maybe Caria was right. There *was* something bizarre about all this—the sudden upswing in energy, the spike in his creativity, the flood of wild, surreal images in his brain. Should he be questioning why all this was happening?

Doubting it seemed like what the old Brandon would do. Try to put a damper on things, hesitate, distrust everything— himself most of all. He was caught up in it, swept along like a boat plunging through rapids.

The whitewater rafting analogy was frighteningly apt. You're not in control, you can't stop even if you want to. You know the power of the river could easily kill you, but while it's happening all you can feel is exhilaration.

At the end of lunch, Caria told him that no, she was flattered he asked, but she had to get back to work and didn't have time to go back to his house with him for a quickie. So he returned alone. Truth be told, he wasn't that disappointed at being turned down. Lately, sex had been second in his mind after painting, but it was a distant second. She'd promised a tryst that evening, and that promise would hold him for the next few hours.

He had paintings to work on.

He opened the door to his studio, and was hit immediately by the unmistakable smells of linseed oil and turpentine. Paintings were everywhere—on easels, leaning against walls and bookcases and cabinets. He went from one to another, and Caria's questions about why all this was happening to him bubbled up in his memory again.

He wasn't on drugs, and in fact hadn't used much since college. Bipolar was a possibility, but did it just come on suddenly like that? Even if it was bipolar, he didn't *want* to go on meds that would bring him down, that would blunt the edge of what he was experiencing. He'd chance crashing eventually to keep the thrill of the high he was on. Whatever was coming, it was worth it.

But then another, more troubling set of questions came to him. What about his conviction that these people and events were real—but lay in the future? That, he had to admit, sounded completely insane, but simultaneously he had no doubt of it at all. They were out there, except maybe some who hadn't been born yet. He was getting communication from the future.

But communication from whom? And why? And why him?

There seemed to be no way to answer this.

He could picture each one of them as clearly as he could picture the faces of his friends and family. He would know them instantly if they walked into the room. He'd expected some of the emotional resonance with them would be discharged after he finished each painting, but he found it only made the charge higher.

It felt like he was getting to know these people.

The little boy, levitating the Earth above his upturned palms. His name was Perry, and he had somehow plugged into the same power that was driving Brandon, although it manifested differently in him.

The old African American woman in the painting he called *Poured Out Like Water*, spilling liquid sunlight from her cupped hands while bearing the weight of heaven on her shoulders. Her name was Julia. He would hear her voice very soon, not just in his head, but in person. She was perhaps the closest of them all.

The blond man in the first painting he'd done, *The Tilted World*, who looked as if he was the pivot of the entire universe, upright no matter what, and protecting the rest of humanity behind his outstretched arms. His name was Soren. He wasn't an oracle like Perry and Julia, but he had a role to play that would determine which of them lived and which of them died.

Brandon knew the names of each one of them. More, he felt that they were growing in his mind, revealing themselves as they penetrated deeper, as if he was probing into their brains as they probed his.

What would be the end result? Would he eventually be mentally linked to all of them?

For some of them, that was fine. He felt their fundamental goodness. They were humans with frailties and faults, he knew that, but there was nothing dangerous about a reciprocal connection, like an invisible cable networking their brains. But there was one…

Reluctantly he turned toward a corner of the room, where a canvas was tilted against the wall. It was called *The Pyre of the Former World*, and the dominant color was red. The central figure was a woman with dark hair flying. Her eyes were closed, but she wore a faint smile, as if she was the keeper of a great and terrible secret. Circling her waist was a rope that bound her to an upright stake. The smoky air was filled with fire and sparks, rising up from the chasm of hell that opened before her bare feet. The flames swirled around her, and streaks of fire, almost too bright to look at, ran up her scarlet dress. Her hands had stigmata like the wounds of the crucified Christ, and blood streamed from them, but it appeared to feed the fire, not quench it.

He hadn't gotten her name yet, and he would only do so if he bared his mind to her. But that felt like opening the door to something dangerous.

Perhaps there was more to her, as well, just as the others had virtues and flaws. Perhaps the fire-woman was, like all humans, a mixed bag of good and bad, and any wrongs she committed had their reasons. He remembered his eleventh grade lit teacher saying to the class, "Every villain is the hero of their own story," and maybe that was true here.

But even so, he wasn't ready to throw himself open to her.

By late afternoon, after working four hours with barely a glance at the clock, Brandon realized he had to take a break for something purely prosaic. He needed to go to the grocery store. He was almost out of a number of necessities, the top of the list being coffee. In the rare moments when his energy flagged, a cup of coffee brought it roaring back full-force.

With some reluctance he wrapped his brush and set it down. No need for a thorough cleaning. He knew he'd be back at it as soon as he got home. He gave a quick stretch to relieve the stiffness in his back, then gathered his wallet and keys and headed out of the door.

Once in the store, he shopped in an abstracted way, paying only enough attention to make sure he wasn't forgetting anything while the rest of his mind went back to the images he'd created and the ones he'd yet to tackle. He ruefully admitted to himself that Caria was right to be a little concerned—this was becoming an obsession—but the quality of the art he was producing, and the fact of his landing a solo show, was enough to buoy him up from any worry he shared with her.

Into his cart went two pounds of coffee, milk, sugar, some items for meals, personal items like deodorant and shampoo. Had he put on deodorant that morning? He couldn't remember, but figured Caria would have mentioned it if he hadn't. Like everything else, personal care had kind of gone by the wayside lately. He was ordinarily fastidious, but his mind was so occupied with his art that he'd more than once had to check his bath towel for dampness to see if he'd showered that morning or not.

He turned his cart into the vegetable and fruit aisle, and came to a dead halt.

Standing by a display of apples, going through them one by one with a critical eye, was the elderly woman in *Poured Out Like Water*.

It was not a chance resemblance. This was her, as certainly as if he'd used her as a live model.

Before he could stop himself, he said, in a thin voice, "Julia?"

She pivoted slowly, and her face registered incomprehension. "Yes?"

His brain went into complete vapor-lock, and he stood there with his mouth hanging open.

A frown creased her forehead. "Do I know you?"

"I… I don't think so."

The incomprehension morphed into suspicion. "Then how do you know my name?"

Brandon's eyes widened. A conviction that the people in his paintings were real was one thing, but bumping into one of them at the grocery store was something else entirely.

"I'm not sure. I just knew it. Somehow."

As lame as that sounded even in his own ears, it seemed to strike some kind of resonance in her.

"You knew?" she said quietly. "My name was revealed to you?"

"I guess." He reached into his pocket and pulled out his phone. "Look." With a few taps, he brought up the image of Julia's improbable portrait.

The frown deepened as she peered at the bright colors of the painting through her bifocals. "You're the artist?"

He nodded.

"And you didn't paint this because you saw me somewhere?"

"No. Except in my mind. And I've done others like it as well."

"I see." She continued to examine the image. "It's good. Your painting, it's really good."

"It's called *Poured Out Like Water*."

Julia glanced up. "Like the Ava Norwood novel."

"I don't know about a novel."

"She's an author. She wrote a novel with that name. The pastor of my church disapproved of my reading it, said that it portrayed Christians in a harsh light. My response was that some of them deserve it, and if we are to represent God's will on Earth, we have to be willing to examine our own people, and call them out when it's warranted."

"I don't think I've ever heard of the book. The title just came to me."

"Like your image of me." She gazed at him with an evaluative expression. "What's your name?"

"Brandon. Brandon Nguyen."

"You're Chinese?"

He bristled, tried not to roll his eyes, and mostly succeeded. He recalled the nastiness back during the pandemic years, when the president and his cronies blamed the virus on the Chinese. He had been only twelve at the time, but still had a sickening memory of the horrible upsurge of violence against people of Asian descent that followed, and the harassment he and the members of his family had to endure. When he spoke, he could hear the defiant anger in his own voice.

"I'm American. Aren't you?"

"All right, point taken."

Her response sounded patronizing, and it was an effort not to sigh. "If you're curious, my father's family is originally from Vietnam, and my mother's is Indonesian and Dutch. But on both sides we've been here for three or more generations."

Her voice took on conciliatory terms, and the suspicion in her face ebbed a little. "I didn't mean to give offense."

It always surprised him to face prejudice from people who

were themselves minorities, but at least she was backing down.

"It's not a problem."

She nodded, then gestured back at his phone. "Why did you paint this?"

"I don't really know. Like I said, the image just came to me."

"Along with my name."

"Yes. And it's not the only one. I've done twelve paintings that came to me the same way."

"Twelve. Twelve apostles, twelve tribes… twelve oracles." She paused, and seemed to be pondering what to say. "Perhaps we should sit down and have a cup of coffee in the café. I think this will take more discussion than we should have standing in the vegetable aisle."

eight

. . .

Julia held Brandon's phone in one hand, using the tip of her index finger to swipe one by one through the jpegs of his paintings.

"They're amazing. I was going to say *beautiful*, but that word seems a little frivolous considering the subject matter. You have incredible talent as an artist." She looked up at him. The young man with the long black ponytail stared at her with curiosity and apprehension in his dark eyes. She took a deep breath before adding, "You believe all these people are real."

"I'm sure of it. I think they're all out there, waiting for me to meet them. Just like you were."

"Have you read the Book of Revelation?"

It must have seemed like a non sequitur. He gave her a look of pure puzzlement. "In the Bible?"

She nodded.

He shifted in his chair. "I'm not a Christian."

"That's not what I asked you."

He didn't answer for a moment. "I think I read parts of it, a while back. It's about the apocalypse, right?"

"Yes. It's an account of the End Times. John of Patmos was

a prophet who received the visions recorded in it, and wrote down what he saw. These images…" She paused, searching for the right words. "These images come from the same place."

"So you believe me that these are real people?"

Julia's long habit of caution around strangers stopped her from acquiescing, even though she felt in her bones that what he said was the exact truth. She'd seen hostility aimed at Christians by the secular, and even though the Bible called on true believers to witness, she was always wary about it. And if this strange young man, a nonbeliever, was truly receiving messages from God, what did that imply about her own place as a prophet during the End Times?

She didn't answer, but swiped forward, pausing at *The Hands of the Magician*. "A little boy who holds the world in his hands."

"I don't understand why. Or what he's done, or what he's going to do. All I see is the picture in my mind, and I paint it. I don't know what any of them mean."

She swiped ahead again, to *The Pyre of the Former World*. A quick frown crossed her face. "The Scarlet Whore of Babylon."

"She certainly looks like it."

"She doesn't just *look* like it. She *is* it." She examined the image through narrowed eyes, then handed Brandon his phone.

"Who are the others?" His voice combined hope and desperation. He wanted answers.

"I don't know. I don't recognize anyone. Neither do I know what place they have in the times to come. I don't think they're mentioned in Revelation, other than the Scarlet Whore of Babylon. But the source of all these images is the same."

"What's the source?"

She gave him an incredulous look. "The mind of God, of course."

Brandon stared at her, and didn't respond.

"You're not a Christian, so I wouldn't expect you to come to that realization right away. But that's where they come from. I'm not speculating, here. I *know*."

"How?"

That one word seemed to encompass all of the doubt she'd heard from people during her life, and in fact, some of the doubt she herself sometimes felt.

"Because I'm getting messages, too. Not images, or at least not the way you do. I'm no artist. But in the last weeks I've had messages from God in dreams, and also during my waking hours. The apocalypse is coming. It's on our very doorstep."

"When did your messages start?"

"You remember the day of the earthquake?"

Brandon blanched, and blurted out, "Mine too. That's when I started getting images."

She gave him a grim nod. "It must have been the signal God was giving us that the End of Days was coming, and that certain of us would be the prophets who would hear and understand His word. It's like what happened on the Day of Pentecost, when God sent what appeared to be tongues of fire down upon the heads of the apostles, and they began to prophesy. He has chosen you and me, and undoubtedly others."

"But I don't believe in God."

"Apparently He has taken a hand in altering your disbelief."

He swallowed hard. "This is terrifying."

"It is. Surely the fact that you painted me before we'd ever met convinces you that you're getting information from something much, much bigger than yourself."

He nodded, but his expression still betrayed terror.

Compassion rose in her. It was hard enough for her, and

she'd been a believer all her life. For Brandon, it must feel like his world had been turned on its head.

She patted his hand. "It's understandable you're afraid. You'd be a fool not to be. I'm afraid, too, afraid I won't be able to do what is demanded of me. Also afraid of the ordinary things—suffering and death, hardship and trials, losing my security and my home. Anyone would be afraid. But don't let your fear cause you to doubt your visions are real."

Brandon took a sip of his coffee and still did not respond. His hands trembled.

"I think we have our tasks laid out before us. You need to seek out the other people in your paintings. There's a reason those images have been given to you." She frowned. "But be cautious around the woman. There is a deep, deep evil there. If she realizes you know who she is, she will not hesitate to destroy you."

"What should I do?"

"Right now? Finish your coffee and your shopping. Go home. Keep opening yourself to the voice of God, however He chooses to speak to you. Keep painting what you see. Other than that, look for the people in your visions, and prepare yourself for the chaos that is sure to come. You and me and the others like us—we will have a lot to face once it all starts."

"When will that be?"

"I don't know. I know that's an unsatisfying answer, but it's the truth. It could be tomorrow. It could be next year. My feeling is tomorrow would be a closer guess." She took a piece of paper out of her purse, jotted down a number, and pushed it across the table to him. "My phone number. I don't give it out often. But I think we need to keep in touch. Let me know if there's anything we need to discuss."

He nodded, then tore the paper in half, wrote down his own, and passed it back to her. "Same. This scares the hell out of me, but you're the only one so far who has been able to make sense of any of it. Call me if you need to."

She nodded. "I'll see you soon."

His face went pale and bloodless again, and for a moment she was afraid he would faint, but he got himself under control quickly. He stood up, a little unsteadily, and left the café.

Poor young man. This had to be a shock. But still—he should have expected *something* after painting all of those images. Surely he realized they had to come from somewhere, and more importantly, they had to have meaning.

It was, Julia reflected, different for her. She'd expected something like this for years. Not this, exactly, but signs and portents. Now that it was almost upon her, it was a relief the waiting was over. She would have to watch that young man carefully. He was important, she could tell that, but he would need help. His lack of belief set him up for collapsing completely once the End Times began in earnest.

The two of them made an odd partnership. She had expected the members of her church to rally around once she told them about the messages she'd received, but had been politely rebuffed at every turn. First Reverend Talcott, the night the messages began. Similar attempts with the director of Ministry and Oversight, the Deacon, the Outreach Committee chair, and various others had been met with nothing more than mild puzzlement.

Odd thing, that. When the real messages from God came, the flock who had been primed for years to listen for them didn't believe it, and the only one who did was an atheist artist who was hardly more than a boy.

God works in mysterious ways.

The next days went much as the previous ones had. Julia devoted herself to prayer, for the world, for herself, for Brandon, and more than once she found herself echoing Jesus's plea that the cup be taken from His lips. She had no real expectation that this would happen, but it was only human to be apprehensive. If even the Lord himself asked to be spared, she supposed God would forgive her for a similar frailty.

She checked in twice with Brandon. Each time, he sounded a little embarrassed, as if his sharing his art with her had exposed a part of himself about which he was ashamed. She tried to be reassuring, but it was hard for her to understand why he felt this way. If these were messages from God —and she had no real doubt about that—he shouldn't be embarrassed to share them.

But then she recalled the reactions of Reverend Talcott and the rest of the church elders, and ruefully admitted to herself that he had justification for feeling reluctant.

"If you've been chosen to receive these visions, it's an honor. A burden, but an honor as well."

"I guess," Brandon answered.

"They have continued to come to you?"

"Yes. I'm still painting every day, all day long. Hardly any breaks. My girlfriend is worried about me because sometimes I forget to eat. She thinks I'm obsessed."

"You have reason to be. In biblical times, the prophets were often seen in the same light."

"I get the feeling that… it's never going to end. That I'm some kind of conduit, and that as long as I keep painting, there will always be more coming. A reasonable person would find this exhausting even to consider, but all I feel is exhilaration."

Julia didn't answer for a moment. Then she spoke slowly, choosing her words with deliberation. "You don't have the sense that there is an end date coming? That the message of the paintings will conclude once the visions you have seen begin to manifest?"

"I don't, no. Like I told you when we first talked, I don't really understand the meaning of the images. They come to me, and I paint them, but I don't see the overarching pattern. It's like if you saw thirty different still shots from a movie, and tried to piece together the plot from those alone."

The downside of not having a background in the history of prophecy. Unfortunate, but understandable.

"I think that will come when you start to connect with the other people in your paintings. You haven't seen any of them, have you?"

"No."

"Keep looking. I feel certain you will. It may not be until the real collapse begins."

Long pause. "And you don't know when that will be?"

"No. I have not been given that information."

"Let me know if you do."

"I will."

Each time, she had followed up her conversation with more prayers for guidance, for information, for counsel. The waiting was agonizing even though deep in her core she knew it was almost over.

But no real change came in the messages she herself was receiving until the evening of Thursday, May 11, 2035.

She was just finishing the dinner dishes, contemplating spending an hour or so reading, and then having an early bedtime, when she was hit with a flood of knowledge so dramatic, so huge, she almost lost consciousness. It was from the same source as the others, but it was like comparing a raindrop to a waterfall because they're made of the same stuff.

When it ended as suddenly as it began, she was a little astonished to find herself still standing.

This was it. The time was finally here. All of it—the chaos, the blood, and her time of trial in leading people through and out of it—was beginning tomorrow morning.

"Lord," she said in a weak voice, "You could have given me a bit more warning."

God did not respond.

She immediately went to her phone.

Her first call was to Brandon. He didn't pick up, so she left a message, hoping she modulated her voice enough that he wouldn't sense the panic she felt. Then she called, one after another, Reverend Talcott and each of the church elders, giving them one more chance to heed her words. Then she went on to call some of her friends and family whom she felt duty-bound to warn.

An hour later, she sat at her kitchen table, weeping with frustration and anger. She had, once again, been met with a uniform wall of resistance. Reverend Talcott, in fact, had suggested that she not call him again, but see a psychologist.

She responded, "Look what happened to the people who didn't listen to Noah."

It made no difference.

A couple of the elders of the congregation had said, "Thank you for letting me know," but there were overtones of amusement in the words that made her wonder if she and her obsession with the End Times had been the subject of discussion behind her back. One friend said, "My word, that's horrible. Why are you thinking about such horrid things, Julia?"

It took all of her commitment to charity not to shout into the phone, "I'm not just 'thinking about it,' I'm warning you so you can save yourself!" Over and over, she found herself incredulous that these people she thought she knew, who each Sunday had listened to Bible verses about the words of the prophets, didn't actually believe any of it. It was nothing more than nice-sounding platitudes to them. In the days of the prophets, they'd have been amongst the scoffers. And now, when the real tribulation was on their doorstep, they were too content in their safe, comfortable lives even to believe it was happening.

Brandon called her back a little before eleven. She had tried to go to sleep at about nine, but couldn't relax even though she knew she'd need all her strength tomorrow to face what was coming. After about twenty minutes of restless tossing, she got up, put on her robe, and sat in her armchair staring into the shadows, wondering how on earth her seventy-year-old body was going to do all of what was going to be demanded of it.

When the phone rang, it jolted her out of her thoughts hard enough that at first, she wasn't even sure what the noise was. She blinked groggily at the words "Brandon Nguyen" on the "caller" screen, and nodded. She knew he'd call back. At least he took this seriously.

"Hello?"

No greeting, no preamble. "Julia, you're sure? It's tomorrow?"

"I'm sure."

"Holy shit."

She chuckled. She had to admit the phrase was appropriate. "You should prepare yourself in whatever way you can."

"Okay, but prepare myself for what?"

She frowned, and didn't respond. That was the question, wasn't it? If the tribulations were beginning tomorrow, what should they do? Flee? Barricade inside their dwellings? Find weapons and prepare to fight?

Finally, with some reluctance, she said, "I don't know. I think we're gonna have to play this one by ear."

"That's not very reassuring."

"No, it's not. But it's the best I can do. I've prayed for more direct guidance, but this is all I have for now. I trust that God will give me what I need to know, when I need to know it." She paused. "I do think, though, that you and I have a long road to walk ahead of us, and we must ready ourselves for hard times."

"I need to call my girlfriend. Warn her."

"Now would be the time."

"Then I should pack up my paintings. If we're going to have to get out, I have to be able to bring them with me."

She felt a pang at this, because she resonated to the same thoughts. She was attached to her little apartment and her few belongings, as spare and simple as they were. She could only imagine how it felt for Brandon, faced with leaving behind his life's work. But she was reminded of the passage from the Book of Matthew that it was better to cut off your own hand and enter the Kingdom of Heaven than to keep it and be given to the eternal fire.

But that seemed too harsh a truth to speak.

"You do that, Brandon. But only what you cannot face leaving behind, and whatever you can carry on foot. I don't know where we are going, nor how, but I do know one thing. When the time comes, we can't let any earthly possessions hold us back. Not even the most precious thing we own. I fear that in the end, it will come down to a choice of saving ourselves and the people under our care, or clinging to what we have and drowning with the rest of those who did not heed the warnings."

nine

. . .

Perry Abraham started saying goodbye to everything around him during the first week of May.

He didn't make a show of it, and if his parents were aware he was doing it, they said nothing. But when he saw something he liked, even set down a toy or a book, he whispered under his breath, "If I never see you again, bye."

The voice still spoke to him in its odd, empty tone, telling him that all the things it'd warned him about were almost here.

"You'd better start saying your farewells," it said to him one night as he lay sleepless in bed. "You don't have much more time to make your peace with everything."

Perry hadn't known what *make peace* was, but he asked Joe the next morning.

"To make peace with someone or something usually means to accept it, to understand that it cannot be changed."

"So being happy about stuff you can't fix?"

"No, not to be happy, specifically. Do you know the word *resignation*?"

Perry shook his head.

"It means to realize that an outcome you do not desire is

inevitable. To understand that it will happen anyway, and that the best thing to do is not to strive against it. Do you understand?"

Perry said "Yes," and was about to ask how you could know something was inevitable, but closed his mouth when his mother came into the room.

"Perry, you need to finish your breakfast. We're leaving for school in ten minutes, and you still have to brush your teeth." Corine Abraham looked at Joe. "Joe, that's all the interaction Perry can have right now. Please shut down."

Joe said, "Very well." His head tilted forward a little, and after a few seconds, the light behind his eyes went out.

School went well enough that day. He said goodbye to the playground equipment, the pretty flowers on Mrs. Gray's desk, and the classroom guinea pig, Ralph. The voice was quiet most of the day, so he figured that whatever awful things were coming, he at least had a little more time.

Time to make peace.

He brought home some art work he'd done and a spelling quiz that he'd gotten ten out of ten on. His mom would be pleased, and he may as well make her happy now since he wouldn't have many more chances.

She did look pleased, and he was glad he'd guessed right about that. Her face relaxed into a smile, something that wasn't all that frequent. She praised his art—a crayon drawing of some mountains with lots of trees and some birds flying through a blue sky—and said, "I'm so proud of you for doing so well in spelling. I knew you'd take to reading right away."

"How did you know that?"

"Because you're a bright boy, and you've always loved hearing stories read to you. I was sure you'd be excited to be able to read them on your own."

He nodded, but it still seemed weird that his mom thought she knew what he would and would not be able to do. He had no idea what went on in other people's minds most of the time. It was kind of incomprehensible that she did.

Or maybe she just thought she did. Joe had said a few days ago that what she was doing was called *making assumptions* or *jumping to conclusions*. He pictured his mom jumping from one thing to another, like a frog from lily pad to lily pad, and had to stifle a smile.

That night, Perry lay in bed listening, knowing somehow that the voice would come. Even so, it was a little startling when it spoke, as if someone were there in the darkness, speaking right behind his left ear. It was difficult not to turn that way, but he knew from experience that if he did, there'd be no one there, so he resisted the temptation.

"Tomorrow you need to make two new friends."

"Friends?" Perry whispered. "Who?"

"Colin Dorn and Emily Banfield."

Perry frowned. "They're big kids. They're not going to want to be friends with me."

"Don't make assumptions."

He recalled his thoughts that morning about his mother making assumptions, and the frown relaxed. "Okay. But why?"

"You need someone older and stronger who will help you on Friday."

"Friday? What happens on Friday?"

"That's when all the things I've warned you about start to happen. But once the two older children have taken charge, the ones who follow them will be safe."

A chill shuddered its way through his body. "What should I say to them?"

"Tell them what you know. Tell them what will start two days from now, and that they have to pull together and try to save as many as they can."

"They won't believe me. Why would they believe me? I'm

just a little kid." He gave a harsh sigh, and realized he was near tears. "I'm the weird kid. That's what everyone calls me."

"You have to try."

"Why me? Why don't you go and tell Colin and Emily yourself?"

There was a long pause, long enough that Perry thought the voice wouldn't answer.

Finally it said, "Because you are the one who can hear me."

"Other people can't?"

"There are others. You will meet some of them. But most people can't. Most people have brains that are closed off, locked up so tight nothing can get in. Nothing except what they already expect. Disbelief is a powerful shield."

Now the tears spilled over, dripping onto his pillow, and he pulled his legs upward until he was curled up into a ball on his side.

"So if I stop believing in you, I'll stop hearing you?"

"You wouldn't be able to do that if you tried. I know it's hard for you. It's hard for the others, too, each in their own way. But it's still a gift. Very soon it will be the only way to find things out. You and the others have to work to get better at listening, not work to close yourself off."

"I don't want to," Perry whispered, and it ended in a sob. He pushed his face into his pillow to muffle the sounds. If his mother heard him crying, she'd come and ask him why, and he couldn't explain it to her. Not without raising a lot of other questions he didn't know the answers to. Not without ending up back in Dr. Lansing's office.

What would he do if his mother burst in right now and was so concerned she kept him home from school tomorrow? Tomorrow was Thursday, and the voice said everything would start on Friday. What if he couldn't talk to Colin and

Emily, not because he was afraid, but because his mother had intervened and kept him home?

At once, the idea sounded wildly appealing. Maybe not let her see him crying, but pretend he was sick, or had a headache. It didn't take much to get his mother worrying about him, and it probably wouldn't be hard to convince her to let him stay home. He'd never feigned illness before—he honestly liked going to school, or at least he had before the voice started—so it wouldn't seem suspicious. Maybe Friday, too, so that when the bad things happened, he'd be safely at home.

But this wasn't possible. Things were going to happen a certain way, and fighting against it didn't help. What had Mrs. Gray called it? *Fate.* Joe had termed it *resignation*, to realize an outcome you do not desire is inevitable. As impossible as it seemed, he had to do what the voice told him—talk to the big kids, tell them what he knew, and hope they listened.

And then, on Friday, face what was ahead as bravely as he could.

During lunch on Thursday, Perry got up from the table where he usually ate, apart and in silence, and walked over to where a group of the older children were eating, talking and laughing with each other. He went up to Colin Dorn, who was seated next to Emily Banfield. Lucky thing—it meant he could talk to them together, instead of having to explain everything twice. But sitting there, they looked almost like adults to him, and he felt small, weak, insignificant. The girls thought Colin was cute—he'd heard them talking about him in the lunch line—tall for his age, curly, dark-gold hair, hazel eyes, shoulders that at fifteen were already starting to fill out with muscle. Emily was physically Colin's opposite, small, dark-skinned and brown-eyed, frizzy hair pulled back into a ponytail.

Both had a reputation for being popular and smart. This didn't make approaching them any easier.

As he came up to the table, one by one the kids stopped talking and turned toward him. He knew only a few by name, and doubted many of them knew him. But for a kindergartner to walk up to the big kids' table was pretty unusual.

"Hi," Perry said in a small voice.

A couple of the kids responded with greetings that seemed friendly enough, but held a good measure of puzzlement.

Colin gave him a smile. "Hi."

"Can I talk to you and Emily?"

Colin's eyes flickered toward Emily, who lifted one eyebrow and shrugged.

"Sure."

Perry looked around at the curious pairs of eyes. "Not here."

This got a quick frown, but his tone was still pleasant. "Sure. I was done with my lunch anyhow."

He and Emily stood, picked up their cafeteria trays and brought them to the counter, and followed Perry out into the hallway.

"What's up?" Colin said, as soon as the door closed behind them. "Your name is Perry, right?"

Perry nodded. "I have to talk to you. Because I know something, and I... I have to tell you." It sounded fumbling and lame to him. He couldn't imagine how it must sound to them.

But Colin didn't seem bothered. "Sure, what do you need to tell us?"

"I... I don't know how I know this. But tomorrow, something bad is going to happen. Really bad." The tears from last night were right below the surface, but crying made people stop listening to you. He had no idea why, but as soon as the tears came, the adults immediately switched from hearing what you were saying to trying to get you to stop crying.

"What sort of bad thing?" Emily asked.

"People dying. Lots of people. Horrible things."

The two older children exchanged glances, and said nothing.

"I know you probably don't believe me. But you have to at least hear what I know. It's going to start tomorrow morning, and when it does, you have to do something right away. Hide, and get as many people as you can to hide with you. Otherwise…" He trailed off, feeling his throat tightening.

"Otherwise what?" Colin said gently.

"Otherwise we'll all die."

Colin knelt on the floor, which brought his face on level with Perry's. "Perry, you have to tell us the truth. Did you hear someone talk about planning an attack on the school?"

Perry shook his head.

"Then how do you know?" Emily said.

"I don't know!" Perry was nearly shouting. He realized that if an adult heard, he'd have no choice but to explain it to them, too. He lowered his volume. "It's just… it's just a voice. It tells me things. That's all."

"Why didn't you tell your parents? Or one of the teachers?"

"Because the voice told me that I had to talk to the two of you. It said telling adults wouldn't work. Teachers wouldn't listen. They'd think I was making things up. My parents would just have made me stay home from school so they could take me to the doctor again. But I couldn't do that. I had to warn you." He paused. "The voice said it's up to us."

"I don't know what you want us to do to stop it," Colin said.

"Nothing. You can't stop it from happening. It's *fate*."

Again, Colin met Emily's eyes in a quick glance, and he remained silent.

"But tomorrow, if you know ahead of time… if you're ready, then when it happens, you can… faster…" Perry grimaced in frustration. "I don't know the word."

"We can react more quickly," Colin said quietly.

"Right. It'll be up to you to get as many to hide with you as you can."

"And you don't want us to tell an adult?" Emily said.

"No!" Perry hitched a sob. "Because… then they'll want to know how you know. And if you tell them I told you, they'll ask me how I know. Then they'll tell my mother, and she won't believe me, she'll just think I'm…" He swallowed hard. "Psychotic. None of that will stop the bad things from happening. It'll just mean that we won't be able to help some people to get away."

"Okay, please don't take this the wrong way, but I have to ask. Are you making this up? Like, some kind of joke, or to scare us, or whatever?"

Perry gave a short, sharp shake of the head.

"I didn't think you were. It didn't seem like something you would do."

Evidently Colin, like Perry's mom, had some kind of idea what he would and would not be likely to do. Weird, but at least a little encouraging. He wasn't dismissing him out of hand.

"Okay. I still think we should tell one of the teachers, or Mrs. Miyata."

"No!" Mrs. Miyata was the principal, and Perry felt a kind of awe in her presence. He couldn't imagine trying to explain all this to her. "You can't. It won't help, it'll only make things worse."

"Maybe one of the adults could get the police to come, if you really think this is going to happen."

He shook his head, feeling desperate to get them to stop

giving suggestions, to convince them none of it was going to do any good. What was going to happen was unstoppable, like once you drop a ball on a hill and it starts to roll away, accelerating far faster than you could ever hope to run.

"I just wanted you to know," he said in a near whisper.

At that moment, the bell rang. Colin and Emily exchanged one more look, then Colin said to Perry, "Okay, we'll think about what you've said." The older boy stood. "I hope you're wrong, though."

"I hope so, too," Perry said, and added bleakly, "If wishing would stop it from happening, I'd do it. The only thing we can do is wait for it to start—then try to save as many as we can."

ten

. . .

D oyle Mallett stood in his bedroom, wearing just his boxer briefs, staring into the closet trying to figure out what to wear for his date that night.

He didn't seem to have much between the two extremes—the tasteful tailored shirts and slacks he wore to work, and various t-shirts, sweatshirts, and jeans. Nothing of the smart but casual fashion he assumed most guys wore when they took a woman out to dinner.

The weather had turned warm, so in the end he settled on a light green short-sleeved button-down shirt and a relatively new pair of jeans. The combo, he thought, might just fit the bill. Lydia certainly didn't seem the type who would be attracted to someone too conservative. Better to err in the other direction.

He'd been surprised to reach the end of the workday that Thursday and not have her come up with some kind of excuse for ditching that evening. She still sounded interested —and a bit amused by his awkwardness—but they agreed to meet at Sakura Japanese Restaurant at seven. He offered to pick her up, but she politely demurred.

"I live in kind of a rough neighborhood. Probably better

that I drive myself. Your nice car would attract all the wrong kind of attention."

"Okay." She didn't look like someone from a rough neighborhood, but he didn't say that. Maybe she was weird about his knowing where she lived. Although he doubted it'd take much effort to find out where her pay stubs were mailed.

Whatever. At least she still wanted to go out with him.

He got to Sakura at seven on the dot. Lydia wasn't there, but he'd made a reservation, so he let the hostess know he'd arrived, and his friend would be there soon. With a smile, the hostess escorted him to a table for two in a secluded corner.

Romantic, he thought. Not that romance was likely on a first date. Or with him, even a fourth or fifth date. But still, the ambience was nice. It was quiet, dimly lit, with walls of some dark varnished wood, decorated with traditional Japanese art. A tall house plant in a huge, ornate pot, decorated with blue and white glaze, stood in the corner.

All in all, a good choice.

Lydia got there at ten after seven, just as Doyle had convinced himself that she'd stood him up. She was shown to the table, sat down with a smile, and for a while the main topic of conversation was the menu.

He couldn't help stealing glances at her. She really was remarkably pretty. She wore a long-sleeved turquoise blouse and a pair of tan slacks, both of which subtly accentuated her curves. Dangling earrings caught the light as she moved, set off against her dark brown hair.

Charming.

After food was ordered—a sushi and sashimi platter to share—the conversation lagged.

"A little warm for long sleeves," he said. The weather seemed like a safe topic, if not particularly inspired.

She shrugged. "It gets a lot cooler at night. I'd rather be too warm than too cold."

"I'm exactly the opposite. I love hot weather."

She smiled. "You live in the wrong place."

Doyle chuckled. "Right? I'd probably have never considered western Washington if I hadn't been born and raised here. Grew up in Bellevue, but didn't like commuting across the bridge every day, so I bought a house in Queen Anne when I got the job at the realty."

She gave him an incredulous look. "You bought a house as soon as you got a job?"

His cheeks warmed. "I know. Lucky. My parents helped me out. I'm an only child, and my mom said it was worth it, that they could stand to miss their yearly vacation for one year to give me enough for a down payment. I could afford the mortgage payment, but the up-front purchase costs were a little beyond me at the time."

"I'll bet. Houses in Queen Anne aren't cheap."

"Like I said, I'm lucky." The heat in his cheeks increased. How had the conversation turned to his parents' wealth? He didn't want her thinking he was some kind of upper-crust aristocrat. "But anyhow. Where are you from? Seattle native?"

"Nope. Eastern Washington, near Prosser. My family lived there for five generations."

"Wow. Doing what? Aren't there a lot of wineries in that area?"

A slight frown crossed her face, but was gone almost before he noticed it. "Yes. The whole Yakima Valley is wine country. My grandfather was a farmer—mainly soybeans and wheat. As unstable as the market is, he couldn't make enough to pay the taxes, so he sold it, back when my dad was a teenager. I guess his acreage got converted to wineries along with most of the rest of Benton County."

"What did he do?"

"Went to work in a fruit-packing plant." Her eyes looked distant. "But look, it's not a nice story. Let's just say we went through some hard times, and leave it at that."

Doyle nodded. His embarrassment at having brought up

his privileged upbringing morphed into acute awkwardness at the contrast with Lydia's story. Why the hell couldn't conversations come with rewind buttons? It never failed. He seemed to realize what topics to avoid only after he put his foot right in the middle of one.

"I'm sorry."

She gave him a faint smile. "It's okay. It isn't your fault. It's just the way things are."

Any response he could have made to that was cut short by the waiter approaching with their appetizers and a bottle of sake. Probably for the best. Surely it was safe to comment on how good the food and drinks were.

But somehow, the evening never really recovered. Both of them were ill at ease, and any direction their conversation went ultimately fizzled into uncomfortable silence. At one point, Lydia's phone pinged, and whatever she saw made both eyebrows rise. She quickly typed in a response, sent it, and returned the phone to her purse, smiling to herself. Whatever it was, she seemed happier about it than she did about talking to Doyle.

Not that he blamed her.

When she reached over to slip her phone back into her purse, her sleeve pulled back a little, and he caught a glimpse of the edge of what could only be a tattoo on the inside of her right wrist.

He gestured toward it. "You have ink? I've always liked tattoos, but I'm too chicken to get one."

Lydia froze, her smile vanishing in an instant, then she reflexively pulled her sleeve down to cover it.

"It's okay. I know a lot of workplaces, you can't have visible tattoos, but it's not like I'm your boss, or anything."

Still she just stared at him, not speaking. What did *that* expression mean? Her eyes had gone hard as flint, and now the contempt he'd always imagined she felt seemed to have manifested into reality.

"What's wrong? I didn't mean to upset you."

"I know you didn't."

What was it, a gang insignia or something? She said she lived in a rough neighborhood. "Maybe we should talk about something else."

"No." She took a deep breath, and her expression registered defiance. Her body, though, was still, like an animal trying to decide whether to flee or attack. Every muscle seemed tensed to spring. She locked eyes with him. "I shouldn't be embarrassed by it."

She reached down with her left hand and pulled her sleeve up.

Jagged lines for eyes. A triangular, downturned mouth with a pair of fangs.

The symbol of the LLA.

An icy jolt twanged its way down his backbone. "You're LLA?" he whispered.

Finally she moved, but made no attempt to cover it back up. She looked down at the symbol inscribed on her arm. Her mouth quirked upward, but still her eyes were cold.

"That surprises you?" she said in a quiet, level voice.

"It does, yes."

"Why?"

"Because I... I don't know, I thought they..."

"You thought I was just a nice, ordinary girl. You never imagined I could be a Lacklander." She shook her head. "Weren't you listening to anything I said earlier?"

"About your grandfather?"

"Yes. My whole family. It's people like us who formed the LLA ten years ago. It's people like us who are why it can't be bullied or compromised or legislated out of existence. Ordinary people who have lost everything."

"I... I didn't know."

"Of course you didn't." It came out in a sneer, as if his ignorance was his own fault, as if not knowing made him the same as the owners of the swanky wineries and industrial farms that in the past thirty years had taken over nearly the entire eastern half of the state.

He felt suddenly on the defensive, but that would just make the situation worse. In the end, he just said again, "I'm sorry."

"Yes. So am I."

Once again, the waiter interrupted at exactly the right time. "Can I get either of you anything else?"

"No." Doyle's voice sounded strained in his own ears. "Just the check."

With a quick jerk, Lydia pulled her sleeve down. Now that the waiter had broken the spell, she wouldn't meet Doyle's eyes. She seemed anxious to leave, and truth be told, so was he.

He paid for the meal with his credit card, which got a quiet "Thanks" from Lydia. The word sounded sardonic, and this time Doyle didn't think his anxiety was making it up. She had grown up in poverty, apparently still lived in poverty—how could he have thought otherwise, given that she was on a temp's salary?—so it was no surprise if any gratitude she felt for getting a free meal was tempered with the embarrassment of being a charity case.

No wonder she'd gone LLA. That night was, truthfully, the first time he'd ever considered how much his privileged upbringing sundered him from understanding how most of the people in the world lived.

As they stood, he said, "I'm sorry for how this evening went. I honestly didn't mean to make you feel bad."

"I know that. I should have known better. I should learn my place." She caught his eyes again, her expression filled with contempt. "Learn my place, then stay there."

Doyle tried to think of some possible response to that, but his mind was a roiling mess. No words came out.

Just as well. She turned, shouldered her purse, and headed for the exit.

A little afterward, Doyle followed. The hostess and waiter gave him a sympathetic look. It must have been obvious that the date hadn't gone well.

As he walked out into the warm evening, he thought briefly about following her, trying to talk to her, trying to convince her that he wanted to erase what had happened, that he never intended to make her feel belittled.

But the sidewalk in both directions was empty.

Doyle made sure to get to work early, so he wouldn't have to pass Lydia's desk while she was occupying it. He had debated calling in sick, but he had already agreed to take the Garritys around again, so he had to go into the office to pick up the listings and blank purchase order forms. He decided to steel himself to the inevitable uncomfortable meeting.

Andrea would say it was the right thing to do. Confront your anxieties, don't let them rule you.

At least it was Lydia's last day. Brittany Tanner would be back at work on Monday. It was a relief to know he only had to deal with one day of awkwardness, and then with luck, he'd never see Lydia Moreton again.

She arrived at a little before nine, settling herself in without giving Doyle so much as a glance. He considered going up and apologizing again, but that wouldn't accomplish anything but bringing the previous evening's debacle of a date back into the conversation. Better to keep to business, and speak to her as little as possible.

He comforted himself with the certainty that she was probably no more eager for an exchange of pleasantries than he was.

Three things happened at just after nine o'clock.

The first was that Lydia's phone pinged. This was strange in and of itself. The company policy was that the front office staff were to keep their personal phones on silent and not to use them unless it was an emergency, and Lydia had adhered to that rule scrupulously during the time she'd been there. But now she pulled the phone from her purse, and in an odd repeat of the previous evening, she looked at the text on the screen, and her expression went from neutral to pleasantly excited.

She said, loud enough for him to hear on the other side of the room, "Finally."

The second thing was the wail of sirens in the distance. Not just one police car or ambulance. That was so ordinary that it wouldn't have been noticed. This sounded like a fleet of emergency vehicles, their sirens in a blaring counterpoint that seemed to come from all directions at once.

The third was that Lydia picked up her purse and walked over to Doyle's desk, still wearing a contented smile.

"I quit," she said.

Doyle goggled at her. First, he wasn't the owner of the realty, and had nothing to do with hiring and firing. Her announcement that she was quitting was a complete non sequitur.

Odder still was that she was quitting on the last day of her employment. Didn't she know how bad that would look to the temp firm, and to any other prospective employers? From her expression, it was clear that she didn't care.

"You… you quit?" Doyle stammered out.

"Yes, Doyle. I quit. You and the rest of the agency can shove this job up your collective asses."

"But… you were doing fine… you seemed happy?" He ended it as a question, holding his hands palms upward.

"'Seemed' is the operative word. As far as my doing fine, let's just say a better offer came along."

"What better offer?"

She didn't respond. She reached in her purse, and drew out a small but deadly-looking gun.

"It wasn't until last night that I made the decision of who would be first. I chose you for that honor not because you're the worst, but because you're the best of them. Good enough that you should know better. Good enough that you should be fighting with us, not ignoring us into nonexistence, living in your fancy house up in Queen Anne never having to worry about someone coming and taking it all away from you. Your privilege should have informed you, but instead it made you blind." She shook her head. "I can honestly forgive stupid people more easily. They don't know any better, so they swallow the pretty lie this entire society has been fed for decades. That justice prevails. That democracy works. That the little guy has as much chance to succeed as the wealthy. But you? You're smart enough that you should have figured it out."

Doyle stared at the black hole at the end of the gun barrel. He felt like all the saliva in his mouth had dried up. He croaked out, "Please."

"You're the first. You won't be the last. We plan to turn the world upside down. You should be thankful that you won't be around to see it."

Their gazes locked one last time. Until the very end, Doyle was convinced he'd see some flicker of uncertainty or remorse, some sign of hesitation, the faintest trace of humanity in her brown eyes.

It never came.

part two
breakdown

eleven

. . .

Friday, May 12, 2035

The sun rose over the Cascade Mountains into a cloudless crystalline blue sky on the day civilization fell.

Soren Conover stood at the window of the little house he and his partner rented in the quiet Seattle suburb of Ballard at a little after six, holding a cup of steaming coffee. He hadn't turned on his computer yet, savoring his mental tranquility before getting online and listening to today's bad news. Awful as it usually was, it all seemed far removed from his life as an academic. The Lackland War was simmering down, with an uneasy peace holding in some countries. In others, hired mercenaries squashed the dispossessed rebels by whatever means necessary.

A nasty business, but at least it was happening elsewhere. Other than a spike in the prices for food, it had little direct impact on him. The situation would have been different if he'd lived in France or Germany. The Lacklander revolts had destabilized the European Union, and much of western

Europe was still experiencing daily riots, not to mention shortages of food and gasoline, power outages, and loss of internet accessibility. No one knew exactly how many people had died there, but it had to be in the thousands. Perhaps tens of thousands.

But even hearing about this on the news left it one step removed from reality. Soren's quiet little cul-de-sac was as peaceful as ever. His neighbors still waved cheerfully at him when he went for a run. He still spent his days at the University of Washington, doing research in historical linguistics and teaching one or two classes a semester. If the number of students was significantly smaller than when he'd started five years ago, it was another thing he could ignore. The lecture halls were open, the university admitting new students. Even if the classrooms were half-filled it was no worse than when he was in high school during the years of the pandemic, when a lot of parents chose to homeschool rather than have their kids exposed, and the schools that did open had student desks a minimum of six feet apart.

A breeze stirred the leaves of the Japanese maple tree outside his window. The scene was idyllic, as far away from the horrors of the war as it was possible to be.

An arm slipped around his belly, and a warm body molded into him, chest to his back, and he felt the brush of a kiss on the nape of his neck.

Soren smiled. "What are you doing up so early? You don't have to be at work until ten."

"If you want, I'll go away," Finn Donnelly said in a sleepy voice, but he didn't let Soren go.

"I didn't mean that. I figured you'd want to sleep in since you could."

"Ah. Well, when do you have to go in? The documents on Old Norse noun declensions aren't going to get any more boring if you stay in bed for another hour."

This got a laugh. "Coffee's on. Shall I get you a cup?"

Finn heaved a sigh. "I guess that means I can't entice you back under the covers. So as second best, that'd be awesome, thanks."

Soren stepped away from both the window and his boyfriend's embrace, and a minute later, returned with a fresh cup of coffee for Finn, and a refill for himself. Finn was shirtless, obviously having dragged himself out of bed moments before, stopping only to pull on a pair of baggy sweat pants. His thick auburn hair stood up in wild disarray, and his eyes—blue-gray like a stormy sea—still looked sleepy. As he approached, Finn put both hands behind his head, stretched and yawned. Soren looked at his lean, sculpted physique with appreciation, the errant thought *Maybe we should go back to bed after all* skipping through his mind.

But Finn extended one hand and took the cup of steaming coffee, sipping it with a smile.

Soren shook his head. "Have to wonder how much longer coffee will be available. The price has gotten ridiculous, and I read in the news yesterday the importers are shutting down."

"Serves them right. The coffee and palm oil plantations have ruined the tropics."

"I know. But still. Coffee." He took a sip. "Why does it have to be good stuff like coffee and chocolate and bananas? I wouldn't mind if the rebels had destroyed the cabbage plantations, or something."

"Cabbages are grown on plantations?"

"Actually, I have no idea."

Finn sat down in an antique rocking chair. "You know when you'll be back this evening?"

"Should be midafternoon. Three-ish. I've got my syntax and semantics class to lecture at ten, then I need to work with Dr. Quaice on some citations and diagrams for our paper. The submission deadline is in two weeks, so we need to get the details cleaned up."

"Quaice isn't still giving you grief about being lead author, is he?"

"No." Soren gave a dismissive wave of one hand. "The research was my baby, he knows that. As the grand old man of the linguistics department, he wanted to make sure I know my place. It was all for show."

"Alpha dog marking out his territory."

"More or less. He's not a bad egg, just can be a little touchy if he feels like the younger generation is getting uppity. He's not as hard to work with as you'd think talking to him. Plus, mostly what he wants to do is lock himself in his office and work on his conlang."

Finn frowned and shook his head. "How many hours has he put into that thing?"

"God alone knows. He teaches an evening class to people who want to learn it, did I tell you that?"

"Okay, I guess I get why someone would invent a language. As hobbies go, it's not the weirdest thing I've ever heard of. And hey, Tolkien did it, so it's got a coolness factor right there. But why would anyone want to learn someone *else's* fake language?"

"I've heard the University of Wisconsin used to offer for-credit classes in Klingon."

"Doesn't mean it makes sense."

Soren sat down on one end of the sofa, a pensive look on his face. "Dr. Quaice calls it *insurance*."

"Insurance against what?"

"You know how convinced he is that the end of the world is nigh."

"Yeah, he cornered me at last year's Christmas party and lectured me about it for at least an hour."

"When he started writing Kalila twenty years ago—so he told me—it's because he wanted a way to communicate that would defy translation. Something he and a few others could use if they wanted what they said or wrote to be a secret."

"And he's got people who are willing to put enough time into learning an invented language just so they can talk to each other if civilization collapses?"

"Apparently."

Finn moved to the couch, sat down next to his boyfriend, and leaned against him. "You've never shared his paranoia enough to learn it?"

Soren smiled. "I know how to say hello, goodbye, thanks, and fuck you."

"Add 'where's the bathroom?' and you've got the necessities covered. How do you say 'fuck you?'"

"*Thó selta.*"

"Cool. Gives me another option for rude people on the Metro. But it sounds a lot more genteel than the English version."

"You should hear Dr. Quaice say it." Soren slipped one arm around Finn's bare shoulders, and kissed the top of his head. "You might be convincing me to come back to bed for a while."

Finn snuggled in, and Soren could feel him smiling against the skin of his upper chest. "Excellent."

"But like I said, I'm not going to be working late today. So if we're short on time, maybe this afternoon…?"

"Why not both? Both is good." He paused. "Oh, damn, I've got a meeting with Kathy about getting closed-captioning done for that new set of video lessons she recorded. I probably won't be home till dinnertime."

"So we'll have to wait till tonight."

"For round two, anyway." Finn stood up suddenly, grabbed Soren by the hand, and brought him to his feet. "C'mon, into the bedroom with you, unless you want me to tackle you right here on the couch."

Three hours later, Soren looked out of the bus window toward the blue waters of Lake Union, still under the cool spring sunshine. The only thing marring the tranquil tableau was a plume of smoke in the distance, perhaps somewhere around downtown. Whatever the cause, it looked big. He hadn't had time to check the news. After his dalliance with Finn they'd both dozed off again in each other's arms, drowsy and sated, and woke up with only enough time to take a quick shower and then run full-tilt to catch the bus.

He made a mental note to see what he could find out over lunch.

His curiosity only climbed further when, just before the bus doglegged onto Pacific Street, two police cars and a firetruck zoomed past, sirens blaring, going in the opposite direction.

Something's wrong.

The thought came out of nowhere. In a city the size of Seattle, you could hear sirens pretty much any time of the day or night, and in fact since Soren moved here five years earlier from his home town in upstate New York, he'd gradually acclimated to the point that he didn't even notice them unless they were right in front of him. Seeing plumes of smoke was less common, but was also hardly unusual.

But there was a sense of visceral unease. Maybe it had come from his conversation with his boyfriend about Dr. Quaice's obsession with the impending collapse of civilization. Most of the time he was able to dismiss the old man's dire predictions, even laugh at them, but for some reason, this morning they'd bitten into him deeply enough that even a highly satisfying romp with Finn before leaving didn't dispel the sense of foreboding.

Something's wrong.

He shook his head as he descended from the bus onto the sidewalk as if to clear the malaise, and forced away the inadvertent frown he wore. By the time he arrived in his classroom, he had convinced himself he was worked up over nothing.

But ten o'clock rolled around, and of his thirteen students, only three had shown up.

This was a three-hundred-level class, composed entirely of linguistics majors, and had a reputation as a technical and challenging subject. Students didn't miss it unless they were deathly ill. He looked at the three who were in their accustomed seats, and the question in his eyes must have been obvious, because one of them, a deferential Chinese student named Mei-Lin Xiao, spoke up.

"Dr. Conover, I think many students are experiencing trouble coming to the university this morning. I heard on the radio that we were advised to avoid I-5 and the Evergreen Point Floating Bridge, and that unnecessary travel was discouraged."

"Why?" The single word came out sounding blunt, almost angry. He went on in a steadier fashion. "Did they say what had happened?"

Mei-Lin gave a quick shake of her head. "No. Just that traffic was stopped. I assumed it was because of accidents on the roads."

"I heard there was some kind of protest." Stephen Kelleher, a lean, athletic-looking young man wearing shorts and a t-shirt for a band Soren had never heard of, gave a shrug. "It was only a matter of time. A couple of weeks ago, protesters in Boston damn near shut the whole city down for three days. I guess it's our turn."

"I saw a big plume of smoke while I was on the bus coming in this morning." Soren tried to keep the concern out of his voice. As the teacher, wasn't he supposed to project calm, keep everyone feeling safe? Maybe he shouldn't have mentioned it. He refrained from telling them about the police cars.

"I saw that, too," the third student, a blonde Californian

named Eva Klayze, said. "It was on the skyline when I looked out of my dorm window."

"Do you live on campus, Stephen?" Mei-Lin asked.

"Yeah. But if the traffic is all fucked up…" He gave a quick side-eye to Soren. "Sorry, screwed up, then it means we're stuck on campus. I was gonna meet my girlfriend in the Pike Place Market for lunch."

"I wouldn't go downtown unless you have to," Soren said.

All three students turned to look at him.

"Why do you say that?" Eva asked.

Why *had* he said that? Of all of them, it seemed like Mei-Lin was the only one who had any reliable information, and she hadn't mentioned anything about downtown.

"I… I don't know. I think that's where the smoke was coming from. But in any case, staying off the roads entirely sounds like a good idea, don't you think?"

"Yes," Mei-Lin said.

Stephen shrugged again, and gave a snort of frustration. "It's a pain in the ass." This time he didn't even apologize for the impropriety.

Soren let it pass, not that it honestly bothered him in any case. "If it doesn't improve by this afternoon, I'm not sure how I'll get home."

"Where do you live?" Eva asked.

"Ballard."

"That'd be a long walk."

Soren nodded.

As usual, Stephen cut to the chase. "So, are we going to have class?"

"We're not even close to a quorum. So class dismissed. But read the chapter on stochastic grammar and Markov models for Thursday. I'll email everyone with the lecture notes, and just do a quick review at the beginning of next class before we go on."

Stephen was already packing up. The two women followed suit a little more slowly.

"Dr. Conover?" Mei-Lin said, as she stood up.

"Yes?"

"What if the problem isn't resolved by Thursday's class?"

The other two turned and looked at Soren, concern in their eyes. Soren's twelve-year age difference had never been so apparent to him. They all suddenly looked very, very young.

"We'll deal with that if it happens." He hoped his words sounded more relaxed and breezy than he felt. He forced a smile. "Don't put aside the reading in the hopes we won't have class. The great likelihood is that I'll see everyone on Thursday."

All three of them looked relieved. Maybe his show of confidence had worked.

But once they left, he stood in the empty classroom, a frown on his face, lost in his interior world. Something was going on outside these four walls, outside this familiar building. Something bad.

And he knew, knew with an unquestioning certainty, that he wouldn't be holding class on Thursday. Might not, in fact, hold class for a very long time.

A gruff voice came at Soren's knock on the office door. "What is it?"

"Soren Conover."

"Oh. Conover. You're early. Come in."

Dr. Anderson Quaice was seated at his desk, long legs stretched out, gawky arms resting a little askew. His gray hair, as usual, was in disarray. He was tall—he had Soren by a good four inches, and Soren was just over six feet tall himself—and Quaice somehow never seemed to have grown into his own body. He was at least sixty years old, so chances were, he never would. But it gave him an awkward, uncomfortable appearance, exacerbated by the fact that he never stood still. Even when he wasn't pacing about, he was in constant motion—rocking back and forth, tapping a foot, shifting his weight from side to side. When Soren first met him, his impression was of a marionette being operated by someone who didn't quite know what he was doing. He'd never been able to shake that image.

"I'm here to talk about the citations and diagrams."

One long hand gave a contemptuous wave. "To hell with the citations. We're not going to submit the paper anyhow."

Soren goggled at him. "What do you mean, we're not going to submit? We've been working on this for six months."

"Pfft. By the time we could get it together, there's gonna be no one to submit it to."

"What are you talking about?"

Quaice raised a bushy gray eyebrow. "Sit down, Conover."

Soren sat.

"What rock have you been hiding under today?"

He swiveled his computer around so Soren could see the screen, and with a click of the mouse turned on the volume. There was a news report already in progress. A frightened-looking man wearing a headset mic was talking.

"... seems to have been coordinated. Lackland Liberation Authority has already taken responsibility. We're not sure how many buildings have been burned and lives lost, and likely won't know for some time, but there is chaos in Washington D.C., Boston, Chicago, Houston, Atlanta, Seattle, and Los Angeles. Reports of multiple assassination attempts against elected officials, some of them successful, are coming in from not only the United States but from several other nations. Confirmed dead in the U.S. are Governor Marcy Tate of Arizona, Governor Bob Delhomme of Louisiana, Governor Jason Goldschmidt of Maryland, Governor Andrew Wiedemann of Washington, Governor Mary Kurnow of Wisconsin…"

Soren stared at the screen. It felt like every drop of saliva in his mouth had dried up, and he wasn't sure he could speak. When he did, his voice sounded thin, weak, almost alien in his own ears.

"They killed him? They killed Andy Wiedemann? I thought… I thought he was negotiating with representatives of the Lacklanders, trying to redress some of their grievances, especially in eastern Washington…"

"Don't you get it, Conover? The Lacklanders never wanted redress. That's been obvious for a while. They just wanted enough time and opportunity to take it all down. They'll burn the world to cinders even if it takes them with it."

"How can we stop it?" As soon as the words were out of his mouth, he knew it was a ridiculous question.

The expected sardonic sneer from Quaice didn't come. When he answered, his voice was thoughtful and a little sad.

"No one can stop it. The door of opportunity to stop it closed twenty years ago." Quaice glanced up at Soren, and gave a sharp shake of his head even though Soren had done nothing to contradict the older man. "No, I'm serious. The whole stage was set when the politicians started enacting legislation funneling money away from ordinary middle-class folks and into the hands of corporations. You can only tilt that so far before the whole thing collapses. They thought they could keep doing it forever, even after the Lackland movement formed and demanded change. They'd get richer and richer, and the money would keep them safe. They neglected two things—they were vastly outnumbered right from the beginning, and once you put a person in a position where he has nothing left to lose, you've created an enemy you can't stop unless you kill him."

Soren stood suddenly, making the legs of the chair squawk on the tile floor. "I've got to get home."

"How are you planning to do that?"

"The Metro…"

Quaice scowled and waved a hand in the air. "The Metro isn't running. Got a notice from the University almost an hour ago. Don't know why you didn't see it."

"I was in class. I turned my phone off." He swallowed. "I guess I'll walk."

The old professor snorted. "To Ballard? The whole city hasn't slipped into chaos yet, but it will before long. You do not want to be out on the street when that happens." His voice softened. "Look, Conover, I live in Madison Park, just east of the Arboretum. Half hour walk, if that. You can come home with me and then figure out what to do from there. I've already told Cassandra Nicolaides and Gavin Liu to do the same. They're in their offices gathering their things up. It might be a while before we're back here."

"But Finn…"

He was suddenly light-headed, disembodied, and he gasped out his boyfriend's name again, unable to force out another word. He fumbled to pull his phone out of his pocket, and with a trembling hand turned it on. There were four text messages. The first was the one from the University administration that Dr. Quaice had referenced, letting employees know that the Metro wasn't running until further notice. No explanation was given, just an adjuration to "find an alternate means of transport for any travel that is absolutely necessary."

The second, third, and fourth were from Finn Donnelly. The first was timestamped a little over an hour ago. He must have written only minutes after Soren had turned his phone off. "I don't know what the hell is happening, but there's some kind of riot and it seems to be getting closer to the house. They've barricaded the street so I can't use the car. Not sure if I should try fleeing on foot. Might have no choice."

Only six minutes later, a shorter message. "Looks like running. Me & Janie Inoue. Not sure where we'll go. They broke Janie's windows but she got out through the back and climbed the fence."

Three minutes after that was a final text. "Soren, I love you. So much. Never forget that. I love you, I love you. Forever."

Beneath that were the words, "User currently offline."

twelve

. . .

Brandon Nguyen never did go to bed the night before the attacks began.

After getting off the phone with Julia Lowell, he immediately called Caria. From her slurred voice, she had obviously been asleep.

"Caria, you need to come over here. Right now."

"Brandon, I'm not in the mood…"

"No!" He waved his hand in the air. "Not for that. It's… it's important. Something terrible is going to happen. Tomorrow morning. We need to be together."

"What the hell are you talking about?"

"I'll explain, but once you get here." He paused, swallowed. "Bring along… whatever you can carry that's important to you."

"Why?" Now she sounded exasperated. "I'm not just going to…"

"You have to!" His voice cut through hers, and she stopped short. "Caria, there's no time. You have to get over here. But assume… assume you're not going to see your apartment again. Ever."

"You're scaring me."

"You should be scared. I'm scared, too."

"This is about your paintings, isn't it?"

He took a deep breath. "Yes. The things in them… they're real. And it all starts tomorrow."

"I'm going to call 911. You're… you sound like you're having a nervous breakdown."

"No. I'm sane. Saner than I've ever been." He forced his voice to calm down. "I'll explain what I can once you get here. Please."

There was such a long pause that he thought she wouldn't answer. He waited for the dry click indicating she'd ended the call, but it never came.

Finally she said, "All right. I'm coming down. But when I get there… I reserve the right to call 911 when I see you."

"Agreed."

After the call ended, he looked around his studio, the paintbrushes and tubes of oil paint, bottles of linseed oil and turpentine, the finished and partly-completed paintings, the blank canvases on their stretcher boards waiting for his next inspiration. What of all of that could he take with him? He wouldn't be coming back here, at least not for a very long time. Julia had said to take only what he could carry. Did she foresee, somehow, that travel by car was going to be impossible? Or was she still just styling herself as one of the prophets of the Old Testament, wandering around the desert in sandals proclaiming the word of God? He pictured himself trying to carry his paintings with him, but it was clearly impossible. The most recent ones still weren't completely dry, and the canvases themselves were large and awkward.

As much of a stab in the heart as it was, he was going to have to leave them behind. He had photographs of each one on his phone, so at least he could take that much of them with him, meager compensation though that was.

In any case, he couldn't leave them here in the studio. He pictured someone breaking into his house and vandalizing the place, kicking holes through each piece, laughing evilly while doing so. In the end he walked each one of them up the narrow staircase to the mostly-unused second floor. There was a small linen closet opening onto the hallway, next to a tiny spare bedroom. Both were entirely empty, and Brandon didn't remember the last time he'd opened either door. Maybe it was three years ago, when he rented the place. Once he saw the huge, brightly-lit room in the back of the lower floor that screamed "art studio," he hadn't cared much about the house's other features, and truthfully he hadn't paid attention to the rest of the tour. As long as there was a place to sleep and eat, and at least one functioning bathroom, he'd take it. Houses with open spaces like his studio weren't all that common.

The interior of the spare bedroom was stuffy, and the floor covered with a layer of dust. He walked in, leaned the first painting up against the wall, and returned for another.

A half-hour later, he had the last one moved. He was coming back down the stairs when Caria opened the front door without knocking.

"What the hell is going on?"

He came up to her and gave her a hug. She did not reciprocate, although he did notice she had an overnight bag in her hand. At least she'd believed him that far.

Brandon told her about Julia Lowell's dire phone call the previous evening.

"She said that all of it—the terrible things involving the people in my paintings—they're starting tomorrow." He consulted his watch. "Well, at this point, it's today."

"How does she know any of this?"

"She says it's messages from God."

Caria gave him an incredulous look. "I thought you were an atheist."

"I am." He shrugged. "But she's not."

"Why do you believe her if you don't even believe in God?"

"Because I've had visions of my own."

"This whole situation makes no sense."

"No. It doesn't. But neither does my painting someone's portrait before I've seen them. Julia says that the other people in my paintings are real, too, and eventually I'll meet them all."

Anything Caria could have responded—and from the expression on her face, she had a lot to say, and none of it good—was cut off by a knock on the door.

Brandon felt an overwhelming sense of relief when he saw that it was Julia. At least now he'd have some backup.

"Hello, Brandon." She walked in, shutting the door behind her, and set down the satchel she was carrying. She glanced over at Caria. "I presume this is your girlfriend? I'm Julia Lowell."

Caria stared at the woman, her mouth hanging open a little, and said nothing.

"This is Caria Sahin," Brandon said.

"Pleased to meet you, although I wish it was under different circumstances."

Caria closed her mouth, cleared her throat. "You really are... you're..."

"The woman in Brandon's painting? Yes. I was incredulous at first, myself."

"I thought..." Caria paused, trying to find the words. "I thought Brandon had just seen someone who resembled the woman he'd painted. But it's... it's you. It actually is you."

"That's what I tried to tell you," Brandon said.

Julia tsked softly. "Be charitable, Brandon. It's a lot to take in. Have you put together whatever belongings you will want to take with you?"

"Not yet. I don't have much." With a pang in his heart, he added, "I can't take the paintings."

"I feared as much."

"Where are we going?"

"I don't know yet. The path will be shown to us when it is time. I'm given to know that our job will be to get as many others to listen as we can, and get them out of Seattle. How we will do that, where we will ultimately end up—that I do not know."

"This is insane," Caria said under her breath.

"I can understand it seeming that way."

"At least you're not still saying *I'm* insane," Brandon said.

"Jury's still out on that," Caria said. "About both of you. But these bad things that are going to happen… what kind of bad things?"

"There will be bloodshed. The innocent and the guilty will perish together. In the end, the land itself will rise up against humanity. It is our responsibility to get as many to safety as possible before that happens. I have no guarantee of security for ourselves—only a knowledge that this is what we must do."

"I'm glad you came here," Brandon said.

"It made sense. My apartment is on a busy street, this house in a quiet neighborhood. It might give us a little bit of extra time to prepare."

Caria sat down on the first step of the staircase. In her face were fatigue, astonishment, disbelief. She still stared at Julia as if she were an apparition from a fever-dream.

Julia went and sat next to her. "I know you are finding this difficult to accept." Her voice was quiet, gentle. "So are we all. You trusted Brandon enough to come here. Let that trust carry you a little further. With time, you will see that what we are telling you is simply the truth. Until then, let your love for Brandon bear the burden of your doubts." She looked up at Brandon. "You should put together the belongings you wish to take. I don't know how much time we have. It's still in the depths of the night, and I'm given to know that the attacks will not begin until it is fully light outside. I've been shown that much. But you should not delay. Once it all starts, we might have minutes, hours, or days to respond—but my intuition is that it's more likely to be minutes than days. We should be ready to flee at a moment's notice."

———

They settled in Brandon's studio, which was the most spacious room in the house, especially now that all the paintings were gone. He got glasses of wine for himself and Caria. All Julia wanted was ice water.

"Where are all the paintings?" Caria's voice still held incredulity. It was the voice of someone who had lost her bearings, and was desperately flailing around for something, anything, normal to hang onto.

"I brought them all to the upstairs bedroom."

"I didn't even know there was an upstairs bedroom."

"It's been empty since I rented the house. I felt like... I couldn't just leave them down here in the studio. Once I'm gone, if people break in... it would be the first thing they'd see. Upstairs, at least there's a chance that my paintings won't be noticed."

"You are serious that you're not coming back to your house."

"I don't know. I'm not like Julia. I'm not able to predict the future. But I'm planning for it."

"I don't predict the future." Julia took a sip of her water. "I'm only given knowledge of certain things. I cannot see all eventualities."

"I was wondering if I needed to call in sick to work," Caria said. "I thought maybe I'd be bringing you to the emergency room. But I guess if everything is going to collapse, calling in is kind of pointless."

She gave a mirthless little laugh, but Julia said, completely seriously, "Yes, it is."

Caria looked at the older woman in amazement. "You're taking this so… so calmly. How can you accept this, like it's just some completely ordinary thing?"

Julia regarded her in silence for a moment. "That's what you think? That I'm calm? I assure you that calm is the last thing I am right now. You're right in a sense, though. I've been expecting this for years. Not this specifically, mind you, but something like it. But just because I'm not running in circles screaming my head off doesn't mean I'm calm."

Brandon gazed at his girlfriend in silence for a moment. It was clear in her face—the perplexity and hurt. The intimacy of their relationship had been invaded by this strange woman, and Caria was realizing their shared ability brought Julia closer to Brandon than she was, perhaps than she would ever be. Even though the oracular vision manifested differently in the two of them, in the few short days they'd known each other, they understood each other more deeply than Caria and Brandon did after a two-year relationship.

There was nothing to say that wouldn't make it more glaringly obvious. In the end, Brandon kept silent.

By first light, the bottle of wine was empty. Caria was dozing, snuggled up next to Brandon on the sofa. Julia was still wide awake and watchful, sitting ramrod-straight in an armchair.

As the light of dawn increased in the studio, Julia said, "We should all get some food."

"I'm not sure I can eat," Brandon said.

"You need to try. My sense is that we'll be on short commons after today, perhaps for a good long while."

Caria stirred at the sound of their voices, and stretched and yawned. "Has anything happened yet?"

"No." Julia frowned. "I don't know exactly when. I just know it's today. Nor do I know exactly what is going to happen. But it will be obvious, as obvious as the starting pistol at a race. There will be no doubt when it begins."

Brandon went into the kitchen, put on the coffee, and made a pot of oatmeal, returning to the studio carrying a tray with three bowls full, three glasses, and a carton of orange juice.

"It's all I had," he said, an apology in his voice. "Keeping the kitchen stocked hasn't been much on my radar since all this started."

"It's easy enough to forget how precarious everything is," Julia said. "It always was, of course, it's just that now it is coming to fruition." She paused, cleared her throat. "'For as a snare shall it come on all them that dwell on the face of the whole earth. Watch ye therefore, and pray always, that ye may be accounted worthy to escape all these things that shall come to pass.' It was true in the time of the apostle Luke. It's true now."

Caria took a bite of her oatmeal, and gave Julia an appraising look. "Who do you believe is going to do all this? The bloodshed you talked about. Who here in Seattle would do that? I mean, there's petty violence, like there is in every city in the world. But not on the scale you seem to be talking about."

"I have a suspicion that the ones who will begin it are the people calling themselves the Lackland Liberation Authority."

"The LLA? Aren't they trying to settle things peacefully? I know they've rioted in other countries, been responsible for bombings. I thought we were safe from all that."

"I don't know for certain. It's merely what I have guessed from watching the news. As far as our being safe, it always seems that way, doesn't it? Right before lightning strikes, everything is calm and normal. It's hard to imagine it ever being different. I think the LLA has been biding its time and laying its plans. The overtures toward elected officials, like the negotiations with Governor Wiedemann, are a feint. I don't believe they had any expectation those negotiations would be successful. It was merely a delaying tactic, giving them long enough to convince us all that everything would be fine. To lull us to sleep, so when the hammer falls, it will be entirely unexpected."

"Except by you."

Julia's expression didn't change. It was clear she had no misgivings about her messages from God, if indeed that was the source of all of the warnings and visions.

"I'm not the only one chosen. Brandon was, and there are others we will meet. But what you are saying is in essence correct. We have one advantage the LLA would not dream of. An ear to the voice of God..." She stopped, her body suddenly stiffening, like a rabbit that has scented a fox.

In the distance there was a sudden cacophony of sirens, and a series of low rumbles that sounded like thunder.

"Those are explosions." Caria's voice was thin. She stared at Julia, wide-eyed. It was clear that until now, even though she was nominally going along with Brandon's dire warnings, she had doubted anything would happen. Now, she looked at one of them to the other, undisguised horror in her face.

"Finish your breakfast," Julia said. There was a tremor in Julia's usually steady, calm voice. "It has started. It may be a while before we have food again, or a safe place to eat it."

thirteen

. . .

Perry Abraham arrived at Cabell Street School that morning at about eight-thirty. He and his sister said goodbye to their mother, and got out of the car.

He doubted if goodbye meant the same thing to his sister as it did to him.

They walked toward the entrance, joining about a dozen other kids whose parents had just dropped them off. He noticed Colin Dorn there, and the older boy gave him a frown.

What did that mean? It could equally easily be that Colin had decided to believe him and was worried about what was going to happen, or had decided Perry was lying and was annoyed.

No way to tell.

Parsing people's expressions reminded him of when Mrs. Gray had shown her class some examples of Chinese script. It was hard to imagine those lines and curves coming together into anything meaningful, but apparently for some people, they did.

He went down the hallway toward Mrs. Gray's room, where she already stood outside the door, wearing a welcoming smile. "Good morning, Perry, how are you today?"

"I'm not sure."

She laughed, although he'd been entirely serious.

"Well, I hope that will change to *good* soon."

Perry didn't answer, but went into the classroom and found his seat.

The bell rang at nine o'clock, and Mrs. Gray came inside and shut the door. After some quick, cheerful greetings, she began the morning's lesson, which was math.

Perry couldn't stay focused on what she was saying. Ordinarily he liked math, but his mind kept wandering. First to the final warning the voice had given him that morning, that he had to act quickly when it all started, not let panic make him freeze. Get as many people as he could into hiding. But then he was distracted by a distant noise that sounded like wolves howling. A whole pack of them.

It took a full minute for him to realize that it wasn't wolves, it was sirens.

They were getting closer and louder. At first Mrs. Gray tried to keep talking to the class about how subtraction was like addition backwards, but the other kids in the class were clearly paying more attention to the noise than to her, and eventually a frown crossed her usually cheerful face.

"I wonder whatever can have happened?"

As if in answer, in rapid succession there were three explosions, one of which sounded quite close. The entire building shook. A bookend on a shelf along the wall bounced and slid off the end, falling to the floor with three of the books it had held back.

Mrs. Gray turned toward the class, her eyes wide with shock. Then suddenly, as if the light of realization had dawned, she met Perry's gaze. Her mouth opened, but no words came out.

Perry knew, knew for certain, that she was replaying their conversation in her mind.

If you had bad news about someone, should you tell them?

What kind of bad news?

Like if you knew something bad was going to happen.

Well, yes, if I knew something bad was coming, I would warn them.

Even if you knew that warning them wouldn't stop it?

Finally, she spoke, and her voice was a creak, so unlike her usual cheerful tone it was almost unrecognizable. "You knew. You were trying to warn me, weren't you?"

Another explosion cut off any answer he could have made, and it was followed by what could only be gunfire. Perry stood, feeling almost as if he'd been pulled to his feet by an impulse outside his own volition. "We've got to get out of here."

"We're safer inside."

"No, we're not. Inside we're trapped." The gunfire again, closer this time. "But it's too late anyhow. We've got to find a place to hide."

The door of the classroom burst open. Mrs. Gray, and several of the children, screamed, thinking the attackers were upon them. Perry saw with relief that it was Colin and Emily, and behind them, a group of children still in the hall.

Thank heaven. They had believed him.

"Come on," Colin shouted. "We know a place to hide! The art storeroom on the third floor. It's big enough, and we can lock it from the inside. But you've got to come now."

"There are people with guns coming up the street!" Emily said.

Perry ran to the older children. "Thank you."

"We're supposed… we're supposed to stay where we are!" Mrs. Gray was in tears. "That's what they told us. Lock the door, curtain the windows, and stay still and silent. You need to come in so we can lock everything down."

Perry looked back at her, his eyes wide, and gave a frantic shake of the head. "You can't! You need to come with us!"

If she really had realized that he'd tried to warn her, why didn't she trust him now? But she didn't. It was obvious from her face.

She was going to stay with the school's official lockdown policy. Which meant she was going to die. But there was nothing he could do about that. He had no way to force her.

He shouted at his classmates, "Come with us! Now!"

Only a couple of them did so. The others sat, frozen. Of course. They'd obey the adult, like they were trained to do, not the weird little kid everyone rolled their eyes at. But he didn't have time to argue, to try to convince them. Maybe some of them would survive.

Perry, and the two children who had stood when he yelled, ran after Colin and Emily as they retreated into the hall. He heard Mrs. Gray shout in a voice that was nearly a sob, "Perry! Becka! Levi! Come back!"

Then the door closed.

Colin was in the lead, the dozen or so kids he'd gathered following him, Emily bringing up the rear to keep track of any who lagged.

Perry felt a wash of relief, and immediately realized how strange that was. Shouldn't he be *more* scared now that the attack the voice told him about had started? But it meant the waiting was over. It was happening, and there was no time to be scared. He also knew, knew for certain, now that Colin and Emily were in charge, he could relax. It wasn't his responsibility any more.

The voice had assured him that after that, the children in their care would be okay.

They ran up a set of stairs, then turned and ascended a second one, rushing out into the third floor hallway. The classrooms they passed, whose doors were usually open and inviting, were shut up tight. They'd done what Mrs. Gray had done. Followed the school rules. Maybe…

There was a crash, and the sound of gunfire, coming unmistakably from inside the building. He heard screams. No, there was no time to pound on the doors, to argue with the adults, to get the people in those locked rooms to follow him.

Ahead, Colin already had a door open. A sign next to it said *Storage*. They piled into the little room, which was lined with shelves laden with art supplies—paper, boxes of crayons and colored pencils, modeling clay, bins with scissors and rulers, bottles of paint, jars with what looked like hundreds of paintbrushes of different sizes.

When the last of them came in, Emily shut and locked the door, then turned and said sternly, "Now, be quiet. Quiet as you can."

Several of the kids were crying, but they stifled their sobs, looking at the two older children with wide eyes.

"I know," Emily whispered. "I feel like crying, too. But you can't right now. We all have to be silent."

Colin looked over at Perry, his face set in a frown. Perry knew he wanted to ask questions, but there would be time for that later.

At least now, they were safe. For the others, the ones who had been left behind… there wasn't going to be a later. But he couldn't help that.

He'd done what he could.

***

They stayed in the art stockroom all day.

The sound of gunfire continued, as did the explosions. There was a heart-stopping moment when a tumult of angry voices got close, and the shots that followed were deafening. More screams, crashes as doors were kicked in.

A female voice give a triumphant shout. "More privileged rich kids. No great loss."

The gunfire started again, and the last of the screams was silenced.

A moment later the handle of the art stockroom jiggled. Perry heard one of the children gasp. Was it audible from out in the hall?

A muffled voice spoke. "Can't you read the sign? It's just a storage room."

"You want me to shoot the lock?"

The female voice. "No. Don't waste the ammunition on the door of an empty closet. We'll need it." A pause. "Come on."

The voices receded, and silence fell.

One hour passed, then two. One of the kids said he needed to pee, and Colin found a plastic bucket that he placed in the corner.

"Anyone who needs it, use it," he whispered. "We don't know how long we'll be here."

The day dragged on, and the gunfire—now from outside the building—grew more intermittent.

Colin came over and sat next to Perry, who was cross-legged on the floor with his back to a wall.

"Is it safe to go out?"

"Not yet."

"You're sure?"

Perry nodded.

There was a long pause. "Perry, how did you know this was going to happen?"

Perry met the older boy's gaze steadily. "A voice told me."

"What kind of voice?"

"I don't know. It's just a voice. But it tells me things, and the things become true. Later. So I knew this would happen."

"You could have warned the adults."

"The voice told me not to. I told you that. It said the adults wouldn't have listened."

"You could have tried." There was a clear edge of anger in Colin's voice.

Why was Colin mad at him? What Perry had said was going to happen, had happened. They'd saved some of the children—without acting as fast as they had, all of them would be dead, shot down in their classrooms.

"I just did what the voice told me," Perry said in a small voice.

Colin shook his head and looked away. That meant he was still mad, but there was nothing Perry could do about that.

Finally, the silence was absolute. And in that silence, the voice spoke to him, so clearly that he looked around to see if anyone else had heard.

"You did well."

No one reacted. Colin and Emily were seated next to each other. Emily's eyes were blank. Colin had his forehead on his knees and his arms wrapped around his legs. Two of the younger kids were curled up on the floor and appeared to be asleep.

"Your task is not over. There is still far to go before the day ends."

"Is it safe to go outside?"

When Perry spoke, several of the children looked over at him, but it was obvious he wasn't speaking to them, and in fact wasn't speaking to anyone who was in the room. Only Colin and Emily stared at him with understanding, but it held a measure of sheer terror.

Colin had been mad at him before. He was afraid of him now.

But the voice continued. "It is safe to go out into the building. But you will have to be brave. You will see things that will upset you, and will upset many of the others. So linger in the building as short a time as you are able. Once it is dark, it will be safe to go outside, and I will tell you how to go to a place where you can stay longer."

"What about our parents?"

Perry knew the answer. There'd been a reason he had been saying fervent goodbyes all week long. When the voice spoke, it was still in the same uninflected, flat tone.

"Your parents are dead."

"So no one is coming for us."

"I told you—it is up to you. You and the two oldest children. You cannot stay here, not past tonight. The people who attacked will return once they realize there is a cafeteria here that has stockpiles of food. Right now they are still bent on killing as many as they can. The thought of finding food and other supplies will not occur to them right away. It will give you long enough to get away."

"Get away to where?"

"I will show you. But not until tonight. For now, rest, and when you feel you are ready, you and the others can go out into the building. But you should warn them that they need to be prepared for what they will see."

Perry gave a start when Emily sat down next to him. He had been so focused on the voice he hadn't noticed her standing.

"It's talking to you?" Her voice was quiet, soothing.

He gave her a small nod.

"Why can't anyone else hear it?"

"I don't know."

"What did it tell you?"

Perry took a deep breath. "That it was safe to go out into the school, but that... it was bad out there. That we'll see bad things."

Emily regarded him solemnly for a moment. "I suppose we can't stay in this stockroom forever. And I think the people who attacked are gone now."

"But the ones they killed are still here."

"I know." She swallowed. "I'm trying not to think about that."

"But we need to leave. The voice said so. It said the people with the guns will come back. We need to go somewhere else. Tonight."

"Where?"

With a horrible suddenness, exhaustion swept over him. He didn't feel sleepy—sleepiness brought with it a sort of comfort. Hunger can be pleasant, when you know dinner is on the table in front of you. Sleepiness, when you're snuggled under the covers, is the same. Instead this was a dreadful weariness, as if even standing up would be more effort than he could manage, and no cure for it would ever come.

There was a long way to go still before he would reach a place of rest, and between here and there were horrors beyond his imagining.

"I don't know where." His voice was slurred in his own ears, as if he could barely make his mouth move to form the words. "It said it'd tell me later, but that we had to get out of here as soon as it was dark."

Emily regarded him in silence for a moment. "Where is this information coming from?"

"I don't know." How many questions had he answered that way since the voice started talking to him? Perry took a shaky breath that was almost a sob. Did he even have the energy to cry? "I wish it would talk to someone else."

She nodded.

"Why is Colin mad at me?"

She looked over at the other corner of the room, where Colin once again sat with his forehead against his knees, completely immobile, possibly asleep.

"He's not mad at you. He's just upset and scared, like we all are. We all deal with it in different ways. But he doesn't blame you."

"I asked the voice why other people couldn't hear it. It

told me they'd closed their minds. They can't hear it because they don't think it's real."

"Have you heard the phrase *seeing is believing*?"

Perry shook his head.

"It means that if you don't believe in something, seeing it for real will change your mind, will make you believe it. But maybe it's the other way around." She paused. "Maybe sometimes we don't see things, or hear them, if we don't believe in them first."

"But that doesn't work for everything. Some things are just fake, and I can't make them real by believing in them."

"No, that's true."

"Then how do I know which are which?"

"I have no idea."

He sighed. "Me either."

Emily's intelligent eyes met his for a moment, and Perry realized that she, perhaps alone of the children in the room, was convinced that what he told her about the voice was true. Her questions were out of a desire to understand, not out of doubt. It was such a relief to have even one person unequivocally on his side that he wanted to hug her, but as with most interactions, he wasn't sure how she'd react, so he didn't do it.

"I'm glad you don't think I'm psychotic."

A flicker of a smile. "I don't. I didn't, even when you talked to us yesterday. I knew somehow that you were telling us the truth."

"I wish everyone else did."

"They'll come around. Colin will, too. But first, let's focus on getting somewhere safe. If that voice is telling you we need to leave, then we need to leave. After what it told you about the attack, and what we needed to do—I think we'd be crazy not to do what it says."

fourteen

. . .

Soren stared at his phone's screen, and the last three messages from Finn Donnelly, in stunned silence.

His mind was blank. His heart hammered in his chest, but it was almost like he was watching someone else experience panic. The emotion was there, trying to reach his conscious mind, but it couldn't quite catch hold.

"Sit down, Conover," Dr. Quaice said. "Sit down before you faint."

He collapsed into the chair, his butt hitting the seat so hard the chair jerked backward with a squeak.

"You're not going to do Finn any good if you freak out. Anyone else, either. Deep breath and then we'll figure out what to do."

He stared at the screen, fighting the desperation to see something else, something encouraging, in the words. With quick, jerky motions he texted, "Finn, call or text as soon as you get this, I'm worried sick about you. I'm with Quaice and a couple others, we're heading to his house in Madison Park."

He hit "Send." Waited for the little smiling pic of Finn to show up next to the text, showing that he'd seen it.

None appeared.

Soren finally pulled his gaze away. He met Dr. Quaice's eyes, and swallowed. "You knew. You knew this was going to happen."

Dr. Quaice shrugged. "I knew it would happen at some point. I didn't know it'd be today any more than you did. I got here at seven this morning. Like you, I figured I'd get down to work and everything would be like it usually is. I didn't hear that anything was up until I decided to have a cup of coffee and check the news."

"But how… how can things go to shit so suddenly?"

His eyes were thoughtful, and he was silent for a moment. "That's always the way. There's a moment that's a pivot. Before that moment, everything is normal and ordinary and calm. After… Well, pick any of those big events in history. JFK's assassination. The explosion of the Challenger space shuttle. 9/11. Natural disasters are usually that way, of course —no warning. The Japanese tsunami and the meltdown at Fukushima, the earthquake in Nepal, the eruption of Mount Nyiragongo. Even when it's something that was planned— like when the United States invaded Iraq—it's still one of those sudden turns to the ordinary people who didn't know it was going to happen. Each time, moments beforehand everything is normal, and moments afterward, nothing is."

Soren stared at the older man, his mouth hanging open.

"Now what do we do?" Even in his own ears, his voice sounded strained to the snapping point.

"Well, that's the question, isn't it? You can't control when these pivots happen, all you can do is prepare as best you can, and determine what your posture toward them is going to be."

"You're not afraid?"

Dr. Quaice barked out a short, harsh laugh. "You think that?"

"It looks like you're not."

"I'm as scared as you are, Conover. Okay, maybe I've been

expecting this. But that's not saying I was ready for it to happen today. That's why I started creating my conlang twenty years ago…"

"Finn and I were talking about that this morning."

He nodded. "I had a hunch eventually we'd need a way to communicate that would allow some guarantee of privacy and secrecy. There's no code or conlang that can't be deciphered, of course, but at least it'll slow them down."

"Them?"

"Whoever ends up in charge."

"You don't think the people in government, the police and military, will put this right? Stop the riots?"

"Honestly? No. You can only do that up to a point. This time it's too coordinated and too widespread. As far as the police and military, they're part of the problem, not the solution to it. Mark my words—once someone starts consolidating power, the enforcers will rally around them. At that point, we need to watch our step like we've never done before. For what it's worth, I think the old order is done. You're witnessing the end of the United States as you knew it."

Before Soren could respond the office door opened, and a woman stepped in carrying a laden backpack. Cassandra Nicolaides, the department's resident expert on Middle Eastern languages. Her demeanor radiated *don't fuck with me.* Not an unusual thing—Cassandra was a serious badass at the best of times—but today she looked ready to do battle with anyone who crossed her. Nearly as tall as Soren, dark hair swept back into a tight ponytail, dark eyes flashing defiance, she was an imposing figure, someone he was glad was on his side.

"Ready," she said to Dr. Quaice. "Gavin's right behind me. He said he'd be down in five minutes." She looked at Soren. "So you're caught up in this, too?"

He nodded. "Had a class this morning. I was already here by the time things started to fall apart."

"Same as the rest of us, then. Although I don't know if we'd be any safer if we'd stayed home."

Soren thought about Finn's text describing a riot and blockaded streets, and just nodded.

The door opened again to admit a slender, bespectacled man, one of those youthful types who never looked his actual age. He had a round, gentle face with nary a wrinkle. Black hair starting to go to gray at the temples was the only clue. Soren knew that Gavin Liu was fifty-one—Soren had been invited to his fiftieth birthday party—but by appearance, he could have been anywhere between thirty and sixty.

"I got a call from Peggy," he said. "She's at her sister's house. They're locked in and as secure as they can be. No violence in their immediate area."

"Yet," Cassandra interjected.

Gavin nodded solemnly. "Yet. I told them I'd get there when I could."

"Where does the sister live?" Dr. Quaice asked.

"Kirkland."

"That'll mean getting across the Evergreen Point Bridge."

Gavin didn't respond beyond a quick, almost imperceptible frown, there and gone in a moment.

Dr. Quaice switched off his computer with a sudden movement and then stood, unfolding his lanky limbs with a groan. "All right, no reason to wait."

"Might we be safer here?" Gavin asked.

"No way to tell. My guess is no. They'll target public buildings before private residences, more than likely. Also, there's hardly any food here, if we end up stuck for more than a day. I've got a stockpile at my house that'll last us at least a couple of weeks. Once we're there, we can regroup and decide what to do."

"I did a quick run up and down the halls," Cassandra said. "We seem to be the only people here."

"Everyone else must have delayed long enough to figure out what was going down," Soren said. "I only had three students show up for my syntax class. Out of thirteen. And all three of them live on campus."

"They better get back to their dorms and stay put," Cassandra said.

Soren nodded. He thought about the three young people he had spoken with earlier, and a thought came out of nowhere—*you probably will never see them again.*

Where had that come from? He took a deep breath. Maybe things weren't as bad as Quaice thought. Surely someone would step in and restore order. The government couldn't collapse that quickly.

Chances were, things would be back to normal in a day or two, and afterward this would be one of those *Do you remember where you were when…?* things you chat about over a glass of wine with friends. But the bleak knowledge rose in him that this wasn't true. This was a fundamental shift into chaos, and there was no going back.

Quaice packed a satchel with some papers, a bottle of water, and a handful of granola bars, then shut the drawer of his desk with a bang.

"Okay. Stick together, and watch for any signs of danger. We'll stay off main roads and thoroughfares as much as possible. We'll have to take Montlake Boulevard across the Cut, but that can't be avoided. Until then, we keep close together and avoid open spaces."

Cassandra and Gavin shouldered backpacks.

Quaice led the way into the hall, closing and locking his door behind him. "You want anything from your office, Conover? You weren't expecting to have to make a run for it. We could make a quick stop if you want to grab something."

Soren thought about what he'd left in his office. A backpack containing folders with lesson plans and graded student work. A thermos of iced tea. He usually caught lunch at a nearby café, so he even didn't have any food.

He recalled Dr. Quaice's words from only a few minutes earlier—*It might be a while before we're back here.*

What would he need from his office? Nothing. The essential things were finding a safe place to stay, avoiding getting caught up in the violence. Keeping his head down.

First and foremost—finding Finn, getting him to safety. He pictured his boyfriend's brilliant, open smile, the first thing he'd noticed the day they met eight years earlier. Dimples, thick auburn hair, eyes a deep blue-gray like ocean water, a spray of freckles across his shoulders and the bridge of his nose. When they were reunited—they had to be, the alternative was pure agony to consider—he would never again take for granted how sheerly beautiful Finn was. He'd hold him close, maybe for hours. He recalled the touch of his lover's hands that morning, the tenderness of his kiss, the passion of his embrace. If he'd known this might be the last time…

But that was too hard even to consider. With an effort he pushed the thought aside.

"No. There's nothing I need from my office. Let's go."

Their footsteps echoed in the empty hallway as they headed toward a staircase with an exit sign. Soren was struck by how ordinary everything looked. Doors of professors' offices, storage rooms, restrooms. Corkboards with schedules, fliers for conferences and lectures, and advertisements for internships and study-abroad opportunities. A few examples of arcane linguistics humor, like the legend in neat Sharpie someone had put on the wall saying, "This is not graffiti. It is a single graffitus."

All so familiar, ordinary, belying the chaos that was happening outside.

Each time, moments beforehand everything is normal, and moments afterward, nothing is.

They descended the staircase, still neither seeing nor hearing anyone else. The window in the exit door looked out onto a green lawn edged by a sidewalk and some cherry trees in full bloom. Dr. Quaice got there first, slowly pushed open the door, peered out, and gave a beckoning gesture with one hand.

They set out southward. In the distance was the circular mirror of Drumheller Pond. The fountain wasn't running, and its surface was glassy and undisturbed, reflecting the cool blue of the sky. Ahead of them was the hulking complex of the University Medical Center.

And everywhere, windows. Soren hadn't thought about that before. There'd been no need to. Even though they'd seen no one, he felt exposed, naked, and imagined hostile faces behind the glass, wearing grim smiles as they watched the four of them skulking along. He'd never felt unsafe walking on campus, even at night, but now he realized how easy it would be for someone with ill intent to hide in ambush amongst the lush trees and shrubs lining every sidewalk.

The open lawn of the Rainier Vista was far too open to view, even if some of Soren's fretfulness was an overactive imagination. They crossed Mason Road and the Burke-Gilman Trail, and ahead of them was the multi-lane concrete expanse of Montlake Boulevard Northeast.

A volley of gunfire broke out somewhere nearby, and behind them a flock of birds exploded from a dense grove of fir trees and rhododendron bushes, squalling angrily as they swirled up into the sky. Soren's heart slammed painfully against his ribcage. Ahead was a square, industrial-looking brick building—Wilcox Hall, part of the College of Engineering, if he remembered right—and someone had spray-painted in huge, uneven black letters, "THIS BUILDING IS NOW THE PROPERTY OF THE LACKLAND LIBERATION AUTHORITY. TRESPASSERS WILL BE SHOT ON SIGHT." Next to the graffiti was the fanged logo of the LLA, depicted with blood dripping from the long downward swoops from the letter A.

"I think we'll be seeing a lot of that logo in the next few weeks," Dr. Quaice whispered.

They gave Wilcox Hall a wide berth.

In ten minutes they had reached the bridge across Montlake Cut, two ornate, turreted towers flanking the roadside on each end. They still saw no one, and odder still, no traffic. It wasn't until he stepped onto the north end of the bridge that Soren saw why. Ahead of them was the broad expanse of Highway 520, that connected Seattle to the Eastside communities east of Lake Washington—Kirkland, Bellevue, Redmond, and Sammamish. There were long, disordered barricades all the way across, and a pileup of cars behind it in the westbound lanes blocked any hope someone might have had of smashing their way through. The breeze brought faint traces of the sounds of screams, muffled with distance, rising and falling with the air movement. Columns of smoke rose from the skyline, billowing gray and black, into the blue spring sky.

"Oh, my God." Soren swallowed hard. "What have they done?"

At the same moment, there was a gunshot and a loud *ping!* as the bullet struck the stone side of the nearest turret, exploding a shower of fragments off its surface. Soren dropped to the ground. Gavin Liu looked around in confusion, as if trying to figure out what direction the shot had come from, but when the sniper fired a second time Cassandra grabbed him and pulled him down behind the bridge abutment.

"Well, that complicates matters," she said, in a completely calm voice.

"At least he doesn't seem to be a very good shot," Dr. Quaice said.

Soren shuddered. "I'd rather not give him a third attempt."

"We don't have a lot of choices, unless we want to head back to Guggenheim Hall and hole up there as long as we can. We'd be safer in my house."

"If we can get there," Gavin said, rather unnecessarily.

There was another shot, but it seemed to come from somewhere else.

"Awesome," Soren mumbled. "There's more than one of them."

"A lot more," Dr. Quaice said.

"Going back doesn't make any sense," Cassandra said. "Dr. Quaice is right. The University buildings are going to be targets before private residences are. The Lacklanders always threatened to go after the elite, and you don't get more elite than a university. Plus, they're big targets. I vote for crossing the bridge. Run, keep your head low. At the other end there's cover."

She looked from one of them to the other.

No one spoke.

Finally she stood, still crouched behind the bridge tower.

"I'll go first. If I get shot you'll have to decide what to do." Before anyone could object, she'd taken off at a dead sprint. The impact of her shoes on the asphalt sounded loud in the silence. But she made it to the other side without there being another shot from the sniper, and disappeared into a cluster of fir trees that lined the roadside on the south end of the bridge.

The three men exchanged glances.

Soren took a deep breath. "I'll go next."

The words sounded foreign in his own ears, as if someone else were speaking. He'd never been a big risk-taker. Even jumping off the high diving board into a swimming pool was past his comfort level. Now, running across a wide-open bridge with an unseen gunman targeting anything that moved not only seemed possible, but inevitable.

Choice didn't enter into the decision. Staying put was not an option, going back was not an option. So it was forward. And once he thought of it that way, it was as if it were a thing accomplished. Only a tiny voice *You could die* skittered through his brain, but by that time he was already sprinting across the bridge.

He reached the trees, panting hard, and nearly collided with Cassandra in his desperation to get off the road. He turned back toward the bridge, where the two older men stood, moving hesitantly but apparently ready to cross as well.

Cassandra took his arm, gave it a light tug, then whispered and pointed. "Look. Over there."

Behind the bridge tower on the other side of the road was the slumped form of a man dressed in camo gear. Cassandra gave a quick jerk of the head toward the fallen man, let go of Soren's arm, and crossed the empty roadway. A little reluctantly, Soren followed.

The man was dead, that was obvious. A bullet hole in his temple trickled blood, and Soren didn't want to see what the exit wound on the other side looked like. A handgun was still clutched loosely in his right hand. Shuddering, Soren reached out and touched the man's slack face. It was still warm, as if he'd died moments before.

Dr. Quaice, breathing hard, came up to them, followed by Gavin.

"Our sniper?"

"I think it might be," Cassandra said.

"So who killed him?" Soren asked.

"Doesn't matter. The enemy of our enemy is our friend."

Soren stood and looked around. No one and nothing moved.

"Whoever killed the sniper is staying out of sight," Cassandra said.

"Is that a good thing?"

She didn't respond.

They continued their skulking path southward, crossing Highway 520 west of the line of barricades, keeping to the shadows as they followed the cement embankment of the underpass. What looked like a dozen more bodies lay slumped near the blockage, but whether those were rebels or motorists who'd gotten out of their vehicles to try storming their way across was impossible to tell. A couple of moving figures wove amongst the stopped cars, but they were moving away from Soren's group and either were unaware of them or else didn't care.

After crossing the Cut, the going got easier and less nerve-wracking. Ahead were the two-hundred-plus acres of beautiful, immaculately-maintained gardens of the Arboretum. Magnolias and peonies and azaleas were in full bloom, and the cool air was redolent of the smell of flowers. As they left the streets behind for the hills, trails, and pathways through the park, Soren's pulse decelerated. There could still be snipers there, but the cover—made up of dense growth of giant rhododendron bushes, hollies, and Japanese maples—would give them at least some protection from hostile eyes. Their path would take them lengthwise across the Arboretum, and thick undergrowth would follow them nearly the entire way.

They followed a trail through a cluster of trees covered with delicate white bells, and rounded a corner toward a massive cedar. Cassandra was the first one to spot her—a woman sitting cross-legged with her back to the trunk, watching them approach with a broad smile on her face. She was perhaps forty years old, and the most remarkable thing about her appearance was how completely unremarkable she looked. An oval face, even features, light brown hair in a loose ponytail, neither particularly attractive nor at all unattractive, she was the kind of person you might pass a dozen times a day and never notice.

But here she sat in the Arboretum as the world collapsed around her, apparently unconcerned.

"Oh, hello," she called out in a pleasant, melodious voice, and waved.

Soren exchanged a puzzled glance with Cassandra, who shrugged.

As they neared, the woman stood, moving a little awkwardly, but with no evident self-consciousness. Soren jerked to a halt until she raised both hands to show that she was unarmed.

"Don't be afraid," she said. "I mean no harm. In fact, I've been waiting for you all."

fifteen

. . .

Lydia Moreton had given some thought to where she was going to live after the attacks started, but finally decided to leave it to luck. She and the other LLA leaders in Seattle had a detailed plan to clear a number of downtown office buildings—by "clear" they meant killing everyone inside—and undoubtedly one of them would have some comfortable sofas to sleep on, perhaps even a cafeteria. A suitable place would turn up.

What she hadn't reckoned on was how little sleep she'd need. Most of the others looked at killing as a necessary task, one to finish as quickly as possible. Lydia didn't. Every time she killed, she experienced a nearly orgasmic rush of pleasure.

Sleep was the last thing she was thinking about. What she wanted was more people to destroy, more opportunities for discharging the deep, razor-edged rage that filled her. The anger had been with her a long time, since she was a teenager living through the deaths of her father and grandfather less than a year apart. The worst part was watching her father, nearly to the end, continuing to drag himself to his job operating machinery in a fruit-packing plant for just above minimum wage.

Her grandfather had gone first, victim of a freak accident involving the machinery that had left his body so mangled her parents had never told her the details. Later that year her father and three others sickened and died in a space of three months, first showing flu-like symptoms, then lapsing into a coma from which they never recovered. After the fourth death there had been an inquiry resulting in the company being found in violation of safety standards—something about volatile solvents, poor ventilation, and no respirators— but their lawyers had argued that there was no indication the problem was of long standing. However, because no one on the production line reported anything wrong, they weren't found financially liable for the deaths of the four men. The result was a minuscule fine.

Paid to the government, of course. Not the victims' families.

That was the beginning of the anger digging its claws into her. They'd pay. The ones who did this would pay, them and everyone like them.

When the attacks began, she quickly took over as executioner. Most of the others seemed just as happy to let her carry out the actual killings. There were a couple who apparently shared her glee in bloodshed, but she doubted they enjoyed it as much as she did.

After her third killing, the thought went through her head that at long last, she'd found her true calling.

Even destroying the school hadn't affected her much. When they came upon Cabell Street School, on the first day of the attacks, there had been a momentary pang of *Not children. You can't kill children.* But the voice of rage in her shouted down her doubts. This was an expensive private school. These were the children of the oppressors, who would grow up to be oppressors themselves, just as it had been throughout history.

They weren't killing *people*. They were eliminating a whole class of wealthy, amoral parasites.

They had been forming the plans for years. The leaders of the LLA recognized what had doomed previous attempts at overthrowing the world order—lack of organization. People got pissed off, rose up, got crushed, and that was the end of it. In order to have any hope of succeeding, the attacks had to be huge, worldwide, and simultaneous. It was all right having small, easily-quelled disturbances beforehand. In a way, that was even to their benefit. It would lull the powers-that-be into thinking the LLA was just another in a long line of amateurish agitators who jabbed at the social and political structure piecemeal, without any real overarching plan. Minor protests and riots and vandalism were what they'd expect.

That expectation would blind them to how big the movement actually was, and stop them from dealing with it until it was far too late.

And that's exactly what happened. Up till the morning of the attacks Lydia had hoped, but not quite believed, they could pull it off. The LLA leaders claimed for years that quick and massive attacks would completely overwhelm the ability of the police to respond. Plus, the plan was not just to set the bombs, then run away. They'd wait for them go off, and for the police to arrive, who they'd then pick off, one by one.

The result was that the police presence collapsed almost immediately. Not only could they not keep up with the emergency calls, there were more than a few policemen who were LLA sympathizers, probably drawn by a combined sense of injustice and that once the chaos was past, a new authoritarian order could emerge. It was doubtful whether most of the police and military who did support the LLA understood that the leadership intended to destroy the current power structure and replace it with nothing, but a lot of them seemed to have the idea that anything was better than the rampant petty lawlessness they saw every day. Whatever the motivation, when it became obvious which side was likely to win, defections swelled the ranks of the rebels and shrank the official response to zero.

Lydia kept half expecting to feel some reluctance, some remorse, something other than glee. By the evening of the first day of the attacks, they'd cleared an office building and decided it would serve as a decent home base, despite the fact that one of the bombs detonated that morning had damaged the façade and front office. She was exhilarated at how well everything had gone, and now had some time to sit back, to act as judge for the few people who had neither fled nor been killed during the day's attacks. Just at nightfall, a young man who'd been taken alive in one of the office buildings was brought to her. He was obviously terrified—shirt ripped, a bloody cut on his face, hands tied behind his back.

"I didn't do anything!" His shout was nearly a sob. "Why are you people doing this?"

"What job did you have?" she asked, in a conversational tone.

He frowned as if he couldn't quite believe what she was asking. "I'm a financial planner."

"Hmm. Okay." She turned toward the guard holding the man's upper arm. The thought went through her mind—and was immediately dismissed as irrelevant—that she found the guard repellent, almost simian, while the young financial planner was actually kind of hot-looking. "Give him to Lachman. He's got a whip he's been wanting to try out." A smile grew on her face. "Tell him to take his time."

The young man's inarticulate shouts of terror as he was pushed out of the room faded for a few minutes, but she clearly heard his screams as the whipping began.

"You like listening?" She looked up to see the face of Jeff Landry, the only LLA higher-ranked than her in the Seattle area. He was also the only one that she herself was a little scared of. The others, mostly of the brute force variety, she didn't fear because she was smarter.

Landry, though, was smarter still. A genius, perhaps. This didn't temper the fact that he was also batshit crazy. His eyes glinted with a frenetic intelligence. His unruly brown hair looked as if it hadn't seen a comb in months. His body was taut as an overwound guitar string. If she hadn't known better she'd have pegged him as a meth addict, but he eschewed all drugs, even caffeine, nicotine, and alcohol.

No, his appearance wasn't from a chemical. He might be a brilliant leader, but he was insane.

She met his eyes. "It sends an example to the others. We can't give them an easy out. They need to suffer like they made the rest of us suffer."

Landry nodded with approval. "I don't mind making an example of a few of 'em. But keep in mind that it takes time. Better to dispose of them quickly when possible."

"I've used my gun plenty today."

"That's another thing. The ammunition isn't going to last forever. We have stockpiles, but no one's making any more, and won't be for a long time. Use the bullets in a combat situation, but afterwards, with any captives…" He gave her a grin. It was light years from an ordinary human smile. It looked like a machine had pulled up the corners of his mouth to expose his teeth. "We have swords and axes for a reason. They're just as quick, and don't use up supplies we need."

"Going medieval, then?"

The grin stretched wider still. "The whole world will have gone medieval by the time we're done."

Lydia nodded. The whistling of the whip and the screams still sounded from the direction of the courtyard behind the building, but the screams were losing intensity. He obviously wouldn't last much longer.

It took less time to flog a man to death than she'd realized.

"What's our next move?"

Landry nodded. "We've got some breathing room. My main concern was taking out the Westin Building quickly. The one thing that could have caused us to fail is if they'd used telecommunications fast enough to mount an effective response. Taking out the internet and cellular service was absolutely critical. But it went off without a hitch. We've still got our radio base stations—along with enough solar generators to keep them going—so we can stay in touch with each other. But them? They're hamstrung." He stopped, and gave a sigh of… gratitude? Relief? What emotions did this man actually experience? "They're cut off from each other, and we can pick apart the remaining resistance at our leisure."

"You make it sound easy."

"Oh, it will be. That's their fatal flaw—overconfidence. They got fat and lazy. They believed that their money would protect them, and if anything did go wrong, they had help coming at the touch of a computer keyboard. Hardly anyone gave a thought to how vulnerable that made them. When you've got one electronic network holding it all together, all you have to do is pull out that one thread, and…" He flicked his fingers upward. "Boom."

"How long do you think the electricity will last?"

"Doesn't matter. A long while, I'd expect. Matteo said that since it's hydropower, it could continue for at least a month with minimal oversight. It'd be different if we ran on coal." He grinned again. "The Northeast is probably already in blackout."

"We could have taken out the hydro plants."

"Waste of time. So they all have electricity, what can they do with it? Cook dinner, have a cold beer? Doesn't hurt us. Doesn't slow us down at all. In fact, if they're idiots enough to turn the lights on at night, it'll help us to track down survivors."

"I suppose that makes sense."

"You're not having second thoughts, are you?" His feverish eyes narrowed a little.

Lydia listened for a moment. The whip was still hitting its target, but the screams had stopped.

"No. No second thoughts. I just want to make sure we succeed, is all. I don't want to meet their overconfidence with overconfidence of our own."

He frowned. "All right. But don't doubt the plan. It's succeeded beyond what even I anticipated. Before the internet crashed, there were reports coming in from all over the world." He paused. "If any governments survive this, I'll be shocked."

"Good."

Landry's face relaxed a little. "Are there any other prisoners to deal with?"

"No. He was the last one."

"One other thing. Have we found out more about that shortwave network? The one that communicates in a foreign language?"

"No. Unfortunately. Whatever it is, it appears to have been going on for some time. We've had people listen in pretty continuously for the last few months, and no one seems to be able to figure out what language the broadcasts are in. People monitoring that frequency have identified by voice at least two dozen different speakers using it, so that would suggest it's a commonly-spoken language, but we've ruled out all of the ones that seemed likely." She paused. "I still think it's a code."

"What kind of code?"

"I don't know. Maybe some kind of artificial language."

"Like Klingon?"

A chill rippled its way down her back as he followed up his comment with a dry, mirthless laugh. Yeah, this guy was fucking insane. Dangerously insane. He'd have to be watched carefully. Maybe eliminated once the dust settled. She'd much prefer to be in charge herself than having to listen to—and act like she trusted—this man.

But she kept her voice light. "Yeah, like Klingon. During World War II they had the Navajo Code Talkers, right? And it worked because the Germans and Japanese had no one who spoke Navajo. But it'd work even better if it was a synthetic language, where the *only* speakers were the ones in the network. It'd be damn near untranslatable."

"But there have been a couple of names identified from the talking, right? Or at least things we think are names?"

She nodded. "Our monitors have picked up a couple of words that sound like forms of address based on how they're used. A few of them are clearly names—Glenn, Davis, Carlson. Not enough information that we can figure out who they are. With one exception."

"Which is?"

"There's one name that's come up over and over. Almost every time we've listened in, we've heard it. And it's unique enough that we've identified who it belongs to. An elderly linguistics professor at UW."

"Linguistics." Landry looked surprised.

It was one of the first times she'd ever seen the expression on his face. Whether it was a safe thing to surprise him, even with good news, was debatable. He was very much the type who distrusted people who knew more than him, even if they were on his side.

"Yes. And it turns out he *is* known for having created a synthetic language. Apparently doing that is some kind of hobby amongst the language nerds. They're called conlangs. This particular one is called Kalila. He offered classes in it."

"Interesting. Sounds like we need to speak with him. Or at least someone who has taken one of his classes."

"Maybe in a week or two, once things have settled. I can't see that it's a priority. We don't even know if they're talking about anything we care about. For now, let's just keep monitoring it."

"I don't like that we don't know." Landry's frown deepened. "What's his name?"

"It's fortunate he has an odd name. Only one in the telephone directory with that last name." She paused. "Quaice. His name is Anderson Quaice."

sixteen

. . .

The sounds of explosions brought people out into the street. Brandon Nguyen heard the murmur of voices, and when he peered out of the window, he saw about two dozen, some shading their eyes while staring southward.

"Come," Julia said. "Now that it's begun, so must we."

Caria still looked at the older woman with some combination of reverence and terror. Brandon touched her upper arm, hoping to reassure her, but she jumped, flinching as if she'd been stung. When she turned toward him, her usually urbane face held such raw emotion she hardly seemed the same person he'd known for three years.

They walked out onto the front porch, then down the stairs to the sidewalk. Brandon scanned the faces of the people standing in the street in a loose cluster. He knew only a couple of them by name. He hadn't exactly been an unfriendly neighbor, but neither had he reached out to any of them. It might have been easier if he had. Maybe they'd be more inclined to believe the insane story they were about to hear.

"People, you need to listen." Julia's voice took on an oratorical quality, and one by one the crowd turned her way.

"This is just the beginning. We are facing tribulation the likes of which most of us have never seen."

A couple of people rolled their eyes. Brandon could almost read their minds—*Religious End Times nutter.*

"What's happening?" a middle-aged woman asked. "What were those explosions? I thought they were earthquakes at first."

"They're not earthquakes. They're bombs. There is an attack in progress on the heart of Seattle. But it's not alone. Cities all over the world are suffering the same fate."

"From who?" The man who asked had a narrow, skeptical face, and was one of the ones who had rolled his eyes.

"And how do you know all this?" someone else shouted.

Brandon cut Julia off before she could tell them her knowledge came from God. They couldn't start the conversation out that way, or ninety percent of people would stop listening.

"It's the LLA," he said. "The LLA is coordinating violence all over the area."

He didn't know this for certain, but it seemed likely.

"The LLA?" the middle-aged woman said. "But they're in Europe."

"They're here," the skeptical man responded. "I've seen the graffiti. But they're just small-time thugs. Don't tell me they have the balls and the brains to coordinate some kind of massive attack."

As if in response, another explosion, this one closer, made the ground shake.

"I'm afraid you're wrong," Julia said. "They are far better organized than anyone thought. They are capable of carrying out attacks on a worldwide scale."

"And once again, how do you know this?" The man's eyes narrowed with suspicion. "Are you one of them?"

"Far from it. But I learned what they were planning. There was nothing I could do to stop it, but now that they've begun I want to get as many people to safety as I can."

Brandon waited for her to add something about divine guidance, but she didn't. She'd told him how members of her own church had responded to her warnings. Maybe she sensed that leaning on the message-from-God aspect wouldn't add to her credibility.

"Where is safety?" A young man who looked no more than twenty-five turned toward her with a worried expression. "Are you saying here isn't safe?"

"It won't be for very long. I don't know when they will attack this neighborhood, but they surely will. These people will kill on sight, without the slightest hesitation, without any pity or remorse. We need to get out of the city. Those who don't flee with us will die."

"Out of the city?" The middle-aged woman sounded incredulous. "Just get in our cars and head off in some random direction?"

"Cars won't help. Very soon the roads will be impassible. Cars will be death traps."

"If you knew this, why didn't you get out before it all started?" The skeptical man's face had gone from doubt to outright anger.

Julia answered without hesitation. "Because I could not leave all of you behind."

All she got in return was a wave of bafflement.

She took a deep breath. "It is my task to gather people together and lead them out of danger. My own personal safety is irrelevant except in regards to fulfilling that duty."

"So you're, like, Moses or something?" the young man asked.

If he expected her to show any discomfort with the comparison, he was fated to be disappointed.

"Yes," Julia said. "Exactly like that."

There was some nervous laughter, but once again it was cut off, this time by the sound of automatic gunfire from somewhere nearby. Brandon looked over at Caria, who seemed to be in the extremity of fear. He would have to help her, and soon, but he had no idea what to do or say. She was approaching the point that fight-or-flight turns into being frozen in place, like a mouse watching a snake ready to strike.

"Caria," he whispered. "It's going to be okay."

But the sound of gunfire stopped his reassurances cold.

"They're coming," Julia thundered. "Follow me, or stay and be lost."

She turned, as if certain they would obey her command. Brandon and Caria followed her, and when he glanced over his shoulder, he saw that about ten people had done the same —including the middle-aged woman and the young twenty-something.

Of the rest, some were running back to their houses, probably to barricade themselves in. Others still stood in the street, peering southward toward the source of the riotous noise.

Brandon trotted ahead to where Julia was striding, her eyes focused straight ahead. "Shouldn't we stay and try to convince more of them?"

"We can't. There isn't time. It is just as in Jesus's day. All I can do is say, 'Leave everything thou hast and follow me,' and let them decide who will and who won't. I cannot coerce, and even if I could, I would not. To coerce would make me just like our enemies."

"But they'll die. You said so."

She gave him a side-eye. "Yes. They'll die. But so will we all, Brandon, when the Lord chooses. Until then, we all have to do the best we can to make our own decisions."

By the time they'd gotten only three blocks north of Brandon's house, the sound of gunfire was already less. It didn't mean they were safe, he knew that, but at least they were going in the right direction, whether from Julia's divine guidance or merely the common sense of heading away from the sounds of rioting.

Twenty minutes more walking brought them into a long, tree-lined street flanked by apartment complexes. Thus far they'd seen only three other people, all of them from a distance and all of them scurrying for shelter, perhaps because they thought Julia and her followers were themselves rioters. About a half-dozen cars passed them, going well over the speed limit and heading in the same direction. Whatever news had reached here about the attacks, it had the effect of either keeping people indoors or inducing them to get into their cars and drive as fast as they could away from downtown.

Whether that was the best decision remained to be seen.

A few minutes later, the two new additions came up to Brandon. They'd probably been having a quiet confabulation, and had chosen him as the most approachable of their trio.

"Your name is Brandon, right?" the young man said.

He nodded. "I'm sorry, I don't know yours."

"Trevor. Trevor Keene."

The woman said, "I'm Veronica Sulzbach." She gave a nervous giggle. "But that's a mouthful, so everyone calls me Ronnie."

"Do you believe all that stuff she said?" Trevor gave a quick jerk of the head toward Julia, still moving forward with a determined stride.

"Yes. I do. She knew the attacks were going to start today. Also... wherever she gets her knowledge from... I sort of do, too. I can't explain it. But I know she's right. We have to get out of here. Now."

Ronnie gave him a dubious glance. "And you don't think she's LLA herself? How else would she know?"

"Does she look the part?"

"Not really."

"Well, she's not. I can say that with a hundred percent certainty. And I'm not a believer in divine guidance, or whatnot, but I can say I believe *her*. She says we need to go, I'm going with her."

"When do you think it'll be safe to go back to our houses?"

Brandon half turned to look at them. Ronnie was pure nerves. It was clear she'd followed because she was alone and afraid the rioters were heading their direction. Trevor, on the other hand, looked excited. Did he think this was some sort of trek, like in a fantasy novel?

"Honestly? I don't think it ever will be safe to return. At least not for a very, very long time."

"You can't be serious," Trevor said.

"Completely. Didn't you hear anything she was saying?"

"I thought..." He stopped, swallowed. "I thought it was just a riot, like they've had in France. People in the street, some fighting, some damage and looting, then everything goes back to normal like always."

"Not this time."

He digested this in silence.

"The LLA scare the hell out of me," Ronnie said.

"They should."

Trevor spoke with a quaver in his voice. "But if... if we're not going back... shouldn't we have, like, packed a suitcase or something?"

"There wasn't time."

There was another distant explosion.

Ronnie jumped. "No, I expect there wasn't."

Trevor turned a frightened face to Brandon. "But where are we *going*?"

"I don't think she knows, honestly."

"Doesn't she think it's, like, God speaking to her? She said she was like Moses. Shouldn't she know where the Promised Land is?"

Brandon didn't speak for a moment. "I can't really answer that, not with any certainty. Yes, she believes it's the Voice of

God. Me, I've never been religious. But a few weeks ago, I… I started having visions. I'm an artist, and I felt compelled to paint what I saw. One of them…" He dug in his pocket for his phone, and after touching the screen a couple of times, held out the image of *Poured Out Like Water* for Ronnie and Trevor to see.

"That's a good likeness," Ronnie said.

"Thank you. But you need to know… I painted that before I'd ever seen her. I first met her *after* the piece was done."

They both stared at him in silence.

"The visions I have aren't like what Julia gets. From what I understand, she hears a voice directly, giving her commands, giving her information. Me, I just get pictures." He flipped through the photos of the other pieces. "Julia said that all these are real people. People I'll meet sooner or later."

"What does your friend think of this?" Ronnie gave a quick gesture back at Caria, who was following a little behind, her face as blank as a victim of shell-shock.

"She's not finding it easy."

"Me either," Trevor said.

"But she believes you enough to come with you," Ronnie said. "She must trust you and Julia."

Brandon shrugged. "I don't know. I think it's more that there's nothing else she can do with what's happened. I paint a woman, and she shows up in real life. The woman tells us there will be attacks starting this morning, and then they do. She doesn't have any choice but to believe what's happening, but that doesn't mean she has an explanation for it. I think she's with us partly because she trusts me, and partly because if she didn't come with us she'd have to figure all this stuff out alone."

"What's her name?" Ronnie asked quietly.

"Caria. Caria Sahin."

She nodded, and a determined look came into her eyes. She half turned. "Caria?"

The younger woman startled. "Yes?"

"Come on up here with us. You shouldn't be back there by yourself. We need to stick together."

Caria sped up her pace a little to match theirs. Brandon reached out and took her hand. Her expression didn't change, but she gave his hand an appreciative squeeze.

"Brandon was just telling us how all this started. With his paintings, and meeting Julia and all."

"You believed him?"

"He showed me the photo of his painting."

Caria gave a bleak little laugh. "He showed me, too, but I still didn't quite believe him."

"But you do now."

"I have no choice."

Ronnie nodded. "Whatever happens, let's look out for each other, okay? I don't understand it either. Maybe none of us do, not really. But we'll be all right if we just have each other's backs." She took a deep breath. "I'm Ronnie Sulzbach. This is my next-door neighbor, Trevor Keene."

Any response Caria would have made was cut off by the sound of a car roaring up the street toward them. Brandon turned to see an expensive-looking white Mercedes paying little attention to the lane markings. It was fortunate no other cars were on the road, because the way this guy was driving, there'd have been an accident for sure.

Brandon watched its approach, frozen, unable to decide whether or not to run. The driver slammed on his brakes, and rolled down his window.

It was a balding man, perhaps forty-five, with a neatly trimmed beard. His tie was askew, and his eyes registered panic.

"What the hell are you doing?" he shouted at them, and his voice cracked. "Don't you know what's going on?"

"We know there have been attacks," Julia said in level tones.

He laughed, a high, wild sound. "Not just attacks. This city is a war zone. It all happened... god, it was sudden. Everything was normal then all at once people started opening fire. Bombs went off. I got out of my office just before..." He stopped, swallowed hard. "I don't know how I got to my car and away. Most of the streets near downtown are either barricaded or are so damaged you can't drive on them. But the rioters—they're headed this way. You need to get indoors where it's safe..."

There was a report and then the whine of a bullet, feeling like it passed inches from Brandon's right ear. The man in the Mercedes jammed his foot on the gas pedal and his car shot forward. He turned right at the next intersection, still accelerating, and was lost to view.

Another shot, this one followed by a sharp *ping!* as the bullet hit the pole of a street sign. Caria's hold on Brandon's hand turned into a death grip. Ronnie and Trevor looked terrified, and even Julia seemed as if she was unsure what to do.

A deep, gruff male voice shouted, "Hey! You! Get in here!"

Another gunshot was enough to galvanize all of them. The front of the building had a set of stone steps leading up to a door, half open, a shadowy figure inside waving them to come in. Brandon took the stairs two at a time, dragging Caria along with him.

Trevor was the last to enter, and slammed the door shut.

In the dimly-lit hallway was a man in a wheelchair, looking up at them with an expression that was half perplexity and half outrage.

"Okay," he said. "Maybe one of you could explain to me exactly what the fuck you think you're doing?"

seventeen

. . .

Soren stared in puzzled silence at the woman walking toward them. The breeze ruffled the leaves of the trees in the Arboretum, as normal a scene as he could imagine, and in the middle of it was a woman who had just said something so weird that he was half convinced he hadn't heard her correctly.

How could she have been waiting for them, when an hour earlier, none of them knew they'd be there?

Her smile was friendly and warm. "I'm Mary Hansard." She stretched out one hand, as if they were colleagues meeting at some kind of business conference. "High school physics teacher. Well, I was until all this happened. I suspect I won't be teaching for a while."

"Soren Conover."

He shook her hand, and his bafflement only increased when she smiled, tilting her head to one side. "You're Dr. Conover? I somehow had the impression you were older."

Reflexively, Soren said, "I'm thirty-two," afterward wondering why he hadn't said, *And how the hell did you know my name?*

"You look younger. But of course, given your position, you'd have to be at least thirty."

"Thanks." He ended the word on a question mark, but she didn't seem to notice.

"And you're Dr. Quaice." She shook his hand. "So by process of elimination, the two of you must be Drs. Liu and Nicolaides. All professors of linguistics, am I correct?"

Dr. Quaice nodded. The other three simply stared at her.

"Well, we should be moving along. There's going to be an armed band of the LLA sweeping the Arboretum looking for you in about"—she consulted her watch—"twenty minutes, give or take. Not looking only for you, of course, but they saw you from a distance when you crossed 520, so that'll draw them in, at which point they'd be happy to shoot anyone they saw. The sniper at the bridge was supposed to take you out, but when he didn't get you, they decided to send some people after you to do the job right." She frowned. "I don't know who killed the sniper, however. Lucky for you. Sometimes things work out in your favor."

Dr. Quaice suddenly shook his head, and when he spoke, it was like a dam bursting. "Who the hell are you?"

The woman smiled broadly. "I told you. I'm Mary Hansard."

"But how do you know who we are? And that we'd be coming here? We weren't even sure of that ourselves."

She shrugged. "How does anyone know anything?"

"That's a bullshit answer," Cassandra muttered.

Mary turned toward her. "Sometimes it's the only answer there is. But we can discuss that later. Because I'm serious about the LLA guerillas. If we're not clear of the Arboretum by the time they see us, they'll mow us all down without batting an eyelash."

That seemed to make sense—insofar as anything she'd said had made sense. She turned away from them and led them back onto the trail, between two huge old magnolia trees in full bloom, their heavy, sweet scent surrounding them like a cloud.

"You know where I live?" Dr. Quaice asked, after they'd walked in silence for a few minutes.

"Of course."

"How?"

"I just know, is all. It's like a memory, even though I've never been there before."

"That's ridiculous."

"Suit yourself," she said in a friendly tone.

Dr. Quaice looked perturbed enough to write her off as crazy and drop the subject, but Soren couldn't stop himself from persisting.

"So you knew the four of us would be coming through the Arboretum."

"Yes."

"And you knew when."

"At least approximately, yes."

"Did you know the LLA was going to launch their attacks today?"

"Yes."

Long pause. "Why didn't you warn anyone?"

Mary gave an easy laugh. "Who would have believed me? I've learned that quickly. You warn people, they write you off as a loony. Then what you were warning them about happens anyhow. I took the chance with you because I thought maybe I could convince you. You're academics, after all. You're convinced by logic and evidence."

Dr. Quaice snorted.

"The only evidence we've got is that you knew our names," Soren said. "As far as logic…" He shrugged.

Mary laughed. "Oh, I know, believe me."

"But you're still claiming what you said is true."

She nodded. "If you'd stayed where you were, you'd have gotten ample evidence in the form of fatal gunshot wounds.

And I understand that this doesn't seem to make much rational sense. It rather flips the whole idea of cause and effect on its head, doesn't it?"

Soren shook his head to clear the confusion. If the day hadn't been surreal enough, with news of riots and assassinations, terrified and terrifying text messages from Finn, and snipers trying to kill them, now they were being led through the Arboretum on foot by a woman who was able to see into the future.

Or at least *said* she could. As far as Soren had seen, self-proclaimed psychics fell into two categories—delusional or fraudulent. James Randi had died back in 2020 without ever having someone win his million-dollar challenge to demonstrate psychic abilities—any kind of psychic abilities—under controlled conditions.

This sort of thing had turned Soren into a devout skeptic. Bring in the scientists, and the claims mysteriously evaporate.

But how did she know their names? The only one who mentioned his name first was Soren himself. The other three she named before they introduced themselves. Somehow, she not only knew who they were, but where they were going.

What the hell was going on here?

"Mary?" Soren said, as they topped a low rise and wound their way through some gnarled, patch-barked conifers and through beds of peonies in full bloom.

"Yes?" She half turned toward him, wearing a trace of a smile.

Soren got the impression she already knew what he was going to ask.

"Look, you said you knew the future. But how? Everything I know about science suggests that's not possible. And so far, all you've done is give us vague answers. If there really was an armed band coming after us, I appreciate your warning us and all, but I think you owe us at least some kind of explanation of how you knew."

Mary's brow creased for a moment. "It's complicated. I mean, what I understand of it. There's a lot of this I don't understand myself."

"Try me."

"Okay. Keep in mind that this is only based on what I've experienced and what I've guessed from those experiences." She took a deep breath. "Have you heard of the 'Arrow of Time'?"

"No, but I can guess what it is."

She nodded. "It's one of the biggest mysteries in physics. Most physical processes are time-reversible. If I were to show you a video of a pool ball bouncing off a bumper, then the same video in reverse, it would be impossible to know which was the forward one and which the reversed one. All the way down to particle physics, the theories work equally well if you run time backwards."

"Then why do we perceive it only as going forward?"

"Exactly. The only exception seems to be the Second Law of Thermodynamics, which states that systems tend to proceed toward disorder. It's why if I showed you a video clip of a glass breaking, then ran it backwards—the pieces coming together and sealing up to form an intact glass— you'd immediately know which is which. But as far as we know, the Second Law is the only physical law that isn't time-reversible, and it's hard to see why that would affect our memories. Plus, the Theories of Relativity suggest that time is just another dimension, and to a person in another reference frame, something that is in our future might be in their past. In some frame of reference, the events that are about to happen to us have already happened. So from the perspective of physics, it seems like our brains should have equal access to the past and the future, and we don't." She gave him another half-turn and quirky smile. "As Einstein put it, time is an illusion, but it is a remarkably persistent one."

"So how does that explain what you can do?"

She didn't answer for a moment, but finally shrugged. "Well, in any kind of scientific sense, it doesn't. All I can say is that for me, memory points both directions, and the Arrow of Time stopped making a difference. It all began a few weeks ago. You remember the day of the earthquake?"

Soren nodded.

"That's when it began."

"You're saying an earthquake gave you precognition."

She laughed. "Oh, come on, you know better than that. You're an academic. You should recognize the *post hoc* fallacy. I just said that's the day it started. I didn't say the earthquake *caused* it."

"Okay, fair enough. But you seem awfully nonchalant about it."

"No. I've just had to accept it, is all. What's up here"—she tapped her temple—"has equal access to the past and present, so much so that I sometimes can't tell them apart, and don't know if something in my mind has happened or is going to happen in the future."

"Must be useful for choosing lottery numbers."

She laughed. "Well, that's just it. The downside is that my future memory—for want of a better term—is no better than my past memory. Do you remember the past perfectly?"

"Of course not."

"In fact, what were last week's lottery numbers?"

"I have no idea."

"Exactly. For most people, memory is a very sketchy thing. True photographic memory is quite uncommon, and is usually limited to a specific type of memory. For example, some people can recall long sequences of numbers, but their ability to remember music or visual images is unremarkable. In any case, the majority of humans have highly unreliable memories. What they think they remember is an amalgam of what actually happened, what they think happened, what they heard had happened from other people, and complete fabrications, along with big gaps where whatever it was simply didn't go into storage. We always think our memories are far more accurate than they actually are. How many times have you heard someone say, 'I know it happened that way, I remember it'?"

"All the time."

"There've actually been experiments to test that. We're not only bad at remembering what happened, we're remarkably suggestible. All you have to do is ask the right questions, and you can confound someone's memory completely. It's why eyewitness testimony is the worst form of evidence."

"Tell the judges and juries that."

"I know. It's mostly because what's in our heads *seems* so vivid and complete. To admit we really aren't remembering anything accurately is profoundly upsetting."

"So how does this...?" He trailed off, raising his hands palms upward.

"Well, that's how my brain works, too, only in both directions. I can see some events in the future, just like I can remember some events in the past. But they're both fragmentary and inaccurate. It can be helpful, like knowing you were going to come to the Arboretum, and that if I didn't warn you, you'd have died. But there are things in my future I don't know, just as there are things in my past I've forgotten, remember wrong, or simply never recorded in the first place. So it's better than nothing, but as a lens into the future, I've learned not to rely on it too much."

"How is it that you can do this, and other people can't?"

"No idea."

"What else do you know about our futures?"

Her perpetual easy smile vanished. "It's not a good idea to know that."

"Why not? You do."

"I've had experiences that..." She paused, and bit her lower lip, frowning. "Where I see things clearly, I've found it's usually better not to say anything. If it's something unpleasant, people try to avoid it, and it never works."

"You warned us that the LLA was after us."

"That's because I knew you'd get away. I remembered that you weren't going to get killed. All I had to do is say, 'You need to get out of here,' and you'd do it."

"So we'll make it to Dr. Quaice's house safely?"

A sidelong glance, and she gave him a quick nod.

"And after that?"

Mary shook her head. "I can't say. Really, I can't."

He gave her a speculative look. "Is it really *can't*? Or is it actually *won't*?"

"Both. There are things I'm pretty sure will happen. Some good, some bad. Some of the things in my mind are probably inaccurate or outright false. Just like your own memory of the past, there's no way to know which are the accurate bits and which aren't. So I can't say more than that, I really can't. I'll tell you what I can, but that's all."

The sound of distant gunfire came from behind them. All five turned. They were on a grassy knoll covered with the soft stems of meadow plants. They were in clear, unobstructed view from of one of the Arboretum parking lots, something Soren didn't realize until they looked back, and as they watched they saw figures, small with distance, pointing and running toward them. There was the confused noise of shouts, but no words were discernible.

"We'd better table the scientific discussion and get a move on, don't you think?" Mary said in a light, conversational tone.

The five of them broke into a jog. Soren knew Cassandra was in great shape—probably better than he himself was—but the two older men wouldn't be able to keep up a running pace for long.

Gavin pointed toward a grove of cherry trees. "We'd be

less visible down there." He panted for breath. "And we must be near Parkside Drive by now."

They found a route leading in the general direction they wanted to go, which at this point was as far away from the armed gunmen as they could get. A path led through a grove of apple trees in full bloom, and after a short walk the winding curve of Parkside Drive East appeared ahead of them.

"Only a little farther." Dr. Quaice sounded as winded as Gavin. "I live on McGilvra Boulevard."

The asphalt strip of Parkside Drive was devoid of traffic, but there were two wrecked cars in view. One had driven into a telephone pole, the other was nose down in a ditch. In the nearer one Soren caught sight of a bloodied face behind the steering wheel, the body tilted at an awkward angle away from a neat, circular bullet hole in the windshield.

He winced and looked away.

"Awful, isn't it?" Mary whispered. "The path we've taken avoids the worst of it. But I think we'd better steel ourselves to a lot more of this, because it isn't the last time we'll see things like that."

"Where is everyone?" Gavin said.

"The ones who were home when it started are still home," Mary said. "Staying out of sight. The ones who were away—at work, or whatnot—are stuck where they are, for the most part. The only ones out are the LLA guerrillas and people like us who have to go somewhere urgently."

"Maybe we should have stayed back on campus."

Mary shook her head. "No. You made the right decision." She swallowed. "By tonight, most of the University buildings are going to be either occupied by the LLA or else on fire. It will be a very long time before the campus will be safe. If it ever is."

They reached Dr. Quaice's house without any further incident. Mary had been right, as far as it went. Whoever was following them through the Arboretum had either lost their trail or else decided they weren't worth pursuing.

But the open suburban landscape around them offered a much better view of the sky than the dense trees they'd just left, and what they saw made Soren's heart pound. Everywhere they turned, smoke rose into the air. It looked like the entire city was on fire. Not far away were shouts and gunshots. The riots were nearby, although Dr. Quaice's street was clear, at least thus far.

And somewhere, out in all that, was Finn Donnelly. Soren had to stop a sob from rising into his throat, and push away the despair. They'd gotten to safety, perhaps Finn had as well.

He had to. He just had to. The thought of his boyfriend being one of those people crumpled by a barricade or slumped over a steering wheel, that the warm, vital man he'd loved and held close so many times was now a cooling corpse somewhere out in the collapsing city, was too horrible to consider.

Dr. Quaice unlocked his front door and with a quick motion urged them inside, turned and locked the door, and drew the curtains tight.

"Here we stay."

"How long?" Gavin asked.

"As long as we need to. I have food stockpiled long enough to last us several weeks if we use it sparingly. But first things first." He went to a desk in the corner of the living room and switched on a computer. In moments, the monitor lit up. He sat down, and with a few taps on the keyboard, brought up *CNN*. The others clustered behind him, reading over his shoulder.

"All around the globe there is chaos. The Lackland movement has launched a coordinated attack in every major city. It is unknown how many world leaders have been the victims of the multiple assassination attempts being reported..."

Fox News Online:

"The president urges calm, but the country is already spiraling into anarchy. We have lost contact with many of our reporters, as television and radio stations have become prime targets of the rioters..."

BBC Online:

"No word yet from Newcastle, Gloucester, Manchester, Birmingham... The rail lines were bombed early today, and it appears that communication links were disrupted as well, but how this was accomplished is unknown..."

Xinhua:

"The military has been deployed and is working to contain the situation. A mandatory hold-in-place order is in effect until further notice. Anyone on the street will be considered part of the Lackland movement and will be executed on sight..."

Pravda:

"The Kremlin has not responded to requests for updates, but the situation in Moscow and St. Petersburg appears to be dire. Clashes between the rebels and the military are ongoing. It is unknown how the attacks were coordinated, but this is obviously the result of long and careful planning by the Lacklanders and those working with them. Civilians are required to remain home with their doors locked until the danger is over, but at present no one knows if that will be hours or days..."

Dr. Quaice snorted. "Optimists." He looked up at the others, who were reading over his shoulder, wide-eyed. "Months. Years. Longer." He flashed a glance at Mary Hansard, whose usual smile had been replaced by tight-lipped anxiety. "What says our resident psychic?"

She gave a sharp shake of the head. "I knew it was bad. I

didn't know it was this bad." She swallowed hard. "This isn't something that will just end with order restored."

"Agreed."

She looked around at the faces of the others, dim in the shadowed room. Soren met her eyes, but she wouldn't hold them. She'd seen it coming, so why did she look so terrified?

When she spoke, it was in a near-whisper. "Is this it, then? Are we witnessing the fall of civilization?"

eighteen

· · ·

Brandon stared at the man in the wheelchair. He was perhaps forty years old, with thinning brown hair and intense, deep brown eyes. His expression held the anger Brandon had heard in his voice, but where that anger was directed was uncertain.

"Are you people out of your goddamn minds?"

"Probably," Ronnie said in a small voice.

He heaved a harsh sigh. "Don't you know what's happening?"

"Enough," Julia said.

"Enough? Not enough to know that if you're walking down the sidewalk like you're on a Sunday stroll, you're going to end up with a bullet in your back?"

Julia didn't answer his question, merely extended her hand to him. "I'm Julia Lowell."

That seemed to take him off guard. He gave her a brief hand clasp. "Marcus Gellert."

"Thank you for calling out to us."

"Jesus Christ," Marcus said under his breath. "What were you thinking?"

Brandon expected her to challenge the impropriety, but all she said was, "We were going where we needed to go."

"Nowhere in this city is safe. I was watching the news and texting with my brother until the internet went out. He said that downtown is very quickly being converted to rubble, but it looks like it's all over. The LLA finally did it. I've been expecting it. And they're not doing it by half-measures. They're killing everyone they find." His lips tightened. "Chances are, by now my brother's dead. He said as much right before the service crashed."

"I'm sorry for your loss."

"Thanks." His voice held a sardonic edge. "Where are you people going?"

"Trying to get out of Seattle."

"On foot?" He frowned. "Yeah, honestly, that's probably the best way at this point. Not that you have a snowball's chance in hell of getting out alive, in my opinion. Most of the main roads have been barricaded, some by the LLA, some by the police, some by people trying to seal off their own neighborhoods. All it's done is make sure no one can get away. They had some footage from an aerial camera, a helicopter or something, and every road you could see looked like a parking lot. The highways that aren't blocked by barricades are blocked by accidents. And non-accidents." He gave a dry, humorless laugh. "You got a car creeping along, you shoot the driver, the car becomes an instant road block."

"The cell service is down?" Trevor asked. "All of it?"

Marcus laughed again. "They're smart, you gotta give 'em that. Shut down all the telecommunications, isolate people from each other. Then you can take apart the resistance at your own pace."

"Where are the rest of the people who live here?" Ronnie asked.

"In their apartments. Well, the ones who hadn't already left for work when it started. Those people are probably dead by now too." He said it flatly, without emotion. "Lucky for you I heard the gunfire and left my apartment to look out the window of the lobby and see what was going on. I'm the last one down the hall"—he nodded toward the dimly-lit corridor —"if I hadn't been curious I'd still be there waiting for the rioters to get here. Not much else we can do, of course. I'm guessing maybe a third of the residents are still here, all holed up in their apartments."

"This place isn't safe," Julia said. "The rioters will get here sooner or later."

"Oh, I know. I'm stuck in any case. I can't go anywhere. So I guess I'll just sit here and wait for 'em."

"What about the others?"

"What about 'em?"

"Do they just want to sit here and wait for the rioters to arrive?"

"What choice do they have?"

"They could come with us."

Another laugh. "What, and walk down the street in full view? My guess is they'll take their chances hiding out in their apartments. Even if I could walk, I wouldn't do that. It'd be different if I had a car."

"You said the roads were already impassable," Brandon said.

"Yeah," Marcus admitted. "I did. And it'd probably be a fool's choice if I tried. But if I had a car, I'd sure as hell give it a shot, and I'd make sure to take down a few of those sons-abitches before they got me."

"Would you object to my knocking on the doors of people here, and seeing who is willing to come with us?" Julia said.

"Why would I object? None of my business what you do. Maybe you can convince some of them, but I still don't see why you think you'll be safer out there on foot than we are here in our apartment building."

"I know," Julia said, "because God has told me that."

Brandon expected Marcus to have some sort of sneering response, but to his surprise, the older man just said, "Oh, really? God speaks to you?"

"Yes."

"Must be nice."

"No," Julia said. "Nice is exactly what it isn't. It's the truth, and the truth is often more painful than a lie."

Marcus nodded. "Can't argue with that. Anyhow, have at it, Prophet-Lady. Like I said, I'm stuck here, it's all one to me if people leave or stay. I don't know my neighbors much. I'm not the sociable type, and they have their own lives. Well, did. I don't know what we all have now."

An hour later, Brandon, Julia, and the others were back in the lobby, along with four new additions.

The trek through the three floors of the building, knocking on every door they saw, gave Brandon appreciation for what door-to-door missionaries went through. Only a quarter of the knocks were met with a response. If the silence was because the residents were away, or because they were there and hiding, was impossible to tell. Two resulted in a threat if they persisted or tried to force their way in. One said if they didn't back away he was going to shoot them right through the door. Three opened the door a crack after being assured Julia and her friends meant no harm and were not on the side of the rioters, but then slammed it shut before she'd had a chance to explain what they were doing there.

But four of them were at least receptive enough to join them in the lobby. Another young man of perhaps twenty-five, two women who were about Julia's age, and a stern-looking middle-aged man with a buzz cut who had the appearance of an ex-military. Brandon was surprised the last had agreed to come along with them. Perhaps it was because someone like him preferred action over inaction, even if the action was more risky.

Brandon watched in some amazement as Julia quietly, patiently explained what she knew and how she claimed to know it. There was nothing of the ranting evangelical preacher in her. No frenetic desperation to drive her point home, no attitude that she was anything special. She had knowledge, that was all, and wanted to use that knowledge to save as many people as she could.

In the end, two of them—the stern man and the twenty-something—decided to come with them.

"Be right back," the older man said, jogged off down the hall, and five minutes later came back with a laden backpack.

And a gun in a holster.

"I'm not going out there unarmed," he said, when he noticed Trevor staring at the pistol wide-eyed.

Trevor just nodded.

From outside, there was still the sound of intermittent gunfire, but nothing sounded especially close. After some discussion they decided to canvass the adjacent apartment buildings up and down the street before moving on.

By midafternoon, their ranks had swelled to three dozen. The ones who responded favorably were an odd assortment. Mothers with their children, fortunately all old enough to walk on their own. A handful of older folks, probably retired. A few college-aged, probably graduate students living off campus.

Very few men or women between twenty-five and sixty. Most of them had probably already left for work by the time the attacks began.

Once they were done, Julia, Brandon, and Caria returned to Marcus's apartment, leaving the now-substantial group of followers crowded into a blind alleyway between two of the buildings. The thought crossed Brandon's mind that if the rioters showed up suddenly, the alley would turn into a trap.

Of course, if Julia was right, they were no safer in their apartments, as difficult as that still was for Brandon to accept. The human drive to hide when faced with danger, to close yourself in some small, safe place, was powerful, probably stretching back to when we lived in caves.

Marcus was no longer in the lobby, and the three of them went down the hall to the door Marcus had gestured toward earlier. A soft knock, and "Marcus, it's Julia," led a moment later the noise of the door being unbolted and opened.

"I thought you'd be gone by now."

"We're leaving soon. But I don't want to leave without you."

"How?" The single syllable was harsh, almost angry.

"We can find a way."

He shook his head. "I'd slow you down. I'd only be a hindrance. Absolutely not."

Julia nodded slowly. "I... I understand." Their eyes met. "I knew that was what you would say. I was told as much."

Marcus's eyebrows rose, but he didn't respond.

"I should know better than to question. Even if I knew, the thought of leaving you behind..."

"Don't worry about it." His features softened, losing the sharp anger. "Look, it was nice of you. I don't know if you're hearing from God, or whatnot, but there's... something. Believe me, I used to slam the door in the face of the Jehovah's Witnesses. Got no time for that Holy Roller bullshit. But you're different. I don't know how I know that, but I do."

"Thank you. And..." She paused, looking upward for a moment as if searching for the right words. "There will be others. Not right away. You will be safe until then if you stay inside."

"God told you that?"

She gave him a slow nod. "And those ones... you must send them after us. A man leading children. They need to find us. We're planning to head northward out of the city, which will mean cutting across Fremont and North Gate. Tell them that."

Marcus's mouth twitched in a quick smile. "I've always been an agnostic. I don't know why the hell I believe you."

"I have learned that recognizing the truth and believing in God are two different things." She gave a quick flicker of a glance toward Brandon. "It is better to believe, but accepting that what I am telling you is the truth is good enough for now."

"When is this guy with the kids supposed to come along?"

"I don't know. Not today, nor for a while, I think. You needn't keep watch. But Marcus..." Her face registered reluctance.

"What?"

"I am also given to know that when you do see them, and tell them what I've said, your time on Earth will not be long."

He stared at her for a moment. "I see."

"I'm sorry."

He shrugged. "As soon as I saw what was going on this morning, I knew I wasn't likely to come out of it alive. At least I can accomplish something before."

She gave him another slow nod. "Thank you."

"You should go. It's getting toward late afternoon. You want to find a safe place once it's night."

"Yes."

"Good luck to you."

"I don't know who amongst us will reach safety, but I can only do what I have been tasked with. That some will survive, I am certain. Beyond that... no one is guaranteed another hour, day, year. I'm no different."

Marcus gave a dry chuckle. "So I suppose that my knowing I'm going to live to see your friend and his kids means I'm more informed than most of us. I can't ask for any more than that. Take care of yourself."

"You as well."

Brandon, Caria, and Julia turned away, and the door shut behind them.

Brandon gave the older woman a sidelong glance, and was surprised to see her cheeks wet with tears.

She met his eyes, then quickly looked away. "I don't know if I can do this. I'm just not strong enough to do what I have to."

Caria took a deep breath, and looped her arm in Julia's. Something in Caria's face changed—Brandon saw it happen, as if she'd had a sudden acceptance of the situation, along with a realization that figuring out why this was happening was less important than helping each other through it.

"You're not alone, Julia. I haven't been a pillar of strength, myself. But maybe together, we can stand as long as we need to."

nineteen

· · ·

All five people standing in Dr. Quaice's dimly-lit living room were silent. Probably everyone had been thinking the same thing—that they were witnessing the fall of civilization—but no one except Mary Hansard had been willing to speak the words. To do so brought up a superstitious conviction that saying it would bring it into being, but to deny it seemed like an outright lie.

In the end, silently, awkwardly, they moved away from the endless litany of devastating news on Dr. Quaice's computer, sitting apart from each other, not speaking, not even wanting to make eye contact. Even that level of acknowledgement of the spiraling chaos they were trapped in was too much for Soren's heart to handle.

But the alternative was sitting there staring into space. He had no real inclination either to chat about other things, nor to find some reading material from Dr. Quaice's packed and disordered book shelves. Doing what his heart urged— texting Finn, "Please respond to me, please, I'm losing my mind with worry"—would accomplish nothing. He'd already texted something similar, only a couple of hours earlier. If Finn had been able to contact him, he already would have.

Continuing to send hysterical messages wouldn't make him respond any faster.

Also, his phone was on vibrate. If Finn or anyone else texted, he'd realize it immediately. But over the next half-hour, that didn't stop him from pulling it out of his pocket and checking it. Six times, in fact. He'd first called his parents in Lake Placid, New York, his sister in Baltimore, and his brother in Houston, leaving voicemails in which he had to exert a mammoth effort to keep his voice steady. When none of them picked up, he'd dashed off text messages to all of them, and thus far had no responses.

Bad news was one thing, but not knowing—there being no way to know, nothing he could do to find out—was agony.

The others, he knew, were going through the same thing, thinking about family and friends whom there was now no way to contact. Gavin had mentioned before they left that his wife, Peggy, had made it safely to her sister's house in Kirkland, on the other side of Lake Washington. But to join her meant crossing the long expanse of the Evergreen Point Floating Bridge that lay between them. From what they'd seen, trying to get to the west end of the bridge, much less getting across it, would be tantamount to suicide. Gavin seemed to take that realization with a quiet despair. Soren could read it on his face as clearly as if he'd spoken it out loud. *I might never see her again.* Gavin sat in a recliner, one of Dr. Quaice's books open on his lap—a book of photography, it looked like—but he hadn't turned a page in twenty minutes, and it was obvious his mind was miles away.

Cassandra sat on the other end of the sofa from Soren, her face set in an inscrutable expression, her body completely relaxed, one arm resting lightly on the cushions as if this was nothing more than a meeting between friends. She and Soren had been hired right around the same time, her for her expertise in Middle Eastern languages, him for his knowledge of Scandinavian ones. He'd never gotten to know her well. She wasn't unfriendly, exactly. More aloof, self-contained, as if she were used to relying on no one but herself, not even needing the camaraderie of friendly acquaintances at work. She was brisk, confident, efficient, seldom smiling, never engaging in small talk, only speaking when she had something salient to say. They'd worked together for five years, and he still didn't know if she had a partner, siblings, or children, what her hobbies and interests were, even where she'd been born and raised. Other than what she contributed professionally, Cassandra Nicolaides was a complete cipher.

Anderson Quaice's gawky form was hunched over his computer, obsessively clicking between various news sources and social media sites, bouncing one knee in a continuous, staccato rhythm. Of the five of them, only he and Mary Hansard had seen this coming, albeit for entirely different reasons. Now, he sat, doomscrolling, unable to take his eyes off it as the horrifying news unfolded.

And what about Mary Hansard? Soren wasn't sure he believed all her wild claims of the Arrow of Time and remembering the future, but she was right about one thing—it was hard to explain otherwise how she'd known their names, and that they'd be coming through the Arboretum when they did. But for someone who had forewarning, at the moment she looked stunned, lost, sitting in a rocking chair but unmoving, staring off into the shadowed room. Once she'd seen the news on Dr. Quaice's computer, and had confirmed to her what she had foreseen, it was as if she'd simply collapsed under the shock.

Five people, all in the same situation, yet all reacting differently.

Soren resisted the urge to pull out his phone again. He knew what he'd see. No responses from anyone. If he were to check the status of the last texts from Finn, it would still say, *User currently offline.*

He couldn't handle seeing that message again.

"Jesus," he said, to no one in particular. "Isn't there anything we can do, other than sitting around here waiting for everything to fall apart?"

Four faces turned toward him. Dr. Quaice's mouth opened to answer. But there was a sudden shock wave, like a sonic boom, that shook the house to its foundations. A crack snaked its way up one of the windows, and from the kitchen came the noise of glasses and plates falling and shattering.

"Earthquake?" Gavin's voice sounded as if there was no breath behind it.

A second long, low rumble came, along with another tremor.

"That was no earthquake," Cassandra said. "That was an explosion."

Dr. Quaice had turned back to his computer, his face close to the screen. He clicked *Refresh* on the site he'd been on—from a distance, it looked like it might be *Al Jazeera*—and in seconds an error message appeared saying, *No internet detected. Check your connections.*

Without turning, he said, "Check your phones."

Silently, the four of them pulled out their phones and switched them on.

"Zero bars," Mary said.

"Same here," Cassandra said in a grim voice.

Gavin just nodded.

Soren stared at the screen. Now, instead of *User currently offline*, his phone said, *No internet connection.*

"What happened? You know, don't you, Dr. Quaice?"

The older man didn't turn away from the screen, although it was strange that he was still staring at it when there was nothing there to see. Maybe it was for the same reason Soren had looked over and over at the screen of texts from Finn. A desperate hope if he just stared at it long enough, it would change to something that would give him some hope.

Finally Quaice spoke, in a low voice so unlike his usual

acerbic, rapid-fire mode of speech it seemed as if it must be someone else's voice.

"Know? No. But I have a guess."

Cassandra raised one eyebrow. "Which is?"

"The Westin Building. I'm guessing the LLA took it out. That explosion sounds strong enough to have destroyed most of downtown, but I think Westin was the target."

Gavin closed his eyes. "So we're cut off."

Quaice nodded.

"Wait," Soren said. "The Westin Building? You mean the skyscraper on Sixth Avenue?"

"It's not just a skyscraper. It's the main telecommunications hub for the Seattle area. Destroy that, and it cuts the links to internet and cell service providers for the entire region."

"Smart," Cassandra said. "Keep people from talking to each other, and they can't organize against you."

Dr. Quaice got up, went to a bookshelf in the corner of the room, and picked up a telephone handset sitting in its charger. He pushed the "Speaker" then the "On" button. Instead of a dial tone, there was a crackle of static.

"Even the landlines are down."

Soren fought down a rising sense of panic. "So there's nothing… no way…" He glanced from one of them to the other, trying to find something hopeful to hang on to. Gavin still sat with his eyes shut. Cassandra looked defiant, Mary scared. Dr. Quaice turned slowly toward him.

"It's the price we're paying for our reliance on telecommunications networks. They powered everything. Take out the hubs, sever the connections to each other, and we're crippled. Not only does that take down business, it shrinks the world for most of us down to a ten-kilometer effective radius. No email, no texts, no telephones."

"Most of us?"

The older man gave him a quirk of a smile. "It's true that

without electronic communication we're back to the mid-nineteenth century, where information traveled at the speed of a horse, and most people on Earth never saw a single human being who came from more than thirty kilometers away from the place they were born. I have a possible alternative to the communication issue, though, which I'll show you later this evening."

"But that doesn't solve the problem that we're still more or less stuck in place."

"No, you're right, it doesn't."

"Cars…" Mary closed her mouth. It was clear in her face she knew the answer to that before Dr. Quaice even spoke.

"You saw what they did to the highways. Okay, they can't barricade every thoroughfare everywhere, but think about it. You break down communications and make travel difficult, and very quickly you've hamstrung industry worldwide. How long will the gasoline last without oil refineries and delivery trucks and the whole superstructure of the corporate petroleum enterprise? Once again, humanity did this to itself by refusing to divest from oil and diversify into local renewable energy. Smart people have been shouting this literally for decades, but the government was too deeply in the pockets of Big Oil to listen. The LLA leaders figured it out, though. Pull out those two threads—communications and petroleum availability—and the whole thing comes unraveled."

"But why would they want that?" Mary said.

"Payback. Their attitude is that they have nothing to lose, they'd already lost everything. At that point all that's left is revenge. You figure you're going to die yourself, so you take as many of your enemy down with you as you can."

"Amoral," Mary whispered. "Brutal and amoral."

"Yes. But inevitable. You keep pulling away rights and livelihood from people, eventually this is how they respond. It's happened before on a small scale. This time, they coordinated worldwide. They're destroying it all."

Soren stared down at the phone still held loosely in his right hand.

"Give it up, Conover." Some of Dr. Quaice's usual sharpness came back into his tone. "That phone in your hand is useless unless there's some kind of miracle and the boat magically rights itself. My guess is the next thing they'll target will be the electricity, and at that point you won't even be able to recharge it. Lights out, both literally and figuratively."

"We've got to get out of here." Mary sounded near panic. "We can't stay."

"And go where?"

"Anywhere." She squeezed her eyes shut. "We have to get to a refuge. Somewhere out of the city, away from all… all this." She moved her head as if she were looking around, seeing things none of the others could see, although her eyes were still tightly closed. "Trees. Trees and mountains. Rebuild somewhere"—she gestured vaguely with one hand—"out there. But here… here is…" She shook her head in a nervous, agitated way, and a lock of hair that had come loose from her ponytail fell forward across her face. She seemed unaware of it. "We're in a death trap. Stay here and we die. It's coming. Remember what happened to Atlantis, Númenor, the City of Ys, Herakleion, Lemuria, Lyonesse… Pharaoh's armies and Lot's wife…" She began to cry, tipping her head forward, her entire body shaking with sobs. "No, it's too terrible, I don't want to see that, don't make me look…"

Soren stared at her. "What the hell is happening to her?"

No one answered.

He went to her and put one hand gently on her shoulder. "Mary, it's all right. You're here with us. You're safe."

Her eyes snapped open, looking right into Soren's with such intensity that he took a step back. "No. That's where you're wrong. I'm not safe. None of us are. I can see it so clearly, the terrible destruction. If we don't get out of here soon…"

"But you said that what you knew of the future was incomplete and often inaccurate. What if this is just a reflection of your fears?"

She gave another jerky shake of the head. "No. Not this. This I *know*. I don't know when, but I know it's not long." She grabbed Soren's shirt sleeve. "We've got to get across the bridge, and then away. As far as we can. It isn't just the riots. It's everything we know. Soon it'll all be gone, and if we don't get away, us with it."

Soren glanced at Dr. Quaice. "Okay, this is scaring the shit out of me."

Mary tightened her grip on Soren's sleeve. "Good. Good. You should be scared. Scared people act." She hitched a sob. "Complacent people die."

"At the moment, we can't go anywhere," Dr. Quaice said. "Trying to get to, much less across, the Evergreen Point Bridge is impossible right now. There's also no guarantee that once we're across the bridge we'd be any safer. There's nothing but a big sprawl for miles on the other side—Kirkland, Bellevue, Redmond. Chances are there's chaos there, too. Here, at least, we're safe for the moment."

Another sharp head shake, but Mary didn't respond. She seemed to be struggling not to cry again.

"And I'm not going anywhere until I find Finn," Soren said.

Dr. Quaice gave him a quick, sympathetic glance. "I understand."

But in those two words the message was clear—*He might be dead. Even if he's alive, there may be no way to contact him, much less find him. Beyond that, there's nothing to do but wander aimlessly through the city hoping for the best.*

"At some point, I'm going to try to get across," Gavin said. "I have to. My wife is over there. It might be a risk, but I have to take it."

"We should at least wait until we know what the danger

is. You won't do Peggy any good if you get killed before you reach the bridge."

"Which means sending out a scout," Cassandra said.

"Perhaps at some point. Mary's right that we can't stay here indefinitely, even if the disaster she claims to know about doesn't happen. I've got food for maybe three weeks. Bottled water if the municipal water goes. After that, we'd have to go out foraging. And the problem is, by then we won't be the only ones doing it."

"That situation will turn ugly fast," Cassandra said.

Dr. Quaice nodded. "So just from a practical standpoint, getting out of the city, to somewhere less populated, is not a bad idea. But at the moment, I think we should try to rest and regroup. Our likelihood of surviving will be a lot greater if we don't act out of panic."

A surprisingly lavish dinner of pork chops, broccoli, French bread, rich red wine, and a cherry pie for dessert was a pleasant coda to what had been the most horrible day Soren could recall.

"May as well use it up," Dr. Quaice said, as he helped himself to a second slice of pie. "There's no guarantee of how long we'll have electricity. Seattle Power and Light mostly runs on hydroelectric from the Skagit River, so we can hope it'll keep going for a while. We're better off than the folks in the Northeast, with all their coal-fired power plants. You stop shoveling in coal, the lights go out."

"It's nice to end the day with a full stomach," Gavin said.

Murmurs of assent.

Soren took a sip of wine, feeling it warm him all the way down. The thought *Finn would love this wine* skittered through his mind and away. If he never saw Finn again, how long would it take before everything, day and night, stopped bringing him back to mind? Did widowed people never stop thinking of their lost loves, however long it had been?

But that elegiac thought was too painful to consider and he pushed it away.

"Dr. Quaice," he said. "You told us earlier that you had a solution to the communication problem, that you'd show us this evening. What were you referring to?"

The older man smiled, looking pleased with himself. "Yes. Kalila wasn't the only precaution I took against civilization collapsing."

Mary frowned, looking from one face to another. "Kalila?"

"Dr. Quaice's conlang," Gavin said. "A synthetic language he wrote and has been teaching others to speak for twenty years."

"Like Klingon?" She laughed. "Seriously? Do you all speak it?"

"The others do," Soren said. "I only know a few words."

"You undersell yourself," Dr. Quaice said.

"Well, I haven't put the time into it that the rest of you have."

"In any case, Kalila was my answer to talking without being understood by people we'd rather didn't. But the communication over distance problem has a different solution." He stood, unfolding his lanky frame from his chair so suddenly that it made a protesting squawk on the tile floor of the dining room. "Come take a look. Leave your food and wine. This won't take long. You can come back to it and finish up at your leisure."

They rose and followed Dr. Quaice toward a study that opened off the living room. Cassandra and Soren exchanged glances, and Cassandra shrugged.

Apparently she was as in the dark about this as the rest of them.

In the study was a metal contraption that looked a little like an electric circuit breaker box, on a heavy-duty tripod stand. Sitting on a shelf nearby was a rectangular plastic device with a wire protruding from the top that was clearly an antenna.

"It's a short-range radio communications base station. It's connected to a 45-amp amplifier, and runs off batteries that recharge from the solar array on the roof. It's hooked to a high-gain antenna that extends its range to pretty much the entire Seattle area and the Eastside up to the foothills of the Cascades."

"But who is out there to talk to?" Soren said.

"About a thousand of my current and former students of Kalila. Whenever someone signed up to study with me, I suggested they set themselves up with one of these. They're not terribly expensive to buy, and cost next to nothing to run. A remarkably large percentage of my students took me up on it. We've kept our language skills fresh by having conversations several times a week. I suspect that like you, they never thought they'd have to use either their language knowledge nor their base stations for anything but playing around, but I think they've probably realized by now that I wasn't blowing smoke when I warned them about what was going to happen."

Even Cassandra looked impressed.

"How do you use it?" Mary asked.

"Watch." He switched it on, and picked up a microphone attached by a coiled wire to the box. He keyed the mic. "*Bak Quaice, dhís lam?*"

"What does that mean?" Mary's voice was hushed, as if she couldn't quite believe what she was hearing. And to be fair, even to Soren—who'd known for years about Dr. Quaice's conlang—the whole thing had a surreal, dreamlike quality.

Dr. Quaice smiled. "Just waving my hand and seeing if anyone waves back."

"What if the LLA has thought of the same idea?" Cassandra said in a low voice. "They could be listening in."

"Let 'em," Dr. Quaice said. "They won't be able to understand what they're hearing. And the source of short-range radio signals is next to impossible to trace. I'm not worried." He repeated his greeting. Within moments, a voice came with a crackle of static. "*Bak Glenn Sonnenberg. Dhís dova?*"

Quaice looked up. "Glenn was one of my first students, almost twenty years ago. He lives up in Ballard, near you, Conover." He keyed the mic again. "*Dovak lóda. Dhís dova tét Leedén?*"

"*Lóda. Áts kéde. Maxas dévad.*"

"He and his wife are safe at home," Dr. Quaice said.

"Can you ask him if he's seen Finn?" The request burst out of Soren with almost no conscious thought. The chance was slim, he knew that—even if Glenn had lived close to Soren's house, Ballard was a big place. Neighbors a couple of streets over usually didn't know each other.

Dr. Quaice looked up, sympathy in his eyes. "I can try." He keyed the mic again. "*Glenn, dhís veser mét kólet, balomna, malaks spena Finn Donnelly?*"

A pause, then Glenn's voice came back after another rattle of static. "*Aps gésar tét.*"

"No," Dr. Quaice said quietly. "He hasn't seen him."

Tears welled up in his eyes, and when he spoke, his voice was thick. "Can you ask him to watch for him? Please?"

A quick nod. "*Shúlaba két vets shúthala tém.*"

The response came back almost immediately. "*Kles, thalats tém.*"

"*Laba két.*" He set the mic down. "I gave him a description, as well as I could. He'll keep an eye out for him. I know Glenn. If he sees him or hears about him, he'll let us know right away."

Soren nodded, unable to speak. His eyes spilled over, and he bit his lip and looked downward, trying not to lose control.

Gavin put his hand on Soren's shoulder and squeezed gently. He reached up and put his hand on top of the older man's, aware that if he acknowledged it further, the unexpected kindness of the gesture from someone whom he honestly didn't know well would undo him completely.

Dr. Quaice seemed to recognize the emotional tension in the room. "You all finish your dinners. I want to try to contact as many of the people in my network as I can and see how they're doing. I'll join you in a little."

It was a dismissal. A good thing, really. The surreal sense of having been transported into an alien world, where nothing was as it had been only twenty-four hours ago, was becoming insupportable. Standing in this shadowed little room, talking to others in an odd, jagged-sounding language that prior to this had seemed like nothing more than a game for linguistics nerds, was too much like some fever-dream.

Soren led the others out of the room, and as he left he heard Dr. Quaice key the mic again and repeat what he'd started with. *"Bak Quaice, dhís lam?"*

This is Quaice, is anyone there?

They returned to the table, finishing up the last of the food on their plates and the last of the wine in their glasses, silent and ill-at-ease. Nothing could make this situation normal. Suddenly Soren was overwhelmed by exhaustion, and realized what he most wanted was to find out where he was sleeping, to put his head down, curl up, and disappear into unconsciousness for as many hours as he could.

Mary's voice cut into his thoughts. She once again had the friendly smile on her face that she'd worn when they met. Was this woman bipolar? She certainly seemed capable of wild mood swings.

"So, how do you all know each other?"

"You knew our names, but not that?" Cassandra said.

"I don't know everything." Mary laughed. "Far from it."

"We all work together for the Department of Linguistics at the University," Gavin said.

"Ah. That explains the synthetic language. I have to say, that's pretty impressive."

"It's the product of decades of work," Soren said. "It's been his passion for years."

"Good thing. Looks like it'll be useful." She glanced around at them. "So, are you all from the Seattle area?"

Awkward silence. Small talk at this point seemed beyond pointless. But someone *had* to speak. They couldn't just leave the question hanging.

She must have recognized the tension in the room, because she added, "I know we've all got to be thinking about our friends and families. I thought..." She gave a shrug.

"I'm originally from upstate New York," Soren said.

"Really? I hear it's beautiful there."

He nodded. "Lake Placid. Adirondacks. Beautiful place, but the winters are kind of brutal."

Her smile faded. "You still have family there."

It wasn't a question.

Soren nodded. "Parents. I'm the youngest of three. A sister in Baltimore and a brother in Houston. We're scattered to the winds."

And what was his family doing right now? As far as his parents, surely a little town like Lake Placid would be safer than a big city. Were they hunkered down in their house? Or was everything more or less normal, and the riots in other parts of the world just a distant rumor of chaos? Heaven only knew what a mess Houston and Baltimore were. They were crime-ridden enough beforehand.

But without phones or email, there was no way to find out.

"How about you, Dr. Liu?"

Cassandra's lips tightened. Her annoyance was obvious in her face.

"I grew up in Seattle. My parents were from Hong Kong and emigrated here when I was an infant." Gavin's tone sounded as if he wasn't inclined to talk but too polite to refuse to answer.

"Are your parents still alive?"

Gavin gave a small shake of the head and looked down.

"And you, Dr. Nicolaides?"

"No," Cassandra said sharply. "I'm not from Seattle." Her dark eyes met Mary's light blue ones as if daring her to ask anything more.

Soren gave his colleague a quick frown. Cassandra ordinarily kept her emotions well-hidden. Even in contentious faculty meetings, she rarely showed anger, or even frustration.

Cassandra cleared her throat. "Sorry. I'm not sure where you're going with all this, Mary, but I'm dog-tired. If you're curious about my life, it'll have to wait."

Mary's smile faltered. "I understand, it's okay. We all feel that way." She paused. "I'm worried about my family just like all of you are. I'm from Olympia, born and raised. I have a brother and a sister still living there. On high ground, fortunately. And my mother's seventy-eight, she lives with my brother."

Soren gave Mary a quick frown. What did she mean by *fortunately*? Probably part and parcel of her bizarre forward-vision, but he didn't have the energy to pursue it.

"My family's lived in the south Puget Sound for ages," she continued. "Back into the nineteenth century. So I've got cousins in abundance down there. Plus, I'm terribly anxious about my students. I've taught at Shoreline High School for—let's see—nineteen years. Physics. The thought that they're out there in all this…" She shrugged again, and fell silent.

He drained the last of his wine, stood, and attempted a smile. Probably not too successful, but it was the best he could do.

"I'm sorry, but I'm falling asleep on my feet. I'm going to go lie down on the sofa in the living room and see if I can sleep. When Dr. Quaice comes back and you discuss sleeping arrangements, if you need me to move, it's no problem, just wake me up."

Three faces turned toward him. Gavin's expression was sympathetic. Mary managed a smile, but it seemed as forced as it undoubtedly was. Cassandra's face as usual had settled back into impassivity.

"Good night, then," Mary said.

"Good night."

Soren walked into the living room. His feet were leaden, so much so that it was an effort not to stumble. He couldn't recall ever being this exhausted.

He lay down on the sofa, facing away from the room. Unbidden, the memory that twenty-four hours ago, he'd been safe, warm, and secure in Finn's strong arms rose in his mind. The tears he'd held back before returned with a vengeance, and his whole frame shuddered with silent sobs until finally, mercifully, he relaxed into a dreamless sleep.

twenty

. . .

Perry Abraham looked down from the top floor of the medical office building. The streetlights were on, illuminating a tableau of wrecked cars and destroyed store fronts that from this distance looked almost like toys, like Lego models and Matchbox cars. Colin and Emily were posted as sentries by the door to the staircase, although what they could have done if people with guns showed up, he wasn't sure. Probably neither were they, but as the two oldest in the group they obviously felt it was their duty.

Perry had learned a lot about parsing why people did things in the last few days.

Most of the other children were sprawled on the floor and on chairs and sofas in the room behind him. He guessed that it had been a waiting room. The space, furniture, and décor reminded him of the waiting room at Dr. Lansing's, although Lansing's office had been in a little one-story building, and this one had twelve.

The streets below were fading into darkness as night fell. It all looked peaceful from up here. Down there it was anything but. The voice had guided them well, taking them past the bodies of their fallen teachers and classmates, then into the parking lot of the school. His mother and sister were there, both shot to death, eyes staring sightlessly at the sky.

He had thought of turning away, but forced himself to look. If this was reality now, he had to know it for what it was.

On their walk from the carnage in the school to the top of the medical building, the sounds of gunfire and explosions had been terrifyingly close, but the voice told him where to go and when to hide and when it was safe to go another block. The most frightening moment was when they caught a glimpse of a woman, a pretty woman with dark hair, leading a group of men down a street that crossed the one the children were on. The voice said, in a commanding tone, "Hide. Now."

Perry tugged on Colin's sleeve, and after a quick exchange, together they got all of the children into the alcove of one of the building fronts.

"Who is she?" Colin whispered.

Perry turned to him, his heart pounding. "She's bad." A tremor rippled through his body. "Really bad. We can't let her see us, or see where we're going. Ever. Whenever we see her, we have to hide right away. If she sees us, she'll kill us all."

"That's what the voice says?"

Perry nodded.

They waited until the woman and her followers were around the corner and out of sight.

"It's clear?" Emily asked Perry.

"It's clear."

After nearly an hour's walk they were standing in the wrecked lobby of the medical office building. There were piles of bodies outside on the street and sidewalk that were probably what was left of the staff, but the voice didn't tell him more about them and he didn't want to ask. In the lobby were overturned chairs, broken glass, walls and desks with bullet holes. In the air there was still the faint stink of gunpowder.

"Come on," Perry said.

They found a door that opened onto a staircase and ascended it, with Colin and Emily encouraging the youngest ones. One of Perry's classmates, Becka Shimada, seemed like she couldn't go much farther, but with Emily's gentle nudging, she made it to the top floor with the rest of them. They didn't give any encouragement to Perry, and he wondered if it was because they knew he could make it to the top without.

Then the astonishing idea occurred to him that maybe it was because all of them—even the older children—looked upon Perry as one of the leaders.

If so, it was a relief that he no longer would have to work to convince them, but it was also a little terrifying.

Having made the supreme effort of getting up one staircase after another, the kids were all glassy-eyed with fatigue. Perry felt the tiredness, too, but he had no inclination to sleep.

So he stood at the window, looked down at the street, and thought.

The world had been turned upside down. Was there anything in his old life—as he was already characterizing yesterday—that was the same? It was as if he were a character who had been picked up from one story and dropped into another. Right now the exhaustion was getting in the way of thinking and feeling anything other than confusion. He sensed that grief and fear were going to show up eventually, and probably sooner rather than later, but right now when he pictured the faces of his parents and his sister and his fallen classmates, he felt little besides puzzlement at how weird it was that he'd never see them again.

"You should rest now. You're all safe for tonight." When the voice spoke, Perry didn't even startle. "Find a comfortable spot and sleep. You've done well."

"What happens now?" He kept his voice to a whisper,

hoping no one would overhear and ask him what the voice was telling him. At this point, he couldn't face more questions, or even more attention.

"You will be here for a while. Tomorrow you will search the top floors, and you will find food to last you for several weeks. Do not be tempted to go back downstairs, or go outside."

"I'm not."

"This place was chosen because the attackers cleared it rather than killing people where they stood. Most of the building is empty, but you will find places where there are dead bodies. Be prepared for that, and warn the others as well."

"Okay." Perry swallowed. "Voice, I have a question."

"What is it?"

"Who are you?"

"I am you."

The answer was so immediate, but so bizarre, that he was unsure if he'd heard it correctly.

"What does that mean?"

"Exactly what it says. I am the voice of knowledge you have and knowledge you will have. All you are doing is listening to yourself now, and listening to who you will be."

"Is that why the others can't hear you?"

"Yes. They could each hear their own voices clearly, if they would allow it to happen. You are wide open, open as the sky, so you can hear yourself speaking in a way that they cannot. Speaking of things you know, and things you will only know in the future."

Perry's forehead wrinkled with puzzlement. "That doesn't make any sense. How can I tell myself something now that I won't know until later?"

"Do not press yourself to understand too much too quickly. Right now you are crushed with fatigue and loss and grief. Let yourself feel those things, but mostly, relax in the knowledge that at least you and the others are safe for now."

"But not forever."

"No one is safe forever."

"I know," Perry said in a small voice. If he had any doubt about that, the events of the past twenty-four hours cleared that up in a horrific fashion.

There was a pause, and he'd just decided that the voice wasn't going to speak again, when it did.

"There is one other thing you must tell the others."

"What?"

"There is someone coming who will help you. He will find you seemingly by accident, and will lead you to the next place. It would be easy to let what has happened convince you that everyone is an enemy, but you must resist that."

"How will I know who he is?"

"You will know. You will explain this to the others. And he will take you away with him."

Perry hitched a sigh that was half a sob. "Why us? Why did you save us and not everyone else? What is special about us? We saw so many people dead. Some of them were probably nice, but they died anyway. I don't understand."

"It isn't about who is nice and who is not, nor about who deserves to live and who deserves to die. The only thing that is critical for you to know is that you and the others are the link to the distant future. Do not doubt your importance."

"I'm doubting everything."

"I know. Sleep. It will not change what has happened, but it will make you better able to deal with it."

Perry nodded, then turned away from the window. They hadn't turned on the lights, but outside the window was a balcony with floodlights, and the interior of the room was a surreal grayscape of shapes and shadows. The children were sprawled on the floor and on furniture, unmoving, sleeping so soundly they looked like statues. He glanced over to the entrance into the room from the staircase, and saw that Colin and Emily as well were sound asleep, sitting on the floor with their backs against the wall and their heads lolling.

Perry found an unoccupied corner and lay down, curled up on his side. It was hard and the carpet was rough and scratchy, but even so, sleep stole upon him within minutes. Silence, both internal and external, fell in the big room at the top of the medical office building, as the first day of the new world came to an end.

When Perry opened his eyes, it was already midmorning. He had no idea how long he'd slept. He sat up, groggy and disoriented. Some of the other children sat in small groups, talking quietly. Colin and Emily were both awake, still at their sentry posts on either side of the door, but when they saw him stir they got up and walked over to him.

The two older children knelt on the floor.

"How are you feeling?" Emily said.

"I'm not sure."

She nodded. "It's going to take time to figure all this out."

Colin met Perry's eyes levelly. "Perry, I'm sorry I seemed angry yesterday. I wasn't mad at you. I was just afraid and upset."

"That's what Emily said."

Colin nodded. "I didn't want you to think I was mad at you. You saved our lives."

"I wish I could have saved more."

"Me too. But you're probably right that it wouldn't have worked."

"I know for sure it wouldn't have worked."

"Because the voice told you that?"

Perry shrugged. "Yes, but also because that's how adults

are. If you're a kid, and you say something they don't like, they look for a way not to believe you."

"Your parents wouldn't have believed you?"

He thought about his distant, job-focused dad and his nervous, overprotective mom. There was no way, no way in the world, they would have given his warnings any credence.

"No. They would have kept me home from school and brought me to the psychiatrist again."

"So you wouldn't have been able to warn us."

"Yes."

"You warned us yesterday," Emily said. "At that point, we would have known and you could have stayed home. That way you wouldn't have had to go through… all this."

"No. Because you wouldn't have known to leave the school last night. You wouldn't have been able to get here. Then when the bad people saw you…"

"They'd have killed us all."

"Yes."

Neither of the older children spoke.

"Since I'm the only one who can hear the voice, I have to stay with you in case it tells me more about what we have to do."

"Has it spoken to you again?" Colin asked. "Since last night, when it told you how to find this place?"

He nodded. "Last night after everyone was asleep. It told me we'd be here for a while."

"How long?"

"I don't know. But it said we had to stay on the top floors, not to go down to the first floor or anything."

"How will we find food?"

"It said there's food up here somewhere, that we just have to look for it and we'll find it."

Colin and Emily exchanged glances, but said nothing.

"It also said that someone was going to come here. An adult. It won't happen for a while, but when it does, he's on our side. He'll come when it's about time to leave here, and we should do what he says."

"Who is he?" Colin asked.

"I don't know."

"And until then, we're just supposed to stay here."

"Yes."

Colin took a deep breath, and to Perry's amazement, the older boy's eyes were glistening with tears. "Can you ask the voice… ask it…" He looked up, took a deep breath, let it out slowly. "Can you ask it if my parents and my brother are still alive?"

Perry nodded. "I'll ask it next time it talks to me."

"I want to try to get home, to see…" Colin began, but Perry shook his head sharply.

"The voice says we can't leave, not until the guy shows up."

"I hate this!" Colin burst out with a suddenness that made Perry jump. "I hate this. I fucking hate this!"

Several of the other children turned to look at them in alarm. Emily put her arm around Colin's shoulders, and he hung his head, his entire body shaking with sobs.

"I know," Perry said quietly. "We all do." Timidly, hesitantly, he sidled over and snuggled up next to Colin, putting his arms around the older boy's waist. Perry had never known when a hug or a touch was okay and when it wasn't, so he pretty much never touched anyone unless they initiated it. But something about Colin's weeping reached to his heart.

Now. This was a time he could help. Colin would help him later. He would help Colin now. Each of the survivors would need support, all of them in their own times and ways, and it was up to them to provide it for each other. Maybe together, they all would make it through this.

And sure enough, Colin reached out one strong arm and pulled Perry close, and they sat like that—each of the three of them propping the others up—for some time afterward.

twenty-one

. . .

S oren woke to a diffuse light coming in through the gap in the curtains above the sofa. He had slept through the night, amazingly enough. He sat up, parted the curtains, and looked across Dr. Quaice's front yard to the empty street. The crystalline blue skies had been replaced by gray—much more common Seattle spring weather, honestly. The warmth and sun had been an unexpected beneficence in a climate that was wet more often than not. He watched for a few minutes, waiting to see if there were any cars coming down McGilvra Boulevard, but soon was driven off the couch by the need to find a bathroom.

That taken care of, he went into the kitchen. Dr. Quaice would undoubtedly have no problem with his impromptu guests foraging about for food, but he still felt awkward and presumptuous doing it. He was about to open a cabinet to see what he could find when Cassandra walked into the room.

"Up early, too, Soren?" she said.

"What time is it?"

"Six-thirty."

"Oh. I didn't sleep in as long as I'd thought."

"It will be interesting to see what happens when the electricity goes. Humans in industrialized countries have become completely dependent on artificial illumination. When we don't have it any more, we'll have to realign our body clocks to the daylight hours, like they did before the invention of artificial lighting."

He pulled open a cabinet door. Plates and bowls. "You think we're going to go dark? Like, long-term?"

"Let's just say I share Dr. Quaice's pessimism about this situation having an easy or quick resolution."

The next cabinet had boxes of cereal, bags of flour and sugar, some canned goods, and most welcome of all—a bag of coffee and box of coffee filters. He set up the coffee maker, and within minutes, there was an encouraging gurgling noise coming from its innards.

"Can I fix you a bowl of cereal?"

She shook her head. "No, thanks. I usually just have a cup of coffee and a piece of fruit for breakfast."

Soren poured himself a bowl of granola and went to the fridge for milk. "What do you think of our resident psychic?"

"Mary?"

He nodded.

"I'm not sure what to make of her. There's something about her that seems… off. Like you're looking at an optical illusion. You know something's wrong, but it's hard to put your finger on what it is."

"I don't believe in precognition, but it's hard to explain how she knew our names otherwise."

Cassandra nodded. "And that we'd be in the Arboretum."

"Exactly. Was she annoying you as much as me last night?"

"I hate small talk at the best of times. I was seriously not in the mood to exchange life stories."

"Same. But maybe it's what she said, that her family was on her mind, so she needed to talk about it."

"You're probably right. I've noticed that about some

people. Worry makes them talk more. Me, I talk less. And get irritated a lot faster with chitchat."

Soren brought his bowl of cereal to a small table by a window looking out into a back yard surrounded by a tall cedar fence. Cassandra filled a mug with coffee and joined him, and her dark eyes regarded him solemnly. It was remarkable how composed she looked—her black hair combed, her clothes neat, wearing gold earrings that set off strikingly against her deep brown skin. Soren wondered how he must look. He'd given a glance in the mirror when he was in the bathroom, and recalled puffy eyes and blond hair sticking up in awkward tufts.

Maybe his stress and worry and loneliness showed in his appearance more. Couldn't be helped.

"I'm sorry about Finn," Cassandra said, as if she'd read his thoughts.

He met her eyes, gave a quick nod, and looked down again.

"I know Dr. Quaice was asking about him over and over on his radio last night. He recognizes how upset you are. If it's humanly possible, we'll find him."

"I'm damn sure not going to stop trying." He cleared his throat. "Are you just guessing about Dr. Quaice querying his friends because of hearing Finn's name? Or do you speak Kalila?"

"I know some. Enough to get the gist of what he was saying, but I wouldn't call myself fluent. When I got hired, five years ago—right around the same time you did, I believe?—I thought it sounded entertaining to study. I'd heard of conlangs, of course, but never tried to write one or even learn one. I found out about Dr. Quaice's crypto-reason for creating it pretty quickly, and honestly, I didn't think it was a bad idea to have a way to communicate if things fell apart, even if I wasn't as convinced as he was that a collapse was imminent. Did you know he's had over two thousand students in the last twenty years?"

"Had no idea it was that many."

"He doesn't make a big noise about it. Nothing like Klingon conventions or workshops for learning Elvish script. He's spent the last twenty years quietly and steadily building up a population in the Seattle area with whom he could talk without being understood by outsiders. To begin with I admired his passion and tenacity, but now I have to say his approach appears to be vindicated."

They sat in silence for a while, looking out into a tricolored tableau—emerald green foliage against the deep red-brown of the damp cedar pickets, above which hung a sky the color of dirty cotton.

"I know it's probably pointless to ask this," Soren finally said, "but what's the next step?"

Cassandra gave him a quick flicker of a smile, there and gone in a moment. "I get it. I hate being inert. We escaped the chaos for now, but we're in what amounts to a cage. Much as I want to take action, there's no action to take that isn't far more risky than it's worth. I hope the rioting dies down without hitting this neighborhood, but we can't get complacent. The best thing is to make the house look unoccupied."

"That'll work until people start raiding other people's houses for food."

"Point made. With luck that won't be for a few days at least. Decorum will break down if the collapse isn't stopped, but it won't break down that fast. We have a breather. We should use it."

"You mentioned last night going out on a scouting run to try to find a way out of the city. I want to be included when it happens."

"I wasn't asking for volunteers. I meant to go myself."

"I know. But I'm volunteering to go with you. Gavin and

Dr. Quaice aren't in the physical condition to manage it, and Mary…" He took a bite of granola and shrugged.

"I know. I don't completely trust her, not yet. Maybe she's exactly what she says she is—a physics teacher with psychic abilities. Her strangeness might be nothing more than the reality of who she is. Plus, a lot of people act oddly in extreme circumstances, which these definitely are. I'm not going to judge her. But I also don't want to depend on someone I don't trust completely. You and I could manage it. If we brought her along, I'd spend the whole time wondering what the hell she was going to do next. You, on the other hand, I know I could count on."

The acknowledgement of Soren's value on a scouting mission was encouraging. He had the sense Cassandra wasn't someone who dispensed compliments easily.

"I'm not a fighter."

"None of us are."

He smiled. "You don't seem like the type who puts up with any shit."

"I don't." No aw-shucks self-deprecation there, just an admission of the truth. "But I'm not a war-hardened veteran, or anything. I can take care of myself, and have done, but that doesn't mean I'm the person you want next to you in a pitched battle. I'm a fast runner and don't get freaked-out scared easily. I'm not afraid to defend myself. But I'm an academic like the rest of us. I don't want you to think I'm some kind of… Lara Croft type."

Soren smiled. "*Tomb Raider*? That goes back a ways."

This got an honest laugh. It may have been the first time he'd seen her laugh, and it softened the severe lines of her face. "What can I say? Love action/adventure movies. Can't have too many kickass archaeologists."

They both turned as Mary Hansard entered the kitchen, cheerful smile already in place. "Hello. Glad I'm not the only early bird."

"I've only been up for twenty minutes," Soren said.

"I know. You were still curled up on the sofa when I went through. I was out as soon as it was light."

"Out?" Cassandra and Soren said the word simultaneously, and exchanged glances.

"Yes. I wanted to see what was going on. Don't worry, I was crafty. In any case, there was hardly anyone out. I saw why there've been no cars—someone barricaded McGilvra Boulevard about three blocks up, and also maybe five blocks down. I went to the closer one, and someone had put a sign up saying, 'This neighborhood is off limits. Rioters and looters will be shot. Crossing this boundary is forbidden.'"

"Hopefully that convinced you that being out on the street was a bad idea," Cassandra said. From her guarded, measured tone Soren knew she was pissed off by the older woman's lack of caution.

"Oh, no one was around. When I left I decided to go up to the near barricade because I knew I could get back safely without being challenged."

More alleged prescience.

"You need to be more careful," Soren tried to find a way to soft-pedal his criticism of her actions, and then decided that he didn't care. "You said yourself that your knowledge of the future is incomplete and sometimes inaccurate. You've got to admit that relying on that as a guide is dangerous."

She shrugged, her smile undimmed. "But I knew for sure this time."

"In any case," Cassandra said, "there's more to it than just getting back alive. Soren and I were discussing how the best approach is to make it look like this house is closed up, dark, unoccupied. Going out for a nice morning walk is risking not only your own life, but the lives of everyone who might be targeted by someone who followed you back."

"I suppose that's sensible. Well, if I'm under house arrest, at least Dr. Quaice has got a sweet little back yard with a tall fence, for when we feel completely claustrophobic indoors." She didn't seem at all upset.

Cassandra was right—there was something off about her, something more than her claims of foresight. He got a sense of there being closed rooms behind that friendly smile, places she would rather not go—and didn't want others to see. They'd had a glimpse last night with her trembling meltdown about disasters. What was it she'd said? Something about Pharaoh's armies and Lot's wife. But afterward, once she pulled herself together, whatever door the day's events opened had slammed shut again, and by the time of the peculiar after-dinner chit-chat, she was back to a smooth surface, so smooth there was nothing to grab on to, nothing to catch hold of.

"I see you've found the food and coffee." Dr. Quaice was dressed in a t-shirt and sweat pants, and his gray hair stood on end more than usual. Combined with the fact that he hadn't shaved yet, Soren was reminded of Jack Nicholson's character in *One Flew Over the Cuckoo's Nest*.

"Hope you don't mind that we rummaged around your kitchen," Soren said. "Didn't know when you'd be up."

He gave a dismissive wave of the hand. "No, of course not, it's no problem. Anything you can't find up here, those are the basement stairs"—he pointed to a closed door in the corner of the kitchen—"and I've got more of just about everything down there. Like I said, at least three weeks' worth, as long as we don't treat it like an all-you-can-eat buffet." He got himself a mug, poured it full almost to overflowing with coffee, and held it up like a toast. "Enjoy it while we got it, folks. Coffee and tea are both tropical imports. Once it's gone, that's gonna be it for a long while."

Soren had said that to Finn—was it only yesterday? "Chocolate and bananas, too."

"Oh, man, chocolate," Mary said, and gave a rueful laugh.

"Did you learn anything from talking to the people in

your network last night?" Cassandra, as usual, cut through the chitchat to the serious stuff. "Is there any way to get information on what's happening out there?"

Dr. Quaice didn't answer for a moment, but stared into the depths of his coffee cup with a frown. "From what people were saying, it's obvious the riots are city-wide at least. The farthest ones in the network are in Everett to the north, Olympia to the south, and this side of Snoqualmie Pass to the east, so it's impossible to say what's going on beyond that. Besides knocking out the telecommunications hub and wiping out email, phones, and internet connectivity, the LLA has apparently destroyed the KING-FM offices on Harrison Street, and probably the main transmitter up above Issaquah. All the local television and radio stations were offline last night. I haven't checked this morning, but I'd be surprised if they were back. I'll be surprised, in fact, if they come back at all."

"So we still have electricity, but can't use it to communicate other than via shortwave," Cassandra said.

"Exactly."

"And no way of knowing whether the attacks have been contained in other places outside of the Seattle area."

"No, but it'd be a miracle if they were. One of the last pieces of information I saw from outside of Seattle was about a series of near-simultaneous assassinations and bombings. This was coordinated nationwide. Probably worldwide."

"But there's one thing I don't understand," Soren said. "If they had this coordinated plot, planned well in advance, there has to have been communication between different places. By destroying the telecommunication hubs, they've cut themselves off along with the rest of us. It's sawing off the tree branch you're sitting on."

"I doubt they care." Cassandra's lips tightened, the only display of emotion she revealed. "I've read some of the Lacklanders' manifestos. They're no different than the suicide bombers in the Middle East back during the Gulf Wars. The point is to destroy the power structure they despise. If they can take down the corporate-capitalist overlords, they still count it as a success even if they go down along with them."

"That makes no sense at all," Mary said.

"I didn't say it was rational."

Mary simply shook her head.

Soren frowned. "So where it stands is that Seattle is a mess, and not likely to improve soon, and there's no way to get information about anywhere else."

"Correctly summarized," Dr. Quaice said. "Some parts of Seattle are apparently worse than others. There was a lot of destruction on Capitol Hill, and also down toward Renton and Kent. We're lucky here in Madison Park so far. The East-side communities sound relatively quiet, although a bunch of the businesses along the Kirkland waterfront were looted and then burned. Downtown Seattle is apparently impassable—the streets are full of rubble, both from the deliberate building of barricades to stop traffic and pieces of bombed buildings. They were selective with blowing things up, though. Communications, law enforcement, and corporate buildings were the main targets, apparently. Like I said, they planned this carefully, and probably a good long time ago."

"How were the other residential areas?"

"Well, be aware it's a skewed data set. The ones who answered were the ones who are still in their houses with access to their radio transmitters. Those folks were mostly hunkering down and hoping to wait the chaos out. But several talked about crowds of people who'd been driven out of their homes and were trying to find a way to somewhere safe."

Like Finn. One of the last messages from him had said, *Looks like running. Me & Janie Inoue. Not sure where we'll go. They broke Janie's windows but she got out through the back and climbed the fence.*

Janie was a retired elementary school teacher, about seventy years old. It was hard to picture her climbing a fence, but apparently she'd done it. It seemed like a fair indication of how bad it already was when Finn texted him.

Now, almost twenty-four hours later, it was anyone's guess what things were like outside of their little protected enclave between the Arboretum and the lake.

"'The restraints on men, as well as their liberties, are to be reckoned amongst their rights.'" They turned, and Gavin Liu was standing in the doorway, face set in a thoughtful frown. "Edmund Burke said that after witnessing the bloody chaos of the French Revolution. He knew how hard it is to achieve order, and how quick and easy it is to lose it."

"Is it possible to re-establish order once it's gone?" Soren said.

Gavin's brow furrowed. "Perhaps eventually. The horrors of the Reign of Terror went on for almost a year. Public executions, sometimes a hundred a day, often of people whose only crime was to annoy the wrong person. The government didn't really pull itself back together in any kind of effective way until five years after the execution of Robespierre, which most people call the end of the Terror. And consider that even after that, France went through the teeter-totter of the Bonaparte years. Stability? I guess it depends on how you define it. But my estimation is it took France a generation to recover from what they'd done to themselves."

A bleak sense of hopelessness rose in Soren's chest. "And this isn't only one country. It's the whole world."

Mary turned toward the others, holding a loaf of bread. "Would anyone else like a piece of toast and jam?"

No one responded. Undaunted, her smile undimmed, Mary went on fixing herself toast and jam.

After they cleaned up the coffee mugs and breakfast dishes, Soren went back into the living room, followed by Cassandra. Mary and Gavin had gone out into the back yard, even though the gray was persisting and it seemed to be drizzling.

Cassandra scowled. "No, I don't want any toast and jam," she muttered under her breath.

Soren snorted laughter. "Right? I don't know what to make of her."

"I don't either. I try not to be annoyed with her, because she's stuck in this situation just like we are. But I feel like I can't get at what she's really about, you know? I think she has a veneer that she expends a lot of energy to maintain. Might come from the fact that she's a public school teacher. You can't put your emotions out on display. You're having a bad day, you fought with your partner, you're having financial problems, you still have to smile and say, 'Good morning, class,' and act as if everything's fine. Maybe that veneer eventually hardens into a shell. At that point, you can't get past it unless you hit it hard enough to crack it."

"Like last night."

"Exactly."

"I was thinking of her as having closed rooms in her personality that she desperately wants to remain closed."

"Decent analogy. But the same idea. It reinforces my determination not to trust her. I don't like relying on people I can't parse. I think it'll be a long time before I'll be able to parse Mary Hansard, and I'm not sure I'll like what I find when I do."

The day crawled by into another silent evening. Curtains drawn, lights out, a meal in which five uncomfortable people ate food that had been set aside for a catastrophe that only one of them had anticipated. Like the previous night, afterward Dr. Quaice vanished into his study to connect with his network, all speaking in the strange synthetic tongue that very likely none of them—with the possible exception of Quaice himself—ever thought they'd have to use for its created purpose. Soren knew enough Kalila to get the gist at least of some of the conversations. Dr. Quaice was arranging for food sharing, mapping out where known violence was occurring so his friends could avoid it. Making note of any observations that might indicate danger—or resources.

After that, another night on the couch, followed by another cheerless morning.

Days went by. With a unanimous vote of approval from the others, Dr. Quaice went down his street knocking on doors, each time announcing himself and saying, "I'm unarmed and mean no harm. I'm just trying to find out who's here and to see if anyone needs help." Only about a quarter of the doors opened. Whether the ones that didn't belonged to unoccupied houses, or that their owners were afraid to open them out of fear, was impossible to tell.

"My guess is that a lot of them really are empty," he said, upon returning. "Because of the way the timing worked out, most people were probably at work when things really shut down, and got stuck. Just like all of us. But I found out that of my neighbors who are in their houses, most of them are getting desperate for food. I didn't volunteer ours—it's dwindling fast enough as it is. Pretty soon, it's going to be everyone fending for themselves. Harsh reality, but reality nonetheless."

"Won't be long before desperation breaks down what's left of the social niceties," Cassandra observed.

Dr. Quaice nodded. "Won't be long before it isn't safe to knock on anyone's door. At least this isn't Texas, where damn near everyone's armed to the teeth."

The nightly radio conversations were more and more about the simple necessities, especially food and medical supplies. Dr. Quaice did what he could to coordinate drop-offs and trades so no one went without, but it was obvious to everyone that this would only postpone running out completely, not prevent it. People were starting to go on raids, first of grocery stores, then empty houses, then occupied ones. As he had predicted, the raiders were met with violence, not only from the people they were trying to rob, but from the bands of LLA terrorists that now controlled much of the central city. Evidently the leaders of the LLA, whoever they were, had given orders to shoot looters on sight, and more than one person who only weeks before had been an ordinary businessperson or shop clerk or student was gunned down for stealing food and left lying where they'd fallen. The network kept track of sightings of the marauders patrolling the streets, warning people about safe and unsafe paths to take, but there seemed to be no predictable pattern to where the LLA foot soldiers went.

It looked as if they had no plans once the coordinated attacks were done, and were content to let the city devolve into anarchy.

Every night, Dr. Quaice asked for word of Finn. Every night, there was nothing. The older man consoled Soren with statements that were technically true but made no emotional impact whatsoever. "It's a big city." "It might be better that you haven't heard. It probably means he's holed up somewhere, safe." "He's probably as worried about you as you are about him."

The exhausted sorrow Soren had felt the first night gradually morphed into anger at the people who had done all this, who had separated them. The rage in him spiked every time he thought of Finn somewhere in the dark, alone, scared, hungry. It was a white-hot diamond-tipped needle of fury that he hadn't even known he was capable of.

The last words he whispered before sleep, like some kind of prayer, were, "I'll find you. I swear. I'll find you. And then I'll never let you go."

But as the days turned into weeks, those words more and

more seemed like the empty prayers of his doubting teenage years, when he still attended his parents' church but didn't believe anything he was saying. "The Lord be with you… and also with you." "deliver us from evil, all who turn to you with confidence…" "… blessed saint, whom we venerate as our protector on Earth, be our intercessor in heaven." Mumbled words, no more able to change what was happening than his fervent promises to Finn.

But some part of him couldn't let it go. He became laser-focused on the words, as obsessed as the churchmen of old who were fixated on getting the words of the prayers exactly right, fearful that one misspoken syllable would incur God's wrath and the failure of the petition. Each night, he recited his mantra three times, whispering into the darkness, even though it felt like no one was listening.

Only then could he let go of his anger enough to relax into sleep. His rational mind told him that his prayer would have no effect—but it was better than the alternative, which at the moment was admitting to himself that he could do absolutely nothing.

twenty-two

. . .

T here was barbed wire stretched across the road, wound loosely around a variety of objects acting as makeshift fence posts. Sawhorses, kitchen chairs, a stepladder, free-standing metal shelves that looked like they had once held house plants. Hanging in the middle from the wire was a sign that said, "This is the boundary of the Free State of North Seattle. Anyone seen crossing it will be shot on sight."

The letters were neat, painted with stencils. Just across the barricade were six dead bodies sprawled on the pavement, all in varying states of decomposition.

Brandon turned away from the horrifying tableau, trying to force down his nausea and mostly succeeding.

It was Ronnie Sulzbach who spoke first.

"Why?" she said quietly. "Don't they understand that we have to help each other?"

"It's understandable." The tough former soldier who had joined them on the first day, whose name was Arden Ballinger, spoke in a grim voice. "There's a catastrophe, you have two choices. You do the compassionate thing and try to save everyone, which increases your own risk. Or you hunker down and protect your clan, to hell with anyone else. When food's scarce, more people will take the second option. More mouths, less food for each one."

"It's so heartless," Ronnie said.

"It's reality."

In the two weeks since the attacks had started, their numbers had swelled to almost fifty. The more time passed, the easier it was to persuade people to come along. Julia's message, which probably would have been looked upon as the rantings of a religious maniac, now offered at least some hope.

Brandon had to admit she was persuasive, partly because of how humble she was. She never claimed authority. She was a conduit of the prophecy, nothing more than a mouthpiece being used by God to save as many people as she could. Strangest of all was how close Julia and Caria had become. The last thing Brandon would have expected was his urbane, modern, secular-minded girlfriend finding common ground with an elderly Christian woman, but whenever Julia's strength—emotional or physical—flagged, Caria was there to support her. Of the doubt Caria had expressed, even after the attacks had begun, there seemed to be not a trace left. Once she realized that Julia spoke nothing more than the plain truth, she had accepted her and her message completely.

Brandon wished his own conversion had been that complete. He still felt disembodied, as if the scenes of destruction surrounding them were something out of a dream. Since the moment he started on the first painting, nothing made any sense. It was all just chaos, a lunatic walk through a hellscape.

More than once he wondered if he had simply had a psychotic break, and was now strapped down in a mental ward somewhere, hallucinating.

But day after day, he woke up to the same thing. The city had collapsed. A large part of the population had been killed or had fled. Julia led them unerringly through it all, avoiding the worst of the fighting, saying that the command was to head north, paralleling I-5 out of the city.

But now there was a barrier across their path, and Julia seemed as mystified as he was.

"What do we do now?" Trevor Keene, the young man who, along with Ronnie, had been one of the first to join them, looked at Julia with expectation in his eyes. He clearly thought she had all the answers.

Up to now, she had.

"I… I'm not sure." Julia frowned, her gaze going past the barricade and up the street, which looked deserted. "I don't think we dare cross. I think those poor souls have been left there as a warning that they mean what they say."

"Maybe we could go around."

"I don't know." She looked down. "I'm not given to know that. I don't… I don't hear a directive. Without that…"

"Let's get away from the barricade," Ronnie said. "They said they'll kill us if we cross, but I'm worried they'll get nervous if we stand here too long and decide on a pre-emptive strike."

"That makes sense," Trevor said.

Arden Ballinger's lips tightened. Brandon could tell he didn't like to respond to a threat by backing down, but he didn't argue. Arden still had his handgun—which he had yet to use—but there were too many places a sniper could hide and get off a clear shot. Even with a weapon, crossing the barricade was likely to be suicide.

They retreated down the street, and only when they'd turned a corner and the boundary was out of sight did Julia raise her hand, halting the entire group.

"We've come upon a barrier I did not expect. That I did not know about." Her voice sounded dull with fatigue, wearier than Brandon had ever heard her. Little food, days of walking and hiding with uncomfortable sleep at best, was taking its toll on them all, but Julia's age was working against her. At the beginning, it was easier to forget that she was seventy years old. In only two weeks, she was showing it.

"Where do we go from here?" The question was asked by a middle-aged man whose name Brandon couldn't recall, but who spoke with a distinct accent that sounded Dutch or German.

"I'm not sure."

"You've never run into a problem you didn't know about."

Julia nodded. "God brought me—brought us—to this place for a reason. But I don't know what that reason is, and I dare not cross. The risk is too great."

"Then why?"

"And how will we get out of the city?" someone else asked.

"I'm not sure," she said again. The first patter of raindrops sprinkled them. She glanced up into the gray sky. "It's getting toward evening, and the weather's turned inclement. We should find shelter, and I will give thought to our next step." She took a deep breath. "Maybe the Lord will speak to me."

They found an open double garage attached to an apparently empty house, the cars it had once housed gone and the door standing open, where they could rest for the evening. The floor was concrete but dry. They'd slept in worse conditions.

But night fell, and if Julia received any divine guidance, she said nothing about it.

The morning dawned bleak and gray, with a thin drizzle hissing its way down from sodden skies. It wasn't exactly cold, but the air felt clammy and chilled. A day that only a few weeks ago would have impelled people to stay inside.

Brandon would have started a cozy fire in his wood stove and spent the day in the studio.

But instead they were displaced, dispossessed, homeless. Ironic thing, that. The LLA originated with the outrage of people who lost their land and their homes. Their response had created thousands more landless refugees.

The logic—if it could be called that—seemed to be that if the poorest couldn't be raised to the level of the affluent, the affluent would be knocked down to the level of the poorest.

Caria and Julia were sitting together in quiet conversation, and Brandon went to join them. He threaded his way through people who were curled up on the cement floor, some huddled together for warmth and comfort. The garage suddenly seemed like the cave home of our distant ancestors. Humanity hadn't reverted to the Middle Ages. They'd gone straight back to prehistoric times. Who was it that said that back then, life was poor, nasty, brutish, and short?

Was that what they all had in store—even if they could escape the desolation of the city and the guns of the LLA and the Free State of North Seattle?

"Sit down, Brandon," Julia said quietly, and he did. "We have been discussing our strategy now that it seems the road north out of the city is closed to us."

"We don't know that for certain."

"No, we don't. It may be that farther east, there's a way to get around the area that's been cordoned off. Perhaps that will become clear once we're moving again. But I think we must plan as if the entire north section of the city is blocked. We can't risk trying to force a crossing, and people dying. We've been lucky so far."

"Because of you," Caria said.

A flicker of a smile of gratitude crossed the older woman's lips. "I've only done what I could manage to do. I still feel sick about leaving Marcus Gellert behind."

"It was his choice."

"I know that. And practically speaking, he was right. Pushing a man in a wheelchair through all this, with all the obstacles, would have slowed us, if it didn't turn out to be downright impossible. Plus..." She stopped, turned away, frowning. "It was what I was supposed to do. I know that. It's only my human frailty that makes me doubt the decision."

"Compassion isn't frailty," Brandon said.

"No, I take your meaning. But doubting what I know to be true—that is weakness of will. Marcus had to be left behind as a messenger to those who come after. But at the same time, leaving him behind was brutal. Cold, calculated. Using him then discarding him when his purpose was done. How is it any different from the people who put up that keep-out sign? I don't agree with Arden Ballinger about much, but he was right about that. When things collapse, you have a choice. Set your own safety aside and help others, or abandon the others and do what you have to in order to survive."

"It's not the same thing," Caria said. "The people who put up that sign didn't have guidance from something greater. I'm not ready to call it God, but there's no way you got us here—without losing a single person, telling us exactly what streets to take, what streets to avoid, which houses were empty and would provide shelter—without that knowledge coming from *somewhere*. That doesn't change the fact that sometimes all the choices are bad. You still have to choose."

"That's true."

"So until proven otherwise, I'm going to trust your knowledge. It wasn't easy at first. I fought like hell even when it was obvious you were right. Finally I had to say, 'Okay, I may not understand it, but that's the way it is.' That's where I am right now. I trust you, even if at the moment you're not quite trusting yourself."

Julia gave her another grateful smile, but her face became serious again. "I appreciate your trust, but I... I don't know what to do next. The voice of God got us to this place, but now… now that we're here, there's nothing. Just silence. There must be a purpose to our being here, but I don't know what it is. Nor do I know where to lead these people now. My suggestion to head east and see if there's a way to turn north again is just…" She gave a helpless shrug. "A guess. Nothing more. Without the guidance, I am just a foolish old woman pretending she knows what she's doing."

"Don't give up yet," Brandon said.

"I'm not giving up. I'm just tired. Lord have mercy on my soul, I've never been this tired in my life, not when I was working eighteen-hour shifts as a nurse in the emergency room. I sleep at night, as well as my old bones can on the ground, and wake up the next morning just as tired as I was. I hope my body can last long enough to get us all to safety."

"You were chosen to lead us for a reason," Brandon said. "I'm with Caria—I've never believed in God, but I do believe in you, and in whatever is guiding you. We'll keep relying on that. It's all we can do."

By midmorning the drizzle had tapered off, but it was replaced by rolling clouds of fog that obscured everything. Houses, trees, roads become vague phantoms, blurred and indistinct ghosts of real solid objects. As they left the garage's shelter, heading east along the suburban street, Brandon kept looking over his shoulder, half expecting the scene would have changed into a nightmare landscape, but all he saw was the pearly gray billows draping the neighborhood like a gauzy curtain.

"I think we're far enough away from that barricade to be safe," Caria whispered. Something about the place made everyone reluctant to speak loudly, above and beyond any enemies that might alert to their presence. "We still haven't seen anyone else around."

"It isn't that," Brandon said. "I'm just… I think it's finally sunk in, everything that's happened, and my brain still doesn't want to believe it's real. The fog makes it worse. It makes it seem like a fever-dream."

She took his hand. "I know what you mean. Having Julia here helps, though. Before I met her, I couldn't understand why you trusted her so quickly. Now I understand. It's like she's solid and real even if nothing else is."

"That's it exactly."

Ahead of them, the sharp voice of Arden Ballinger barked out, "Stop. There are people ahead of us."

As one, the group halted, crowding together on the side-walk. Brandon peered down the street. Near the next corner, indistinct in the fog, was a shadowed group of figures, perhaps four or five of them. They were standing around a trash can with fitful flames burning inside it. The people had seen them, too. He caught the sudden tension in their postures, like rabbits that had scented a predator and were ready to bolt.

Julia stepped forward. Despite strong characters like Arden, to most of them she was still clearly in charge, and even he stepped aside to let her pass.

"We don't want any trouble," she said in a commanding tone. "We just want to go past you peacefully. We're no threat to you as long as you intend none to us."

There was a moment during which they obviously conferred with each other, and a male voice said, "That's okay. We're not armed. Besides, you outnumber us by a lot."

"Why do you all think it's a good idea to start with 'we come in peace'?" Arden grumbled. "Makes us sound weak and scared."

"Because it's the truth," Julia said. "There's still value in that."

She moved toward them, and the rest followed. As they got closer, the figures resolved, their outlines sharpening into a lean, athletic-looking thirty-something man with thick auburn hair, freckles, and a deep gash on his right cheek, a thin, tiny older woman with a round face, glasses, and a pixie cut, two teenage girls who looked like they might be sisters, and a balding bespectacled man wearing a flannel shirt and jeans with his left arm in a makeshift sling.

The younger man stepped forward to meet Julia, scanning the group as if looking for someone. His face relaxed back into disappointment and resignation, but when he spoke, his voice was friendly.

"Where are you going?"

"We're trying to find a way around the barricade so we can head north."

The woman with the pixie cut gave a little gasp. One of the teenage girls said, "You don't want to do that. You seriously don't."

"Why not?"

The other girl said, "Because the people in there are fucking insane. You wouldn't make it two blocks."

"How do you know that?" Julia asked.

"Because we came from there," the young man said. "When the riots started, a bunch of us got together to see if we could get away. We honestly thought it was just our neighborhood, you know? Like if we could walk far enough we'd get clear of it. It became obvious quickly that it wasn't just confined to one area. We doubled back to see if things had simmered down in our neighborhood, maybe hunker down in one of our houses, you know? Wait it out. But there was no way to do that. We found a place to shelter—a school gymnasium—until they got there and we had to run for it again. Since then we've gone place to place. Nowhere is safe."

"But what's going on behind that barricade?"

The man's expression was grim. "Maybe a week after the riots started, a bunch of people up in the north end decided they needed to close the borders. It started with the police— they were armed, and figured all they needed to do was seal up the perimeter. Some military types, probably from the naval station up in Everett, joined in. They did battle with a bunch of the LLA rioters, and won. Killed maybe a hundred of them, and the rest took off. But instead of saying, 'Okay, things are all better, you can go home,' they decided to tighten their grip rather than slackening. They figured if there was a strong presence, it'd keep the peace."

"The Free State of North Seattle."

He nodded. "The name made me laugh. Inside there, the last thing you are is free. It's like the Democratic People's Republic of North Korea, you know? But they're serious about the borders being sealed. You stay this side of the barricade, they don't bother you. You touch it, you're dead. They have snipers posted 24/7. No one in, no one out."

"You got out," Arden said.

He nodded. "You might want to know that before we got out, three days ago, we were a group of about twenty. We're the only ones who made it." He touched his cheek. "I got grazed. Danny took a bullet to his arm."

"Flesh wound," the man with the flannel shirt said.

"But the rest weren't so lucky. They shoot people and let them lie, as a warning to anyone else who wants to try to breach the barricade in either direction."

When Julia spoke, she sounded as if she were near tears. "Have pity on me, O Lord, have pity on me, for I lie prostrate in the midst of lions that devour men. Psalm 56. Heaven help us all."

"I dunno. Given the choice, I'd take my chances with the lions rather than my fellow human beings."

"There are still good people left." Julia shook her head and took a deep breath. "You're right, though. It's senseless. There's a threat from outside, and we immediately turn on each other." Her voice became resolute. "We're trying to find a way out of the city. If the northward road is blocked all the way across, we'll have to try for one of the bridges. You can come with us if you like."

The man looked at his companions. One of the teenage girls shrugged.

The other said, "Strength in numbers."

"All right," the man said. "Thank you. We were running out of ideas of where to find food and shelter. We happened on an empty house with a stash of granola bars and Pop-Tarts three days ago, or we'd have gone without."

"I don't know we'll be any better at it," Julia said. "More mouths to feed might mean less for each, but it's the only thing we can do. Help each other to survive." She put out one hand and said, "Julia Lowell."

He took it in a firm grip. "Finn Donnelly."

"Thank you for the information, Finn. I'm afraid at some point we might have been tempted to cross the barricade."

He gave her a solemn nod. "I have to ask you something. Every time I've seen someone new, I've asked. I'm trying to find out if you've seen—if anyone's seen—a man my age, six-one, a hundred eighty pounds or so. Blond, hazel eyes, nice-looking."

"Doesn't sound familiar. Family member?"

"Boyfriend. Partner. We were separated the day the riots started and I haven't had any word from him since. His name is Soren Conover."

Brandon's head snapped up as if he'd had an electric shock. Heart pounding, he took a step toward Finn, reaching his hand into his pocket. He pulled out his phone, pressed the button on the side. He hadn't touched it since the first day—there was no service, so no reason to—and even though the power bar was in the red, it still had enough juice for the screen to light up. In a moment, he had called up an image he hadn't looked at in two weeks, one that seemed like it was from another life. A tall blond man standing with his feet firmly planted on the tilted world, and behind him a crowd of children he was protecting from harm.

Soren. His name is Soren.

Hand trembling, he held the phone up in front of Finn. "Is this him?"

Finn's eyes startled open wide, and he gave a gasp that was almost a sob.

"How…" He stared at the image as if it were a dream, as if it would vanish when he looked away, severing a lifeline to a hope he'd almost given up on.

"Now I understand why we came this way." Julia put her hand on the man's arm. "I think you'd better come with us. We have a lot to discuss."

twenty-three

. . .

Two and a half weeks after their flight from the University to the safe haven of Dr. Quaice's house, it became obvious to Soren they couldn't hold out much longer.

"I mentioned earlier sending out a scout," Cassandra said over a meager breakfast. "It needs to be soon. We're down to the last boxes, bags, and cans of food. Somehow the electric and water are still on, but I can't imagine it'll be for much longer. We need to get across the bridge and over to the East-side and beyond."

"Yes," Mary said under her breath. "Finally."

No one acknowledged her.

"Keep in mind we don't know that things are any better on the other side," Cassandra continued. "My guess is Kirkland, Bellevue, and Redmond are as much a mess as Seattle is right now. But if we can get out of the city, and go east and north, we can get past the sprawl and into some smaller towns that might have been less affected by the chaos. It's a chance, but one I think we have to take. We can't stay here."

"I've already volunteered to go on a scouting expedition," Soren said.

She nodded. "Soren and I discussed a while back that he

and I should be the ones to go. We're both runners. We're fit and have good stamina. From a physical perspective, we're the obvious choices."

Dr. Quaice leaned back in his chair and tented his fingers. "What you're saying makes sense. I've got binoculars you can bring to scan as far down the length of the bridge as you can. Evergreen Point is over two kilometers long, and over open water most of the way. From our enemies' perspective, that makes it easy to defend. From ours, it's a huge risk to cross. We need a good assessment of how well it's being watched."

"That's exactly right."

"It's possible they've already blown a hole in it somewhere to prevent people getting out," Soren said. "Easier than guarding it 24/7."

Mary shook her head. "No, it's passable. I'm not sure how well it's defended, but it's passable."

"Would it be better to try to go up I-5, and get out of the city northward?"

Gavin looked at him and gave a quick frown. He had forgotten that Gavin's wife was in Kirkland, at the east end of the bridge. Going any other way would take them farther away from his family, and Soren had the sense that Gavin's quiet demeanor hid a steel-hard determination to rejoin his wife or die trying.

A conviction Soren understood all too well.

"Only if Evergreen Point is impossible," Dr. Quaice said. "Going either north or south along the interstate is a very long walk through heavily-occupied areas. Even if we stay off the interstate itself and try to find a way parallel, you don't get out of a solid stretch of city and suburbia until Everett northward and Tacoma southward. Here, we're placed well, close to the west end of the bridge. It's the obvious way out, unless going that way is completely blocked."

"Agreed," Cassandra said.

"Just remember that this is a reconnaissance mission

only," Dr. Quaice said. "No heroics. You do us no good if you get foolhardy and are captured or killed. Quick out, quick back, gather as much information as you can, and do your damnedest not to be seen by anyone, friend or foe. Once you're back, we'll lay it all out, along with the latest updates from my network, and figure out our strategy."

"All that matters is getting across the bridge as soon as possible," Mary said.

"No argument there," Dr. Quaice said. "Let's take a look at a map and plan out a path for you."

"There's no easy way out of Madison Park to the north." Dr. Quaice smoothed out a map of the city across the dinner table, and Soren peered down at the tangle of streets, squinting in the dim light of another gray, drizzly morning. "Everything runs into Union Bay. If you go straight north on McGilvra eventually it tees out, and after that it's nothing but marsh. Probably better to cut back across the Arboretum, heading northwest as best you can. Depending on how far north you go you could also cross Broadmoor Golf Course, but that'll give you less cover, so I'd avoid it. Once you hit Lake Washington Boulevard, head generally north. Eventually it doglegs around to the east and merges right onto Highway 520."

"Lake Washington is a major thoroughfare," Cassandra said.

Dr. Quaice nodded. "True, but it can't be helped, at least not once you get close to the bridge. You can stay off the road and parallel it as best you can, but it's a danger either way. You're on the road, you get seen. You're off the road, you're crossing private property and risk getting taken for a raider and shot by some trigger-happy homeowner."

Cassandra gave him a wry eyebrow. "Cheerful outlook."

"Realistic outlook."

"I'm not doubting that."

He gave another sharp nod. "The network is reporting more and more attacks every day. Some of them are LLA, others are people defending their property from trespassers. Some of it seems to be random violence by people who've reached the end of their tether."

Soren glanced at Cassandra. She was a good person to partner with on a job like this. She looked completely calm and ready to go despite Dr. Quaice's warnings. He tried to hide the fact that he was already sweating and his heart pounding, and they weren't even out of the front door yet.

Hopefully she had as much faith in him as he did in her.

"Try your hardest to get back by nightfall," Dr. Quaice said. "Darkness hides you, but it also hides anyone trying to target you, and at night it won't be possible to get a good look down the entire length of the bridge. I wish there was a better time to send you out, but can't be helped. You'll just have to fly by the seat of the pants."

"Pretty much what everyone's doing in the last three weeks," Cassandra said.

Dr. Quaice folded the map and slipped it into Cassandra's backpack. She picked it up and elbowed her way into the straps, then cinched it up.

"You ready, Dr. Conover?"

"Ready as I'll get." Soren pulled on a backpack as well, this one borrowed from Dr. Quaice. They'd split the food and water between them, and each carried a hunting knife—the only weapons Dr. Quaice had. He thought of his own pack, full of student work and folders of notes on linguistics, sitting in his office in Guggenheim Hall. Just one of thousands of pieces of detritus, left behind by people fleeing the chaos.

Did they think they'd eventually be back to collect their belongings? He'd had a premonition he'd never return there. It wasn't true foreknowledge, of the sort Mary said she experienced, but simply an overwhelming sense that things had changed permanently, that the world would never go back to what it had been. Wherever he ended up, it would not be as a college linguistics professor.

"Good luck," Gavin said.

Mary came up to Soren, and clutched at his sleeve. Her eyes looked far distant, and he was suddenly certain he was once again seeing that other Mary Hansard, the one she hid, the one who was diametrically opposed to the breezy, cheerful woman she appeared to be most of the time.

"I have to tell you something. Two things. One for this time, one for the next. For today—it sounds a little ridiculous, I'm sorry."

"That's okay, what are you trying to say?"

"It's cats. Look out for cats. When you see a cat, the danger will be behind you."

"Cats."

"I told you it sounded ridiculous. But that's the best I can do. I don't know anything more than that. It's all kind of foggy." She passed a hand over her face. Soren got the impression she saw something other than what was around her in the room, a tableau that was invisible to everyone but her. "But other than cats, you'll be okay. You'll be home tonight, no problem."

"Okay, we'll look out for cats." There was a sardonic ring in his own voice, but it seemed to make no impact on Mary.

"But the real danger is the next time. The second time you go out, away from here."

"There'll be a next time?"

She gave a jerky nod. "Of course."

"Okay." He let the word draw out. "So what do you need to warn me about for the next time?"

She leaned in close. "Don't tell her," she whispered to him. "Whatever you do, don't tell her. It will be hard, but you can't. Everything depends on it."

He frowned at her, resisting the urge to yank his arm away. "Don't tell who? Cassandra?"

Her eyes registered incomprehension, as if for a moment she didn't even know who he was talking about. "No, not Cassandra. This woman… I don't know her name. It doesn't matter what she calls herself. She threatened you, they all threatened you. Horrible threats. You have to hold steadfast."

That weird confusion about past and future again. A chill tingled the back of Soren's neck. "What can't I tell her?"

She looked up at him, her pale blue eyes flickering across his, then away. "Anything. Silence. The only thing that defeated them was silence."

"Why aren't you telling this to both Cassandra and me?" He looked over at the others, clustered near the front door. Only Dr. Quaice was looking back at Soren and Mary, frowning, whether with curiosity or concern was impossible to tell.

"She doesn't believe me. I can see that. It's obvious. She won't listen. But about the second warning, about remaining silent—she doesn't need to hear it. Doesn't affect her. This is for you." Her grip tightened, and she pulled him close, looking up into his eyes. "I'm sorry. I'm so, so sorry. But there's really nothing I can do that will make this any easier. I'd volunteer to go in your place, but it… it didn't happen that way. It was you both times. It was you the whole way."

"But you're not trying to talk me out of it."

She shook her head. "No. It wouldn't work anyway. You went, and that's that. It's more that I want you to be prepared. It won't stop it from happening as it happened, but at least you'll be more ready for it."

"I'll do the best I can, Mary."

She gave a quick, jerky nod. "That's all we can ask."

She let go of his sleeve suddenly, stepped back, and turned away. As he watched, she went to the back door and let herself out into Dr. Quaice's fenced yard, sitting down on a plastic chair underneath a fir tree.

Soren joined the others at the door.

"What the hell was that about?" Cassandra said.

"I honestly have no idea. Something about watching out for cats and how I'm not supposed to tell her anything."

"Her? Who is her?"

He shrugged. "She said I'd find out the next time we go out scouting. For this one, we just have to watch out for cats."

"That woman has a screw loose."

"You're not wrong."

"Even if this is some kind of precognition, I still don't trust her." Cassandra frowned toward the window looking out into the back yard. Mary looked forlorn, staring at nothing, a personification of emptiness and despair. "If she actually does see the future, it'd be a lot more helpful if she could tell us whether the bridge is crossable and save us the trip."

"She'd probably tell you that her foresight doesn't work that way."

"Convenient." She snorted, and adjusted her shoulder straps. "Well, enough delay. Let's do this. Lock and load."

McGilvra Boulevard was quiet and empty. The houses lining it, mostly beautifully-maintained homes with expanses of garden in full bloom, were—like Dr. Quaice's—dark, with curtains drawn, garage doors shut, no sign of life. There was no good cover without crossing onto private land, and most of that was lawn now in need of mowing but not offering much in the way of hedges or fences that could prevent them from being seen by hostile eyes.

In any case, who should they hide from? It was impossible to know. The houses' inhabitants might be ordinary folks trying to survive, just as they were, but the bands of LLA marauders now in control of large sections of Seattle could be anywhere. Chances were, the only reason Madison Park hadn't been attacked yet was the physical boundary of the Arboretum separating it from the rest of the city. But that couldn't be any more than a temporary thing. Sooner or later the LLA would see the wealthy subdivision as ripe for attack, if for no other reason than supplies and resources.

The quiet was not going to last. Not here, not anywhere.

Cassandra pointed to the left and they went down a side street that was at least marginally better from the standpoint of visibility. This took them directly toward the boundary of the Arboretum, and after a short walk during which they saw and heard no one, the wooded hills of the park became visible ahead.

"Stay on the trails, but continue generally northwest as much as possible," Cassandra whispered. "But I think Dr. Quaice's suggestion of avoiding the golf course is a good one. Two people traipsing across the green would be visible from a long way away."

Under the eaves of the trees, everything was peaceful. He could close his eyes and pretend he was in some tranquil park, far removed from any violence and chaos. But as they approached the northwestern boundary of the Arboretum, more disquieting sounds began to filter through. Intermittent fire of automatic weapons. Low booming noises. Farther along still, the thin, distant remnants of raised voices, torn apart by the breeze, rising and falling like some kind of spectral chorus. No words were audible, but it didn't take much imagination to hear violence, anger, and fear in the chaotic noise carried into the park by the cool spring air.

"Where's all that coming from?" Soren whispered, as the Arboretum parking lot appeared through the trunks of fir trees.

"Not as far away as it sounds." Cassandra gestured toward her left. "Voices don't carry that far. Volunteer Park, maybe Capitol Hill. This side of I-5, anyway. We need to be careful. As soon as we're out of the Arboretum, we should act as if we're visible for miles."

"We haven't seen anyone so far."

"Doesn't mean they haven't seen us. Spotting movement is easy. We haven't hit the dangerous parts yet. I'm not sure if it was luck or planning, but it's a good thing Quaice's house is in Madison Park. It's like a little island of peace, at least for now." She half-unshouldered her pack and pulled out the map. "Oh, for the days of Google Maps. Anyhow, let's get our route planned here so we don't need to stop and reconnoiter out in the open." She pointed toward a green space. "There's the main parking lot. That's straight ahead. If we can skirt around it to the north, we'll hit Foster Island Road. That'll take us west to Lake Washington Boulevard, which is the best access to the bridge head."

"We don't have to stick to the roads. We don't need to think like we're driving. Is there a better way without going along a major thoroughfare?"

She shook her head. "You're right, of course, but not this time. That whole bit of land, near the western end of the bridge, is marsh. Foster Island Road is mostly through trees at the north end of the Arboretum—no problem finding cover there. Lake Washington Boulevard will be trickier. Even so, it'll be better to follow the general line of the road, even if it's more dangerous. We want speed, here. Quick in, gather information, quick out."

They passed the main parking lot on their left. The piece of the visitor center that was visible was spray-painted over and over with the stylized, fanged face of the LLA logo. They'd been here, that was obvious, but there was no sign of them now. Through the trees were glimpses of the cars belonging to visitors and staff that had been there since the riots started. Where were the owners? Fled, holed up in a house somewhere? Dead by the side of some road? They, like the vandals, were gone.

Smart. Being outside in the Arboretum parking lot was a bad idea.

Foster Island Road was a short walk north, and when they went down a hill and out from under the trees, it seemed like a sudden revelation of where they were to the entire watching world. There were finally breaks in the cloud cover, blue streaks through the gray, and while sunshine would be a cheerful change from the omnipresent gray and drizzle, it felt to Soren like a searchlight trained on their position. They peered out from behind the trunks of fir trees, up and down the road.

Foster Island Road was a series of tight curves, so it was impossible to get much sight distance. Even in the short section of it they could see, there were four wrecked cars, one of them blackened and burned. The nearest one had silhouettes in the driver's and front passenger's seat that were almost certainly corpses, but he didn't want to confirm that by looking more closely.

They hugged the trees on the left side of the road. The broad sidewalk would have been easier walking but would leave them far more exposed. The sound of gunfire was louder now but more sporadic, as if whatever melée they'd heard earlier was dying down, at least for the moment. Ahead was the intersection with the main thoroughfare of Lake Washington Boulevard, leading to Highway 520 and the long span of the bridge.

At that point it would be nearly impossible to stay out of view. Not only was the Boulevard lined with houses—mansions, most of them, with a beautiful lake view, worth millions—but there was no way they could expect the comparative peace of Dr. Quaice's neighborhood and the meandering path of Foster Island Road. It was too near the heart of things, too exposed, too wealthy. Obvious targets.

Even expecting it, though, their first clear glimpse of the Boulevard was a shock. Soren stared, unmoving, as if his will simply would propel his feet no farther. Just north of the intersection was a multi-car pileup. It looked as if someone had barricaded the road with a makeshift wall of sawhorses, lawn furniture, and pieces of lumber, but someone—probably several someones—had tried to smash through. There were at least a dozen cars, most with shattered windshields, sitting at random angles and blocking the road more completely than any deliberate barrier would have. Bodies lay on the sidewalk, and the sickening stench of decay struck his nostrils. This calamity must have happened early on, and the corpses left where they'd fallen.

His gorge rose and he gagged, keeping his breakfast down with an effort.

Cassandra grasped his upper arm, her fingers digging into his triceps. "Center, Soren. Center. Don't stare, it makes it worse. Close your eyes, breathe through your mouth."

He followed her instructions without speaking, although closing his eyes brought images of enemies coming in from all sides, as if shutting his eyelids alerted them to the fact that he was standing there, uniquely visible, alone in being blind and unaware. But Cassandra was right—it steadied his nerves. His stomach settled into an uneasy grumble.

"You okay?" She'd dropped her voice to a near whisper.

He gave a quick nod and opened his eyes.

"It's a tossup which is the best way to proceed. The right side of the road is almost all open space and parkland. We'd be visible to anyone who glanced that way. The left side has more cover, but is nearer to houses if anyone is doing guard duty against looters. What do you think?"

He knew it was a courtesy, a formality—Cassandra was the type who was never without a plan and a strong opinion about why it was the right course of action. She was taking his focus away from the horror scene in front of them, giving his mind something to concentrate on other than the terrible knowledge that only a few weeks ago, these had been ordinary people leading ordinary lives, never realizing they were destined to be killed on the side of the road in their own home town.

And also turning him away from the reality that they might end up that way.

Mary, though, said they'd come back. She was sure about it. As dubious as he was about the psychic, both in terms of her alleged abilities and her peculiar personality, her certainty gave him something to hang on to. They'd make it back by evening.

As long as they could avoid the cats. Whatever the fuck that meant.

"I'd vote for the lake side. It's open, you're right, but even if that means we can be seen from farther away, we can see farther ourselves and have more warning if there's any danger nearby."

Cassandra nodded. "That's my thought as well. It does narrow when we get closer to the on-ramp to 520, but at that point we should get off the road entirely if we can and look for a vantage point to see the bridge. Going all the way to the on-ramp and then standing out in the middle of the road looking down the bridge with binoculars would be a pretty stupid move."

"Can't argue with that."

"You okay to keep moving?"

He took a deep breath. "As long as I don't have to get too close to… all that."

"Sounds like a good idea to me."

They crossed to the north side of the road, closer to the still waters of Lake Washington that they could just glimpse between the trunks of trees. Soren had to steel himself not to look more closely at the scene of carnage near the intersection. The smell was bad enough, and the one glance he'd taken was sufficient to fuel weeks' worth of nightmares.

Fortunately, past the pileup it wasn't as bad. There were

cars in the middle of the street, some with windshields and windows bashed in, but the doors were open and it looked as if the owners had fled. Strangers or not, he hoped they'd gotten to safety, and weren't some of the limp, lifeless bodies now receding behind them.

In the distance was the snarl where Lake Washington Boulevard met Highway 520, angling to the right and turning into the long, slender expanse of the Evergreen Point Floating Bridge. There was another car pileup right at the intersection, probably explaining why there was no movement nearby. If it was as horrific as the one they'd just passed, it would be about as effective a "Keep Out" sign as he could imagine.

Fortunately, there'd be no need to go that far. Between them and the lakeshore was an increasingly narrow triangle of land, with only scattered trees and a low stone wall to obstruct their view of the lake and the bridge. The only unsettling part was another fanged LLA logo someone had spray-painted on the wall. After a ten-minute walk, Cassandra motioned silently for him to follow her across a grassy field and up to a chain-link fence with a sign saying, "Washington State Department of Transportation Property. No Trespassing. Violators Will Be Prosecuted."

She shrugged, muttered, "Prosecute away, my friend," and after jiggling the latch on the gate and confirming it was locked, climbed over in one quick, graceful motion.

Soren followed, a little more clumsily, and they continued their walk downhill, moving past the trees until they had a clear view of the long, low line of the bridge, and a scraggly hedgerow to at least partly shield them from view if anyone was on the road behind them.

Cassandra sat on the ground, unshouldered her pack, and pulled out the binoculars. After a quick adjustment of the focus, she peered along the part of it they could see, from the descending slope coming off the on-ramp down onto the water-level surface of the bridge floating on its enormous concrete pontoons.

"Looks fragile, doesn't it?" Cassandra said. "Like a touch would snap it in two."

"I always get creeped out crossing it on a windy day. Being on a bridge and having waves crest over the railing is a little unnerving."

She nodded, and handed him the binoculars. "The I-90 bridge actually did collapse, you know. I think it was back around 1990. They were doing maintenance, and a storm blew up suddenly, making the watertight doors on one of the pontoons fail. The pontoon filled with water and sank, bringing a big piece of the bridge with it. I've seen photos and video clips. It doesn't look real—this huge slab of concrete tilting upward then sliding underwater like the sinking of the *Titanic*."

"How earthquake-proof is that thing?"

"Probably not very. When it was built they didn't know how earthquake-prone Seattle is. I remember reading some kind of exposé—I think it was in *The New Yorker*—when I was in graduate school. It said that geologists have been holding their breath for a while waiting for the Cascadia Subduction Zone to rupture. And when it does, it could bring down half the city. Then, what doesn't fall down from the quake would get destroyed by the tsunami fifteen minutes later."

"Cheerful."

Cassandra's mouth twitched a little. "Yeah, well, I'll take natural disasters over what humans do to each other any day of the week."

Soren scanned along the bridge. As they'd guessed, it was clogged with cars and debris. How many of the cars had been set there deliberately to stop traffic and how many were accidentally caught fleeing was impossible to tell. A little farther along the span was movement, small human figures walking along the edge with uncertain purpose. At least two of them he could see had some sort of large gun slung over their shoulders.

Not encouraging.

"They're guarding the bridge. It's not going to be easy to get out that way."

"Don't think it'll be easy to get out *any* way. But it makes sense from their perspective. The two bridges are bottlenecks preventing anyone from getting out to the east. Block those two, and you've effectively stopped anyone from leaving unless they walk the entire length of the city northward or southward."

"If we could get past that pileup right at the west end, it looks clearer farther out."

"If."

"I know." He handed the binoculars back. "It's like saying handling a lion is easy except for their teeth and claws."

She gave a low chuckle. "That's accurate. In any case, I think we've seen enough. We've confirmed what we suspected." She looked up, frowning. "And the sound of gunfire is getting closer. We should get back to safety."

"No argument from me."

Cassandra shoved the binoculars back into her pack, and after taking a sip of water from her water bottle, shouldered her pack and stood. The open space between them and Lake Washington Boulevard still showed no signs of movement. They climbed the fence and went back uphill toward the road, stopping several times to look for danger.

Nothing.

Retracing their steps would mean going past the horrific scene of carnage they'd passed earlier. There was no easy way around it. It was still a good twenty minutes' walk ahead, but Soren was already steeling himself. He'd never thought of himself as having a weak stomach, or an unrealistic attitude about the violence the human race was prone to. But confronted with it, here and now, in the peaceful and wealthy suburbs of his adopted home town, was beyond his ability to process. Dozens dying by the roadside, killed by people who only a month ago had been their friends, neighbors, coworkers.

The breakdown of the social order. If Quaice was right, this was only the beginning. It'd get worse before it got better.

A lot worse.

The first signs of the wreckage appeared as they rounded a gentle curve in the road. Soren took a deep breath. Nearer were two other cars, both fancy sports cars, angled across the road, one of them with its front wheels up on the sidewalk. Both had open doors and smashed-in windows, and lying alongside was a long piece of two-by-four that had obviously been used to do the damage. Cassandra was ahead, and edged her way around the nearest car, a sleek black Jaguar.

Sad to see such a beautiful machine destroyed and abandoned. But car travel was going to be impossible for a while, not only because of the road blockages, but because of gas running out. It was a shame, but at present owning a Jag was about as useless as anything he could think of.

He brushed his fingertips along the car's hood. And that's when his eyes landed on the hood ornament.

A shiny, chrome-covered figure of a leaping cat.

It's cats. Look out for cats. When you see a cat, the danger will be behind you.

Soren felt a clench in the pit of his stomach, and started to turn. There was a sudden movement toward him, so fast his brain didn't even register it, then the razor-sharp tip of a hunting knife caught his shirt and slit a long rent in the side. He cried out, stumbling backward and almost falling. In front of him was an elderly man, unshaven, clad in a dirty t-shirt and sweat pants. He had a crazed look in his eyes.

"Looters," he wheezed out. "Fucking looters. Can't have it, it's mine, you can't take what's mine." He slashed out again with the knife, making Soren take another step back.

His heel caught on the piece of two-by-four and now he did fall, landing in a seated position in the road.

The old man's eyes glittered, and he gave Soren a vicious smile. "Gotcha."

Cassandra turned and sprinted toward them, shouting out something incomprehensible. It distracted the attacker enough for Soren to scoot away on his butt and then scramble to his feet, holding the piece of two-by-four like a club.

Cassandra yelled, "We're not looters, back off!"

It had no effect on the man's behavior. He reversed his grip on the knife, to stab rather than slash downward, and took two steps toward her, leering.

"You're kinda pretty. Sorry I gotta mess you up." He advanced on her, jabbing at her wildly, but for the moment had his back turned to Soren.

Almost without thought, Soren brought the two-by-four up, and yelled, "Leave her alone!"

The man began to pivot back to facing him, mingled fury and confusion in his eyes. "Whadja say?"

Soren took two quick steps forward and swung his weapon like a baseball bat, putting his considerable upper body strength into it. The blow caught the old man on the side of the head with a sickening crunch. His body was knocked sideways and toppled, and the knife flew from his hand to clatter onto the sidewalk.

He didn't move again.

Soren stared at the prone figure of the attacker. The words *I just killed a man* ricocheted through his brain. And then he fell to his knees and his breakfast did come up. He retched over and over, coughing and gagging, and Cassandra knelt by him with her hand resting gently on his back.

Once the paroxysms of vomiting had passed, he sat up, breathing hard, and wiped the back of one hand across his mouth.

"It's okay, Soren," Cassandra said. "You had to do it."

Soren shook his head and looked up at her, bleary-eyed.

"No," he croaked out. "It's not okay. It will never be okay."

He looked around at the scene surrounding them, the darkened and silent houses, the crashed cars and dead bodies a little farther down the road, the lake with its line of guarded, impassible bridge barely visible through the trees. And in front of him, the dead attacker, whose body would be left here like the others.

Left for the scavengers. Left to rot.

He struggled his way to his feet. She gave his shoulder a quick squeeze.

"Let's get going."

He nodded and silently followed her, past the Jaguar and the other sports car, toward the much larger pileup near the intersection with Foster Island Road.

Is that what was going to become of them all? Kill or be killed? Would smashing an attacker's head become okay to them, a sad necessity, but nothing to lose sleep over?

In only a few short weeks the world had turned into a place he'd never imagined. But what was he turning into?

In another month, a year, ten years, would any of them be recognizable?

twenty-four

. . .

"That's what I was afraid of." Dr. Quaice's voice was somber.

"Why do they want to stop people from leaving?" Gavin said. "With food running out, it seems like the LLA would say, 'Go ahead, take off if you think you can make it somewhere else, and good riddance.' Fewer people means more food for the ones still here."

"Nothing they've done makes sense." Mary seemed to be teetering on the edge of the shaking nervous wreck she'd been the first night here. Her relief that Soren and Cassandra returned unharmed, and that her premonition about cats had likely saved their lives, was once more giving way to the hopelessness of the situation as a whole.

"I don't think we should give up," Cassandra said. "They can't guard the bridge 24/7. And my guess is sooner or later they'll get tired of watching it, and turn their attention to more pressing matters like getting food themselves. The good news is that past the first blockade the rest of the bridge looks wide open. We get over the hurdle on the west end, then it's a clear run."

"A clear two-kilometer run." Gavin gave her an uneasy

look. "I suspect anyone who was set to guard the bridge will be able to run faster than I can. I'm no athlete."

"Whatever happens, we're not leaving anyone behind." Dr. Quaice's tone was unequivocal. "Even if that means we all stay put until we have another option."

Mary shook her head and looked down, but said nothing.

After another five minutes of discussing, and with nothing further decided, they all dispersed—Mary back outside, Gavin to the armchair, Cassandra to the sofa. Dr. Quaice touched Soren's shoulder and gave a jerk of the head, then turned toward his study. Soren followed, and once in the room, Dr. Quaice shut the door behind them.

"You're gonna be all right, Conover?"

"I don't even begin to know how to answer that."

The older man frowned. "I asked if you were going to be all right, not whether you were unaffected. All right means you can deal with what happened even if it was terrible. All right means you're choosing to survive rather than collapse."

Their gazes met. "I'm honestly not sure which way it's going to go."

"That's a fair answer. But you've got more strength and toughness than you know. Taking someone's life won't ever be a pleasant choice, but I think it's one we're going to have to face more than once before this is over."

"I don't feel tough. I feel like a pampered academic who's lived the easy life." He shook his head. "I read the news, you know? I read about places like Syria and the Congo and North Korea, where you aren't safe anywhere, any time. You say goodbye to your family, you get on a bus, you head to work, it's never out of your mind that you could die. Me? I've never known real danger. I've never known shortage or hunger. I always thought I'd be able to go to the grocery store and find fresh food in nice clean plastic packaging. Come home after work to my nice quiet house, spend the evening with my partner, all peaceful and calm and always the same.

Everything you read about, it seems unreal until you experience it, until you're dropped into the middle of it. Then it's real. Then you find out if you're one of the survivors—or one of the ones that collapses."

"I'd say the fact you killed your attacker to protect yourself and Cassandra puts you in the category of survivor."

Soren shrugged. "I hope so. I puked my guts up afterward, though."

Dr. Quaice chuckled. "Like I said, all right doesn't mean unaffected. I'd be more concerned if you'd killed the guy then just dusted yourself off and said, 'Okay, let's go.'"

"I never thought I'd kill someone. Hell, I can't even kill spiders. I pick them up and put them outside."

"We never know what we're capable of, for good or bad, until the time comes."

There was a pause, and the only sound was birds twittering in the bushes outside Dr. Quaice's study window. Stop, close your eyes, and it all seemed so ordinary. Then open your eyes, and it all comes crashing back that nothing will ever be the same again.

"So what now? Mary said we were going to go on a second scouting expedition, but I'm not sure what more that'd accomplish."

"She saw that, did she?"

"Yes. She said there was some sort of danger to me in particular."

"Danger from what?"

"It was her usual vague pronouncements. Something about a woman and how she could only be defeated by silence."

Dr. Quaice gave an annoyed snort. "Damn psychics. She's as bad as Nostradamus. Says something obscure, then after the fact says, 'Yes, that's what I was talking about.'"

"She was right about the cat."

"Okay, I'll give her that. But you have to admit you'd have

reacted a lot faster if she'd said, 'If you see a black Jaguar, there'll be a guy with a knife standing behind you.' Are you concerned about her prediction of your being in danger?"

"I'd be lying if I said I'm dismissing it entirely. For what it's worth, she didn't say I was going to die. By implication, I was going to come out on top somehow."

"By staying silent."

"Yes."

Dr. Quaice frowned thoughtfully for a moment. "There's no reason you'd have to go on any subsequent outings."

"I know. But I also know Cassandra and I are in the best shape to run. Or to fight, although I hope it doesn't come to that because my last fight was with a bully in seventh grade and I had a black eye for the next week. If it's anything where speed is important, Cassandra and I are the obvious choices."

"Agreed. But there's nowhere to go immediately. Based on what you saw, we couldn't get all five of us across the bridge alive as things stand. Tonight after dinner I'll do some more reconnoitering over the network and see if I can come up with another idea of how to proceed."

But three more days passed, and there was no change except the basement shelves were now empty.

"We've got maybe till the end of the week," Dr. Quaice said. "Then we have to find food. I'm flat-out astonished the power is still on. I guess the LLA thought ahead enough at least not to bomb the hydropower. That bodes well for the quality of any food we might find, but at the moment the main concern is quantity."

"Where do we look that won't already have been stripped bare?" Cassandra spoke what was in Soren's mind, but that he'd been reluctant to say. Finding a new source of food seemed at the moment as impossible as crossing the bridge.

"We waited too long," Gavin said in a defeated voice.

Dr. Quaice gave a harsh sigh. "You're not wrong."

Soren gave the older man an astonished look. Surely he had a plan? He had foreseen this twenty years ago. How could he not have thought ahead about the most basic of human needs?

"I'm still in contact with the network. The random violence has died down, at least near the University District, Capitol Hill, and Queen Anne. There's no word from downtown. It seems to be entirely in the hands of the LLA. Same up on the north end of the city. Just silence. But one by one, we're losing people from the network. Whether they've been killed or captured, or stopped transmitting for some other reason, I don't know. But everywhere I'm hearing the same thing. Food is running out. People have gone from working together to get supplies where they're needed to every man for himself." He gave a mirthless laugh. "It's amazing how thin the veneer of civilized behavior is. Underneath we're just another species of animal doing whatever it takes to survive."

As always, Cassandra seemed uninterested in philosophy. "Okay, grocery stores are the obvious targets that would get picked off first, but other places would have stores of food. Schools, churches, hospitals, even museums that have cafeterias. They can't all be emptied out this quickly."

"It'll mean another scouting trip."

Mary looked up sharply, not at Dr. Quaice who had spoken, but at Soren, then just as quickly lowered her gaze again.

"We'd have to go a lot farther afield," Soren said. "The last time was a quick, fairly short walk. This would require covering a lot more ground. It'll be risky."

He met Cassandra's eyes, and she gave a little nod. "I don't see that we have much choice."

Mary stood suddenly enough that Soren startled. She opened her mouth as if she were going to speak, then shut it again. The whole time she kept her gaze locked on Soren's, as if no one else were in the room.

She turned on her heel and strode toward the kitchen and the door into the back yard. There was the sound of a door opening and closing.

"What the hell is wrong with her?" Cassandra's usually impassive face registered annoyance bordering on anger. "Did she get a funny sensation in her little toe, and now she knows which of us is going to die first?"

"I'm a lot less likely to discount what she says since her warning very likely saved my life," Soren said. "If I hadn't reacted when I did, I'd have gotten a knife in the back instead of just a ruined t-shirt."

"Be nice if she could tell us where to find food." She still sounded dubious. "I'm not saying she doesn't have some ability I don't understand. What I don't like is the histrionics. How about giving us the information she has without doing the whole mystical psychic thing?"

"I'd better go talk to her." Soren stood. "I got the impression she knows something she's not saying."

Cassandra made a scoffing noise. "Like I said. She's not the Oracle of Delphi, or something, sitting in her cave and waiting for her devotees to bring offerings. Whatever she's doing, whatever the source of her knowledge is, she's just another human being. Like Dr. Quaice said, another animal trying to survive."

Soren went out through the kitchen and into the back yard. It was still and foggy, droplets of dew hanging from every leaf and every fir needle. The kind of damp chill that could persist in western Washington well into June, and which would return with a vengeance in October.

Despite that, Mary sat in the plastic lawn chair, her head turned away from him, even though she must have heard him approaching.

"Mary?"

She still didn't turn, but spoke in a low, uninflected voice so different from her usual cheer that it sounded as if it came from a different person.

"I wish they didn't hate me, but I can't help being who I am. Knowing what I know. I didn't choose this."

"I don't think they hate you."

Her head pivoted toward him, but her expression was still blank. "I'm not one of you. I'm the outsider."

"We just work together…"

She shook her head. "It's not that. Or, it's more than that. I can try to be part of the group, but I can't keep it up. I've never found making friends easy, but in the weeks since I changed, it's impossible. I've taken a leap into the void, and everyone has become a stranger. When I look at people, I know things I shouldn't know, that there's no way I *could* know. Some of them bad things. Can you imagine it?" She gave a faint smile, her eyes still focused on the middle distance, on some point in the fog. "Imagine knowing, knowing for certain, that your next door neighbor was going to die in three days. Seeing it as clearly as if it were right in front of you, as if you'd seen it happen. Because you *did* see it happen. After you endured kind of thing, over and over and over, wouldn't you learn to self-protect?"

"I suppose I would. Truthfully, I can't imagine it."

"No. You can't. I've heard people say they wished they knew the future, but they don't understand what they're asking for." She frowned, and turned her pale blue eyes on Soren's. "Why did you come outside?"

"More than one reason. One of them was to check on you. You seemed upset."

"That was kind of you."

"Also, what was it you saw? You realized something when we were talking about going to search for food. If you have information, you should tell us, even if it's bad."

"These days, it's all bad."

"No argument."

She didn't speak for a moment, then seemed to come to some kind of decision. "I already said there'd be a danger, danger to you specifically."

"Yes."

"I could see…" She passed one hand across her face. "I see you. They're hurting you. You're such a gentle person. I can't stand seeing you hurt." Tears formed in her eyes, but she seemed unaware of them.

"Will they kill me?"

"No. No, you didn't die there. You didn't die in Seattle."

A shudder twanged its way up Soren's spine. It was bad enough hearing her talking about his death, but referring to it as if it had already happened was downright terrifying.

"But they hurt me."

"Yes."

"How bad?"

"Bad enough to change you. That's what I saw when I was in the house. What happened to you on this raid—what you see—you'll never be the same man again."

"Will I find Finn?" The question blurted out of him before he could think to stop it.

Her face relaxed into a smile. "You love him very much, don't you?"

"I've never loved anyone more. He's my world. I just wish I'd told him…" He shrugged. To voice the rest of it would have been to risk tears again.

"He realizes it. I'm sure he realizes."

"But will I ever see him again?"

"I know… I know that you got another chance to tell him you love him."

So Finn was still alive, out there in the city somewhere. It should have been reassuring, but why had Mary phrased it that way? That'd he'd get another chance to say "I love you"? Unbidden, an image came to him, an image of himself sitting on the ground cradling Finn in his arms, stroking his hair, telling him that he loved him… and holding him as he died.

He stopped himself short. He wasn't psychic, and any troubling visions he conjured up came from his imagination, not from knowledge of the future. He took a deep breath before he spoke again. "By 'a chance' do you mean a moment? Will we have a life together, or only meet long enough to say goodbye?"

She paused, and her eyes searched his face."You both made it across the bridge."

He let out a long breath.

Her expression turned bleak again. "After that, I can't see anything."

There was a long pause, during which the only sound was the droplets of condensation dripping from the branches of the Douglas fir tree.

"Where should we go to find food?" Soren finally asked.

"Cassandra was right. Schools. School cafeterias."

"Which school? Seattle must have two dozen of them."

Mary frowned, and again seemed to be looking into the fog, seeing something Soren couldn't.

"I don't know the name of it. Set in some trees, near a park. It's one of the places they haven't broken into yet."

"Which school are you talking about? Damn near everything in Seattle is near a park and some trees." He suddenly found himself understanding why Cassandra got so impatient with her.

"I don't know the name of it. But it's between the park and I-5. She'll find it."

"She?"

"Cassandra."

"Not me?"

"No."

Reluctant understanding came to him. "Because by then I'll already have been captured."

A quick nod.

"Should I just stay here? Let the others go?"

Now a panicked look came into her eyes. "No. You have to go. I'm sorry, but you *have* to. When the time comes, you can't resist it or run away. I know running toward danger doesn't make sense. But trust me, I see it as clearly as if it were in front of me right now, and that's exactly what you have to do. If you hadn't gone, if you hadn't seen the risk and plunged forward anyhow, you'd never have seen Finn again. And the two of you must be together."

"Must be?" He was certain she didn't mean Love Will Triumph. Whatever else could be said about Mary's pronouncements, they didn't err on the side of romantic optimism.

"You'd never connect otherwise. Then Finn would have had no way of getting out… before…" Her voice trailed off.

"Before what?"

She locked gazes with him again. "Before it's all destroyed. What we've seen so far is only the start. Soon it will all be gone."

"And there's no way around my being captured and… tortured?" She hadn't used the word, and saying it aloud sounded like the ominous clang of a bell. "You warned me about the man with the knife. The cat, remember? Why can't I avoid this?"

"That's different." She pressed her knuckles to her forehead, wincing as if she were in pain. "How can I explain it to you? What I see… to me, it already happened. It's there ahead of me, ahead of you, ahead of everyone, just like a stretch of the road you haven't come to yet. You're not creating the way as you go, you're merely traveling a road already laid out before you." She grabbed his forearm with such speed that it was an effort not to pull away. "You can endure this, Soren. It's terrible but you can endure it. Remember, go toward the danger, not away from it. You'll have to do it more than once, however crazy it sounds. And when she talks to you, stay silent. That's the only thing that will work, even if it seems otherwise. Don't resist capture, don't run away—but don't trust her, and don't tell her what she wants to know."

"That scares the shit out of me."

"I know. I'm sorry." She squeezed his forearm, then let go.

"I'm a complete wuss about pain."

"That's okay. Just keep focused on the fact that you love Finn more than you fear being hurt."

He nodded. "I hope I can do that. I've never been tested."

"None of us have."

"You should come back inside. It's chilly out here."

She gave him a wan smile. "I don't mind. I'll be in shortly. Don't worry about me."

"All right." He paused. "And thanks."

When he returned indoors, three faces turned toward him, all with questioning expressions. He couldn't bring himself to tell them about Mary's warning—it felt too much like the old superstitious belief that speaking something would make it inevitable.

"She's okay. She's just struggling like the rest of us."

Dr. Quaice nodded. "I'm concerned about her mental health."

Cassandra was unexpectedly supportive. "It's no surprise she's struggling. As frustrated as I am with her sometimes, we need to help each other through this, not only physically but mentally. She's not the only one who will be at risk of emotional collapse over the next weeks. This is untrodden ground for the vast majority of us."

Time to change the subject. "When do you want to go on a food search?"

But this question brought up another. *When will you be ready to offer yourself up to torture in order to find Finn?*

When he was a child, he'd been terrified of the dentist. When he had an appointment, even for a cleaning, he'd start worrying about it as soon as he knew, and by the day of the appointment he'd have worked himself up to a state of near panic. His parents quickly realized that the lead-up was worse than the experience itself, and took to telling him about dentists' appointments only an hour or two before they were scheduled. It was a shock every time, but at least one of short duration.

He'd learned from that to get unpleasant things over with as quickly as possible. The worry about what could happen was almost always worse than what did.

Here, though—torture? He couldn't even watch torture scenes in movies. The thought of what he would undergo, if Mary's prediction was correct, made his stomach turn a lazy flip.

How bad would the pain be?

Bad enough to change you… You'll never be the same man again.

He took a deep breath as Dr. Quaice responded to his question.

"We can't do it today. It's too late in the day to start. I'll cast about on the network tonight and see how things look. We can use that information to plan your route. Until then, relax and recover. We've got food enough for at least a couple more days." He gave Soren a frowning glance, as if he guessed more about what Mary had said than he was letting on. "We've got to make as rational a decision as we can manage, given all the information we have."

Soren dozed on the couch after dinner. Gavin, Mary, and Cassandra had already retreated to their sleeping quarters— the little room that served as a library, the capacious but unfinished attic, and the spare bedroom, respectively. His awareness came back slowly at the sound of raised voices, voices he was at first unsure weren't a dream.

One of the voices was Dr. Quaice, and the others were clearly from the network, and had the flat, mechanical quality of human speech rendered by cheap speakers. It was all spoken in Kalila, too fast for Soren to decipher completely, but he picked up the verbs *leave* and *flee* and a word he thought meant *urgent* or *immediately*. Dr. Quaice was arguing, at first vigorously, but then with alarming suddenness, his tone sounded resigned, defeated.

"Shúnelsar ké súemne."

I will tell them.

Silence.

After a moment, Dr. Quaice walked out of the study. His face was ashen.

"Soren. Can you… can you get the others?"

The older man collapsed into a chair.

Soren came back minutes later followed by the others. Gavin was blinking groggily—he'd been sound asleep. Cassandra looked curious, Mary apprehensive.

He wondered if Mary already knew what Dr. Quaice was going to say.

"I'm… sorry," the older man said. "I thought we'd have longer." He swallowed, and rubbed his eyes with a weary gesture. "The LLA has been intercepting the broadcasts between the members of the network, and realized that it was being used to avoid raids and coordinate food drops. They can't understand the words, of course, and it's suspected that one of the network members was captured and induced to explain." He paused. "It's unlikely that even in that case, the LLA could learn Kalila quickly enough to translate what they hear, but what seems certain is that somehow they found out that I'm coordinating it all, and they want it to stop. Apparently I'm a wanted man."

"So you're saying…" Gavin looked from one of the assembled group to another.

Dr. Quaice nodded. "Once they have my name, finding out where I live is as easy as opening up a telephone directory. We have to leave. Tonight. If it's already not too late."

twenty-five

. . .

They each had only a small amount of personal belongings to get together. Dr. Quaice had given changes of clothes to the others early on, but they were so large for both Cassandra and Mary that they only used them when their own single set of clothes was in the wash. But each of them packed up as much as they could fit in their backpacks.

Dr. Quaice disassembled the shortwave radio with quick, practiced motions. He obviously had done this many times before. Knowing him, it was in preparation for just such an eventuality. The whole thing came apart in minutes and was stowed into waiting carrying bags, then added to the pile of packs at the front door.

"When I left my office at the University I felt pretty certain I'd never be back," Dr. Quaice said to Soren. "It didn't affect me much emotionally, even though I worked there for over thirty years. But this house..." He gave a gesture. "Leaving it feels so different. It's like losing my anchor. After that, the current can take you anywhere it wants."

"Where will we go?" Gavin asked.

"That I don't know." Dr. Quaice pulled on his pack, then

looped the antenna bag over his shoulder. Cassandra had offered to take the heavier console in addition to her own pack, and Quaice had acquiesced without arguing. The older man was going to have enough of a struggle as it was.

"Do you have an idea for a direction, at least?" Cassandra asked.

He frowned. "Maybe due west. Cut across the south end of the Arboretum. If we aim right, we could stay in parkland, which at least gives us some hope of cover—first Interlaken Park then Volunteer Park. They almost share a boundary at one point."

"But staying out of sight isn't our only problem."

"No. Finding shelter is the big one. That and finding food. The network said that things had quieted down some in general, which is hopeful. Andy Sirrine, my contact in Capitol Hill, said that there'd been fewer people of all sorts in the streets last week—LLA, raiders, roving bands of thieves, and what-have-you."

"Their motivation doesn't make much difference at this point."

"No. But any of them are potentially dangerous, so lower activity of all sorts is good news."

"Might your friend have room for us?" Gavin asked.

"Only very temporarily. He lives in a small apartment. Top floor, which is probably how he's escaped notice. He's scoured the building for food—enough of the apartments were empty that breaking-and-entering has kept him from starving, and he hasn't had to go outside and risk getting killed. He might be able to hide us for a day or two, but going to his place isn't a long-term solution. I'd still like to head that direction first."

"If we're followed, it could get him killed," Gavin said.

"True. We can't help that, though. I'd like to talk to him before we settle into the longer-term problem of finding an empty house somewhere. It's lucky in a way that the attacks started when they did. A lot of people were already at work, and we have a better chance of finding a place that's not occupied."

He opened the door quietly, peered out, and glanced up and down the street. Empty. The barricades at the north and south end were intact, and anyone still in their home was staying out of sight.

A peaceful haven, but not to be trusted any longer. If the LLA was as eager to find Dr. Quaice as he'd implied, the tranquility in Madison Park wasn't going to last much longer.

The shadows were already lengthening as evening approached, and there were clouds on the horizon that presaged rain. The temperature was dropping. A late-season cold front. It made it all the more critical to find shelter. A cold, wet night was an unpleasant prospect, and if it really got cold, it could be a dangerous one.

They walked out onto the sidewalk, stepping silently, their movements stealthy and guarded. There was no need to caution them to be wary. The danger was all too real. Soren thought again of the horrific scene they'd come across on the outing that morning, and with a shudder of anxiety, pictured himself sprawled dead on the roadside somewhere.

But no, Mary had said he'd survive at least long enough to see Finn again and get across the bridge. He had to hold onto that thought. It was the only thing that would impel him to do what she'd said he had to do—run toward the danger instead of away from it.

He was so deeply lost in thought about Mary's odd prophecies that when the attack came, at first Soren had no idea what was happening. They hadn't even walked half a block. From a quiet, if tense, peace, the night was shattered by shouts and footsteps pounding the pavement. Beams of high-intensity flashlights swung in their direction, drawing crazy loops on sidewalks and houses.

"That's them!" a voice called.

Another yelled, "Take 'em alive! He wants 'em alive, and it's our skins if we don't do it!"

So this was it. The thought *I'm not ready, I thought I'd have more time* skittered through his head. But perhaps, like his childhood fear of dentists, it was better this way. If this was going to happen the way Mary predicted, best to get it over with.

Soren took a deep breath, and bellowed, "Run! Scatter!"

Mary turned her head and locked eyes with him for a split second, then pivoted and ran. Cassandra had already taken Gavin and Dr. Quaice by the arms and vanished into the shadows. Soren closed his eyes for a moment. The thought *Maybe I should say a prayer* flitted through his brain and away. He opened his eyes wide, took a deep breath, and ran toward the lights, which were now less than twenty meters away.

Whatever the attackers expected, it wasn't having someone sprint toward them. He covered the remaining distance in seconds, and plowed right into one of them, knocking him off his feet. The man went over backwards and there was a sickening crack as his head hit the street. Soren grappled with another of them, a broad-chested man with a stocking cap, but in short order he was pulled away and had his arms pinioned behind his back.

He continued to struggle, but whoever held him knew how to do it. His arm was yanked upward, and he yelped in pain as it twisted the muscles in his shoulder.

"Clay, Lachman, Boland, go after the others. At least find Quaice. He's the one who's wanted. If the others get away, we can always lie about how many there were. They'd probably be worthless to us anyhow, and a nuisance to deal with."

Three men, their features invisible in the darkness, peeled off silently, running in the direction the others had fled.

"Abbott, how's Nordin?"

A man who was hunched over the attacker Soren had

knocked down looked up. "Unconscious. He's alive. I don't know how bad he's hurt."

"We have to leave him."

"We leave him, he's a dead man."

"He may die anyhow. It's the risk we take every time we go out. We don't have enough people to carry him back. If he can't get there under his own power, those are the breaks." The spokesman gave Soren's arm another jerk. "We got one of 'em, at least. If we can make him talk, it'll be worth it."

"You think he knows their code?"

"He'll tell us if he does. Voluntarily, or with some encouragement."

The other man gave an ugly laugh.

"All right, let's go. We need to move. The longer we stand here, the more opportunities we're giving them to attempt a daring rescue. You still have the rope?"

There was a rustling noise as the other pulled off a backpack and rummaged around in it. Quickly and efficiently Soren's wrists were tied behind him, the other end of the rope held by his captor.

"All right. Don't try to run. I've got a good hold of this. Be a good doggie and heel, and you'll get back to home base and still have all your teeth."

An hour later, Soren's captors—he still had not gotten a good look at their faces—dragged him along, yanking at the rope that tied his hands every time he slowed or stumbled. He was exhausted, so this was often. A cold rain fell, and his light windbreaker was insufficient to keep him from getting soaked and chilled to the bone. One of the two men snarled, "Move your fucking feet," after Soren tripped on a curb and almost face-planted, and he snapped back, "Sounds like you're afraid of something. Need to get off the street quickly? You're not the biggest dogs in the yard?"

This earned him a fast backhand across the face, and he tasted blood. Then another yank on the rope, and the three of them went down the shadowed street at a near run.

They'd crossed the Arboretum into a neighborhood, but between the darkness and his fear he lost track of where they were. At one point they crossed under the twin spans of I-5, but the interstate ran the entire length of the city from north to south, so that gave him little information. They seemed to be heading in the general direction of downtown. The closer they got the worse the conditions of the streets were. Few of the buildings they passed had intact windows. The façades were riddled with bullet holes. More than one had been entirely destroyed, leaving nothing but chunks of concrete and pieces of lumber and siding spilled out into the road.

He'd known this level of destruction was likely, but still, seeing it was like a punch in the gut. How quickly everything had gone to hell.

Another hour of walking. The hiss of rain, the sound of his footsteps and those of his captors, the sound of his own teeth chattering.

As they got closer to the city center, there were people out, more people than he'd seen in weeks. Running, some chasing, others being chased. Shouting, screams of pain and fear. Gunshots and the sound of fists striking flesh.

No one approached the three of them, however. Four of the rioters, their genders unknowable beneath thick layers of clothing, got close, took one look at Soren's captor's face, sprinted away, and disappeared around a corner.

Apparently this man was known by sight, and feared.

This made Soren considerably less hopeful about his fate.

Was it midnight yet? The front had passed, and the temperature was falling. The clouds were clearing away fast, but the rain had done its insidious work. Not a stitch of clothing he wore was dry. Despite his exertion, the combination of cold and adrenaline left Soren shivering uncontrollably. After another half-hour of increasingly difficult and uneven walking, they ducked into a doorway. The door itself was a twisted ruin, hanging by one hinge. They squeezed past it, one of his captors in front, one behind. Inside was in deep shadow, but from a desk behind a partition and what looked like the remains of a potted plant, it must have been some sort of office before the collapse.

"Bring him up right away?" one of them whispered.

"No." This from the one who had hit him. "Tie him up and leave him to contemplate his fate for a while. It'll make him more cooperative when the time comes. They'll get him when they're ready for him." The man reached into Soren's hip pocket and pulled out his wallet. "Look, he's got ID. At least we won't have to piss away time trying to figure out who he is."

At that, he was dragged off into a side room. An overturned table and three dirty plastic chairs were visible in the pale, silvery moonlight coming in through the only window, set high in the far wall. Too high, he realized, to provide any kind of reasonable means of escape. Even if he reached it somehow, he'd have to break it and maneuver his way through it without cutting himself to shreds.

Last resort, possibly.

He was pushed roughly into one of the chairs, and the rope tying his hands undone then quickly re-knotted behind him and through the metal frame. Two more pieces secured his ankles to the chair legs. He got a good look at one of his captors—a lean, haggard, desperate face, wide eyes in an angry stare, unwashed hair in a snarl. All that was in a flash as the man stepped into the narrow beam of moonlight, then was gone, disappeared back into the shadows.

Of his other captor, he got barely a glimpse.

Without another word, the two who had abducted him left

the room. They closed the door behind them, and Soren heard the sound of a piece of furniture dragged across the floor, presumably to block his exit if he were to get loose from his bonds.

They were taking no chances.

Once their footsteps receded, silence flooded the room.

He took a deep breath. Now that they knew his name, would they know who he was, and his connection to Dr. Quaice? He could easily imagine they'd think if he was Quaice's associate, he must know the conlang, too. It explained why they'd captured him instead of just killing him. Why waste time dragging along someone of no value? Abducting him spoke to some kind of utility they thought he had.

The only possible reason was they'd assumed either he knew where Quaice was, or he knew how to speak Kalila. Would they believe him if he told them he had no idea where Quaice and the others had fled? Quaice had intended to connect with his friend in Capitol Hill, and Soren even remembered the man's name. Andy Sirrine. So any denial of that knowledge would be an outright lie. His captors had asked about the "code"—surely meaning Kalila—but the truth was he only had a rudimentary knowledge of the conlang, not nearly enough to do more than guess at it when it was spoken by someone fluent.

But would they believe that?

Probably not. The Lacklanders hadn't gotten where they were by trusting people—or by leaving anything to chance. If he couldn't convince them of his ignorance, both of the conlang and of Dr. Quaice's current whereabouts, they'd surely kill him.

He gave a mirthless chuckle. If he *did* convince them he knew nothing, they'd still kill him. They wouldn't leave alive someone who was entirely useless to them.

But Mary said he'd survive this. It was a thread of hope.

He'd survive, he'd find Finn, and they'd make it across the bridge. She said she didn't know what would happen afterward, but for now, that was enough. Once they got to land on the east end of the bridge, they'd figure out the next step.

The tickle of the thin thread of blood from the corner of his mouth, from where one tooth had been driven into his lip by the blow to his face, impelled him to try several times to wipe it against his shoulder, but he couldn't quite twist his head at the right angle. The feeling was maddening. The cut throbbed, he was still chilled to the bone, and he had a splitting headache, not to mention the angle his arms were cinched at causing him to lose feeling in his hands.

Also, he had to pee.

More gunfire and shouts in the distance. Nearer at hand, a piercing, high-pitched shriek of terror was cut off suddenly, and silence fell again. The thought that he was near downtown Seattle, which had been a vibrant and thriving city only a month ago, was surreal. It was more like he was in a thousand-year old ruin, some temple built by the hands of a fallen civilization now long gone to dust and their relics crumbling away, the only ones left a savage remnant of the people who had once lived there.

Some unknown amount of time later—perhaps two hours— his captors returned.

The one he'd gotten a glimpse of before put his face and flashlight beam right in Soren's, and gave an ugly smile at his flinch. "You're wanted, Pretty Boy."

The other captor was behind Soren, working at the knots on his wrists and ankles.

"I need to take a piss first."

The man scowled. "It can wait."

"No, it can't. My other option is wetting my pants, and I don't think I'll smell very good after that. Your choice, dude."

The scowl deepened for a moment, then his grin returned. "Fine. Maybe it'll be an opportunity to show you our little playground. Put the fear o' God in you before you get interrogated."

The ropes came away from Soren's wrists, and he moved his arms forward with a groan, rubbing the red chafe marks on his skin. When his legs were free, he stood stiffly.

"Okay, follow me. Don't try to run or fight back or anything. We have permission to kill you, just so you know. Apparently whatever they think you know isn't important enough that they'll tolerate any bullshit."

Soren followed the men through the door and down a dark hallway. At the end, a glass door—surprisingly intact—opened onto a courtyard enclosed on all sides by buildings. He glanced around, trying not to make it obvious, but saw no way out of the square of stone-paved open space unless it was through one of the buildings.

And that was provided he could get free of his captors.

"Go ahead." The lean man pointed. "Wall's over there. Don't have a posh men's room like you're probably used to, sorry."

Soren took a couple of steps forward, unzipped, and peed on the wall. The relief was instantaneous, but now that he was free of the discomfort, his brain returned its attention to the hopelessness of his plight. He finished, rezipped, and turned back toward the two men, waiting only an arm's reach away, ready to grab him if he'd attempted to bolt.

The spokesman gave a jerk of his head. "Before we go back in, got something to show you." He took Soren by the upper arm and pivoted him around, then swung the flashlight beam up to the opposite wall.

A hook protruded from the wall. It probably had been used for a hanging basket or some other decoration. Now it bore a grim burden—the body of a man, hanging by his wrists, the rope that bound them together looped over the hook so his feet dangled a good six inches off the ground.

He was naked, and his back looked as if it had been flayed.

"That's what happens to people who don't cooperate." The hand holding the flashlight swung the other direction, where there was a stack of wooden pallets, dark stains showing against the gray wood in the yellow-white beam. Lying nearby were three bodies, two men and one woman.

All decapitated.

"That's another option. I guess beheading is a quicker way to go than being flogged to death, don't you think?"

Soren's stomach did a slow barrel-roll. Fortunately, he hadn't eaten anything in the last few hours or he'd have thrown up again.

Dr. Quaice had been right about seeing a lot more death. Soren just didn't expect it so soon—and for it to be talked about so callously.

"Okay, come on, then." The flashlight beam dropped, and the horrifying image of the pile of bodies mercifully slipped back into darkness. The man, still holding Soren's upper arm, swung him around and led him back into the building.

Terror. Nausea. When Mary saw that he'd be hurt, how much did she see him endure? Could he take being stripped and flogged? Realistically, he'd probably be begging for mercy and telling them whatever they wanted to know after the tenth lash. But what if he didn't know the answer to what they were asking?

Had the man they'd beaten to death not had the answer, and not been believed?

He was pushed roughly down the hall, past the room where he'd been captive, through what had once been the foyer and into a large space that looked like it had been an executive office. Furniture and faces glowed white and gray, spectral in fluorescent glare reflecting from walls and ceiling. Soren squinted against the harsh brightness.

When had he last seen electric lights used? A month?

It seemed like years. Since the attacks started, smart people didn't dare turn them on and signal to the rest of the world that they were there. Here, though?

Apparently they were in enough of a position of power that they didn't care.

Sitting behind a desk was a man of about Soren's age, perhaps thirty years old, with an unruly mop of brown hair and a fevered look in his eyes, who watched silently as Soren was pushed forward. The only thing on the desk was his wallet, open, with credit cards and driver's license and other miscellany pulled out and strewn across the surface. They hadn't taken out the money—money at this point was worthless.

Once he was shoved forward till he almost ran into the desk, his two captors separated. One closed the door, then went behind Soren and pinioned his arms. The other flanked him, watching the man behind the desk, apparently waiting for orders.

Soren tried not to think about what those orders could be.

"Your name is Soren Conover." The man had a light voice, a pleasant voice, but what Soren had seen gave an implicit threat even to innocuous questions.

"Yes."

"You were a professor of languages at the University of Washington."

Close enough. "Yes."

"You know Anderson Quaice."

"Yes."

"You were staying with him."

Useless to deny it. Probably dangerous as well. "Yes."

"Where is he now?"

"I don't know."

There was a long pause. The man stared at Soren with a frightening intensity. The thought *He's insane* crossed Soren's mind.

"It seems likely that you're lying."

Panic gripped his heart. Had the man picked up something in his voice, or was he just assuming Soren would lie?

He swallowed. "I'm not. When we left his house, we had no idea where to go next. We were just hoping for the best."

The man gave a flicker of a glance to the guard standing next to Soren. The guard pivoted on his heel and gave Soren a hard slap across the face. The blow rocked his head backward, and he staggered a step, his back pushing against the other guard, who was holding his arms.

"What was that for?"

"The first payment if you're lying."

"And if I'm not?"

A backhanded slap knocked his head the other direction.

"I'm asking the questions." The man's voice went up in pitch, losing its pleasant tone. It sounded like a fiddle string stretched to the snapping point. "What do you know about the language Quaice invented?"

"Very little. I know a few words, no more than that."

Another vicious forehand slap stung his cheek.

"Fuck," he said breathlessly. "Is he going to hit me regardless of what answer I give?"

"Give the right answers and I'll instruct him to stop."

"I swear to you. I don't know enough of the language to help you."

"You expect us to believe that? When you worked with Quaice? You're a language professor yourself, so don't pretend ignorance. Why would he have chosen to take you into his home if you weren't one of the inner circle?"

He thought of saying *Because Dr. Quaice is a compassionate man and a friend*, but decided against it. In the end, all he said was, "I don't know."

This time his captor's fist made solid contact with his abdomen. The blow was so fierce and disabling that Soren doubled up, his knees buckling, and the only thing that stopped him from sinking into a kneeling position was the other guard still behind him pinioning his arms. He looked up at the man behind the desk through watering eyes, trying to find the breath to respond.

Finally he was able to gasp out, "I saw the body of the man you flogged to death. And the ones you beheaded. I understand what you intend to do to me. But I can't tell you what I don't know."

The guard cocked his fist again, but the man behind the desk raised a finger and the other froze.

"Listen to this." He brought out a phone, switched it on, and a moment later Soren heard a recording of a conversation in Kalila between Dr. Quaice and two others, a man and a woman. The recording was under a minute long, but Soren picked up only a few words he knew—*food, secret, careful,* and one he thought meant *danger.*

"What are they saying?"

"I only get a few of the words. It's something about food. Probably coordinating a food drop. But I can't do any more than that."

This earned him another brutal slap.

He glared at the guard who had struck him, then at the man behind the desk. "God! What do you want from me? Do you want me to make something up? Torture only works if the victim actually has the information you're looking for. Enough pain and people will tell you anything, true or false."

Another tiny gesture with one finger prevented a backhand that at this point might well have caused him to black out. His ears were ringing from the blows he'd already taken.

"Unfortunately, I still think you're lying. Unfortunate for you, that is. I think that your guards would thoroughly enjoy another opportunity to whip someone to death." He raised one eyebrow, and Soren realized it was the first time any part of his face had moved except his mouth. Despite the feverish intensity of his eyes, his face had been immobile until now. The gesture seemed alien, horrifying, surreal, as if he were looking at a fright mask and it winked at him.

Soren choked out, "Can you answer one question for me before you kill me?"

"Why should I?"

"To get me to shut up."

The eyebrow went up another fraction of an inch. "When the flogging starts, I doubt you'll be much inclined to talk except in screams."

Soren took a deep breath. The imminence of his being tortured to death swept over his brain, and if he didn't distract himself somehow, he was going to faint. "I just want to know one thing."

"Which is?"

"Why? Why did the LLA do this, not only here, but everywhere? It makes no sense. We're running out of food, but so are you. We're cut off from communicating with people, but so are you. How is any of this going to get you what you want?"

The man behind the desk leaned back and tented his fingers, and his mouth twisted with disgust.

"When a limb is gangrenous, you amputate it. The whole superstructure of corporate capitalism was a gangrenous limb. We are willing to undergo deprivation ourselves to free the people who have been oppressed by the rich for years. It serves them right, hoarding their wealth while millions starved. The privileged are getting what they earned."

"And what are you replacing it with? Sending humanity back into the Stone Age, and the survivors banding together only to be ruled by whichever fucking strongman can come up with the ugliest way to slaughter them if they resist?"

This time the blows were expected. He tensed up and

resisted the worst of the punch to the belly, but it still winded him. The guard let go of his arms and he collapsed to his knees, then fell forward onto his face. Kicks followed, to the back, to the legs, to the head, to anywhere they could connect that he wasn't protecting with his arms. Finally it stopped, and he lay on the floor curled into a fetal position, unable to rise, his breath coming in ragged sobs.

"Put him back in the lockup. Give him a few hours to think about his situation. If he doesn't cooperate after that, I turn him over to you to dispatch in whatever way, and at whatever speed, you choose."

He was somewhere in the gray, foggy area between consciousness and unconsciousness as he was first hauled to his feet, then dragged back to the room where he'd been confined. He had no strength to resist as they shoved him into the plastic-backed chair. He finally caught a good glimpse of the second guard, the one who had been behind him during the interrogation. Soren frowned, dazed.

"I know you." Recognition flooded his brain. "You're Doug Abbott. You were the custodian for our building at the university. I liked you, we talked sports, you loved the Mariners and the Seahawks. I thought we'd shared something, become friends. How could you be part of this?"

No answer but a forehand then a backhand blow to the face that rocked his head first one way then the other. Afterward his head tipped forward, as if his neck was unable to support its weight. The two guards rapidly retied his wrists and ankles, but he was barely aware of it.

He tried to make sense of where he was, but he no longer could think, process what was around him. If they had dragged him out to his execution in the courtyard, he couldn't have lifted a finger to save himself.

Within minutes, his consciousness drifted away.

Soren woke to a dragging sound, like someone moving furniture, but his ears were still ringing and a part of his mind didn't want to reconnect. His eyes were swollen nearly shut, and his body felt like one enormous bruise. But he was still alive, at least so far.

It was dark, without even the moonlight there had been earlier. The objects in the room were dim shadows, dark gray against black. It took him a few moments to make sense of the noise, and he finally realized it was the same noise he'd heard when he'd been confined here the first time—someone pushing a heavy object in front of the door.

Or, apparently, moving it away. Soundlessly, the door opened, and a slim figure slipped in. He? She? carried a small flashlight, unlike the heavy-duty ones the two guards had, but it reflected from the floor and walls and gave him at least a sense of what was around him. The shadowed figure moved toward him silently, then knelt down by his side.

A whisper in his ear. "Sit still. Don't struggle."

"What are you doing?" His voice sounded thick, sludgy, his battered mouth unable to form words clearly.

"I'm rescuing you."

twenty-six

. . .

Mary Hansard sat on the wet ground behind a boxwood hedge, trembling uncontrollably.

When the attack came, all five of them ran in different directions. It was a good move, even if it wasn't planned. Their pursuers would have to choose to follow one, or else split up themselves. Soren had run toward them, just as she'd instructed him, so at least one thing went right.

She shuddered. The poor young man had a lot of pain to endure, but she knew it was the right thing to do. No, more than that—she had known it was what he *would* do. That was the way the future was laid out. It crossed her mind to wonder what would have happened if she hadn't told him, but simultaneously she knew it was impossible. Past, present, and future all made one seamless, unchanging whole, and could not be altered. It was the way the universe was.

The only difference was she, alone amongst them, saw it all. The rest were confined to their uncertainty about the future.

As far as their attackers, they'd clearly been after Dr. Quaice, but did they even know which he was? Did they know his appearance as well as his name? No way to tell. All she knew was that they hadn't caught him, or wouldn't catch him, whichever it turned out to be.

She peered around the end of the hedge. They'd left their fallen comrade, the one Soren had knocked down, where he lay. Typical heartless LLA behavior. Once someone's usefulness was past, their response was entirely utilitarian. Discard the broken tool, and don't think any more about it. She had no idea if he was dead or merely injured. That information formed no part of her knowledge, either future or past. She knew she would never find out.

What would happen is that she would strike off, aiming west in the general direction Dr. Quaice said his friend lived, and she'd never see this place again.

She stood, and after a moment, took a deep breath and struck off west.

She'd only gone two blocks when she encountered signs that the riots hadn't spared Dr. Quaice's sheltered neighborhood after all. A car sat diagonally in the middle of the street, windshields shattered. In the rapidly failing light she peered hesitantly into it, verifying her knowledge that its owner was not present.

Fortunately. Thus far Mary had been spared seeing the worst of the carnage, but that wouldn't last.

Past the car, she slowed her steps, frowning, and turned into a steep driveway leading up to an ornate gabled house with a wide front porch. There was no hesitation. The owners weren't there.

Killed trying to get to the bridge. Two of the bodies Soren and Cassandra had seen.

Pity. They were nice people. But so were many of the dead and displaced. Nice people caught up in something very like hell.

"Cassandra," she said in a whisper.

Cassandra peered around the corner of the house, the relief evident in her face when she saw who it was.

"How did you know I was here?"

Mary shook her head. "You know the answer to that."

Cassandra didn't seem disposed to revisit that subject. "Have you seen any of the others?"

"No. I saw Gavin running in this general direction, but lost sight of him when I hid. Dr. Quaice went this way, too. Makes sense given that his friend lives in Capitol Hill."

"Why the hell did Soren run toward the attackers? Yeah, it probably gave the rest of us time to escape, but I thought he knew better than to engage in heroics."

"It wasn't heroics."

The younger woman frowned. "What do you mean?"

"He ran toward them because I told him to."

"You…" Cassandra's lips tightened. "Another of your premonitions?"

Mary nodded. "It's okay. He'll be okay. It's the only way he'll ever see Finn again."

"So he got captured."

Another nod.

Cassandra's anger seemed to boil over. "I don't know what you were thinking…"

Mary interrupted, speaking in a more commanding voice than she'd thought she was capable of. Cassandra's disbelief was beginning to grate on her nerves, as understandable as it was.

"It had to happen this way. How many examples do you need to believe that what I'm seeing is real? At this point, it's beginning to look like you value protecting your fragile worldview more than you do using my knowledge to help. It's one of the only real advantages we've got, and you're ready to throw it away rather than admit you were wrong."

Cassandra didn't respond. It was evident from her expression that the bolt had hit home. For the first time, she seemed uncertain, shifting her weight from foot to foot, her eyes gazing past Mary toward the street.

"I'm sorry to put it that way…"

"No. You're right. And you're right to call me out."

Well, that was a more sudden about-face than she'd expected. "Thank you."

The younger woman shrugged. "I'm an academic. I respect the facts. I needed to be reminded of that. I don't understand how you do what you do…"

"Neither do I."

"But you've proven yourself more than once. I can't argue that point any more. So like it or not, I have to accept that you're an oracle."

Mary took a deep breath. "It wasn't easy for me to accept, either. I'm a science teacher, remember. Well, an ex-science teacher. I value logic and evidence, too."

Cassandra gave her a quick nod. "So, Oracle. Where do we go?"

She pointed off down the street. "That way."

"It's safe?"

"As safe as anywhere is."

They walked in silence for a while, trying for as much stealth as they could manage. Most of the houses had fences, so cutting across private property would be difficult at best, so by tacit agreement they kept to the sidewalk, hoping the shadows would hide them from any hostile eyes.

"I never told you my background," Cassandra said quietly. "When you asked us all where we were from."

"You don't have to tell me. I didn't mean to pry. I just thought we might want to know each other better." She paused. "I know it pissed everyone off. Sometimes when I'm nervous, I talk too much. It gives me a way to deflect from the anxiety."

"I get it." Her mouth twitched. "I was just being a class-A bitch because I was tired, scared, and confronted with someone who had an ability I didn't understand. I'm still tired and scared, but at least I've accepted the latter."

Mary gave her a grateful smile. "It's nice to be believed."

"I can see how it would be."

"So you said you're not from Seattle?"

Cassandra shook her head. "No. West coaster, though. I'm from San Francisco. Youngest of five. My father was half Greek, half African American. My mom was Syrian—came here as a refugee in 2000 or thereabouts. I'm the first member of my family to go to college. Hell, on my mom's side I'm the first one to finish high school. I always felt a little like a fish out of water, like my parents and siblings loved me but we didn't quite speak the same language. That, along with harassment I had to deal with because of my ethnicity— didn't make for a happy time growing up. But it made me resilient. I've always been able to take care of myself."

"I feel lucky to have had the quiet, pleasant childhood I did."

Cassandra nodded. "It was tough. So I became tough. Had to."

"Your parents are both gone? You speak of them in the past tense."

"Yes. Died eight months apart, about five years ago. My dad from a heart attack, my mom from breast cancer."

"I'm sorry."

A long pause. "Maybe it's better. I don't think I could handle knowing they were immersed in all... this." She gave a sweeping hand gesture.

"So you think San Francisco is this bad?"

"Yeah. I do. If you heard the news reports the first day, you know this thing is worldwide. I don't know if every- where is as much of a hellscape as Seattle is, but given what's motivating the LLA, there's no way they would miss San Francisco. Bastion of wealth and privilege, home of Big Tech —it probably was one of their principal targets." She sighed.

"If my parents were still alive, with me trapped here, unable to help them—I'd be out of my mind."

"What about your siblings?"

"We're not close. Cast to the winds. Three in the US, but my oldest brother lives in Italy. I haven't seen or talked to any of them… well, since my mother's funeral."

"That's sad."

"Yes." Cassandra smiled wryly. "What gets me about all this is that here I am, child of relative poverty, daughter of a refugee. I clawed my way up through school to finally achieve a professorship. But the LLA would kill me on sight because of my supposed privilege. Their stance is fundamentally hypocritical. To hear them talk, they care about the 'little guy,' but how many little guys have died in all this? Their actions didn't improve anything for anyone. It was just an excuse for angry people to take out their rage on the innocent."

"That's a decent definition for war in general."

"Can't argue with that. By the way, do we know where we're going?"

Mary frowned. "Heading toward Capitol Hill. Dr. Quaice said he had a friend who lived there, who might give us a place to hide out for a while."

"What does your foresight tell you?"

"That's the thing. I don't have any memory of getting there. I remember his friend's name is Andy Sirrine, but I have no memory of meeting him."

"Memory?"

She gave a frustrated shake of the head. "Sorry. I honestly can't tell the difference. I know some things are in the past and some in the future, but it all *feels* the same."

"I can't imagine what that's like."

"No. You can't."

"But you know whether we succeed in finding Dr. Quaice and Gavin, right? And if we get out of the city safely? You knew Soren would survive and be reunited with his partner."

"Yes. Those things I'm certain of. But the problem is, it's still fragmentary. Just like ordinary memory, you know? Some parts are accurate and relatively complete, but we have these… holes. Missing pieces."

"Lacunae."

"That's what they're called? I didn't know there was a term for it."

"Well, that's what linguists call them. The formal definition is that they're concepts for which no word in the language exists. Holes in the lexicon."

"How can there be a concept with no word for it? How could we even think about it?"

"They're more common than you'd think. Like consider the names of domestic animals. We usually have a name for the male animal, a name for the female, and a generic name. Ram, ewe, sheep. Boar, sow, pig. Rooster, hen, chicken."

"Okay."

"So, what about this one: bull, cow…"

Mary gave her a puzzled smile. "I'd never thought of that."

"No word in English for a single generic animal of that species. But we have a plural. Cattle. How weird is that?"

Mary glanced at her. Here they were, walking through the ruined landscape of a fallen city, discussing something purely academic. It was strangely comforting. Despite their differences, they shared a sense that the cerebral was solid ground, even when nothing else was.

Cassandra gave a dry chuckle. "Sorry. Digression. Bizarre features of languages give linguists multiple orgasms."

Mary snorted laughter. "It's okay. But the sense of what you're describing is exactly what my memories—past and future—are like. Some clear, some fuzzy, and some odd missing pieces."

"I don't see how you could navigate through that."

"It's not easy." She gestured at a street corner. "Speaking of which. Turn right here."

They did, Cassandra not questioning her direction at all. Evidently once she'd decided to accept Mary's odd ability, it was settled in her mind and she didn't need to consider it further.

It must be nice to see things in such a decisive fashion.

"Do you know where we are?" Mary asked. "I don't really have my bearings. It's strange how different things look when you're on foot."

"You know where to go, but you don't know where we are?"

"I know. Bizarre, isn't it? I can tell you where we go, because I know we went there. It's a recursive loop. A snake swallowing its own tail. At the same time, I don't know the geography and street names any better than I did."

Cassandra didn't answer for a moment. "Well, it's hard to be sure in the dark, but I'd say we're somewhere near Miller Park. We just crossed 23rd Avenue East. I saw the street sign. And I think that big building over there is Holy Names Academy."

"I don't know this part of the city well."

"Me either, not really. But if we're where I think we are, Capitol Hill is due west."

They walked for another fifteen minutes in silence. As they moved out of the residential neighborhoods of the wealthy eastern part of the city and approached downtown, the sprawling houses and tall apartment buildings were gradually replaced by businesses. Restaurants, ethnic grocery stores, clothing and shoe stores, and the omnipresent coffee shops. The damage was worse here, too. Many of the buildings were severely damaged. An entire block of businesses here had burned, the skeletal remains a haunting reminder of how much had changed in only a month. The darkness hid much of the devastation, but there was no ignoring it. The heavy smell of decay hung over everything like a sickening cloud.

Maybe it was better they were traveling at night. Mary wasn't sure she could handle what horrors they might see in the bright light of day.

Another hour, then two. They were only able to keep going because some of the streetlights were still on. Some individual ones were out—perhaps shot out deliberately. The blocks that had sustained the worst damage were completely dark, probably because the destruction of the buildings had damaged wiring.

"How much longer do you think we'll have electricity?" Mary whispered. The farther along they got, the more it seemed unwise to speak loudly.

"No idea. I'm surprised it lasted this long, frankly."

"Me too." She pointed toward the once-elegant front of a spa and nails salon, its row of wide windows now devoid of glass. The barely-visible interior looked like it had been completely trashed. "Over there. Gavin and Dr. Quaice are hiding over there."

Wordlessly, they crossed the street, avoiding the wan circles of light under the streetlights. They had yet to see a single living person since fleeing their attackers in front of Dr. Quaice's house. Where had they all gone?

Fled, hiding, or killed. Those were the only possibilities.

The front door of the spa stood open, twisted almost off its hinges. There wasn't enough light to see clearly into the inside, but Mary didn't need to. She knew what was going to happen, what had happened, in the crazy, time-independent block universe she had lived in for the past two months.

"Dr. Quaice?" she said, in a hissing whisper. "Gavin? It's us. Mary and Cassandra."

There was a rustle of motion from within, and in a moment the gawky form of Dr. Quaice unfolded itself from the shadows, followed by Gavin saying, "How on earth did you find us?"

Mary didn't answer that. Now that they'd found their two companions, she was suddenly completely exhausted, as if trying to convince even someone as genial as Gavin Liu about her knowledge of the future was beyond her. "Did you find your friend, Dr. Quaice?"

There was a long pause. "Andy Sirrine is dead. Looked like it happened shortly before we got there. His body was still warm. We found him in front of his apartment building. He and three others had been hanged from tree branches with signs around their necks saying 'Food thief.'"

"Good lord, I'm so sorry."

"Me too. Andy was a good guy. He didn't deserve this."

"None of us do," Cassandra said.

"At this point, we're all food thieves," Mary said. "What do they expect? That we'll just sit and quietly starve to death?"

"None of this has anything to do with rationality," Dr. Quaice said. "But it wasn't safe to stick around and mourn, so we headed back east. We've hardly seen anyone, honestly. My guess is that anyone left here is staying out of sight. We thought that'd be smart, too, and we were both dead on our feet, so we found a promising-looking spot to bed down for the night. This place still has some furniture that hasn't been completely destroyed, including a sofa and a couple of armchairs. Safe as anywhere would be."

"Where is Soren?" Gavin asked. "I didn't see what happened to him."

"He got captured," Mary offered no further explanation.

"Fucking hell," Dr. Quaice said, his voice harsh.

"He'll be okay. They didn't kill him. He got away."

Dr. Quaice gave her a curious glance, but he looked as if he were also tired enough that discussion was out of the question.

"Come on. Let's get some rest. Tomorrow we'll have to reconsider our strategy. Not that running like hell is a strategy, but this evening we didn't have much choice."

"Only one thing is important," Mary said. "We need to head for the bridge as soon as possible. Time is running out."

twenty-seven

. . .

Fingers began working at the knots, first the ones on Soren's wrists, then those tying his ankles to the chair legs. Once free, he stood—a little too fast, and the lightheadedness forced him to sit again.

"Come on," his rescuer urged. "I know you're in bad shape, but you've got to try. We don't have much time. Most of them are asleep, but they never leave a prisoner completely unwatched. I was able to grab a moment when the guard went off into another hallway. He'll be back."

Soren stood, steadied himself on the back of the chair, and squinted toward the slender figure next to him. His rescuer wore a black stocking cap pulled low, and dark, nondescript clothes. Nothing much else was visible. It was still night, although a hint of pearly gray in the high window told him dawn was coming.

A firm hand on his upper arm guided him out of the open door of the room and down the hall. The scrunching of his feet on the dirt and debris that littered the floor sounded as loud as hammer blows. No one came. At the end of the hall, his rescuer peered around the corner into the foyer, then gave a quick beckoning motion.

"All clear."

They crossed the foyer without being challenged, then ducked underneath the twisted ruin of the front door and were out on the street. This was his first look at it in daylight, and even though he knew what must be there, it was horrifying. The once-busy street, lined with high-end office buildings, stood empty. It had been converted into a wasteland of rubble, abandoned cars, and huddled mounds that looked like—and probably were—fallen bodies. Everywhere was the fanged face of the LLA logo, and graffiti that made Soren's blood run cold.

CRUSH THE UNWORTHY BENEATH YOUR BOOT HEEL

PAYBACK'S A BITCH WHEN YOU OWE YOUR LIFE
DIE PIGS

And nearby, on a wall riddled with bullet holes and dark stains:

THE FASTER YOU DIE, THE LUCKIER YOU ARE

He shuddered. The air was chilly, damp, and still, and wreaths of fog snaked their way through the ruined city.

"This way."

Soren followed without question, trying to match the other's speed despite the deep ache that permeated every part of his body. He stumbled only once, on a piece of siding that had been blown out of a shattered storefront, but his rescuer caught him under the arm and steadied him. In the slot of open sky between the tall buildings that lined both sides of the street, the light was definitely growing. Morning was coming, with a blossoming radiance in the sky Soren had expected never to see again. It looked like in an hour or two the mist would burn off, and it would be a fine spring day.

With luck, he'd be alive to see it.

After walking for about fifteen minutes, his rescuer pulled him into the recessed front of a clothing store with gaping rectangular holes where the windows had been. Sparkling shards were scattered both inside and outside, but decorative brick columns provided at least a partial screen from view from the street.

Before his rescuer could speak, Soren said, "Who are you?"

The stocking cap was pulled off, freeing a twist of wavy, deep-brown hair. The improving light revealed a fine-featured face with intense dark eyes, a narrow nose, high cheekbones. "I'm Lydia."

"How did you know I was there?"

She shrugged. "News travels fast. You were seen when they abducted you, then followed. The radio network broadcast your location. I was the nearest person who was willing to attempt a rescue." She smoothed back her hair. "But we can discuss all that later. It's not safe here, or won't be for long. You need to rejoin Dr. Quaice."

Soren opened his mouth to speak, then shut it again. As clear as if she were standing next to him, he heard Mary's voice.

When she talks to you, stay silent. That's the only thing that will work, even if it seems otherwise. Don't resist capture, don't run away, but don't trust her—and don't tell her what she wants to know.

This was the first woman he'd seen amongst his captors. Is this who Mary was talking about? But if this woman intended him harm, why had she rescued him?

He wondered how much of the sudden shock of fear that shuddered its way through his body was visible in his swollen, bruised face.

"Where was Dr. Quaice planning on hiding if the location of his house was compromised?" Lydia's voice was light, conversational.

He stared at her. Did not respond. The urge to run was nearly irresistible, but Mary had cautioned him not to resist or try to escape by force as strenuously as she had cautioned him not to talk. So far, all that had earned him was a brutal beating, but it was all he had to go by.

The cat. She'd known about the cat, and it had very likely saved his life, and possibly Cassandra's as well.

Wherever Mary Hansard got her information from, it was at this point the only thing that might save him once again.

"I know you're dazed and in pain." Her tone was kind, and she reached out and gently stroked his cheek. "God, they hurt you so badly. I wish I'd been able to free you before they did this to you, but there was no opportunity until now."

No response. He simply stared at her. His heart was thudding against his ribs so hard he felt it must be audible.

"Where's Dr. Quaice? You need to focus, Soren. We don't have long before daylight, and it won't be safe to be out. If we're *both* recaptured… well, they'll certainly kill us."

Their gazes locked, and there was something in Lydia's eyes that hadn't been there before, or that he hadn't noticed in the hope of his rescue. Ruthlessness. Her dark eyes were as hard as quartz, even though her mouth still wore a gentle smile.

"Please. You've got to tell me."

He knew he should remain silent, but the urge to end this charade was too strong. He opened his mouth and said, in a rough growl, "If you're already in the network, why don't *you* know? And why do you know more about the people who abducted me than you do about Dr. Quaice?" He stared at her, and took a deep breath. "You knew just where to find me. You knew when the guards would be away. It sounds like you know who they are. But if you're part of the network, you should know where Dr. Quaice is better than I do. I've been separated from him for what, twelve hours now? If you're telling the truth, you talked to him since I did."

She looked at him searchingly for a moment, as if she were debating how to respond. Then her smile vanished, her lips tightening with anger. She gave a harsh sigh, pulled a small, deadly-looking gun from her waistband, and aimed it right at Soren's face.

"I told Landry this wouldn't fucking work."

Of course. It had been too easy, this seeming heroine slipping in unchallenged. They thought if a vicious beating wouldn't get him to reveal Dr. Quaice's whereabouts, maybe playing on his trust would.

Good cop, bad cop. Only here both of them had no intention of letting him live.

She pulled a walkie-talkie from her jacket pocket and keyed it, without moving the gun aimed at his head.

"He's not talking. I knew he wouldn't. He either doesn't know or isn't going to tell."

A flat, disembodied voice came over the speaker. "Shit. It was an outside chance. Get him back here. We'll let the boys have their fun with him."

She returned the walkie-talkie to her pocket, and gave a tiny flick with the gun's barrel. "This way, asshole. Don't even think about making a run for it. I will shoot you—and aim for the leg. Can't have you die that easily."

He stepped back out into the street, and she moved behind him, poking the gun into his back.

"Move."

Streaks of orange, pink, and crimson showed in the bit of the sky he could see past the tall buildings. There was movement nearby, the furtive scurrying of people who obviously didn't want to be seen. Twice he saw frightened faces peering from behind corners and the broken remains of doors.

A voice called from somewhere close. "Fuck you, you murderous bitch." The words echoed from the walls, making it impossible to tell where they'd come from.

Lydia seemed unperturbed.

"Only fair." Her conversational tone had returned, and she gave a careless shrug. "I did a good job as chief executioner when we first took over this part of the city. I lost track.

Hundreds. Maybe over a thousand. Quick and easy, a bullet to the brain. Much faster and more merciful than what you're in for. We didn't have time to mess around, and it was doubtful they knew anything worthwhile. The important thing was to thin out the crowds and scare the shit out of the survivors. I can't imagine the ones still alive and lurking around here are especially fond of me."

"You're LLA?"

"Of course I am."

"How did you get to Doug Abbott? I knew him… before all this. He was the custodian for the building I worked in on campus. He was nice."

She grabbed his upper arm and spun him around, pressing the barrel of the gun into his abdomen.

"You think so? It figures you'd think that. You fucking elites. You assume as long as your life is going fine, the whole world is. Did you ever stop to ask Doug how much he made? If it was enough to make rent, put food on the table?"

"No. It was none of my business."

Her mouth twisted with fury. "No. Of course not. Never your business to see reality. Your position as one of the privileged meant you had the luxury of being willfully blind. You know what I did before? I was a temp. A fucking temp. I went to college because I believed the lie that if you got a degree, you could get a job and buy a house and live comfortably. The only job I could find was temping. Fifty thousand dollars in student loans, what the fuck was I supposed to do? I worked sixty hours a week and I still couldn't afford to rent a decent apartment."

"I'm sorry."

"It's too late for being sorry." She spat the words, and Soren wondered if she was angry enough that she'd just kill him right here on the street. "It was too late for that decades ago. For a century, what you call society has been about one thing—making the rich richer and getting the poor to shut the hell up. Believing the lie that hey, if we just work hard enough, we could be rich, too. The problem is, people started waking up and realizing that it had been a lie all along. When suddenly thousands, tens of thousands, of people recognize they have no hope, that the elite have been laughing up their sleeves the whole time and never did have any intention of helping, it leaves us nothing but anger and a desire for revenge."

"But why didn't the Lacklanders at least *try* to fix things? To replace the system with something better? What good is all the destruction?"

"If you want to get into philosophy, that's Landry's area. Me, I just do it because I want to." She jabbed his belly with the gun. "I spent way too much of my life being the victim. Time to be the perpetrator. I'm making the elites pay for a century's worth of willing, knowing exploitation. Lining them up against a wall, watching their faces change when they go from hopeful, to scared, to resigned. The moment they know, know for sure, they're going to die." She gave him a cold smile. "It's worth it just to see them finally get what they deserve." She stared into his eyes, her mouth set in a sneer. "Your turn is coming, Mr. University Professor. Your willful ignorance makes you as guilty as the rest of them."

"It's not my fault I didn't know."

"Easy. You people left the lions' cages open, then you act surprised when the lions maul you to death." She yanked on his arm, pushed him forward, and jammed the barrel of the gun into the small of his back. "Enough talking. Move."

Ten minutes passed, their footsteps loud in the silence. There were still furtive noises from the buildings they passed. They were being watched, but it was impossible to know by whom. Soren recalled the fearful look his captor received the previous evening. These people were known on sight—and hated.

Just like the Nazi SS, the Stasi, the Cheka, the Mossad.

Ruling through fear and bloodshed wouldn't last forever. The oppressed always ended up rebelling, and people like this woman and her friends inevitably found themselves on the other end of the firing squad.

If he was in the midst of lions, so were they.

But that didn't help him. It wasn't going to happen today. By the time Lydia and the rest of the LLA faced any consequences for their brutality, the likelihood was that he'd be long dead. However hated the LLA were, none of those frightened lurkers in the shadows were going to risk their lives to save a total stranger.

Another block farther was the damaged entrance into the office building where he'd been held captive. One block was all the opportunity he had to try to get away, to fight back, something. Anything, to avoid the fate of those poor bloodied corpses in the courtyard.

But Mary had told him not to run, not to fight or try to escape. How the hell did that make any sense?

There was a sudden rustling noise, then a quick cry cut off sharply. A rough voice said, "Gotcha, bitch."

Soren turned, and froze, his brain barely believing that his thoughts only moments before had been proven wrong. A middle-aged man, bald, paunchy, had jumped out of a narrow alley between two buildings and caught his captor around the throat with a thin rope. He yanked her backward, almost off her feet, and she dropped the gun to clutch with both hands at the rope.

"You killed my best friend," he snarled. "I've been waiting for you."

But it was far from an even match. She fought like a wildcat, and twisted in the man's grasp so that the rope no longer cut across her windpipe. It was clear he was no fighter, and that she was younger and stronger. They grappled, for the moment neither able to completely subdue the other, but he wasn't going to be able to hold her long.

Soren, temporarily, was forgotten.

This was damn close to a miracle, and there would be no other. He lunged forward and picked up the gun from where it lay on the sidewalk. He had little experience with guns—in college a friend of his had persuaded him once to go to a firing range and try some target practice with a trainer—but he lifted it, sighting down the barrel as well as he could, aiming at the woman who had been ready to deliver him to torture and death. She and the bald man were still struggling, and he hesitated. There seemed to be no way to shoot her without taking the chance of hitting him. His finger was on the trigger, but every time he thought he had a clear line of fire, one of them jerked the other out of the way.

Stay there, and he'd be recaptured and killed. Even if he succeeded in killing her, there were other LLA close by who would hear the gunshot. His chances dwindled the longer he delayed. He looked around desperately, trying to gauge his hopes of escape. Run, certainly. But where? Where was safe? Away, put as many miles between himself and the LLA as possible.

Then the words rang in his head again. No. Run *toward* danger. That, Mary had said, was the only way he'd ever see Finn again.

Seconds remained to make the decision. He teetered on the cusp between what his gut wanted to do and what Mary had told him.

His paralysis broke. "You better be right about this," Soren whispered, then took off at a sprint toward where he'd been held captive.

It was an inspired choice, in an insane fashion—it was certainly the last place they'd expect him to seek shelter. He ducked under the tilted, splintered door, and crossed the foyer at a run, then back into the room where he'd been held. It was empty other than the broken furniture and the twists of rope that had been used to tie him up.

There was a commotion, and he heard a shout—it sounded like the guard who had beaten him, but he was uncertain— "There's trouble! Get Abbott and Lachman!"

Pounding footsteps across the foyer. No one bothered to look into the side room where Soren was hiding. A chaos of inarticulate shouts and gunfire from outside. A piercing bellow, cut off by another gunshot.

The paunchy man, probably. His life in trade for Soren's. He'd think about the morality of that later. For now, he was still in enemy headquarters. If it was safe now, it wouldn't be for long. He still had the gun, but any of the guards would be better trained and faster to use a weapon than he was. The best choice was still escape, if that was possible.

He peered around into the hallway.

Empty.

Okay, where now?

Once again, where was the place he'd be the least likely to run *toward*? Almost without thinking about it, he left the room, turned down the hallway deeper into the building's recesses—and exited through the doorway into the courtyard, still without seeing any sign of the men who had held him captive.

He flattened himself against the wall, feeling utterly conspicuous. The walls of the buildings surrounding the courtyard were covered with rows of windows, and bright sunlight angled its way down toward the flagstone patio. Any of those windows could be between him and hostile eyes. He glanced around frantically, looking for a way out.

The metallic smell of old blood struck his nostrils. He had to get out of here as quickly as he could, or his would be spilled there as well. Across the courtyard, and all too near the pitiful, mangled body of the man hanging by his wrists from the hook, a door was slightly ajar.

Without giving himself time to question his decision, he sprinted across the square, past overturned benches and planters that had once made this spot a place of beauty and not a scene of cruelty and carnage. He pushed through the door, swinging it shut behind him with a bang.

With luck even if they heard the noise, they wouldn't know which building he'd gone into.

Once through the door, Soren fumbled for and found a latch that threw the deadbolt. With a click, it locked, just as there was a rising welter of noise. His pursuers had come into the courtyard.

Had anyone seen him before the door closed? If so, they would shoot the latch until it broke, and he'd be done for. There was no way he could elude pursuit for long considering the shape he was in. He looked down at his hand, still holding the gun. If someone came bursting through that door, he'd have to be ready to kill them.

A minute passed, then two. Nothing happened. The expected pounding on the door and rattling of the handle never came.

He couldn't stay where he was. He wanted to put as much distance between him and the men who had tortured him as he could. He turned and ran through what had obviously been a storage room. File cabinets lined the walls, their drawers open and contents thrown onto the floor. Down a carpeted hall, past office doors with nameplates edged in shiny brass. Amy Hiroda, N.P. Tania Salcedo, R.N. Deanne Cho, R.N., Administrative Nurse. Dr. Lee van Zandt, M.D., Orthopedic Surgeon.

Past a room with a copy machine and more filing cabinets. Into another foyer, the front windows shattered, open to the sidewalk. He looked around, weighing his options.

The front door, out into the street, was directly ahead of him. The glass in it and the adjacent windows was shattered, the shards sprayed in glittering splinters across the carpet. There was no one in view, but that didn't mean he was safe. If they'd seen him enter the courtyard, they'd know eventually he'd have to leave. Even if they didn't know which building he was in, all they had to do was circle the block and keep an eye on the exits.

Was he that important to them?

He had a feeling that woman—Lydia—would want him recaptured purely because he'd gotten away, even if his escape was because of someone else. She didn't seem the type who would accept being thwarted.

The wall facing the broken windows had elevator doors, behind and to the right of what had obviously been a receptionist's desk. The power was still on, but if he risked the elevator, anyone looking in would see the glowing number display flickering its way upward. Next to it was a door labeled "Stairs," and before he could question his decision he sprinted across the foyer and through the door, taking the stairs two at a time.

One staircase angled into a platform, then into another staircase, over and over. He lost track of how many floors he'd ascended. His chest burned with exertion, but he was determined not to stop till he reached the top, until he could put no more distance between him and his pursuers.

Finally he was on a platform that had no higher staircase, and he shoved the door open, running into a shadowed and empty foyer much like the one he'd crossed on the first floor. He went up to the windows and looked out, then down.

Past a dizzying drop, the street looked narrow and impossibly distant. How high up was he?

At the moment, he didn't care. He was in comparative safety, in a place where they wouldn't find him unless they searched every building on the block from top to bottom. Exhaustion finally conquered him and he half knelt, half fell, until he was in a crumpled heap on the thick beige carpet. He let the gun slip from his hand.

Silence washed over him. That, with his injuries, the comedown from the adrenaline, and the exertion of running, combined to swamp his brain. Moments later, he was deeply asleep.

Soren woke slowly, so sore and bruised that at first he didn't want to move. From the light coming in through the window, it looked like late afternoon or early evening. He'd slept for a good twelve hours, and woke in the same position as he'd fallen, seemingly without having moved a muscle the entire time.

He groaned and opened his eyes.

Standing in a loose circle around him, their faces spectral in the shadows, were about a dozen children. They varied in age from perhaps five to fifteen years, a fairly equal mix of boys and girls. They were thin to the point of scrawniness. Their clothes were stained, and looked as if they hadn't been changed in a month.

Which, he realized, they probably hadn't.

He groaned again and tried to tilt his body upward, leaning on one elbow. The youngest girl startled backward, eyes wide, like a wild animal scenting a predator. The youngest boy, on the other hand, studied his face with something like relief.

What was that about? Was he relieved simply to have an adult around?

The oldest boy, however, stared at him with undisguised hostility.

"I told you we should have killed him while he was still asleep," he whispered to the girl standing next to him. He was tall, with the awkward features of coltish adolescence, but had a clean-lined face that would one day be handsome. Curly, dark-gold hair, a straight nose, hazel eyes that gleamed with intelligence—and suspicion.

"I'm not going to hurt you." Soren's voice came out in a

dry croak. "I'm just trying to get away from… some bad people. Who were also trying to kill me. So I'd appreciate it if you didn't."

None of the young faces relaxed. Wariness combined with a feral wildness in their expressions.

"Why should we believe you?" the boy who had spoken said, his voice still in a near-whisper. "You had a gun."

Soren scanned the floor, his heart racing in a sudden panic. "Where is it?"

"We hid it. We didn't know what you'd do with it when you woke up."

"I wasn't going to do anything with it."

"Then why did you have it?"

"I took it from the people who were trying to kill me. I'd rather not have to use it on anyone. Ever." Soren started to sit up, then thought better of it, both because of the pain and because any movement he made seemed to increase their alarm. "But I want it back. If I have to defend myself."

"Maybe if we trust you more we'll tell you where it is."

Soren sighed. "I understand why you're fearful, and if the people you're afraid of are the ones in the building across the courtyard, who killed those poor folks, then I'm on your side."

"No one is on our side." The boy didn't say it with any trance of self-pity or rancor. He merely said it.

"Well, at least I'm not an enemy. If I hadn't escaped, I'd be one more dead body in that courtyard. And I'm telling the truth that I have no intention of harming you."

"Why did you come here?"

"I told you. I was trying to get away. At that point I didn't care to where. I got into this building, found the stairs, and basically kept running until I ran out of floors."

"Are you going to stay here?"

"I don't have any plans at the moment other than recovering. After that, what I really want to do is get far away from here and rejoin my friends."

"Where are your friends?"

"Unfortunately, I don't know."

The girl standing next to him raised a wry eyebrow. She was small, dark-skinned and dark-eyed, frizzy hair in an untidy knot, and her expression held the same combination of intelligence and caution as the boy's did.

"If you don't know where they are, it will be hard to rejoin them."

"Believe me, I know. Right now, I'm focusing on the 'get away' part. I'm still way too close to those horrible killers than I want to be." He frowned. "Why are you here?"

The boy and the girl who had spoken exchanged a quick glance. "We don't want to be," the girl said. "But we don't know where else to go. We're students—we *were* students—at Cabell Street School. But the raiders broke in and killed the teachers. When our parents started to arrive to pick us up…"

One of the youngest ones startled at the girl's words, and was staring at her wide-eyed with alarm.

The boy gave the older girl a glance and a quick shake of the head. "That's enough of that."

The girl nodded. "Anyway, afterward, Colin and I—we're the oldest—got together all the kids we could find and hid in one of the rooms in the school. But we were afraid the raiders would come back, so that night we left and came here. By that time it was empty, at least as far as we could see. We thought we'd be safe on the top floor. We figured as long as we weren't seen going inside, they wouldn't bother to search the whole place looking for us. The main thing is we wanted to get the littles somewhere safe."

"Ourselves too, of course," Colin added.

"And you've been here for a month?"

Colin nodded solemnly. "There's a cafeteria where there's food. By now there's not much left, though, so pretty soon we're going to have to find another place. But you're the first person who has come up here since… since it all happened."

Soren struggled up to a seated position, taking care to move slowly. Any trust these children had of him wouldn't take much to destroy, even if it was accidentally.

"I know I probably look awful. The people you call raiders —they beat me up pretty badly. But I swear I don't mean you any harm. I'll help you if I can." He tried for a smile, but wondered if with his swollen mouth and split lip, it just made him look worse. "My name is Soren Conover."

Still no smile in return, but the boy said, "Colin Dorn."

"Emily Banfield."

One by one, each of the children added their names.

"I'm glad you decided to trust me."

Colin stared at him for a moment. "We don't, yet. But we don't distrust you."

"I guess that's the best I could ask for given that we've only been talking for five minutes. So thanks. Also, thank you for not killing me in my sleep."

A quick troubled look flashed across Colin's face, and then was replaced by the still, wary expression he'd worn. "I don't know that we'd have done it. But we thought about it. We used to think we could trust adults, that they'd help if we needed. We all had nice families and nice teachers, and even if we knew that bad people were out there, it didn't seem real." He stopped, swallowed. "Now we know that there are adults here, right here, who are evil. They're the same adults who were here before, and looked all right, but they weren't. They were already evil, we just didn't see it. We didn't know it. Now we do. And the problem is, all of them, evil and not evil, look alike. You can't tell—until they act."

That was wisdom beyond his years. How many children had done some rapid growing up since the collapse began— and how many children hadn't been so lucky?

"I hope I can prove to you I'm one of the not-evil ones."

"He doesn't sound evil," one of the younger children said.

"They never do," Colin said.

"You're right to be careful. It'll keep you safe. So keep being suspicious, even of me, until you're sure. But I'll tell you that right now, I just need a place to rest and recover. I know the raiders are looking for me. I got away purely by dumb luck. They were going to torture me to death, but they tried to trick me into telling them information they thought I had first. Then the person who was guarding me was attacked. I ran away before she could get free…"

"She?" Emily's expression became grim.

Colin gave her a solemn nod. "The Bitch."

Soren gave a dry chuckle. "If we're talking about the same person, it's apt. She told me her name was Lydia."

One of the youngest children shook his head rapidly. "That's not her real name."

Soren turned toward him, a gray-eyed, pale-skinned boy with a mop of over-long blond hair, wearing a *Spider-Man* t-shirt. "What is it, then?"

The boy regarded Soren, wide-eyed. "Her name is whatever she wants it to be. Lydia is just who she is now. She can be anyone or anything. They're all masks, and they all have different names. Behind the masks is a monster, and it has no name."

A shudder of a chill zinged its way up Soren's backbone. "You said your name is Perry, right?"

The little boy nodded. "Perry Abraham."

"How do you know that about her, Perry?"

"I hid in the school with the others. When I came out of our hiding place I saw my mom and my sister. They were dead, and I know she killed them. Then after we came here I saw what she was doing. I watched her kill people. She was smiling the whole time. But then—when I saw her do that, it let me see behind her mask. That's when I knew."

Soren had realized as soon as he saw them that these

children had all been through trauma, but hearing Perry describe it so directly was like a sickening punch to the gut. The boy's young face was set in a preternatural calm, as if he were beyond the reach of sorrow, lost in a world where there were no rules, where anything could happen.

"I'm so sorry about your family, Perry."

He nodded. "Me too. But the Bitch… she thinks she won. She thinks she got away with it, but she didn't. It won't be long. All of us here will outlive her." A flicker of triumph showed in his eyes, the first emotion Soren had seen there. "Even monsters can drown."

Soren started to speak, but Emily put a hand on his arm and shook her head. Perry watched them the whole time, his face still.

"Maybe you can come help us get food," Colin said. "It's time for us all to eat something, and there's not much left in the cafeteria, but what's there is too much for me to carry."

It was obviously a tacit request to speak to Soren alone.

"I'm glad to help." He struggled to his feet, wincing at the pain in his abdomen and back. The movement gave him a head rush that left his temples pounding and almost forced him back to the floor, but he kept his feet.

"The rest of us will get the spoons and forks and meet you in the downstairs place," Emily said.

"We usually eat in the big room one floor down," Colin said. "There are tables and the chairs are more comfortable."

"Come on." With a gesture, Emily led the other children toward the stairwell. They followed her like ducklings after the mother duck.

Evidently the authority of the two eldest had been well-established by this point. It was probably the only way they'd survived this long.

Soren followed Colin out of the room and down a hallway.

Once they were out of earshot, Colin said in a whisper, "Don't encourage Perry. The other littles are afraid of him."

"I'm sorry."

"It's okay, you didn't know."

"Do you think there's anything to what he said?"

Colin gave him a long look. "Yes. Yes, I do. Perry is how we knew to hide when the raiders came. He knew beforehand and warned us. Then, when it was safe, he led us here. He's why we're alive."

"He can see the future?"

"I know it sounds stupid."

"Not to me. I have a friend who can do the same thing, and she is why I'm alive right now. Her ability to know what's going to happen has saved my life at least twice. It sounds like Perry has the same ability."

"I don't know how he knows what he does."

"Me either. Maybe my friend could tell you. I know she wouldn't discount what Perry says."

"I'm not discounting it. Not knowing is not the same as discounting."

"That's true. But if you file what he says under 'Weird stuff Perry comes up with,' it makes it easy not to act on it when you need to. Believe me, it almost happened to me."

Colin gave him a curious look. "This friend of yours. What's her name?"

"Mary. Mary Hansard."

"And she told you what was going to happen to you?"

"Yes. At least she gave me enough information that it saved my life. Twice."

"I really didn't want to believe him at first, you know? Before the attack, I honestly thought he was making it up for attention. Afterward, when he told us we'd be safe, and the Bitch would die before we do—it was easier to think it was just him reliving seeing his family murdered, and hoping their killer gets what she deserves. I still go back and forth. I don't understand him. It's hard to accept what you don't understand."

"That's the truth. But if he's anything like my friend, you might want to take him seriously. A month ago, I'd have been the first one scoffing. Now—well, if he gives you advice, I'd do what he says."

"You're strange." Colin gave him a curious frown. "Adults almost never listen to kids. The younger the kids are, the less the adults listen. Even the good adults. They just pat your head and immediately forget what you said."

"I wonder how much important stuff never got heard because the adults weren't listening."

"I don't know. But I know sometimes I do the same thing to Perry. I guess it's good you reminded me to pay attention." His face twisted with anger. "I hope he's right, actually. The Bitch deserves to drown. I hope it's slow and painful."

"Do you know why he says she'll drown? Has he mentioned any other details?"

Colin shook his head. "He's said it before, but won't say why. He just says that's what will happen. Myself, I don't care how she dies as long as she does."

"I can't argue with that."

They neared the end of the hall, and Colin pointed to an open door next to a sign that said, *Cafeteria*. "In there."

Soren followed him in.

The room was filled with folding tables and uncomfortable-looking hard-backed plastic chairs, all in considerable disarray, as if the last people to vacate the room had done so in a hurry. Along one wall was a counter with a glass front, where once snacks and beverages sat on wire racks. It held nothing now, the shelves stripped bare. Large cabinets, a refrigerator, and a microwave all stood open, the refrigerator light showing an interior as empty as the shelves.

"Amazing the power's still on," Soren said. "It's the one thing they didn't destroy."

"Doesn't do us much good. We don't turn the lights on. They'll see us through the window."

"Good idea. When I was staying with my friends, we did the same thing."

"We've done some scouting on other floors. Most of the office doors are unlocked. I guess when the raiders attacked the building people were already at work, and they just ran away."

"All of them?"

Colin gave him a troubled look. "No. There are a lot of places that have…" He paused, swallowed again. "Dead people. We—Emily and me—tried to figure out which rooms those were, and we marked the doors. We don't go there."

"Horrible."

Colin nodded. "A few other places in the building have a little bit of food, but not much. Not enough to last more than a few days. There's another cafeteria on the first floor, but we decided to stay off the first three floors because there was more chance of getting seen. I guess if we get desperate…"

Soren shook his head. "No, you're right. Staying out of sight is the most important thing."

The two of them maneuvered their way behind the counter, and peered into the cabinets. The shelves weren't completely emptied yet, but were running low. Colin gestured at packs of single-serving cereal.

"Take a box of those and some bottled water, and I'll bring granola bars and what's left of the packages of chips and nuts." He sighed. "We don't have much left. We're going to have to leave in a day or two. I don't know where we're going to go or how we'll get there, but once the food is gone, we can't stay here."

"Getting away from the Bitch and her friends is a good idea in any case."

"That's true."

Soren followed Colin out of the cafeteria, both of them

laden with food and water, and headed back out into the hall, turning toward the foyer where the children had found him. Even the minimal exertion was making his injuries ache.

"Thank you for allowing me to stay here and sharing your food with me. I don't think I have the strength to leave here tonight."

"They hurt you bad." It wasn't a question.

He nodded. "My face usually doesn't look like this."

Colin looked up at him with a thoughtful frown. "You have two black eyes."

"Not surprising given how many times they hit me in the face."

"Why didn't they kill you? The ones we saw them kill at the school—they didn't beat them up first, or ask any questions. They just lined them up against the wall and shot them."

"They thought I had information they needed."

"Do you?"

"What I know isn't enough to help them."

"But they didn't believe you."

"No. Of course not. So they tried to beat it out of me, and when that didn't work, they got the Bitch to pretend she was helping me in the hopes I'd trust her and tell her. Didn't work either. After that, they were ready to kill me, but I was able to escape."

"Lucky."

"No shit."

Colin's mouth quirked into a quick smile, there and gone in a flash.

"After we eat, it won't be long before it's time for the littles to go to sleep. Once they're taken care of, maybe me and you and Emily can sit and talk and see if we can come up with a plan for where to go once the food here runs out."

twenty-eight

. . .

Mary Hansard woke to a gray morning, wreaths of fog snaking their way around the ruined buildings and wrecked cars. She was chilled to the bone. Groaning, she pulled herself up from the love seat where she'd slept. Dr. Quaice's gawky form stood silhouetted in one of the glassless windows. Indistinct in the shadows, Gavin and Cassandra still slept in armchairs.

She joined Dr. Quaice. "Horrifying, isn't it?"

"I've never been this sick at being right about something."

"I feel the same way."

"I'm not prescient." Dr. Quaice gave her a quick side-eye.

"There are different ways of accessing knowledge. You knew because you're smart and read the handwriting on the wall. A pity more people didn't."

"And you are certain we need to get out of the city? Not just because of the riots?"

She gave a quick, jerky nod. "Much more than that. There's worse. The whole city is going to be wiped out. 'The righteous and unrighteous alike will be destroyed.' I forget where I read that. Maybe the part of the Bible about the people of Israel being conquered by Babylon. I don't know. But it's appropriate."

He nodded. "All too. You want us to head toward the bridge?"

"That's the way we got out of the city, yes."

"Just the four of us?"

"No. We met others. Lots of others. But the evil will be right on our heels. We…" She paused, swallowed. "Some of us didn't make it across."

"Do you know who?"

She shrugged. "I shouldn't say."

"Your forewarning saved Soren's life."

Mary rubbed her hands across her eyes. "That's only because… that's the way it happened. I knew he'd see the attacker in time and kill him. It's not that… not that I *cause* anything to happen that way. It's like rewatching a movie. You know what's going to happen, but can't change anything. You can't warn a character, 'Hey, don't open that door, there's a monster behind it.' Everything's already spun out in a particular way. The fact that you know about it doesn't mean you can alter it."

"So telling me I'm going to die before I get to the bridge wouldn't allow me to avoid that fate."

"No." She took a deep breath. "All it would do is make the last hours of your life feel like you're waiting to be taken to the headsman's block."

He nodded. "I didn't realize what a burden you were under."

"I have spent the last two months wishing I could stop it."

"Why do you think this ability suddenly appeared?"

"No idea. I never had the slightest inclination toward psychic anything prior to that. In fact, I'm a scientist. I didn't even believe in psychic phenomena of any kind. And I can tell you, if I had my choice of psychic abilities, this is *not* the one I'd have picked."

Under an hour later, they were prepared to leave their safe haven and strike out for the bridgehead. Mary was relieved that finally, none of them argued with her goal and sense of urgency. After a hurried breakfast on the small amount of food they'd been able to bring along from Dr. Quaice's house the previous evening and a discreet taking-turns to relieve their bodily needs, they headed back out onto the ruined street.

This part of the city was a ghost town. The chilly breeze rustled pieces of litter along the broken sidewalks and past hundreds of decomposed bodies. All of this couldn't be the work of the LLA. It seemed as if the rebellion had shattered the social order, and the survivors had finished the work by turning on each other. There was still intermittent gunfire, but it was distant.

Even the rebels were running out of targets, apparently.

It was drawing to a close, this episode of humanity's saga. Propelled back into the Stone Age. A shame, considering how far they'd come. Mary looked at the faces of her companions. How would they fare in this new world? Cassandra, she suspected, would manage. She was tough. A survivor. It'd be harder for Gavin, gentle soul that he was. Dr. Quaice was canny and smart, but he was also the oldest of them. In prehistoric times nature had not dealt gently with the elderly and infirm. How would he—how, ultimately, would any of them—survive without the modern safety net of medical care, clean food and water, maintenance medications and electricity and communications technology?

Same way as humanity always had. Some wouldn't. The rest would learn from the mistakes, find a way to survive despite everything. Humanity wasn't finished. This was only a setback.

As for her, she had one more hurdle to face before she'd

find herself standing in the middle of the bridge, facing westward as the final ruin approached. She recalled sending Soren off to be captured and tortured, her heart aching for the pain he would undergo.

Was part of her empathy due to her knowledge of what she herself would soon feel?

Probably, but just as she'd told Dr. Quaice, that knowledge wouldn't change anything. On the other hand, it did bring an odd sort of comfort. Soren had told her something like that, the day all this started, when he described how he had the courage to cross the Montlake Cut while a sniper was taking potshots at them. He knew he had to do it, so at that point it became like a thing already accomplished. His fear was no longer relevant.

That was one advantage of her foresight. The confusion between future and past meant it was all one thing. It was the *not-present*. And being *not-present*, it couldn't hurt her. If pain lay in the future, it was as removed from her as her memories of a broken arm when she was twelve. Neither one had any impact on the present as it slowly glided along, a moving flashlight beam following her footsteps through the wrecked cityscape.

Around lunchtime they stopped for a quick snack. They still hadn't seen anyone close by, only a few figures in the distance, probably people like them who were lost in the debris, foraging for anything that might keep them alive. Afterward, they packed back up, and Cassandra excused herself to take a quick pee on the other side of a low wall.

The man with the gun seemed to come out of nowhere. All three of them startled like rabbits when his voice rasped out, "Don't move. Hands in the air."

Mary slowly turned toward him. He was a man of about forty, so thin the clothes hung from him like fluttering rags. He held a gun in one trembling hand, and was sight-lining down it toward Dr. Quaice.

"We don't mean you any harm," Dr. Quaice said.

"No. Probably not. But they said you'd be coming this way. You're Anderson Quaice. You're the one they've been looking for."

No one answered.

The man gave a grim smile and nodded. "Not denying it. No use anyhow. We had your description, and had tracked you in this direction. Lost you once night fell. But you're wanted, Quaice."

"All right," Dr. Quaice said slowly. "But let my companions go. You have no reason to harm them."

"Sorry. Orders. You, they want alive. Anyone with you is to be executed on the spot."

Out of the corner of her eye, Mary saw Cassandra moving stealthily from behind the wall where she'd gone to pee. Had the man not seen her? He showed no awareness that there'd been a fourth member of their group. It was obviously just an opportunistic capture. He'd stumbled on them. The man himself didn't look to be in great shape. Emaciated, with a sickly cast to his skin. If it hadn't been for the gun, he wouldn't even have been a threat.

He swiveled the gun toward Mary. "Okay." He grinned. "Ladies first. Sorry about that."

Cassandra moved suddenly—hurling a piece of a paving block she held in her right hand. It struck the man in the temple, knocking him sideways. The gun went off, and Mary felt a searing pain in her upper leg. She collapsed, trying not to scream.

The man didn't move again. Cassandra bent over, taking the gun from his limp fingers, and without hesitation, shot him once.

"Not taking any chances."

Dr. Quaice and Gavin knelt next to Mary.

"How bad is it?" Gavin said in a panicked voice.

"It looks like the bullet went right through the muscle," Dr. Quaice said. "Didn't hit an artery, thank God."

Mary nodded. "It's not good. But not fatal. And we can't stay here. The gunshots will attract attention."

Cassandra had already unshouldered her pack, slipped the gun into a side pocket, and removed a t-shirt. She tore strips from the cloth, and with Dr. Quaice's help, tied them around Mary's leg, cinching them tight.

"Hopefully the pressure will slow the bleeding. But if they're too tight, let me know. Cutting off the circulation completely would be worse."

Mary nodded. She was lightheaded, and the sweat was beading on her skin despite the cool weather.

"Can you stand up?"

Another nod. She not only could, she had done so. It hurt like hell, but she had done it, and after a few moments, she'd been able to walk with one arm around Cassandra's shoulders.

"I need some help getting up."

The two men gently lifted her to her feet, and Cassandra stepped forward, taking Mary's left arm and placing it around her shoulders.

"Give me a moment."

Mary took a deep breath, and together they slowly walked forward.

"This could have ended a lot worse," Gavin said quietly.

Mary didn't answer, just concentrated on managing the pain, putting enough weight on her injured leg to support her but not enough to make it collapse.

That's what it took. Determination. The wound wasn't what killed her. It slowed them all down, but with focus and concentration, they continued their walk toward the Evergreen Point Floating Bridge. Everything was sliding together, aimed at that one point, as if the bridgehead was the end of a funnel into which they were inexorably being drawn. Others were now heading that way, too, and would be there waiting for them.

Or had been waiting for them. Whichever it was. Her pain-fogged mind stopped trying to sort out which direction her memories aimed. There was no point to it anyway.

There was only one thing more that was clearly in the future, a point where she would stand in the middle of the bridge, the wind howling around her, doing what she must do—what she had, in some sense, already done.

Beyond that was only silence.

twenty-nine

. . .

"So you have no idea where your friends are?" Emily regarded Soren with a frown. "Hadn't you already left your friend's house when you got caught? You didn't know where you were going?"

"Only a general direction. The man whose house I was staying at, Dr. Quaice, said we could go try to find a friend of his first, at least temporarily. But I don't know where that guy lives. I was just following Dr. Quaice and hoping for the best."

She nodded. "It's going to be hard for you to find them. Seattle is a big place."

"Believe me, I know."

"Do you know if anywhere *is* safe?" Colin asked. "This whole area is trashed. But we haven't heard anything since the day they attacked the school, when we went into hiding. Maybe it's just around here that's bad." The hopeful tone in his voice was unmistakable.

"It's not just around here." Should he be so blunt? Colin and Emily, although the oldest of the children, were still children. But what they'd experienced in the last month meant they were no strangers to bad news. May as well be truthful.

"So it's everywhere."

"Everywhere I've seen. Some places worse than others. This area is the worst one I've been in. But nowhere is completely safe."

"Better than here, though," Emily said.

"Better than here. I want to get as far from this place as I can. I'd like to rejoin my friends, but if I can't find them, I've got to try to get away on my own. I won't last long around here."

"What about the gun?" Colin gave him a speculative look.

"I presume that means you're willing to give it back to me?"

"I think so." He turned to Emily, who nodded.

"I'll take it with me. It's better than being completely unarmed."

"Do you think you could actually shoot someone with it?"

"Maybe. But I don't know how to use it well enough to feel confident it could save me. I ran all the way here with it in my hand because I didn't know what to do with it. I figured if I stuck it in my pocket, I'd probably shoot my own balls off."

Colin snorted laughter.

When had he last laughed? The boy's face, just for a moment, lost its drawn, tired, wary expression, and Soren got a glimpse of the carefree adolescent he'd been.

Hell of a way to make the jump into adulthood.

"So the gun is better than nothing. I'll take it with me when I leave. But like I said earlier—I hope I never have reason to use it."

Emily frowned. "So if you don't know where your friends are, and you don't know where's safe, where are you planning to go when you leave here?"

Soren smiled at her. "Get right down to the pragmatic? I've thought some about that. The first thing to throw out is that the friend I mentioned earlier—Mary Hansard—said it was critical to leave Seattle. Not just because of what's happened, but because there's worse still to come."

"Worse?" Emily gave him a wry eyebrow. "How could it get worse?"

"If I was superstitious, I'd recommend not asking that question. But as far as Mary goes, she wasn't exactly clear on *what* was going to happen, just that if we stayed behind, we'd die. She was that blunt about it. She said we need to get across the Evergreen Point Floating Bridge as soon as possible."

"That's a long walk."

"Yeah, it is. And another friend of mine, Cassandra—she and I went to check it out and see if it was safe. The place we were staying was near the western end of the bridge. We found out it was being guarded by the LLA."

"So there's no way to cross it."

"I didn't say that. My opinion, and that of my friends, is that the LLA can't continue to guard it long-term. They're spread too thin. At some point, they'll decide if a few people try to cross and get out of the city, it's not worth the effort to stop them. But Mary—she said we had to go soon, the danger she saw is imminent."

"And you believe she can see the future?" Colin's voice sounded more curious than skeptical. If Perry Abraham had saved the children's lives because of a similar ability, it would certainly make him less likely to doubt the same strange skill in someone else.

"It's not a matter of belief. I saw it happen. When Cassandra and I were checking out the bridge, Mary had warned me to be careful if I saw a cat. I saw the logo on a car's hood—a Jaguar—and there was a guy creeping up behind me with a knife. If I hadn't reacted when I did, I'd be dead. She warned me I'd get captured, and that I wasn't supposed to resist, and when I had the opportunity, to run *toward* danger. That's how I got away. I ran back into the LLA headquarters and through it, and found my way into this building without being seen. If I'd run just about any other direction, I'm sure they'd have seen me and shot me in the back." He paused. "She also said if I did that, I'd see my partner again. He and I got separated the first day of the attacks. I haven't seen him in a month. I don't know… I don't know if he's dead or alive, except that Mary said I'd find him again. I'm holding onto the fact that everything else she's told me has been right."

Colin nodded. "Okay, so head toward the bridge. What's between here and there?"

"A mess. I'm not sure exactly where we are except somewhere a little north of downtown."

"We're close to the Space Needle, if that helps."

"It does, a little. I'm way more used to the city via bus or car than on foot. It's hard for me to visualize a path when you don't have to stay on the streets. But I think we need to head generally east—away from the Space Needle, and away from downtown. Once we get across I-5 I'll have a better idea of where exactly we are, and what direction we should head."

"Okay," Emily said. "But how do we get there without getting caught?"

Soren chuckled. "Yeah, that's the real question, isn't it? I'm not gonna lie. I'm not a fighter. I've survived as long as I have because of a combination of help from friends and dumb luck. I think I'm tougher than I was a month ago, when the worst I had to contend with was bad traffic and long lines at the grocery store. But we'll have to be incredibly careful, especially since we'll have the younger children with us."

"You really want to take us along?" There was a mixture of doubt and hope in Emily's voice. "Wouldn't you go faster and be safer if you went alone?"

"Maybe, but I'm certainly not going to leave you behind. Since all this started, I've become convinced the only way any of us will survive this is by helping each other. So far, I've mostly been on the receiving end of the help. It's my turn to give back. I just hope I can get us all to safety, and that I won't be leading you from a bad situation into a worse one."

"If your friend Mary is right," Colin said, "staying here would be the worst of all. I think we need to leave as soon as possible tomorrow. There's usually no one out on the street early in the morning, so we'll have a better chance of getting away unseen."

"At this point, every advantage we can gain is good." Soren took a deep breath. "I'm holding on to what Perry said, that all of us here were going to outlive the Bitch."

"Maybe," Emily said. "But by how long?"

After their conversation ended, Soren headed off to use the men's room. Having flush toilets was a weird luxury after so much else had crumbled into ruin. Afterward, he went back upstairs to the reception area and lay down on a sofa. Despite his long sleep earlier, he was exhausted, and his entire body ached. Letting himself drop into sleep, to have at least a few hours of escape from the pain and the anxiety, was a gift. If they followed his plans, it might be the last time he had a comfortable place to rest for a while.

He woke after hours of dreamless sleep to see the faint light of pre-dawn glimmering in the window. He forced his eyelids open, and had to stifle a shout when he saw a shadowed figure standing near him, watching him intently.

Fortunately, he realized quickly that it wasn't one of his captors, only one of the children—Perry Abraham, the little boy whose pronouncements the previous evening had reminded him of Mary's prophecies. Soren sat up, and they stared at each other in silence for a moment, Soren trying to get his heart and breathing back to normal, Perry with that eerie, preternatural calm that he always wore.

It was Perry who spoke first. "The electricity is out."

It should have been obvious, even in his groggy state. The low hum of the refrigerator, the air handlers, the other mechanical devices deep in the guts of the building, all left going as long as there was power to run them, had finally shut off. It was completely silent, a silence very few people in the modern world had ever experienced.

"I guess it's a surprise it lasted this long."

"Do you think it'll come back on?"

"No way to know. I'd guess probably not. Even though Seattle runs almost entirely on hydropower, it can't just run itself. My guess is the LLA tried, but eventually they didn't have the expertise to keep it running. It's also possible we were just lucky and it's run unattended for the last month." Soren paused. "We'll probably never know for sure."

Perry watched him in silence for a moment, his large gray eyes almost luminous in the dim predawn light, as if they looked right into Soren's mind. "I knew you were coming. Yesterday, when the others found you, it's because I told them you'd be there."

He had to stop himself from saying "How did you know?" It was obvious that Perry no more knew the source of his information than Mary did. "So you came to look for me."

The little boy nodded. "We were down a floor. The big room there has better places to sit. It's pretty boring being here. Nothing to do but sit around. The older ones like to talk. Everyone else just looks out of the windows and thinks about stuff. Sometimes we make up games, but it never lasts long."

"Why did you come here this morning?"

"'Cause I wanted to talk to you. Colin doesn't like it when I talk too much. He thinks what I say will scare the others."

"I think maybe he takes you more seriously than you realize."

Perry shrugged his thin shoulders. "I'm not trying to scare

anyone. But if I find out about bad stuff, I have to tell everyone, right? It's my… um… it's… I don't know the word."

"Responsibility?"

"Yeah. Responsibility. But I knew I wanted to talk to you
because I knew you would understand."

"What did you want to tell me?"

"Two things. One of them the voice told me a long time
ago. That we had to stay here, in this building, until an adult
came along, and after that, we should follow him. So I've
been waiting for you."

"Okay. I hope I don't lead you into worse danger."

"Even if you do, it's what we have to do. The voice said."
He stopped, his eyes locking on Soren's. "But there's something else I need to tell you. I wasn't telling the truth when I
said the Bitch was going to lose. I mean… she will. But that
doesn't mean we will win."

"What are you trying to say?"

He looked away, and Soren got the impression he was
listening to someone, someone only he could hear.

After a moment he said, "You know how a lot of stories
have endings where all the good guys survive?"

"Yes."

"This isn't one of those stories."

Soren stared at the little boy, whose face was still set in an
expression of utter calm.

"Why haven't you told the others?"

He shrugged. "Sometimes… sometimes it's better not to
tell people about everything I know."

A chill ran up Soren's spine. Another commonality. Mary
had also talked about learning to self-protect, to hide what
she knew because others wouldn't understand. "What do you
actually see?"

"Some of us won't make it. Not just the ones here, but the
ones who will join us soon. I'm not sure why. The voice told
me that, and even told me who. Some of the names I don't

know. They're people we will meet. But even if I know, I don't think I should say. It'd scare them and not change what happens. Right?"

"I guess. I don't know. I don't even know how you'd decide what's the best thing to do about that. Maybe if we reconnect with Mary, I can introduce you. You two would have a lot to discuss."

"There's one other thing."

"What's that?"

"You're right that we have to get out of here today. And it's not just the food. The Bitch and her friends—they're looking for you. The voice told me that this morning, and said I needed to warn you. She's furious you got away. You're the first person who ever has. We don't have long."

Soren shivered. "When do we need to leave?"

The little boy shrugged. "As soon as we can."

"Am I one of the ones who doesn't make it?"

Perry's luminous eyes locked on Soren's. "Would you want to know?"

"Yes. Yes, I think I would."

The little boy frowned. "People say that. They say they want to know, then they're only happy if it turns out to be good news."

"I think I really do want to know."

"You do get away across the bridge. And you're not just looking for your friends, right? There's someone else. Someone you… someone you're in love with. You want to find him, too."

Soren nodded.

"The voice told me that piece is hanging by a hair. That's what it said. It means, 'it could happen either way and we don't know which.' Like in the movie *Clue* where there are different endings. In one of them, you're crying and crying and can't stop."

A sick feeling rose in Soren's gut. "Mary… my friend who

sees the future, like you do… she told me I'd find Finn and we'd both get away."

A long pause. "Maybe she was doing what I do. Telling people what they want to hear because telling the truth hurts too much."

When Mary had told Soren he and Finn would make it, she had taken a long time to get the words out. It was as if she'd been waging an internal argument about what to say. Was it the truth, or had she seen a far bleaker future and been afraid to admit it?

"I don't know."

"But even if she lied, it's important to listen. I could tell you were listening to me last night and not just laughing or getting scared or whatever. It's why I wanted to talk to you this morning. I knew you'd believe me."

"I do believe you."

"Now that everything's changed, people need to listen. I'm not the only one who sees things and hears things. Your friend does, too, but there are other people. In the future… from now on, there will always be people like me, but there will be more people who don't believe. Who don't want to believe. That's gonna be the hardest thing. We had the internet and stuff to find out things before. Now we find out things a different way. People just have to believe that it's real."

There was a rustle, and Soren turned to see Colin enter the room. The older boy frowned when he saw Perry standing there, but he said, "Hi. You're both up early."

"I woke up as soon as there was light in the sky," Soren said.

"We should get going soon."

"Perry and I were just discussing that."

Colin looked at Perry, and seemed to be trying to figure out what to say to him. Finally he just patted the little boy on the shoulder. "You should go to the bathroom and then get something to eat. We'll be leaving soon, before the sun's up."

Perry nodded mutely, and left the room.

Soren got up and stretched, his back cracking pleasantly. He was feeling better than yesterday, and a tentative touch to his face told him the swelling had gone down some. He walked to the window, looked out and then down. The dim light of an hour before sunrise made the street below indistinct in the shadows.

"What did he tell you?"

"Just that we need to get out of here quickly," Soren said without turning around. No way did he want to get into the rest—if he could even find the words to explain it.

"You really think what he knows is real?"

"I think there's a good chance of it, yes."

"He said a voice tells him that stuff. How could a voice know the future?"

"I don't think even he knows the answer to that." Soren stretched again. "But you're right, and so is he, about getting out of here now. Let's discuss this once we're somewhere safer."

Colin nodded. "Your gun is in the drawer of that desk over there." He pointed toward the receptionist's desk, then turned and left the room, leaving Soren alone once more.

So this was it. Today it was out into the unknown. The first priority was to get as far away from the LLA headquarters as possible. If one of the guards spotted them, this would be the shortest escape attempt in history.

He went to the desk and quickly found the drawer where Colin had hidden the gun. He took it out, holding it gingerly. The backpack he'd borrowed from Dr. Quaice had gotten lost somewhere between his being captured and arriving at the LLA headquarters. He couldn't recall where. A lot of that night seemed surreal, like a nightmare or fever dream. He looked down at the gun in his hand for a moment, found the safety, clicked it on, then tucked it into his pocket. At least that reduced the chance of accidentally discharging it, but it would slow him down in using it if they were attacked.

Oh, well. Couldn't have both speed and safety. Given his lack of experience with firearms, better err on the side of safety.

Fifteen minutes later they were assembled in the reception room one floor down.

"The most important thing is stick together." Emily's tone sounded like that of a stern, no-nonsense teacher talking to an unruly class. "No matter how scared you are, don't run away from the rest of the group. You're safer with us than you would be alone."

"Why do we have to leave?" One of the younger children sounded on the verge of tears. Surprising, really, that more of them weren't.

"Because we've run out of food." She gave a quick glance at Colin. Had Perry talked to her about his knowledge that Lydia—the Bitch—would be searching the buildings that day, and she was choosing to keep it to herself because she was afraid it'd make the rest of the children panic? She looked like she knew more than she was saying.

"Okay, come on." Colin led the way from the room. The children followed him without question. Soren took up the rear, and together they went toward the stairwell and the many flights of stairs leading down to the ground floor.

One thing was obvious—living in these circumstances for a month had cemented them as a group and established Colin and Emily as the leaders. There was no complaining, and little noise, as they descended flight after flight. It took almost ten minutes to get them all to the first floor. By the time they did, the sky was rose and gold, but the sun still below the horizon. They went to the smashed window of the front of the office. There was no movement from out on the street, but the many windows of adjacent buildings looked far too much like staring eyes. Soren felt horribly visible even though he saw no one and heard nothing from the ruined street.

They pushed open the frame of the front door—the window of the door was also smashed to splinters—and went into the recessed alcove of the building's street front. Soren peered up and down the street, still seeing no movement.

"C'mon," Colin whispered, and beckoned with one hand.

They followed, staying as close as they could to the wall. They passed three buildings with only narrow alleys between, but still there was no sign of anyone nearby, no indication they'd been seen.

When they reached the end of the block, Soren peered ahead. They were headed northeast, he could tell that from the growing light in the sky, and at some point they'd have to turn due eastward. But this block of buildings was way too dangerous to stay near. Better to go up a few blocks before turning to the right. They could still run into an LLA patrol, but the farther they got from headquarters, the less likely that was.

He hoped.

Emily tugged on his sleeve, and he turned. She pointed across the street. On a long cement wall—part of the base of a parking garage—someone had spray-painted a message in bright red. Drips of paint streamed down from the letters. It looked like blood.

"Soren. You'd better run. If I ever see you again, you're a dead man. Love, Lydia."

Underneath was the fanged face of the LLA logo.

"Fuck," Soren said under his breath.

"C'mon," Colin said again, urgency in his voice. "She's just trying to scare you and slow you down."

They quickly crossed the street, still heading north, passing another block of office buildings. Three blocks farther, the street they followed hit the major thoroughfare of Denny Way, which looked like one long pileup of cars. Too far to the north, and they'd run into the complex of Amazon headquarters, something that was better avoided. Surely the LLA would have occupied it early along given its promise of valuable resources. In any case it wasn't far that they'd run into Lake Union and have no convenient way of going farther north. If Soren remembered right, eastward—the general direction they wanted to go—were more apartment complexes, restaurants, and small businesses, but whether they were occupied or empty shells was uncertain.

A lot of obstacles remained to cross. Getting past the multiple lanes of I-5 was a daunting prospect—underpasses surely were being used as shelters, whether by LLA and their sympathizers or people who were simply refugees like he was.

After crossing Denny, the road angled north, down a narrow tree-lined street with tall apartment buildings. Most of the ground-level windows were shattered. The LLA insignia was painted everywhere they looked, but it was impossible to tell if it meant the buildings were claimed and occupied, or if it was simple vandalism. By that time, the sun was just below the horizon, and in the brightening light Soren felt uniquely conspicuous. Twice he thought caught movement in one of the open, shadowed doorways, but when he turned that direction, there was nothing.

Whoever was still around had obviously survived the same way the children had—by staying out of sight.

"Where are we going?" one of the younger children whispered. She was a tiny wisp of a child, straight black hair in an untidy pony-tail, her face smudged with dirt despite Emily's exhortation to clean up before they left.

Soren looked down at her. "Your name is Becka, right?"

She nodded. "Becka Shimada."

"Honestly, I'm not sure where we're going except for 'as far away from where we were as we can get.' I know it's scary."

"I don't want to die."

Soren was stunned into silence. A child her age shouldn't have to think that way. In only a month, what kind of world had it become? He started to say, *I'll protect you, you won't die,* but he couldn't force the words out. He couldn't promise to protect any of them, nor himself. These children had seen their teachers, parents, and classmates gunned down indiscriminately. Becka would recognize vague statements of false comfort for exactly what they were.

There were no guarantees of safety, or even of survival. It was impossible to pretend there were.

In the end, he said the only thing he could think of. "I don't want you to die, either, Becka. I don't want any of us to die. I'll do whatever I can to keep us all alive."

Another block forward. Looking left down the intersection, Soren caught movement, but it was there and gone too quickly to see what, or whom, it might have been. In that same direction was a heap of what were obviously badly decomposed corpses, and the nauseating smell of decay hung in the air. They were near another pile-up of wrecked cars, but unlike the bodies Soren had seen in Dr. Quaice's neighborhood, who had been left where they fell, these unfortunates were thrown together into a loose pile.

Look away. Don't think of who they were, ordinary people with jobs and loved ones and pets and hobbies. Don't think of their lives, nor how they ended here on a ruined street in a destroyed city.

Even the dead bodies, though, were far fewer in number than he would have expected. Everywhere around here were apartment buildings and condos—but where were the residents? Surely not all of them were hiding inside. The furtive movement he'd seen was infrequent, and if most of the people who had lived there had stayed put, there was the issue of food. Most of the buildings had an air of desolation. They didn't feel like hiding places.

They felt abandoned.

Worse, they felt haunted. The blank, dark windows were like the staring eyes of specters, ghostly remnants of the people who had once lived here.

Soren had always thought people's fear of cemeteries was kind of silly, but now he understood it on a visceral level. It represented the unknown and unknowable fate all humans had in store. This city wasn't dying, it was dead. It was a graveyard.

But the piles of corpses he'd seen weren't close to accounting for all the people who had lived, worked, studied, and played here.

So where was everyone?

No way to know. In any case, getting the kids to safety was the first thing. He could ponder the sickening details of what had happened here later.

Past more apartment complexes. Each one had the ground-floor windows shattered and front doors gaping open. The quiet was unnerving. Their footsteps echoed from the brickwork. One of the children, he wasn't sure which, was crying softly.

No time to stop for comfort. The jittery, unnerving sensation of being watched, not by humans but by throngs of ghosts, was nearly unbearable. Much more and he'd have been impelled to run, even though there was no way to tell if the danger was behind them or ahead of them.

Or everywhere.

"What the hell are you doing?"

The voice that spoke to them from an open doorway, at the top of a low set of stairs with an ornate wrought-iron railing, caught him so by surprise that Soren nearly screamed. One of the children did—a quick, animal-like yelp that caused both Colin and Emily to whirl around in alarm.

"Quiet!" Emily hissed, and for a moment, the only sound was terrified, rasping breaths.

Soren looked up the stairs. In the shadowed doorway was a spectral, white face, nearly skeletal in its thinness. He could almost convince himself this was one of the ghosts, that his fear had conjured one of them into life. But no, this was a living man, even though the sunken cheeks and thin lips made his face look as if it were all eyes. Wide, horror-filled eyes, staring at them as if he couldn't believe what he was seeing.

"What the hell are you doing?" the man repeated. "You've got to get off the road. The patrols are coming."

"Patrols?"

"Get in here."

"How can we trust you?"

"Suit yourself. But if you don't get off the road, you'll be dead in under fifteen minutes."

Emily and Colin both turned and looked at him, a question in their eyes.

From behind them, perhaps only three blocks back, there was the sound of gunfire.

Almost without thinking, Soren said, "Up the stairs! Quick, all of you!"

Emily gave a gentle push to the children nearest her, and once a few started to move, the rest followed. Up the cement stairs and into the doorway, into the darkened hallway of an apartment building. Once they were all inside, Soren dragged the door closed, grating against rubble and dirt on the floor.

He turned and looked at the man who had called out to them. He was perhaps forty years of age, with thinning brown hair and deep brown eyes. He sat in a wheelchair, his skeletally-thin legs tilted to one side.

"What were you doing out there, walking down the street? Don't you know what's happened here?"

"I know some, yes."

The man rolled his eyes. "Then you're either stupid or desperate. Or both."

"Desperate for sure. Stupid or not, I'll let you decide. I'm Soren Conover."

"Marcus Gellert. The patrols always come through here about this time. Looking for anyone who might be around. They capture the ones who look strong enough to be helpful, and who don't seem inclined to fight back. Ones they can turn into more soldiers. Of course, it's slim pickings now. Just about everyone is gone already. The ones they don't take, they kill." He gave Soren a wry eyebrow. "I'm guessing you'd be one of the ones they'd kill. And the kids, too. They don't take kids."

God, did he have to be that blunt in front of the children? There was no need to terrify them any worse than they already were.

"Why did you call out? Weren't you afraid of getting killed yourself?"

Marcus shrugged his bony shoulders. "They can kill me, I guess. I'm going to die sooner or later anyhow. Probably sooner. The food's run out, and I can't get out of here. It's why I got left behind."

"Where did everyone go?"

Marcus raised an eyebrow. "Where have you been? Never mind, it's obvious you haven't been around here long. The LLA started three-times-daily sweeps of this area—must be four weeks ago. To start with, people thought it was safe just to stay indoors, but you can't stay inside forever, you know? You have to go out for food and stuff, and that's when they got caught or killed. So a bunch of them got together and decided to take off northward, try to get out of the city that way. I don't know why they didn't just head for the bridge…"

"It's guarded."

"Yeah, I guess it would be. In any case, a group of people who lived in this area, they all got together and left. The leaders were this weird pair, some old lady and a young hippie guy. But they were charismatic, I'll give them that.

Somehow they convinced people to follow them, to get them out of the city. How they'd gotten this far without getting caught, I don't know. They picked up a few more recruits from the apartments on this street, then took off. Maybe about three dozen, all told. I know they at least got out of the neighborhood here. I haven't seen 'em since, not that I would. Whatever happens, they wouldn't come back here."

"And they just left you?"

"Tactical decision, and honestly, it was my idea. The old lady didn't like it, but there really wasn't any option. I'm in this chair, and I'm chronically ill. MS. I'd be a liability. They couldn't take anyone who would slow them down. It's the way things are now. Old Mrs. Thorpe, who lived down the hall from me, she was type-one diabetic. She knew there was no way she could go. She died last week when her insulin ran out. There were a couple others in this building, but I haven't seen them in days. I don't know whether they died or tried to get away on their own."

There was a low whimper from one of the children, and Soren half turned.

"We shouldn't be talking about this stuff," he said to Marcus, immediately realizing how lame the words sounded.

"Why not?" Marcus's voice was harsh. "It's reality. I'm guessing if these kids have survived this long, they know what's what. Maybe better than I do."

Soren felt outrage at the man's brusqueness. "They may know, but they still feel."

Marcus shrugged. "All right. And it's not like I have any answers. I haven't been outside this building since all this started. I'm just about out of food, and I know I'm done for. Most of the food that's left will spoil now that the power's out. How long do I have? A week, two at the most. I'm okay with that. The world's falling apart. Honestly, I'd just as soon check out. And I'm going to, pretty soon. The old lady told me that."

"She told you you'd die?"

"Yeah." His voice became thoughtful, losing something of its abrasive edge. "She said my time would be about up once I met a man leading some children, and sent them on. She said to tell you they were heading north, trying to get out of the city that way, and you need to follow them." He looked up at Soren, and in his eyes was something like relief. "I've been waiting for you to get here. Because God almighty, I'm tired and I'm ready for the long sleep."

thirty

· · ·

Mary Hansard had known she was going to get shot. She knew it would hit her in the leg, that the bullet would pass through without hitting the bone or a major artery, that she wouldn't die from the injury, that with assistance she would be able to walk afterward. It had all been there, like an unpleasant memory of an experience that was, fortunately, over.

The problem with her foresight-is-hindsight, of course, was that the knowledge didn't mean it *was* over. Now, here in the present, she had to deal with the throbbing pain and the sick lightheadedness. She, Cassandra, Gavin, and Dr. Quaice went as far as she could manage—a distance of perhaps two miles—until she had the sudden realization that she needed to rest or she was going to faint and halt them completely.

Another ruined building, this one looking like it had been partially destroyed by a fire, blocked the view of anyone out on the street who might wish them harm. Not that anyone would. They would be safe overnight in this burnt-out shell.

She lay on her back, trying to find a position in which her injured leg might ache less, her restless mind pursuing at least a fleeting understanding of what had happened to her.

In the past two months, it felt like the universe had changed shape. The linear slow march of time was clean gone, and what was left was a block that was unalterable, the people and events in it frozen in place like butterflies in amber. Her own position in it had become as observer rather than participant. She could see a wedge of the block, extending back into her distant past and forward into her all-too-short future. Anything outside that wedge was invisible.

The oddest thing was that it had expunged almost all her anxiety. She still had flashes of her old worries about what would happen, but they were becoming fewer and fewer. When they were at Dr. Quaice's house, she'd ramped up into a near panic attack a few times, but was able to reestablish her equilibrium when she returned to seeing everything, past and future, as fixed. When the news stories rolled in on the first day of the attacks, she'd known it all ahead of time. That the moving beam of her attention had focused for a moment on those events made them no more real than any of the others that were locked in place somewhere in the crystalline solid the universe appeared to be.

Getting upset about it was about as sensible as thinking your emotional reaction could change the words of a book that was already written. The only option other than reading the book was to close it and set it aside.

Which was what she was going to do, and very soon.

She woke just as the sun rose. Another gray, cloudy, cheerless day, but at least it wasn't raining. Her leg had stiffened up badly, but her pride wouldn't allow her to wake one of the others so they could help her. With difficulty, she finally got to her feet and hobbled around the back of the ruined building to attend to her bodily needs. Returning, she maneuvered herself back down to the floor with equal difficulty.

By this time Gavin was stirring—whether he'd been awakened by her clumsy movements was uncertain—but he got up, stretched, went outside for a brief time, and when he returned knelt down next to her.

"How are you feeling this morning?"

She tried for a smile, and mostly succeeded. "As well as I could expect. Hurts like crazy, but it's tolerable."

"We should try to find something today to keep you from getting an infection."

"Doubt there are any antibiotics to be had. Pharmacies will have been stripped clean, probably within the first week." She paused. "In any case, I'm not going to get an infection. The bullet must have been nice and clean."

The attempt at levity didn't bring a smile to Gavin's face. He still looked worried.

"You know that through your… ability?"

She nodded. "Nice to be aware of something positive, actually."

"I've been wanting to ask you something."

"Go ahead."

"My wife… will I see her again?"

Mary gazed up into the face of this gentle, quiet man, and saw there a combination of love and grief so intense it nearly brought tears to her eyes. He hadn't spoken about his family much. Honestly, he hadn't spoken much at all, simply following along with the others and doing whatever he was asked. He wasn't as acerbic and defensive as Cassandra, although the time Mary had spent alone with her was enough to show that there was a lot more behind her façade, too. She and Gavin both shielded themselves, just in different ways.

Maybe all of them did. Mary's own tendency to feign good cheer certainly wasn't entirely authentic. She'd learned how to do it from many years as a teacher, where wearing your emotions publicly could be an active hindrance.

They all had their coping mechanisms.

How could she answer Gavin's question, though? It was inevitable that her precognition gave the impression that she saw the entire future laid out like a grand tableau. Getting them to understand how it really was seemed beyond her. She barely understood it herself.

In the end, she said, "I'm sorry, Gavin, I don't know."

"You would tell me if you knew, even if it was bad?"

She nodded. "Yes, I think I would. I honestly don't know."

He looked a little relieved, as if he'd been certain the news would be bad.

"I used to read a lot of science fiction. There's a trope in a lot of it that if you have knowledge of the future, you can't tell anyone because it could change what's going to happen."

"That's not how it is." She looked away at the overcast sky, the tops of some fir trees barely visible over what was left of the charred and blackened wall. "If I did know, and I told you, it wouldn't change anything. You can't change anything."

"Like the 'fixed points in time' in *Doctor Who*?"

Mary smiled. "I love that show. But yes. The only thing is, they're *all* fixed. What's going to happen will happen whether we know about it or not."

"Makes the whole free will/determinism argument a bit pointless, doesn't it?"

"That it does."

Dr. Quaice sat up, blinking groggily. "City's a wasteland, we're fleeing for our lives, and here are the two of you discussing philosophy."

"It's not like we can pass the time discussing how the Mariners are doing this season," Mary said.

That got a laugh. "Touché. How are you feeling this morning?"

"Won't be running a marathon, but I can walk. Slowly. Tried it out a bit ago, and it'll support my weight. I'm lucky."

"If you can call anyone lucky these days."

An hour later, they were making slow progress in the general direction of the Evergreen Point Floating Bridge. Orienting by obvious landmarks like the Space Needle—still amazingly intact, its disk seeming to float above the devastated city— they were able to head generally northeast toward the bridgehead.

At about midday they took a short break for food and water—they had little of either left by this point—and Mary, despite her injury, was the first to rise. They'd taken refuge in a small park, strangely peaceful and intact despite being surrounded by a horrorscape of destruction and death. It was astonishing how quickly someone could become inured to seeing dead bodies. They hardly made her flinch any more.

The part of the city they were in was largely depopulated, but evidently during the first days of the attacks it had been the site of a significant battle. There were no walls without bullet holes. Corpses were left where they'd fallen to rot. By this time, they were nothing much more than picked-over bones. The crows and other carrion-feeders had done their job. They did see signs of a few living—furtive scurrying, there and gone in an instant—but there were no attacks or confrontations.

She stretched, wincing, and said, "We need to go. There isn't much time left."

It was a sign of how completely Cassandra had turned about-face that she didn't question Mary at all, simply shoul-dered her increasingly lightweight backpack and followed as she hobbled her way out of the park.

Past the shattered front of a Safeway grocery store and a bank. How many banks were broken into during the first days, before it dawned on people that very soon, money would be completely worthless? A bookstore, ransacked, shelves overturned, the literature of an age strewn about on the stained and torn carpet. This was the one that made Mary the saddest. It seemed emblematic of all that had been lost. How much of the cultural heritage of the human race would vanish forever? She had always had a deep fascination for the European Dark Ages, between the fall of Rome and the rebirth of central governments during the time of Charlemagne and Alfred the Great, simply because of the fact that so little was certain about it. It was a great gaping hole in history, unknown and unknowable, because even the few records had been made when it was happening had ended up being destroyed.

In five hundred years, would a new civilization arise from the ashes of the old, and look on this period as being the modern Dark Ages—a mysterious gap, populated by the ghosts of thousands of people whose lives, struggles, accomplishments, and deaths were lost forever?

Would she herself be one of those ghosts? It seemed all too likely.

But no time now to worry about that. Now there was only one thing that was important—getting to the bridgehead. The chess pieces were all arranged. All that remained was to set the end game in motion.

part three
the tilted world

thirty-one

. . .

"So the two of you are some sort of… prophets?" Finn Donnelly looked from Brandon's face to Julia's, still registering disbelief.

"Julia is," Brandon said. "I don't know what you'd call me."

"You are a prophet as well, Brandon," Julia said in a quiet voice. "Your messages are as prophetic as mine, even if they take different forms. They come from the same source."

Finn had scrolled through the rest of the photographs of Brandon's paintings, but hadn't recognized anyone else but Soren. Of course, that was enough. His mind had tried to piece together another explanation for how Soren's image ended up on a jpeg of a painting in this man's phone, and came up with nothing. Perhaps it was just the emotional punch of seeing his face, so familiar and so loved, when he'd thought there was no chance he ever would.

That alone made their wild claim easier to accept.

Still, Brandon and Julia made an unlikely duo. A young artist, his long, straight black hair held back in a ponytail. A stern and ramrod-straight woman who looked like she would be at home in a revival tent. Despite their obvious differences, they were linked on a fundamental level, linked in a way that defied understanding. They shared a burdensome gift that gave them a common language, overcame the disparate worlds they had inhabited before the attacks started and everything changed.

What about the others? Finn looked around at the ragged group who were following Julia and Brandon. Arden Ballinger, whose buzz-cut and tough demeanor shouted *military*. Why had someone like him followed a street preacher and a hippie artist?

There was a confused-looking young man named Trevor Keene who seemed lost, as if he'd joined their group thinking it'd be a fun adventure and gotten way more than he'd bargained for. Another of their group, Ronnie Sulzbach, was a pleasant middle-aged woman who looked like the "see the best in everyone and everything" type. She was garrulous and friendly, telling Finn that "before all this" she'd been a hair stylist, and was a fitness nut who ran six miles daily.

Brandon's girlfriend, Caria Sahin, on the other hand, didn't say much but stuck by Julia as if she were a lifeline. If anyone else's trust in Julia's divine inspiration was shaky, Caria's was as solid as granite. Whatever had convinced her had done a thorough job of it.

A strange group, but what could be expected of three dozen people who had been thrown together by random chance?

Of course, the people he'd been with hadn't been any better. They were a loose group of neighbors who pulled together after the attacks swept across Ballard, alternately hiding and running. Lou Colligan, the lunatic ex-cop who came up with the idea of sealing up the north end of the city and declaring it a sovereign nation, had very quickly escalated into executing anyone who argued with him and his chosen band of cronies. It had quickly become obvious to Finn that the only way they would survive was by getting out of the Free State of North Seattle as fast as possible.

The result for their group had been fourteen deaths and two injuries. The people posted as sentries on the borders knew how to handle guns, that was obvious. The members of Finn's group were picked off one by one as they ran. Finally five of them forced their way through. Besides Finn, the survivors were a retired elementary school teacher named Janie Inoue who had been his next-door neighbor, two teenage sisters named Stacy and Josie Alleman, and a relentlessly cheerful factory worker named Danny Andersen who had taken a bullet to the upper arm but seemed thankful, well aware that a few inches to the right, and he'd be one of the dead bodies just inside the barricades.

Finn himself had a stinging graze across his left cheek. When he thought about how close he'd come to having his brains blown out, he shuddered. Maybe Danny found his close escape from death encouraging. To Finn, it just highlighted the probability that the next time, he might not be so lucky.

After crossing the barricades, they'd headed south for far enough to be out of sight by the snipers—who, fortunately, showed no inclination to follow them. Apparently "sealed borders" applied to everyone, and once someone was across the boundary, they were no longer in the jurisdiction of the Free State of North Seattle, and not worth the effort of pursuit.

Since then they'd spent most of their time split between finding food and finding places to hide. They'd seen only a few other people in all that time. Some looked like LLA and others were probably refugees like Finn himself. By mutual agreement the five survivors decided to avoid both. The former were clearly dangerous. The latter were furtive, doing their best to avoid contact, and there was no guarantee that if anyone tried to get close to them, they might not react violently out of fear. As a result, before Julia and Brandon showed up, Finn hadn't spoken to a single person from outside their group in almost four weeks.

Finn's mind kept returning to Brandon's painting of Soren. That had been a shock. Not only because of the bizarre origin of the image, but because it had reawakened hope in Finn's heart. For the past month, Finn had been whittling away at his conviction that Soren was still alive, and that he'd find him eventually. Four weeks with no word, weeks filled with a struggle to find food and to stay alive, brought home the bleak likelihood that Finn would never see his partner again, that almost certainly Soren was one of the corpses lying dead in the streets everywhere they went.

But Julia Lowell had said Soren was alive, at least for now. Heard that from God, she claimed.

Finn wasn't religious, but if that was the message, he'd happily believe in God any day of the week.

Finn's group traveled with Brandon and Julia and their followers for a day, heading southeast as well as they could, in the general direction of the bridge. They hunkered down for the evening in a building that had housed the Seattle Branch of the National Archives. The place had been ransacked, like everywhere else, but was in better shape than a lot of buildings. People desperate for food and shelter didn't care so much about destroying books and microfilms. It was a mess but the roof was intact and would keep the incoming rain off their heads.

They were all trying to find spots that provided some level of comfort for the night despite the cool, clammy air and coarse, rough indoor-outdoor carpeting that provided little in the way of cushioning. Brandon, Caria, and Julia appeared to be having some kind of confabulation, and when they saw Finn looking their way, Julia motioned for him to join them.

"We thought you should hear this," Brandon said. "Since you're the leader of the group that joined us yesterday…"

"I'm not, really, but okay."

"Seems that way. The others you were with obviously looked to you for direction. But anyway, Julia has some new… instructions."

The hesitation before the word *instructions* made it evident that Brandon, for all his visions, was still having some difficulty accepting Julia's word about the source of her information.

"We have to get out of the city," Julia said flatly. "By tomorrow evening. The door is closing. Those who are not out by sunset tomorrow will die here."

Finn looked from one of them to the other. "What's going to happen?"

She didn't answer for a moment. She seemed to be choosing her words carefully.

"I don't know, not for certain. My presumption is that it will be an earthquake. The End Times began with an earthquake. Perhaps it will end with one, as well. That's a guess. Whatever it is, there will not be a building left standing afterward. This will be a destruction as complete as when God's hand smote Sodom and Gomorrah."

"And this will happen tomorrow."

"Yes. Our job will be to get these people to, and across, the bridge before then."

"I…" Finn stopped, swallowed. "I still don't know where Soren is."

"I know." Julia's voice was sympathetic. "But you must leave that in God's hands. What is certain is that you cannot stay behind to search for him, or you will die when the cataclysm strikes."

The thought swept across his mind like a bitterly cold

wind—if Soren was left behind to perish, Finn would choose to die with him rather than face a life without him. He'd thought the hope of finding his lover alive had withered and died over the past month, but there it was, as powerful and aching as ever. If he had to stay behind, let the others cross to safety, and face alone whatever calamity Julia had foreseen, that is what he would do.

No way could he choose to save his own skin and leave Soren to his fate.

But he didn't say that. Julia would try to talk him out of it. She had obviously taken Moses's role, and was determined to get as many of them as possible to safety. When he asked her directly if her pipeline to God had told her whether Soren and he would be reunited, she had demurred, but Finn wasn't certain if that was because she honestly didn't know, or because the answer was no and she was afraid to tell him straight out.

He suspected that lies of any kind, white or not, did not come easily to Julia Lowell's lips, but even so, there was a niggling thought in the back of his mind that the older woman knew far more than she was telling them.

The next morning dawned gray and windy. There was a heaviness in the air that seemed to presage a storm. When Finn wearily opened his eyes, he rolled over with a wince at his stiff joints and looked around. He seemed to be the first awake. Along a wall, Brandon and Caria still slept, nestled in each other's arms, giving Finn a pang of combined grief and envy. He had always thought the fictional trope of someone being willing to give everything for one more night in their lover's arms was saccharine foolishness worth no more than an eye roll, but he understood now. He imagined Soren's strong arms pulling him close, and it was only with an effort that he stopped the anguish and loss from overwhelming him.

He forced himself to focus on the prosaic. He went outside, peering out carefully in both directions. Seeing no one, he took a long pee against a tree, and afterward stretched and tried to work the kinks out of his sore muscles. Five minutes later, Arden Ballinger came outside with far greater nonchalance, without hesitation unzipped, peed against the wall of the building, zipped up, and said, "Anyone else moving?"

Finn shook his head.

"It's amazing that in only a month, the city is close to a ghost town."

"I think within the first week, people fell into three groups. The ones who got out before it was too late, the ones who got killed trying, and the ones who went into hiding. A lot of the latter have probably died since then, of starvation or lack of medical care."

"You forgot the fourth group."

"Who's that?"

"The ones doing the killing."

Finn nodded grimly.

"But you're right about the survivors dying anyhow. The first day, when I decided to go with Julia and Brandon, we left behind a guy with MS. No way could he come with us, confined to a wheelchair, chronically ill."

"Harsh."

"Unavoidable. Actually, he's the one who said he wouldn't go, that it was ridiculous to think he could keep up even with help. Julia had some kind of divinely-inspired message for him that he was supposed to tell the next group to follow us, but that might just have been to give him some kind of purpose to hold on to."

"I don't think she'd do that."

Arden shrugged. "No idea. It's pretty clear she believes

what she's saying. Whether it's actually true or not is something else entirely."

"But you followed her anyway."

The older man didn't answer for some time, but stared off in the direction of the lake, his eyes distant.

"I'm honestly not sure why I did. Maybe because it seemed like doing something was better than doing nothing. I'm not religious, never have been. Not even what the mystical types call 'spiritual.' I've always figured this is what we have." He gave a gesture around him. "That's it. When you're dead, you're gone. No higher purpose, no reward for the good and punishment for the bad. Didn't bother me, it just seemed obvious."

"Didn't? As in, now you're not sure?"

Again, there was a long pause.

"I'll admit she's got something." His voice sounded reluctant even to say that much. "What it is, I have no idea. As far as what this means regarding God, religion, and whatnot… I'm not going to worry about it. She's right about one thing for sure. We need to get out of the city. Whether she's right about some sort of catastrophe coming or not."

"There's no guarantee anything will be better once we get across."

"No, there's not. No guarantee of anything, far as I can see. But like I said, I've always preferred doing something over doing nothing. And maybe I can be some use in helping us get to, and across, the bridge. At least I'm armed. If we get into a serious skirmish I'm not sure how long my ammunition will last. But given that it's been a month since all this shit started, I'm guessing the LLA is in the same boat. With the number of bodies we've seen, it seems like they were using up their bullets pretty fast."

Finn didn't answer, and for a time the two men stood in silence, watching the rising wind swaying the branches of the fir trees against the distant backdrop of the lake, gray under the clouds.

Finally Arden said, "You lost someone in all this, right?"

"Yes."

"A guy? You're gay, right?"

Finn gave him a quick side-eye, but Arden's face held no hostility, just the same serious, guarded expression he always wore.

"Yes. His name is Soren. I last saw him the day the riots started. No word or sign since."

The older man seemed to pick up on Finn's reluctance.

"Just to say, I got nothing against gays. None of my business who fucks who as long as it's consensual. I wanted to use the right pronouns."

"Thanks." He looked at Arden with a frown. "How about you? You lost someone in all this?"

"Nah. At least, no one close. Parents are both gone. I've got a sister in Minneapolis, but we don't much get along. Ex-wife I haven't spoken to in years. I'm not even sure if she's still in Seattle. Other than that, a few drinking buddies and friendly coworkers. I'm pretty used to being on my own." He paused. "I'm sorry about your boyfriend."

The words sounded odd, spoken in his gruff voice, but he seemed sincere, not mocking, and Finn decided to respond in kind.

"Thanks. It's torn me up inside. Julia says he's still alive, but then in the same breath tells me if we don't get out of the city today we'll all die. So I don't know whether to follow her, or stay behind and keep looking for Soren and take my chances with facing God's wrath."

"No idea how you'd make that choice."

"I guess I'll figure that out once we get to the bridge."

They both turned as Ronnie Sulzbach came outside, yawning and blinking. "Let's call room service. Full breakfast, orange juice, hot coffee."

"I wish. God, I miss coffee."

Arden snorted. "I miss any kind of food that doesn't come in foil-wrapped packages. Maybe once we get out of the city, there'll be game to hunt. I'd just about kill for a t-bone."

"With a glass of red wine."

A flicker of a smile crossed Arden's face. "Guess we'll keep dreaming. Nearest cows are probably down near Puyallup, and that'd be a hell of a walk. Until then, do we have any of those Pop-Tarts left?"

A half-hour later, they were all assembled in front of the ruined archives building. Ragged, dirty, underfed, but resolute. Finn had to agree with Arden—Julia had something. The fact that she'd led her group for a month without a single casualty was nothing short of remarkable. People gravitated toward her, believed what she said, even ones who a couple of months ago would have scoffed at the idea of prophecies.

"Today, we have to reach the bridge and then cross it." Her voice was steady and strong. "We will have one chance at it. I do not know how well it will be defended. I cannot guarantee safety, then or afterward. But I do know this is the day we have to do it. If you stay behind, you will be dead by nightfall."

A ripple shuddered its way through the group, but no one spoke.

"You must be brave. Do not let your doubts slow you down. But don't take any foolish and unnecessary risks. Stay close together and stay alert."

Ronnie Sulzbach, who stood near Finn in what had been the building's parking lot, frowned and raised one hand to shade her eyes. "Um… I think there's someone over there." She raised one hand to point.

A shot rang out. Ronnie made a sound like someone

being punched in the solar plexus, collapsed to her knees, and fell forward onto the asphalt. There were screams and shouted obscenities as all order vanished, and everyone scattered for cover. More shots—Finn was too panicked to look behind and see if anyone else had been hit—and he ducked behind the corner of the building, his entire body shaking.

Two other people ended up in the same place—Trevor Keene, the young man who'd been with Julia's group, and Janie Inoue, the retired elementary school teacher who had been Finn and Soren's next-door neighbor.

Janie, who despite her size and age had a resolute toughness Finn could only pretend to, said, "What do those horrid people think they're accomplishing by attacking us? What threat could we possibly be?"

"It's *Lord of the Flies*," Trevor said. "Take away the veneer of civilization, and we're all savages underneath." His voice caught. "They killed Ronnie. She was such a nice person. It isn't fair."

"No," Finn said. "No, it's not."

"What do we do now?"

"I have no idea. I don't have a weapon."

Finn peered carefully around the corner toward the now-empty parking lot. Three figures—two men and a woman—came out of a thicket of bushes across the lawn, walking cautiously and slowly. All three were emaciated, their cheeks sunken, eyes staring wide in nearly skeletal faces. One of the men had a hunting rifle under his arm.

The woman said, "We only hit one of 'em."

The man with the gun said in a hoarse voice, "Better than nothing."

They grabbed Ronnie's body by the arms and started dragging it away, back toward the shelter of the undergrowth.

Trevor stared with undisguised horror in his eyes. "They... they're going to..." He stopped, his Adam's apple moving convulsively in his throat. He looked like he was about to vomit.

Finn forced his own nausea and revulsion down. When he spoke, he tried to keep his voice steady. "Desperate people do desperate things."

Moments later they were joined by Julia, Brandon, Caria, and several others, who came around the back side of the building and edged carefully along the wall to where Finn and the others stood.

"Give them a few more minutes to move away from here, deeper into the trees," Julia whispered. "Then it'll be safe."

"You know that for sure?" Janie Inoue asked.

Julia nodded.

"Those people..." Trevor started, then took a deep breath. "Those people are... they're..." He didn't seem to be able to force himself to say the word *cannibals*.

"I know," Julia said. "I saw. I heard. I'm grieved for Ronnie, who was a lovely person, but her soul is in God's hands now. I will weep for her later, but now my responsibility is to get us out of here." She got a distant look in her eye, and frowned slightly as if listening to something none of the others could hear. "Comfort yourself knowing that vengeance will be had upon them. Them and the others like them. They've killed our friend, but their own deaths are mere hours away." She paused. "Now, let's go. We need to find the others who hid from our attackers. We have several miles to walk, and I do not know what obstacles we will face. But like Ronnie's soul, we must commend ourselves to God and trust that whatever happens, it is unfolding as it must."

thirty-two

. . .

Lydia Moreton and Jeff Landry faced each other across the dust-covered surface of a large desk. Every muscle in Lydia's body was tensed, ready to spring. Jeff's body was still to the point of complete immobility. Only the nervous darting of his eyes and the feverish flush of his cheeks gave any indication that he was wound to the snapping point.

Lydia had been certain for two weeks that Jeff had been looking for a pretense and an opportunity to get rid of her. She was second-in-command, and he had a history of eliminating seconds-in-command when they got too smart, too powerful, too cocky. Too whatever. Jeff didn't get where he was by taking chances. And now that all laws had been effectively suspended, and a murder would carry no consequences?

No fucking way would he be comfortable with any kind of challenge to his authority.

Lydia liked challenges to her command as little as Jeff did. The problem was, Jeff had become increasingly erratic since the attacks began, as if the actual fruition of almost ten years of planning had entirely overthrown the precarious balance of his mental state.

First, there was the business of Anderson Quaice and the radio transmissions. She had urged him to pursue the man, find out what the transmissions were. She was certain they were important—and important to stop. He'd shrugged her off. More urgent things to deal with, he said. Lydia tried to convince him the mysterious broadcasts were being used to coordinate resistance, but Jeff downplayed the relevance.

As a result, when he finally did decide to search for Quaice and his cohort, they missed capturing them by mere minutes. Then Guy Nordin, one of Lydia's staunchest allies, got his head cracked open on the pavement and was left for dead, and the only one they captured was a young associate of Quaice's named Soren Conover who appeared to know next to nothing about the broadcasts.

Then, to make matters worse, Landry decided to try to trick Conover into cooperating by staging a fake rescue. Lydia had gone along reluctantly, but the whole thing came to pieces when she was attacked unexpectedly and Conover escaped.

The worst indignity was that he took her gun with him. Guns were precious commodities. Hers could be replaced, but the idea that Landry's idiotic scheme had not only freed a potentially valuable captive, but armed him, infuriated her.

She left Conover a message painted on a wall nearby. Whether he ever saw it, she didn't know, but it at least vented a little of her anger at being thwarted. When Landry found out about it, for some reason it made him apoplectic with rage —she'd honestly expected he'd kill her then and there. At that point, she hadn't replaced her gun, so if he'd wanted to get rid of her, she wouldn't have had a chance. Instead he confined himself to screaming in her face about how useless she was, and how the great goals of the LLA couldn't be buried beneath her own personal vendettas. Did she understand him?

She said she did, speaking as meekly as she could manage.

At the same time, she stored up all of what he said in her mind. Every single word would be paid for.

She also made sure to find a new gun the next day.

Since then, Landry's mental state had gone from bad to worse. He refused to sleep—didn't need it, he said, but she was convinced it was because he knew he would be vulnerable while he slept. His appearance went from disordered to haggard to emaciated. As his body withered, his paranoia intensified. He randomly had his own associates executed, for any reason or no reason at all.

That was when Lydia began, surreptitiously, to talk to the strongest and most intelligent of their people, priming them to question Landry's sanity, and to consider whether he was going to be able to lead the rebellion long-term—or if it might be that he'd outlived his usefulness to the LLA.

It was a dangerous game, that. She knew it. One word to the wrong person, then passed along to Landry, and she'd be dead. Knowing him, it wouldn't be a quick gunshot to the head or axe to the back of the neck. He'd come to call anything contrary to his will *high treason*, and given those guilty of it a fate as prolonged and excruciating as the old hanged, drawn, and quartered sentence the sixteenth-century English had been so fond of.

She looked for opportunities to catch him alone and undefended, but it seemed like Landry and his most trusted guard could never be caught dozing. It would never do to kill Landry and ten seconds later have one of his guards shoot her in the back.

It took almost a month before she had the chance she'd been waiting for. A minor skirmish just south of their headquarters, in an area they'd thought had been completely emptied, brought all the armed men and women available running out to deal with the problem. Landry, for a few minutes—she couldn't anticipate how long—was left unattended.

Lydia edged her way into the room. Her superior stared at her, his glassy eyes looking furtively to one side or another as he realized that in ordering his guards to deal with the skirmish, he might have made a serious tactical error.

"Lydia," he said. "Why aren't you helping to destroy our enemies?"

"There are enough people already there. They can take care of it."

"My orders were that every available person needed to join in."

"I had other priorities."

The corner of his mouth twitched. "Priorities? Such as?"

"Such as having a little discussion with you."

"About what?"

Okay, here it was. No other option than the truth. "About your continued role as leader of the LLA in Seattle."

He gave her one of his ghastly smiles. They'd been terrifying before. In a face that was now nearly skeletal, they were like something out of a nightmare.

"By whose authority are you questioning my leadership?"

"My own. I thought that'd be obvious."

"You know what happens to people who have these kinds of ideas."

"That's if we get caught at it."

Landry's right hand twitched. Ordinarily, he kept his body under such tight reins that he could remain completely still, but maybe the prolonged lack of food and sleep over the past month made his control slip.

Lydia wouldn't have a second chance if that twitch meant what she thought it did.

In one smooth movement, she pulled up her gun and shot Landry directly in the midriff.

He rose with a jerky motion. His left hand clasped the wound, but blood spurted between his fingers. His right felt blindly for the handle of his gun, but missed once, twice, and with a fluttery motion, gave up trying. He fell to his knees.

Lydia went around the side of the desk. Landry gazed up at her, his eyes wide and astonished. Blood trickled from the corner of his mouth. He said, in a conversational tone, "Dying hurts more than I thought it would," and pitched forward onto the floor.

She watched his body for a good thirty seconds to see if he would move again.

He didn't.

After that, there was nothing to do but to wait for the return of the guard and see if her estimation of how they'd react was correct. The first one made his noisy entrance only a couple of minutes later. One thing she'd been right about—how little time she'd had. It was fortunate she'd seized the opportunity, because the great likelihood was she wouldn't have gotten another.

Luck was with her in another way. The man who came in first was Pete Lachman, one of the ones she had trusted enough to talk to about her plans for Landry, three weeks earlier. He looked at her, looked at the bloodied corpse on the floor, and spoke in a flat voice.

"Finally decided to take care of things?"

She slipped her gun back into its holster. "It was the first chance I had."

He nodded. "You shouldn't have any trouble getting the others to rally around you. You're not the only one who has been concerned about Landry."

"Any loyalists I should know about?"

"None you need to concern yourself with."

Other LLA came into the building. She heard their talking and laughter—evidently the action against the uprising had been successful—but as they came into the office, they fell into stunned silence except for someone who said under his breath, "Holy fuck, she actually did it."

Lachman turned around and swept his eyes across the group.

"As you see, the situation has changed. You now take your orders from her. Is that clear?" His voice was commanding. A challenge.

No one spoke.

"Are there any objections?"

Lydia had to stifle a laugh. No one who wasn't crazy would take that bait.

Again, there were no responses.

"Good. Abbott, Boland, Leekirk, you stay. The rest of you are dismissed."

There were soft murmurs as they obeyed. None of them, Lydia observed, looked obviously hostile. There was relief in more than one face, something that boded well for her takeover.

Doug Abbott gave her a curious frown. "What made your mind up? Not that I object, mind you. Landry was nutty as squirrel shit, and you never knew from one moment to the next whether he'd be thanking you or ordering your immediate execution."

"Opportunity. Combined with a realization that things couldn't go on in the same way much longer. He was near the breaking point. So, in a different way, was I."

Abbott seemed to accept that without any reservations.

"What now?" Lachman's transfer of allegiance, at least, had been instantaneous. She was completely in charge.

"First, did you get rid of the little insurrection we had this morning?"

He nodded. "A dozen or so people. Must have been hiding in a building, or maybe they were coming up from south Seattle. Everything south of downtown is still pretty much a wasteland—we've got control of maybe ten percent of it. The rest is run by gangs and bands of refugees who decided to take matters into their own hands. In any case, what made them think that a dozen ragged men and women could attack our headquarters and survive, I don't know. But whatever they were thinking, they aren't thinking it any longer."

"All dead?"

"All dead."

"Good." She leaned her butt against the edge of the desk, relishing the thrill she got from her ankle being mere inches from Landry's dead fingers. "Any other immediate issues we need to deal with?"

"No. We're still in decent shape with food. The warehouse we took over on the first day had enough to keep us going for quite a while. Whoever thought that was a good first move…"

"That was me."

"Well, it was spot-on. My guess is if we hadn't done that, we'd all be dead of starvation by now. Other than the warehouse, downtown Seattle has fuck-all in the way of non-perishable food."

"So no other immediate concerns, then?"

He shrugged. "Nothing pressing."

She gave him a satisfied nod. "Good. Then we have a little time to deal with a personal vendetta. I'm still pissed at our former leader for his decision not to pursue Anderson Quaice and take out his foreign-language broadcasts. They're still going, yes?"

"Not as frequently as before, but yes, we still pick them up now and again. He must have a battery-powered transmitter of some kind."

"It's time we put an end to it. Whatever its intent, it's not about helping us. Plus, I promised a smug academic asshole named Soren Conover that I was going to see him tortured to death, and I intend to keep that promise. Has there been any word of the ones associated with the radio broadcasts?"

"Only a few questionable sightings. We're spread too thin

to do any more than that, at least when we don't know where exactly they are. Patrols have spotted what we believe to be some of them, but always from a distance and always at a time it was impractical to pursue. Conover was seen for certain a few days ago, leading a bunch of little kids. He was on the other side of the Fremont Cut, heading north, so by the time we'd have found a bridge across the cut and then doubled back, he would probably have been long gone. At that point we figured it wasn't worth finding a way across then running around randomly trying to chase him down."

"Reasonable decision at the time."

Lachman looked relieved.

"But now I want them found. All of them. I'm no longer interested in finding a way to translate the messages. I just want them stopped permanently. First, we need some reconnaissance to find out where they are and how many. After that, we go after them. And then I need to finish with Conover. I plan on handling that one personally."

Two days passed. Patrols were sent out with the order to observe, not confront. The evening of the second day one of the men foolishly told his patrol leader he saw some movement near a burned-out building and would go investigate it, and—even more foolishly—the leader agreed to let him do it. The scout succeeded in shooting one of them in the leg, but was rewarded by having his head smashed in and getting shot for good measure. The remaining three on the patrol decided the "don't confront" order was probably a good idea.

One of the people in the group was definitely Quaice. No doubt about it. Two of the others seemed to answer the description of some of Quaice's associates. So they had at least his party accounted for, although it wasn't immediately obvious from their movements where they were heading.

The woman's leg injury would slow them down. Knowing the general soft-heartedness of people like Quaice, no way would they make the strategic decision and leave her behind, as Lachman had done with Guy Nordin. They'd help her along, and that would leave them even more vulnerable.

Where would they likely be going? Conover's group had headed north, but apparently found the way blocked by the lunatics who sealed the borders of North Seattle. Those particular lunatics, Lydia knew, were heavily armed and as ruthless as the worst of the LLA. Still, they'd have to be dealt with eventually.

For now, though, at least the North Seattle barricades served one purpose. They hemmed Conover and his group in, forced them to turn east instead of north. Only a fool would try crossing the Free State's barriers without massive numbers and heavy weapons. So if Conover was trying to get his followers out of the city—which, presumably, he was—there was only one reasonable guess as to where they were going.

The Evergreen Point Floating Bridge.

Quaice, it must be presumed, had orchestrated the plan, so chances were he'd be heading in the same direction.

Other, more incidental, information came in as well. Another large group spotted by the patrols were apparently heading the same way, coming down Sand Point Way along the west side of the lake. This particular group was led by an old woman who looked like some kind of revivalist preacher. They were perhaps two or three dozen, but didn't look like they posed any danger. Lydia doubted any of them were even armed.

She gave orders that their progress toward the bridgehead was not to be impeded. Let them get there, thinking they were getting away. Let them start across the bridge, get to the point there was no way they could turn back.

Then spring the trap. They'd be caught in a narrow spot

that had nowhere to hide, nowhere to run except the two-kilometer span over to the east side of Lake Washington. They'd be outgunned, and—given that they had at least one person with an injury and another leading a bunch of little kids—unable to outrun her and her chosen squad of assassins.

The light was fading fast in the office, where Lydia Moreton now sat behind the desk of command. Shortly after she'd killed him, Landry's body had been dragged away and added to an enormous pile of corpses a few blocks over that now stank so bad they were detectable from a mile away. Of the former leader, the only trace was a bloodstain on the wooden floor that wouldn't come out despite several attempts at cleaning. Lydia watched as a gray fly edged its way across the blackened stain, moving slowly and unwarily.

Her foot came down with a smack and crushed it flat.

Tomorrow. They would pull together everything they had, and tomorrow they would set out for the bridgehead. With luck, they'd get there in time.

At which point Quaice's little gang would be smashed as completely as the unfortunate fly.

thirty-three

. . .

Brandon Nguyen squinted into the distance at the long expanse of the Evergreen Point Floating Bridge. This far off it looked like two parallel bands, each narrow as a bootlace. He could barely make out wrecked cars all along its length. The westbound lanes looked clearer. No surprise there. When the riots started, there had been a great many more people trying to get out of Seattle than into it.

All around him stood what was left of the buildings on the east side of the University of Washington campus. Several were burnt-out shells, with streaks of black soot running up the stone and brickwork that was still standing. The ones untouched by fire had been smashed by the riots. There was not an intact window or door to be seen, and everywhere was the logo and brutal graffiti of the LLA. There were multiple signs of the violence of the last month, but they saw no one, and their walk down Sand Point Way had gone unchallenged.

Even the horrifying attack by the desperate and starving individuals who had killed poor Ronnie Sulzbach wasn't repeated. It was as if some mysterious force had cleared out all the dangers between them and escape, leaving the way wide open.

Or maybe Julia's prophetic gift was showing them the safest path.

A rising wind ruffled Brandon's long hair, and he automatically brushed it back out of his eyes. The clouds were gray and fast-moving, presaging an oncoming storm. Lousy weather to try to cross a long bridge on foot.

"Don't you think it's odd that we haven't been attacked today as we've gotten closer to the bridge?" Finn Donnelly's handsome face was creased with worry. "I thought any exits from the city would be guarded."

"Maybe they figured out they couldn't stop up every way out, and thought if some people left, they weren't worth pursuing."

"That sounds like wishful thinking."

Brandon couldn't argue with that. "Are you still intending to wait on this side if you don't find your boyfriend?"

Finn didn't answer for a moment.

"I have to," he finally said in a low voice. "I know it sounds like some kind of romantic cliché, but I can't leave him behind. I honestly would rather die myself than abandon him. I know he'd do the same if the situation were reversed."

Brandon nodded. "I understand." He took a deep breath. "I wonder if Caria would do that for me?"

Finn didn't answer.

"I feel like since all this started, we've taken off in different directions. Before—well, we were kind of in a humdrum relationship. Mostly my fault, I'll admit. Then, when the visions started coming, it was like I'd been supercharged. Everything seemed brighter, more vivid, more alive. It jolted everything, all the way down to my sex drive. I haven't felt that continuously horny since I was a teenager."

Finn chuckled. "Nothing wrong with that."

"No. And Caria was fine with it. But I could tell she was struggling with the other parts—the focus on my art, how hyper I was, and especially where the visions were coming from. I couldn't think about anything but painting, except when I was desperate for my next orgasm."

Another chuckle.

"It seemed like despite our physical relationship getting hot and heavy for the first time in forever, we had somehow been pulled into different worlds. It was like, we'd talk, but weren't speaking the same language. Then the attacks started, and she met Julia."

"I've noticed she never gets far from Julia's side."

Brandon nodded. "It's not that I mind, you know? Caria needed an anchor when everything fell apart. What I regret is that I wasn't that, for her. That I couldn't help her when she was desperate for it."

"Even if you care about someone, you can't meet all of their needs."

"I guess. I just wonder if… if Julia's right, and we do make it across the bridge to safety… if Caria and I will ever have what we had."

"If it's meant to be, it'll happen." Finn gave a rueful wince. "Speaking of romantic clichés."

"Maybe." Brandon paused. "I suppose the first step is getting across the bridge. If we get ambushed by the LLA, my love life isn't going to be top priority."

Twenty minutes later they were assembled, following Julia and Caria downhill toward the south campus, the bridge across the Montlake Cut, and—if all went well—the bridgehead leading across the lake itself. After that, there'd be only the two-kilometer hike to the other side between them and the Promised Land Julia had hinted at.

The cover was poor, at least up to the short bridge across the Cut, so they went warily. Brandon felt like they must be visible from miles away. The lack of a challenge wasn't reassuring to him. It seemed sinister, as heavy with ominous possibilities as the lowering cloud bank and freshening wind. Whatever the cause, it was better than being attacked outright, but he still was increasingly jumpy, starting at every noise, at every wind-blown piece of litter skipping across their path, at every sharp cry of a gull or crow.

After a half-hour's walk through the deserted campus, the twin towers of the Montlake Cut bridge appeared ahead, each side flanked with rhododendron bushes and tall fir trees. Maybe they'd actually get across it, then across the longer bridge spanning the lake, without being ambushed. Maybe they really were the only people around. Maybe…

"There's someone moving down there." Caria pointed toward the Cut.

Instantly Julia stopped walking, peering nearsightedly in the direction Caria had indicated. Everyone else, following in an obedient flock behind her, stopped as well.

Brandon shaded his eyes from the wind and frowned. She was right. The woman had good eyes. There was a group of people down there, perhaps two hundred meters from where they were. Some figures—it was uncertain how many—were moving toward the little bridge across the Cut, their motions slow and wary.

"What now?" Brandon whispered to Julia.

Without looking at him, she said, "I have no idea."

"So your divine guidance didn't mention this?" Brandon was immediately aware of how snarky that sounded, especially given that he'd gotten information as well, ostensibly from the same source as Julia did.

But Julia seemed to take it at face value. "No. I do not know whether these are friends or enemies, nor what we should do. They're between us and the bridge across the Cut."

"I think at least some of the people down there are kids," Caria said, in a puzzled voice.

"So they're probably not…" Brandon began, then trailed off.

"We have no choice but to keep heading toward the

bridge," Julia said. "Our time is running out. We will find out if they are friends or foes soon enough, but in any case, we cannot delay any longer."

They continued moving downhill toward the Cut. A hundred meters, fifty.

"It's one guy," Brandon said. "One guy and a bunch of…" but before he could finish the sentence he was cut off by Finn, who was standing a little behind him.

"Oh. My. Dear. God." Finn's voice was high, wild, triumphant, and ended with something that was halfway between a laugh and a sob. Then he was running, sprinting down the hill, his long legs driving against the ground as if he were trying to launch himself bodily into the air.

"Soren!" he called out. "Soren, wait! It's me!"

One of the figures turned, and after a moment, he was running as well, until they collided in a tangle of arms and just held on, overcome by emotion.

Julia and the others started down after them and finally joined the two men by the roadside.

Soren reached out and touched Finn's cut cheek. "What did they do to you?"

"Near miss with a gunshot. But what about you? Your poor eyes."

"Doesn't matter. Nothing else matters now." They kissed, and for a time there was no sound but the wind and the soft footsteps of about a dozen children, coming up from behind where Soren and Finn stood. They looked fearful, almost feral.

One of the youngest, a thin wisp of a boy with blond hair and a *Spider-man* t-shirt, spoke up and said, "It's okay. Don't be afraid."

The others—even some considerably older—immediately looked relieved, and their faces lost some of the wariness. For some reason, this little boy was the group's leader, despite his age.

Then Brandon's heart stuttered in his chest. "Perry?" His voice was thin. "Perry Abraham?"

The little boy turned, his large, luminous gray eyes fixed on Brandon's.

"Yes."

He seemed unsurprised that Brandon knew who he was. In his face was nothing but a deep tranquility, a stillness that was unassailable, perhaps unreachable.

"You're…" Brandon stopped, fumbling in his pocket for his cellphone. Amazingly, it still turned on, but there was almost no juice left in the battery. He quickly flipped through the images until he found *The Hands of the Magician*, then held it out for Perry to see.

Perry peered at the image for a few moments. Still, nothing in his face registered surprise.

"That's me."

Brandon nodded.

Once again, no questions about how Brandon had known. Here, Brandon sensed, was a boy who was of the same ilk as Julia and himself. Whatever power they'd tapped into, Perry had as well, although it might manifest itself differently just as it had in Julia and him. There was an instant connection between the artist and the little boy, as there had been between Julia and Caria, just as there was between Finn and Soren.

Links were forming. Now they had to see if those links would form a chain strong enough to pull them all to safety.

But Brandon's phone finally gave up the ghost. The image winked out. Forever. No electricity to charge it, no way to access those paintings ever again. Lost, like so much else in this devastated city.

Julia spoke in a gentle voice.

"We need to keep moving. There will be time for celebrating reunions later."

Finn and Soren separated, both of their eyes glistening

with tears, and when they turned away toward the Montlake Bridge, their hands clasped in a gesture that said, *I will never let you go. Never again.*

In an unconscious mirroring, Perry reached up and slipped his hand into Brandon's.

"You and me are oracles," he said in a calm, uninflected voice, as if it were the most natural thing in the world.

"Is that the word for us?"

Perry nodded. "Soren taught me that word. He said that's what I am. So are you, and so is she"—he gestured with his free hand toward Julia—"and there's one other one. We'll meet her once we get across that little bridge." A quick frown crossed his face. "There was supposed to be one more, but the Bitch killed him."

"The Bitch?"

Another nod. "You know who she is. You've seen her, too."

Brandon immediately thought of the woman in scarlet, tied to a stake but smiling as her blood fed the flames. *The Pyre of the Former World.*

"Yes. I do know who she is."

"There was a guy named Doyle. He was supposed to help us, but she killed him. He was the first one she killed, the day it started."

"Because he was an oracle?"

"I don't think it mattered to her." Perry's expression darkened. "She kills because that's all she knows how to do."

"Julia said the same thing about her."

"She's waiting for us, too," Perry said. "She thinks she's going to surprise us. But she can't, because I know where she is. So does the other oracle, the one we'll meet next. The Bitch thinks that her guns are going to kill us all. That she's going to win. She's wrong."

Brandon gave a little shudder, partly from the coolness of the wind fluttering his clothing, partly from how Perry spoke, as if what he said was no more remarkable than commenting on what had happened in school that day.

"You're sure? You're sure we'll succeed?"

"Yes." Perry paused. "But that doesn't mean... it doesn't mean we're all going to get across the bridge. Some of us will fall." He gave a fluttering motion with his free hand, like a leaf tumbling downward on the wind. "But so will she. She and all the ones following her."

"Do you know which ones of us will die?"

There was a long silence, and when Perry spoke, his voice was reluctant.

"Yes. But there's one..." He stopped, swallowed. "One I'm not sure about. One who the voice hasn't decided about yet."

"The voice?" But Brandon immediately knew what Perry was talking about. This was how it manifested in Perry, just as Julia's messages from God and his own oracular visions.

"I don't know if it's telling the truth." The little boy sounded troubled. "It's always told me the truth before, and it's never told me two things that could happen, where it didn't know which *would* happen. So maybe it doesn't want me to find out that something bad is going to happen."

"It's told you bad things before, though, right?"

"Yes. Lots."

"So maybe it really isn't certain."

"Maybe. I hope so. Because sometimes when things have been bad for a long time, you just need one good thing to happen. Just one. It doesn't make up for all the bad things. Nothing ever could. But at least it means you shouldn't stop trying." He took a deep breath. "That's what I think. I believe the good thing will happen, because we need to not give up."

thirty-four

· · ·

Soren's heart pounded. Despite what was ahead for them, who could be lying in wait, at the moment all he could feel was delirious happiness.

Finn. Beyond all odds, they'd found each other. He had to fight down the urge to pull him into an embrace again. Not only to feel the comfort of his warmth and strength and solidity, but to reassure himself he wasn't hallucinating, the trauma of the last four weeks finally drowning him in delirium.

He gave Finn's hand a little squeeze, and was rewarded by one in return.

Whatever happened now, Finn was really here. And it would be a very long time before anything would induce Soren to leave his side.

He looked down at the little bridge over the Montlake Cut, recalling the first time he'd crossed it on foot, the day the attacks began. That time their group had been under fire from a sniper. He wondered what had happened to the others—Cassandra, Gavin, Dr. Quaice, and the enigmatic Mary Hansard. He hoped to see Mary again to thank her once more for giving him information that saved his life. He was quite certain that however she knew, her instructions to allow himself to be captured and then to run toward danger were why he was here, now, reunited with Finn Donnelly and finally facing the path out of the city.

They crossed the bridge over the Cut without incident. Dare he hope there would be no attempt made to stop them? After all they'd been through, it seemed impossible it'd be that easy. But only a short walk lay between them and the bridgehead, the path straight as an arrow between East Montlake Park and what was left of the Seattle Yacht Club.

Soren looked down the road ahead of them. No movement other than the wind swaying the branches of the trees, no sound except the thrum of waves against the lakeshore. The westbound lanes of Highway 520 looked reasonably clear. So up the off-ramp, then…

"Hello, we meet again."

A friendly voice made Soren whirl around, only afterward wondering why he hadn't drawn his gun. Would that response ever become automatic? But there'd been no need— the voice belonged to a familiar face, and Soren was immediately brought back to the first time he'd heard it, when it had said something even more outlandish.

I mean no harm. In fact, I've been waiting for you all.

Mary Hansard smiled broadly at him. "Hello, Finn," she said, still in the same light tone.

Finn frowned, looking from her to Soren then back again. "Um… do I know…?"

"No," she said cheerfully. "But that's okay. We're over the first hurdle. Now for the second one, right?" She turned, and said in a loud voice, "Come on out, I told you it was them."

Walking from the direction of the bridge were the three others—Dr. Quaice, Cassandra, and Gavin—all of their faces registering some combination of surprise, relief, and anxiety.

"I really should stop questioning what you say, Mary," Dr. Quaice said. He walked up and gave Soren a firm handshake.

"Honest to God, Conover, I thought we'd never see you again." He frowned. "You look like hell, though."

"Had a bit of a rough time getting here."

"We should probably wait for catching up until we're on the other side of the lake," Mary said. "We don't have a lot of time left, and I'm not moving so quickly at the moment."

Brandon, Julia, and Perry approached her slowly, almost reverently. Brandon, especially, looked like he'd seen a ghost.

"Well, hello there," Mary said cheerfully. "I'm so glad to finally get a chance to meet you all."

"You're one of us." Perry's face was solemn. "You're the last one."

"Oh, not really the last. Just the last one you'll meet today."

"You're another of the people I painted." Brandon reflexively reached for his phone then stopped. "Oh, right, it's out of battery. Damn."

"That's okay. I don't need to see it."

"You were standing at the end of a damaged roadway. You…"

"I know." She spoke gently. "I know what you saw. It's okay."

"You are steadfast in what you need to do?" Julia asked.

"Of course. Don't worry about me. In my mind, it's already happened. Everything is all of a piece, forever, unchangeable. There is nothing to fear."

Julia nodded. "The blessings of God be upon you."

Mary smiled. "Thanks." Then she looked at Soren, and a flash of a frown crossed her face. "There's just one more thing…"

She stepped toward him, and Soren caught a glimpse of the woman he'd seen a couple of times while they were still in Dr. Quaice's house, a face pinched with pain, whose knowledge of the future was agony, giving lie to her claim that she wasn't afraid. Her features settled back into their previous calm almost too quickly to register, but for a moment, he got a sense of what it must be like for her to know what was going to happen, good and bad, and to be unable to stop it or even alter its course by a centimeter.

"Before we go I need to give you something." She reached out one hand and touched Soren's forehead. There was a jolt, like a spark of electricity, where her fingertips contacted his skin. "I'm so sorry."

His head snapped back, his eyes opening wide. "What did you just do?"

"It's a gift that you may regret receiving, but I can't help that. I gave it to you, and that's the way it is."

"Gave what to me?"

"Once I'm gone. You'll be the oracle in my place. The knowledge can't simply die. You carried it after me, then you gave it to another, and on and on. The lineage must contin-ue." She gave him a faint smile. "You'll find it's a mixed bless-ing. The knowledge of what's to come, with no ability to change it. One thing I've learned, though, is that it has completely erased my fear of death. If my death is just another frozen event in the not-present, something that is already fixed, then it loses some of its power. A lot of our fear of death is because we never know when it will happen, or how, so we're always apprehensive. When everything is locked in place—well, worrying is kind of pointless, isn't it? What is simply is, and that's all."

"Are you telling me you're going to die?"

She laughed. "At some point, yes."

"And you know when."

"More or less."

"But how…"

She waved him off. "Not now. It's time to cross, finally. The philosophical discussion can wait. Just remember you aren't alone. The other oracles will help you when you need it."

She gave a quick smile to Brandon, Julia, and Perry, then turned and hobbled down the street, wincing whenever she put weight on her injured leg.

"Do you need help?" Soren called after her.

"No," she said, still facing forward. "My leg will get me where I need to go."

"Who the hell…" Finn started, as they began to walk downhill, following her.

"Her name is Mary Hansard. And I don't understand any better than you do. But I trust what she says despite that."

Finn looked at Julia. "She's one of you."

Julia nodded. "We each hold the gift differently. But yes."

"And all of you gained it the day of the earthquake."

"It's a little premature to say *all* when you've only met four of us, but as far as we know, that is the case."

"So whatever unleashed all this destruction turned some people into oracles."

"Yes."

"And now Soren is one?"

Soren looked at his partner and shrugged. "I don't know what she did to me. I don't feel changed."

"She said it wouldn't transfer until she died."

"We should follow her," Julia said. "She was right about putting off the discussion until later. It is time."

She followed Mary, and after a moment, so did the others.

Once they were out of earshot, Finn said quietly, "Do you buy that this is a gift from God?"

Soren didn't answer for a moment, and when he spoke, his voice was thoughtful. "I don't know. I think if there is a cause behind what's happened, it's pretty far from my concept of a benevolent God. The old idea of 'everything happens for a reason' kind of falls on its face if the reason turns out not to care much for humanity."

Finn gave his hand a squeeze. "In any case, we found each

other. At the moment, I'm going to lean on that and assume everything else will work out."

Soren smiled at him, but as they walked he recalled the words of Perry Abraham.

It could happen either way and we don't know which… There are different endings. In one of them, you're crying and crying and can't stop.

Could things still go wrong, badly wrong? Or did finding Finn mean everything was going to end happily?

Mary certainly seemed cheerful about the whole thing. But then, she usually was.

Ahead lay the off-ramp from the westbound lanes of the Evergreen Point Floating Bridge, less than a quarter-mile away. Soren looked behind him. Colin and Emily herded the children along, and the adults trailed in a ragged line of perhaps three dozen people. Brandon and Julia seemed to be in close conversation, but he couldn't pick up what they were saying. What did the two of them think of their chances of making it across?

Soren considered asking, then decided against it.

The wind fluttered his hair, and he felt the first sting of raindrops. The lake was gray under the pall of clouds, the water stirred into a chaos of waves and spray. The roadway ahead lay open. Wrecked cars had been cleared to the side, beckoning them.

Come into my parlor, said the spider to the fly.

Was there an ambush waiting for them? They'd seen no sign of it, but the back of Soren's neck suddenly prickled. This was too easy.

Up the off-ramp, and onto the rising span of the bridge. It looped upward then down onto the lake surface, where the concrete was held up by huge pontoons. Soren motioned the children to go ahead of him and Finn, and drew abreast of Brandon and Julia.

Without preamble, Julia said, "Keep watchful. Our enemies are almost upon us."

The last of them moved onto the bridge and up the steep incline, and that was when another crowd of people closed in from behind them. Out from every bush, tree, car, concrete wall—anything big enough to hide behind—were dozens of men and women, all armed, all wearing triumphant smiles. They'd timed it well. The fleeing group was already well up the incline, too high up to jump over the side safely, too far along to run back to land.

"Go," Soren said in a sharp voice to the others. "Keep moving."

He turned back with Finn to face the ambush.

A woman stepped toward Soren, grinning.

"Gotcha."

Soren's stomach clenched at the sight of her, but he said, "Not yet."

Lydia laughed. "You are seriously going to try to outrun us across the bridge?"

"If I have to."

Lydia's eyes flickered to the side, and Soren gave a quick glance. Mary had come up to join them, and the three of them —Mary, Soren, and Finn—stood near the highest point of the upward span of the bridge, looking down on Lydia and her followers.

"We want Conover and Quaice," Lydia shouted. "If you turn yourselves over to us, we might consider letting the rest of you go."

"Keep moving!" Soren shouted, without turning. "Don't listen to her. She lies."

A derisive snort. "What will stop me from killing the three of you where you stand, and taking the others down at my leisure? You escaped me once. It won't happen again."

Mary laughed—an honest laugh of pure amusement, a

strange sound in this place, where the wind was whipping up from a destroyed city across a desperate band of refugees.

"You're right in one way," Mary said to Lydia. "He's not going to escape, not really. No one ever does."

"Who the hell are you?"

"Oh, it doesn't matter. But I just wanted to say that I'm sorry. I'm so sorry for all of you. My besetting sin is that I can't help but sympathize even with people who deserve what they get. But honestly, you brought this on yourself." Without turning, she said, "Soren, Finn, you might want to move back."

Lydia drew her gun. "If any of you moves, I will shoot you dead."

Mary frowned. "You poor child. Oh, you poor, poor child. I know you've been hurt terribly. I can't imagine it, not really, but responding to pain by inflicting it on everyone around you was never the way. When you're hurt, you should take that burning pain you feel and let it melt your heart. Then you help others, to make certain no one else ever has to experience the agony you did. That's what you should have done. But I suppose you never had a chance. Truthfully, none of us do. It's just that some of us make this frozen universe more beautiful, and others make it uglier. You couldn't help it. And Lydia…"

The woman startled at the use of her name.

Mary's face relaxed into a smile. "I forgive you."

From the direction of the city came a harsh, ruinous noise, a low rumble like thunder. Lydia and her followers turned.

"Now," Mary said quietly, "you'd better run, Soren. You and Finn. I can't manage it, not with my injured leg. But that's okay, really it is. Whatever you see, don't turn back."

Soren backed up, pulling Finn by the hand, and together they sprinted up to the top of the bridge rise.

That's when the earthquake reached them.

The bridge slewed from side to side, and Soren almost lost

his footing. When they got to the top, he turned and looked over his shoulder one last time.

The entire lower span of the bridge buckled and then collapsed. Lydia was the first to fall, screaming her thwarted outrage until her voice was cut off by the thrashing water. Some of her followers tried to outrun it, either up toward where Soren and Finn were, or else back along the bridge toward the city.

None of them succeeded.

Finally the only one left was Mary Hansard, standing at the very edge of the broken bridge, the wind catching her long hair. She gave a quick turn toward Soren. Her face looked fearless, transcendent, almost transfigured into something more than human. She closed her eyes and smiled.

Then the piece of roadway collapsed under her feet, and she was gone.

Soren shouted, "Mary!" and started to turn back, but Finn grabbed his hand. "No. We've got to keep going. She said so!"

At the same moment, a lightning-fast jolt shook Soren like a rat in a dog's mouth, and he almost slumped to the ground. He saw it—saw the whole thing, past and future, spread out before him like pieces on a board game. He knew what to do —because in his mind, it had already happened, it would always happen that way, world without end, amen.

Soren and Finn turned and sprinted together down toward the two-kilometer expanse of the floating bridge.

The others were spread out in a long, disordered line along the bridge, some running, some walking. Cassandra and Gavin were herding the children along, pushing them to go faster.

Soren came up behind them, shouting, "We've got to move faster! There's going to be a tsunami!"

The rest of the run across the bridge was a chaotic nightmare—thrown from side to side by the earthquake, near miss after near miss as more of the bridge collapsed behind them, the chill spray of lake water drenching him to the skin. The second rise, lifting upward and then down onto the east shore, seemed to be intact, but there were cracks in the concrete that shifted and ground against each other as the tremors pulled the pontoons this way and that. Up, up, up to the crest, then downward toward dry land...

One of the children, a little wisp of a girl with long black hair, stumbled and fell, and they were past her almost before Soren realized what had happened. Finn let go of his hand and turned back to help her.

This is it. Soren knew for certain that this was the moment Perry Abraham had warned him about. Perry had known Lydia would fall. There was no doubt in the little boy's mind that their enemy would die. But about Soren himself, Perry had said it was uncertain, that it was hanging by a hair.

"Finn!" He turned back himself, watching as Finn scooped up the little girl, throwing her into a fireman's carry, and began to run.

Another huge tremor, and more chunks of the bridge fell into the lake, raising towering plumes of spray.

Go. Was that Mary's voice, speaking in his mind? *Catch him before he falls. If you don't, he'll be lost, and so will you.*

Soren sprinted toward them, blinded by the flying droplets of ice-cold water, leaping across cracks that hadn't been there moments ago. There was a sudden cry of terror, and he reached out one hand...

... and caught Finn's just as he and the girl he carried were about to topple backward into the torn gap in the roadway. His weight almost was too much, and Soren very nearly went over the edge along with them, but in a moment they had found their feet and were once more pelting their way toward safety.

Down onto the lower span of the bridge, then onto dry land.

"Don't stop!" he shouted, nearly colliding with the nearest

of them, standing gasping for breath. "We've got minutes before the water rises. We've got to get to higher ground."

Off the bridge and down the on-ramp, then any path they could find that led uphill. How high was high enough?

They got to the top of a long, steep slope before Soren looked back. In the distance the horizon rippled as the sheet of water pushed its way across the landscape, tearing up what was left standing, turning the ravaged city into flotsam.

Once again Mary's voice spoke inside his mind.

The righteous and unrighteous alike will be destroyed in the cleansing flood.

The others clustered behind him as he stood between them and devastation, watching the water rushing its way onto the east shore and toward them, rising, rising, reaching out toward where the survivors huddled, exhausted, soaking wet and shivering on top of a hill, unable to move a step farther even to save their lives.

The water rose until it kissed the toes of Soren's shoes as he stood, upright and strong, on the fragments of the tilted world. He put out both arms in a gesture that said, *No. You shall not take one of these. Not one. They are under my protection.* Then as if the flood heard his unspoken words and dared not harm him or the people who stood behind him, it halted and turned backward, rushing away from them, sweeping the debris of the fallen civilization out to sea.

thirty-five

. . .

Julia Lowell had never felt so dog-tired in her life. The rain fell steadily, and when she said over and over, "Come on, now, children, just a little farther," she was reassuring herself as much as the kids she was speaking to. Everyone was shivering, stumbling with fatigue, and a couple of the littlest ones seemed close to collapsing. Finn still carried the little girl who had fallen—Becka Shimada was her name—she'd twisted her ankle badly. She had her arms around his neck, legs dangling, and appeared to be dozing despite the cold and wet.

When they finally found shelter in the ruins of a car dealership that had somehow remained standing despite the riots and the earthquake, she saw to the comfort of the others before finding an unoccupied armchair in what had been the waiting room, settling in, and trying to drop off to sleep. But despite her fatigue, slumber eluded her.

She'd known Mary Hansard was going to fall. God had told her that much. Mary obviously had known as well, and accepted it completely. She'd received no information about the others. The voice was silent about who might live and who might die, so she expected at least some of them to die.

But other than Mary, of the group who had made it to the bridgehead, they had all come safely across. That by itself seemed like a miracle.

One of the children, a slender little boy with a mop of blond hair, had come up to her as they were arranging themselves to get some rest, and looked up into her eyes with a serene expression. It was the little boy who'd been traveling with Soren, the one who seemed to be a leader despite his age. The one who had come up to stand next to her and Brandon as they spoke one last time to Mary Hansard.

"You're one of us." It was the same thing he'd said to Mary herself.

"I know," Julia said. "We're all going to help each other as much as possible."

"I don't mean that. I mean that you're an oracle. Like me."

Julia had stared at him for a moment, then knelt down next to him. "You're the little boy in Brandon's painting. The one he called *The Hands of the Magician*."

He nodded.

The child whose outstretched hands held the entire Earth.

"Will we go to the special place tomorrow?"

She frowned. "What place is that?"

"The new place. Where we'll be safe."

"The valley, you mean?"

Another nod.

"You know about it?"

"I know what the voice told me. That we'd find a special place. A place of rest."

Julia assured him she would help them all get to safety if it was in her power to do so. "I don't know whether we'll get there tomorrow, or some other day. But I do know we'll find our way there soon. I think the worst is past, and we're safe for now."

"That's right." His wide gray eyes had held hers with a steadiness that was beyond his age. "But nothing is ever going to be really safe. That's why people have to learn to listen to the oracles. We have information they don't. That was one of the first things the voice told me. That when the internet and all was gone, this is how we would find things out. It said we'd been chosen to know things, and we needed to tell them to everyone who would listen."

The exchange haunted her as she tried to relax her cold, aching body into sleep. In only a month, the world had changed in ways she had never anticipated. The End Times she had been expecting for years had come and gone, only... the world hadn't ended. It was more like someone pressed *reset* on civilization. Left behind to pull together the broken pieces and survive as best they could, the remnants were not living in the world of Jesus's triumphant Second Coming, but looked as if they'd have to struggle even more against the hazards of the world than they always had.

She still didn't doubt that her knowledge came from God, but even so, nothing had played out like she'd thought it would.

Besides her, who was left to lead them? The oracles. An atheistic artist. A six-year-old boy. A gay man who had somehow assumed Mary's role when she was killed in the bridge collapse.

Not whom she would have picked to resurrect God's kingdom on Earth, but then, who was she to put herself on a pedestal? She was a completely ordinary retired nurse, getting old enough to feel it and certainly nothing special in any way. She'd been chosen... why? She'd thought it was because of her steadfastness to God's word, but looking at the other oracles, there had to be more to it than that. Parsing what that might be, though, seemed impossible. She gave a rueful chuckle at her own presumption. God hardly needed her permission for His choices. It was not her place to question. It was her place to accept what had happened and then do the best she could, just as she had tried to do all her life.

There would be other oracles they'd meet. That much she was certain of. They'd find their way to the valley—the "special place," Perry had called it—and after that, be safe enough for a while. Then, the priority would be finding a way to feed themselves, stay warm, help anyone who became sick. Survive, just as all the generations of ancestors had done.

Some, of course, *wouldn't* survive. That was inevitable. She just hoped she would be able to live for a time in the shelter of the valley, that she would not, like Moses, be denied entry into the Promised Land.

After that, what then? Would she ever find out what had happened to the rest of the planet?

The last she'd heard, it was clear the LLA attacks had been worldwide. Had other places been hit as hard as Seattle? Given the LLA's philosophy, it had probably been chosen for especially savage treatment because of its reputation as a technological hub and center of wealth and privilege.

Were there any national governments still standing? No way to know, but it seemed unlikely. The fact that, since the riots began a month earlier, there had been no sign of anyone coming in from outside to render aid suggested that everywhere else was in dire straits as well. Maybe some state and regional governments were still functioning. And perhaps overseas, there were countries managing to hang on.

In the here and now, though, it made little difference. With the collapse of the internet and long-distance travel all but impossible, the survivors were disconnected, adrift, just as the tiny communities of humans had been for millennia, never knowing what was happening in other places. Back then, most people never in their entire lives traveled more than twenty kilometers away from the spot they were born. The modern world hadn't just collapsed, it had shrunk to the diameter of how far you could walk in a day.

How much of their culture and history would be lost in the process? The grand repository of the internet was no more. Books, at least in some places, would last longer, but when people's main concern is trying not to starve, the textual records of a civilization would hardly be a priority. Paper would crumble to dust, faster in this damp climate. In ten years, twenty, a hundred, what would be remembered about the people they had been before the fall?

She shifted uncomfortably in her chair. In Matthew chapter six was written, "Take therefore no thought for the morrow: for the morrow shall take thought for the things of itself. Sufficient unto the day is the evil thereof."

She looked around her at the shadowed room. Most of the children were already asleep, curled up on the floor. She smiled. Kids could sleep anywhere. Others had found what comfort they could. Brandon and Caria were curled up together, and Finn and Soren snuggled tight, holding each other in an unbreakable embrace.

Reverend Talcott had always spoken against homosexuality as an affront to God, but looking at the two of them, blissfully asleep in each other's arms, she could only feel happiness that they were so deeply in love.

If there had been more love in the world, she thought, maybe none of this would have had to happen. They had fallen into darkness not because of abandoning the hundreds of harsh laws from the Book of Leviticus, but because they'd broken the most fundamental of God's rules—the command to love thy neighbor as thyself. Who was she to criticize how that love manifested? She'd seen the outrages that came from its opposite, and whatever her training in the authority of the Bible, she couldn't find any room to judge the righteousness of who was loving whom. It was the love that mattered. Everything else was trivia.

As if in response to her gaze, Finn moaned softly, nuzzled his face against Soren's neck, and subsided back into sleep.

No, there was no sin here, whatever she'd been taught. It

seemed there were a lot of things she'd believed that were going to take some reconsideration.

Sufficient unto the day is the evil thereof. There was no arguing with that. She'd always had trouble letting go of worry—worry about her loved ones, worry that she was doing the best she could, worry about things outside her control. That verse had brought her comfort before, and it did now. She took a deep breath, listening to the patter of the rain on the roof, gave a quick prayer of thanks that they had gotten this far and found a dry place to rest, and moments later, she drifted to sleep.

epilogue

...

Twenty years later

Brandon Nguyen and Caria Sahin avoided places where there was the smoke of cooking fires. They'd run into a few other survivors, most of whom turned out to be friendly, but there was no sense risking contact with anyone hostile if it was possible to avoid it. Even those few were left behind as they traveled into the area that had suffered the worst damage. Their path took them along the cracked surface that had been Interstate 405, looping northward through Kirkland, Totem Hill, Woodinville, Bothell, and around the north end of Lake Washington. They found signs of the old Free State of North Seattle—tangles of rusted razor wire, pieces of concrete barricades—but of the people who had defended it so viciously, there was not a trace.

The farther west they traveled, the worse the devastation was from the floods. There were still buildings standing despite the double punch of the earthquake and tsunami, but there was nothing that was undamaged. Much of the city had been turned into a wasteland of rubble and rotted wood. They saw skeletons, picked clean by animals and time, but once they rounded the top of the lake and began to work their way southward, not a single living human being.

"It's weird no one's come back." Caria spoke in a whisper despite there being no one there to hear.

"The place is full of ghosts. That'd be enough to keep just about anyone away."

They'd been planning the trek for a couple of years, ever since their three children, Mary, Derek, and Veronica, had grown old enough to leave with friends. The community of survivors that had found Julia's promised valley were still there—fighting the day-to-day struggle to survive, but managing well enough with each other's help. Julia herself had died eight years earlier at the honorable age of eighty-three, after passing her oracular gift on to Trevor Keene, the earnest young man who had joined her and Brandon on the first day of the attacks.

They'd lost Dr. Quaice the previous year as well, to a sudden heart attack while he was working in the settlement's vegetable garden. He'd taught the entire community how to speak Kalila—never a bad thing to be able to communicate with friends and not be understood by anyone with ill intent, he said to anyone who would listen—and to his final days, the old man never stopped trying to raise someone on his short-wave radio. He'd found a hand-cranked electrical generator at what was left of a hardware store soon after they'd arrived, and used it to power up the unit, but no matter how long he listened, all he heard was static.

Either other survivors had no access to communications technology, or perhaps there were no other survivors near enough to talk to. Impossible to tell which, but the fact in two decades they'd only been joined by a handful of stragglers, and seen very few other traces of humanity, argued that the destruction had been far more extensive than anyone realized.

Soren and Finn were still there, living together in a cabin on the edge of the settlement. Neither one had ever completely recovered from the trauma of spending a month with each thinking the other was dead, and they rarely were seen apart.

Perry Abraham and Becka Shimada were partners—no one seemed anxious to resurrect the old ceremony of marriage—and had two children, a boy and a girl. Perry was a gentle and loving father, and his devotion to Becka was downright touching.

Colin Dorn and Emily Banfield were together as well, and they had four children of their own, now about the age Colin and Emily themselves had been when Brandon first met them.

Gavin and Peggy Liu reunited the day after the earthquake, something both of them considered to be close to a miracle, and were in their seventies, still alive and healthy. They lived in a small cabin next to Cassandra Nicolaides, who had taken over teaching Kalila when Dr. Quaice died. She seemed as passionate about it as he had been, and was determined that the conlang would not be lost to the rigors of life and the simple passage of years.

Time slides away. There is no slowing it down.

Brandon and Caria made their way southward through what had been North Gate and Fremont. They skirted westward on the edge of the University District. The LLA graffiti on what was left of the walls of buildings was blurred and nearly unreadable. Tree saplings and underbrush crowded in every open space, coming up through gaps in the roadway. The dominion of humanity was ended. Nature was taking over again.

How long would it take to erase every sign? It had happened before. Pompeii, Santorini, Crete, Mycenae. The empires of the Celts, Romans, Chinese, Indians, Zulu, Hausa, Songhai. All gone, all lost, ground to dust by natural disaster and the ravages of time. Vanished and forgotten, along with everything but the few shards dug up by the archaeologists.

So it would be here.

What would the humans a thousand years hence know about them? By then, surely almost everything would be gone. Wood decayed, books mildewed and fallen apart into unreadable fragments, stone and brickwork crumbling until there was little left. Even a trained archaeologist trying to reassemble the pieces would miss the truth by light years. Might as well try to figure out what life in ancient Rome was like based on broken chunks of pottery, a few coins, a headless statue, the foundation of a building or two.

When Brandon got to his old neighborhood, it began to look familiar despite the devastation. Ronnie Sulzbach's house was mostly collapsed—poor Ronnie, shot not by the LLA but by starving and desperate hunters. Her death had hit him hard, a sign that the world had changed irrevocably, and when they named their younger daughter after her, it seemed a fitting tribute. The duplex where Trevor Keene had lived was a bare foundation. It looked like it had burned to the ground, but with the vegetation crowding in from all sides and coming up through cracks in the concrete, it was impossible to be sure.

Then, there it was.

Brandon's house.

The structure was still substantially intact. Soren had told him it would be. With his peculiar forward-and-backward knowledge, he'd told them they'd found the house, taken what they wanted, and returned safely. As if it was a thing already accomplished, the way Soren spoke about anything that was in the future. But even with that reassurance, it didn't seem real until he and Caria were standing in front of it, staring up at a crooked façade that showed dark cracks through the siding. One corner of the roof sagged precariously. It was good they'd come. The house would collapse, sooner rather than later.

They climbed the front steps, pushed open what remained of the door, and went inside.

The interior was a shattered mess. What had been the art studio was filled with a thick layer of debris and hardened mud, probably left by the tsunami. The worst damage was at the back of the house. The kitchen wall had mostly caved in, and through what had been the window, the reaching branches of a maple tree twisted as if trying to grasp the frame and pull it and the rest of the house down.

Wordlessly, they ascended the staircase. The steps were rotted and unstable, but with caution they were able to make their way to the second floor, down the hallway—avoiding a giant hole in the floor where some of the supporting joists had given way—and into the tiny bedroom near the end.

The room smelled like dust and mildew, but had sustained little damage except for the loss of the glass in the window. It was almost as if some power had shielded the room from the harm that had destroyed the rest of the city. The tattered lace of cobwebs hung from the ceiling, and there was a drift of dead leaves underneath the window, but other than that it was like a small time capsule from two decades and an entire lifetime ago.

"They're here," Brandon whispered, and suddenly found himself forcing back tears.

Caria went to the stack of canvases leaning on the wall. They were brittle and had streaks of mold, but the colors of the oil paints were as vibrant as ever.

The Hands of the Magician. Perry as a child, looking up at the Earth suspended above his hands.

The Pyre of the Former World. Brandon shuddered, looking at Lydia's gleeful countenance, her stigmata dripping blood, feeding the flames that consumed her.

Poured Out Like Water. Oh, Julia. Now the tears spilled

over. How he missed her staunch and compassionate wisdom. She had been with him from the beginning, the first one he'd found, before he'd even understood the significance of his visions. He looked at her familiar, gentle face with a pang of grief. Love and knowledge filled up her cupped hands, glowing like a beacon, spilling over, offered freely to anyone who would partake.

The Tilted World. Soren standing upright, arms outstretched, his face turned to the side, every muscle in his body radiating a fierce and relentless strength. No, these people are mine to protect. You cannot touch them.

Finally he picked up the last one. *Sacrificial Offering.* Mary Hansard standing on the edge of the shattered bridge, the wind whipping her hair. Knowing she was about to fall to the same fate as their enemies, yet wearing a transcendent smile that said, *I may die, but I have still won.*

Brandon dropped his backpack, then knelt and unzipped it. He pulled out a hank of rope, and in a few moments had all the canvases tied securely together. With some help from Caria, he strapped them against his backpack, and shouldered it again.

It was heavy and awkward, but that was okay. He'd known it would be. It was why he was here. The effort would all be worth it once they arrived back home with their precious finds.

"Are you glad we came?" Caria still spoke in a whisper.

Brandon understood the impulse to remain quiet. The ghosts he'd felt earlier were pressing in, watching them with curious and unblinking eyes, hordes of the dead wondering why their habitation had been invaded by two audacious flesh-and-blood interlopers.

"Yes," he whispered back. "But I don't want to stay here. I think it'll be a long time before this place will be somewhere people can live. We can leave now. I got what I came for."

They maneuvered past all the obstacles and damage, and

in a few minutes had made their way outside. Caria took his hand, gave it a squeeze.

"There's no need for us to come back. Ever."

"No." He recalled Julia saying years ago that they shouldn't return, not at least for a very long time.

"Jesus said, 'Let the dead bury their dead,'" she'd told him. He hadn't understood it then, but he did now.

Let the ghosts occupy the place in peace. It was no longer fit for the living.

They turned, and began to pick their way back north through the ruins, their faces turned toward home.

from "the scattering winds"

. . .

*(book two of **Arc of the Oracles**)*

The nine statues in the Hall of Images gazed down at Syra Cheraskin, and for once, she tried to meet their eyes. The light of the Eternal Flame flickered over their solemn faces, making the carved wooden folds of their clothing seem to move.

Leda Banfield, the twenty-sixth oracle of the lineage of the Blessed Martyr Mary of the Bridge, was one of the longest-lived oracles since the Fall and the establishment of the community of Klen over six hundred years ago. Syra had been her apprentice for almost fifty years, so she'd seen the statues daily for as long as she could recall. By now, she was so used to the position of apprentice that she had given up thinking about when she might become Guardian of the Word in her own right.

She looked from one of the statues to the next. Beautiful work, and old. No one knew how old. Were they carved from life? Did the images actually look like the people they had been created to represent? They resembled the faded paintings stored carefully with the other relics of the Flight, which were supposedly painted by the Blessed Brandon himself—but no one knew if that was true or only a legend.

Syra kept her skepticism to herself. It wouldn't do for people to think the future Guardian of the Word had her doubts about whether any of it was true.

The only one of the images that was smiling was the Blessed Mary of the Bridge herself. Her countenance seemed to glow with welcome and good cheer, one arm outstretched toward Syra as if saying, *Take my hand. I will guide you where you want to go.*

Which was odd in and of itself, because if the legends were true, Mary of the Bridge was the only one of the nine founders who died without ever reaching safety. Despite that, her face radiated happiness.

Syra was glad she belonged to Mary's lineage. She'd always liked her best, even when she was little and had no idea she'd be chosen as apprentice. The other faces seemed aloof, distant, almost inaccessible. She looked up at the nearest, the statue of Blessed Finn. He stood, broad-chested and upright, strength radiating from every inch of his powerful frame, gazing down at her with stern pity. He held one hand up, palm toward her. Whether this gesture was intended as a greeting or a warning was impossible to know. His other arm was at his side, the fingertips just touching the hand of the statue next to him, Blessed Soren, the next of Mary's line after Mary herself died on the bridge during the Flight. Syra remembered when she first learned why Soren and Finn's hands touched like that, when all the others stood alone and separate.

They were lovers in real life. Soren saved Finn's life, and brought them safely above the flood waters, both his beloved and the rest of the ancestors. Without Blessed Soren, there would have been no Founders, no oracles, no Klen at all.

Soren and Finn deserved that, to have the hands of their images gently touching, as they had in real life. She liked that thought. It made them more human.

She shook herself out of her reverie and returned to her duties, anointing each statue's feet with scented oil, then tending the fire. The silence echoed around her, magnifying every little sound of her movement. She was always cautious and deliberate in this holy place, but today it was as if everyone and everything was holding its breath.

Syra knew why, as did everyone in Klen. Today was the day that Leda Banfield would die. Then after the three-day period of mourning, Syra would be invested as the twenty-seventh oracle in the lineage of the Blessed Mary of the Bridge. Leda of course knew when she was going to die, and had given Syra and everyone else plenty of warning, but the status quo had been unchanged for so long it didn't seem real.

Syra sensed it the moment it happened, as Leda said she would. Her hand stopped halfway to adding a cedar branch to the fire to make the smoke smell sweet, the knowledge of Leda's death hitting her like a physical blow. She took a step back, giving a sharp intake of breath. The flames flickered and crackled, the firelight playing over the carved faces of the nine Founders standing in a semicircle around it. They seemed to be watching her to see what she'd do next.

She heard it, almost as if someone had spoken the words aloud: *You are one of us now.*

After a moment, Syra took a deep breath and added the cedar branch to the fire. She watched it crackle and burst into flame, then took unsteady steps away from the brazier and sat down, her back against the wall, trying to regain her equilibrium.

Leda had told her what it was like, long ago. Syra herself was only about fifteen at the time, just become apprentice— such a lot yet to learn—but the memory was undimmed with time. "Your mind expands in all directions," Leda said, one long, graceful hand sweeping through the air, her eyes focused somewhere far distant. "The future becomes as clear as the past. It isn't like the oracles of the other lineages, where the knowledge comes in interior voices or prophetic pronouncements or brightly-colored pictures. It is all one piece, the past and present and future all laid out before you, and everything you have experienced or will experience is silent and unmoving and unchangeable. Bubbles frozen into a block of ice. Look at it from this way and that—your perspective changes, but the events never do. You see it all at once."

Syra hadn't understood what she meant then, but she did now. There was the sudden and disorienting sensation of watching her own life from above, seeing the whole thing spread out like the pieces on a game board. Things she knew were in the past: her childhood, her choice of Eliane Shimada as a partner, Eliane's death from a sudden illness six years ago. Things that were in the future: the solemn burial ceremony for Leda Banfield, Syra's installation as Guardian of the Word, choosing a new apprentice, who that apprentice would be.

Syra's own death. The oracular gift of the lineage of Mary of the Bridge conferred a knowledge of one's own mortality but at the same time a complete loss of fear. Once you know something will happen, that it's a fixed point in space and time, it is very much like it's already happened. Syra felt some sadness at the knowledge that her lifespan was limited, but truthfully, wasn't everyone's? That she knew when it was going to happen was the only difference. It was all part of the beautiful, never-changing frozen landscape that was the reality of time.

After a few moments, the dizziness passed. The sensation of what Leda called "all-in-one" didn't diminish. It just was. It always had been there, Syra knew that. Until she received the gift at Leda's death, she just didn't see it.

She stood slowly, and when she was convinced she could walk without staggering too obviously, she made her way out of the Hall of Images. She needed to talk to the other three oracles immediately. Certainly they knew that Leda was going to die today, but they may not have been aware the instant it happened. The oracular gifts were unpredictable, but they had always proven true in the past. And whether they knew or not, she needed to give them formal notice so that the three-day ritual of burial, investiture, and appointment of a new apprentice could begin.

"Are you ready to accept your role?" Garlin Abraham caught her gaze, concern in his dark eyes. He was of the lineage of the Blessed Brandon, so the yearly repainting of the statues in the Hall of Images was his duty, as was creating whatever new inspiration came from his visions.

"I don't think it matters if I'm ready," Syra said. "The gift happens when it happens. We can't control that."

Garlin was only thirty, and it hadn't been long since his own investiture. "Of course," he said. "I remember. It was a foolish thing to ask."

"It's all right. It's been a bit of a shock. Even knowing Leda was ill—and that she'd told me when she would die—it felt impossible. It's like when you're little, and it seems like it'll be that way forever. Your parents will always be alive and will always care for you. Then one day, you realize that it's all changed."

Bastian Nguyen, the oracle in the lineage of the Blessed Julia, gave her a raised eyebrow. "That is true, but there's also readiness in a practical sense. You have the prayers memorized? You'll need to be able to recite them by heart."

Syra allowed herself a quick frown. "Of course I do. I've had long enough to learn them, haven't I?"

Bastian's lips tightened, but he didn't respond. Syra was apparently not the only one with some adjustment to do, and she'd always sensed that Bastian didn't like her much. In one step she'd risen from a mere apprentice to being one of the four sacred oracles. The fact that she might have to fight to achieve the level of respect that the others got automatically had never crossed her mind.

She could just barely recall the grumbling when she was appointed apprentice, at age fourteen. She was naïve enough at the time not to understand it completely. Leda shielded her from the worst of it—the Guardian was a tough-minded and demanding woman, right from the beginning, determined that her apprentice would not have to deal with ignorant bigotry as well as all of the other difficulties that came naturally with the position. But Syra had still been aware, even so.

"Why couldn't she have chosen someone who was one of us?" an old woman said in a loud whisper, at the annual celebration of the Founders' escape from destruction and death, the year after her investiture as apprentice. At the time, Syra thought the old woman didn't know she was there, sitting quietly only two rows back, and could hear everything she said. In the five decades since, she'd become convinced that the woman knew perfectly well Syra was within earshot, and didn't care—or, perhaps, was glad for the opportunity to let Syra know what she thought while still giving the impression of a private conversation.

"She's one of us," the old woman's companion said. "Sort of."

The woman made a scoffing noise. "Half. Her mother was an outsider. Pale skin, hair that was nearly white. Abnormal, I call that. Why her father took up with that woman I'll never know. Against all the rules, yet he got away with it somehow."

"The Guardian allowed it." His voice sounded reluctant,

almost apologetic, as if he didn't want to be in this conversation but didn't have a graceful way to end it.

Another snort. "Said he foresaw it would be good for Klen. Well, it's fifteen years since, and I don't see any good that's come of it. And now she's not only allowed to be here and take part in what is rightly for true community members, but she's been appointed as apprentice to the most important office in Klen." A pause, then she continued in a sneering tone. "The girl takes after her mother, too. You'd never know she was one of us by looking."

"Hopefully Leda will have a long life as the Guardian. Syra might be nothing more than an apprentice for decades."

"Perhaps she'll die first." The old woman's voice was nearly a snarl. "Then Leda can rectify her mistake and choose someone who is suitable."

Then the recital of the prayers started, and the two fell silent. But Syra never forgot it.

Perhaps she'll die first.

She never told Leda about the overheard conversation, at first out of shame, then because she grew to trust that the Guardian knew what she was doing. If Leda chose her, it was because she foresaw that Syra was the next in the lineage, that it wouldn't matter what the grumblers and bigots thought.

But now, fifty years later, with Leda dead and a three-day mourning period and an investiture ceremony between Syra and becoming the Guardian of the Word in her own right, it was a slap in the face to see the doubt in Bastian Nguyen's eyes, to find that the old prejudice was still there.

And from one of the other oracles, no less.

Syra knew the prayers by heart. All the rituals, orders, legends of the Founders, knowledge stretching back six hundred years. She was fluent in the sacred language, had every pronunciation and inflection so deeply within her that she sometimes dreamed in it. Those dreams were often of an elderly man, tall and thin but vital, who spoke to her in the sacred language as easily as if it were common speech. Through cautious questioning of the other oracles, she was convinced that this man was the Blessed Quaice, who had written the language himself six centuries ago. The man in her dream certainly resembled Quaice's statue in the Hall of Images, but there was a big difference between a living man and a wooden statue, however beautifully made.

The Blessed Quaice—if that was who the dream-man was—reassured her each time that everything was happening as it should. Her own self-doubts were nothing to fear. She would prove herself, and the naysayers would have no choice but to accept her.

Of course, Quaice himself had not been not an oracle, however important he was as one of the Founders of Klen. So his words of encouragement might not mean much, might not be any more than her own subconscious engaging in wishful thinking.

Syra sighed. Three days till her investiture as Guardian of the Word. Three days during which she would be going over and over the prayers, making sure to have every word perfect. Perhaps others had the freedom to make the occasional mistake. Even Leda Banfield had sometimes, and had always accepted her own fallibility with a shrug and a smile.

Syra didn't have that latitude.

And before then, she would have to talk to the young man who would be her apprentice. At least there could be no criticism of his appointment, not that Syra had a choice in the matter. The oracular knowledge informed her of who the next apprentice would be, and that was that. But still, it was a relief when she learned his identity.

Unlike her, he was of Klen ancestry through to the bone. Which, she realized, would make his decisions—his life, even—more of a shock to the community. They had expected Syra to do something outlandish, half-outlander that she was, and she had responded by trying to prove herself a woman of Klen every time she had a chance.

Her apprentice?

She smiled.

He would be the opposite. If they blamed her for his heresy and transgressions to come, that'd simply be the way it was. She could no more change that than she could change anything else—past, present, or future.

a request

Please do us a favor to help other readers find Gordon and his books.

On social media: likes, comments, and shares go a LONG way. Links are in the next section.

Follows and reviews are critical: If you liked this book, please tell the world! It just takes a moment of your time and will really help us out.

On Amazon: https://www.amazon.com/stores/Gordon-Bonnet/author/B0BT6XQVL4

On BookBub: https://www.bookbub.com/authors/gordon-bonnet

On GoodReads: https://www.goodreads.com/author/show/4779649.Gordon_Bonnet

And anywhere else you search for or buy books.

Thanks! - GB and CB

about the author

Gordon Bonnet has been writing fiction for decades. Encouraged when his story "Crazy Bird Bends His Beak" won critical acclaim in Mrs. Moore's 1st grade class at Central Elementary School in St. Albans, West Virginia, he embarked on a long love affair with the written word.

His interest in the paranormal goes back almost that far. Introduced to speculative, fantasy, and science fiction by such giants in the tradition as Madeleine L'Engle, Lloyd Alexander, Isaac Asimov, C. S. Lewis, and J. R. R. Tolkien, he was captivated by those writers' abilities to take the reader to a fictional world and make it seem tangible, to breathe life and passion and personality into characters who were (sometimes) not even human. He made journeys into darker realms upon meeting the works of Edgar Allen Poe and H. P. Lovecraft during his teenage years, and those authors still influence his imagination and his writing to this day.

This fascination with the paranormal, however, has always been tempered by Gordon's scientific training. This has led to a strange duality: his work as a teacher, skeptic and debunker on the popular blog *Skeptophilia,* while simultaneously writing paranormal and speculative novels, novellas, and short stories. Gordon explains this, with a smile: "Well, I do know it's fiction, after all."

He blogs daily, and is never without a piece of fiction in progress—driven to continue (as he puts it) "because I want to find out how the story ends." From historical fiction (*Kári the Lucky*), to murder mysteries (the Parsifal Snowe Mysteries, beginning with *Poison the Well*), to paranormal fiction with a humorous twist (*Periphery* and *Lock & Key*) to the truly terrifying (*Gears* and *Descent into Ulthoa*), Gordon's fiction has something for all tastes!

Find him conversing with his dogs (and perhaps his wife) in Trumansburg, NY, or the following platforms:
- Website *http://www.gordonbonnet.com*
- YouTube *https://youtube.com/@skeptophilia1509*
- Skeptophilia blog *http://www.skeptophilia.com/*
- Twitter *@TalesOfWhoa*
- TikTok *@LittleBustardBooks* and *@gordonbonnetauthor*
- Instagram *@skygazer227*

Or, ya know, the Google.

also by gordon bonnet

The Scattering Winds (Book 2 of Arc of the Oracles): *October 2023*

Chains of Orion (Book 3 of Arc of the Oracles): *November 2023*

Lock & Key

Behind the Frame

The Communion of Shadows

Gears

Sephirot

Descent into Ulthoa

The Shambles

Kári the Lucky

Kill Switch

The Fifth Day

Snowe Mysteries *(beginning re-releases 2024)*

Book 1: Poison the Well

Book 2: Dead Letter Office

Book 3: Face Value

Snowe Mysteries *(available now)*

Book 4: Past Imperfect

Book 5: Room for Wrath

Book 6: The Obituary Collector

Book 7: Slings and Arrows

Stay tuned for releases *(and re-releases for ones you may have missed)*

Sign up for Gordon's Little Bustard Books Newsletter and Obscure Weird Tidbits at his website: http://www.gordonbonnet.com

9 781960 370112